ISAAC
AND HIS
DEVILS

ISAAC

❧ AND HIS

DEVILS

Fernanda
Eberstadt

Alfred A. Knopf

New York

1991

THIS IS A BORZOI BOOK
PUBLISHED BY ALFRED A. KNOPF, INC.

Library of Congress Cataloging-in-Publication Data
Eberstadt, Fernanda [date]
Isaac and his devils / by Fernanda Eberstadt. — 1st ed.
p. cm.
ISBN 0-394-58496-1
I. Title.
PS3555.B484I8   1991
813'.54—dc20   90-52909   CIP

Manufactured in the United States of America
First Edition

For Mummy and Dad

BOOK ONE

Chapter 1

THERE IS NOTHING sadder than the sight of a clever, nervy young man, agulp with ambitions enormous and vague as a headache and flaming with an almost chivalric love of a world he hasn't yet met, relinquishing his urgent purposes almost imperceptibly, slowing down, retreating, and fizzling out like a planet still shining but dead. His children who patronize him would never dream their father was once alight with such promise. His former champions wonder idly how he lost it, scan his life for the combination of character and circumstance that tripped him up, search for the hidden flaw that made this medlar mushy before it was ripe: a proud refusal to be caught competing, to be judged; a fastidious sluggishness that made distant success not worth the slog; immaturity of desire, a failure of nerve, a wandering and impatient concentration? What fatal sequence of misturnings led into this wilderness of compromise, silence, flinching mediocrity? Was it that he didn't want fame and greatness brazenly enough, or did he not want it because he feared he couldn't get it, or did he not know what he wanted and never found a prize worth the fight?

It isn't vices do a person in. Vices are his consolation for failure. A senator isn't kept from the presidency by frantic skirt chasing or love of the bottle; he gets to tolerate women and liquor because a man who will never be President must keep busy somehow.

The day Isaac Hooker was born he had already spoiled his mother's evening. That's what his father claimed, and Isaac liked to reproach her jokingly for still begrudging him her night out. "Don't be ridiculous," said his mom, but it was true.

Sam and Mattie had gone to the movies in Gilboa that night (the night happened to be December 3, 1963), to a double bill at the Marquis, which in those days was owned by a French Canadian with artistic taste and was called the Cameo. They used to go to the movies constantly when they were first married: to the Cameo and to the drive-in near the airfield at Sturgis, which Sam liked best. Not only could they stay in the front seat of their '54 Ambassador, of which he was mawkishly proud, he could maul Mattie freely while imagining and even glimpsing what the other couples were doing in the darkness all around them.

Other nights they would drive miles and miles east along icy country roads to Rockingham and Ulster and westward across the Vermont border to Bellows Falls, one strange evening even down to Northampton, Massachusetts, and back, towns they never set foot in again, just to see movies they hadn't seen before. And once Mattie was pregnant she longed for gunfire and chases the way other women hankered after Concord grapes or tapioca pudding. Besides, their apartment was so small there just wasn't room to sit around in the evenings.

Sam, underneath his sheen of knowing cynicism, always expected too much and was always disappointed. In truth he didn't even like movies all that much, and became edgy and distracted as soon as he sat down, but he simply refused to admit them to the list of things—country fairs and cigars and hockey—of which he preferred the idea to the experience. And indeed, every time, the prospect of going to the movies thrilled him as electrically as if he were slipping off on the sly to a broad-hipped mistress or driving to the seaside on a moment's whim.

After the picture was over and the audience was uncoiling itself and shuffling out into the lobby, Sam would stay glued to his seat, morosely poring over the credits, memorizing the names of stuntmen (they often had the same last name; it was clearly a family business), gaffer and best boy, and finally announce in lame triumph, "Mattie, I told you it wasn't really China—see, it was filmed in Spain." When the lights went on, the curtains closed, and the two of them reemerged into the floodlit darkness of Central Square, he felt fully deflated. But five days later he was eager for a new one, and by the time they changed pictures at the Cameo, he was raring to go. And besides, Mattie pointed out: it beat sitting at home.

Mattie was different. Whereas Sam, once the lights were out, became conscious of how cramped the plush seat was, how his knees were crunched up against metal, of the abominable hairdo of the lady in front of them, and began fussing about how he should be at home working on his thesis, Mattie was like a four-year-old at the circus, screaming with laughter at the punch lines (or else, elbow in his ribs, loudly demanding to know what was so funny), yelping at emerging knives, hissing warnings to unsuspecting victims. And Sam beside her would find himself watching Mattie and not the movie, half-admiring half-resenting the ease and gusto with which this wife of his became one with the collective roars and roilings of the crowd. When you married a woman you expected to melt into her and join forces; instead, every day she seemed more wonderfully alien to him, more a baffling stranger. Except with strangers you were more polite, more forbearing.

Afterward they'd go to Sadie's for a nightcap or pull up at a roadside diner for a frappe, and then she would start up.

"So how come they drove all the cows into the pen and shot them?"

"Because they had *anthrax*."

"Who did?"

"The cattle."

"What's that?"

"Foot-and-mouth disease."

"So what? Don't they have vets in Texas?" Pebble-blue eyes gazed through him over the rim of her chocolate frappe.

"Don't you know anything? It's highly contagious and it's fatal. People catch it and die like flies. They could have caused a national epidemic."

"I wouldn't have destroyed my whole livelihood just because some punk from the government came along and told me to. How come the kid's mother left town in such a hurry?"

"*Mother*?! That was the housekeeper. She left because Paul Newman tried to rape her."

"But I thought she was hot for *him*."

"Yeah, but that doesn't mean she didn't want him to be a gentleman about it."

Mattie would lean over, long-handled spoon poised, and scoop up like a raiding seagull the maraschino cherry bobbing in the froth, or dive for the hot fudge bedded on the ocean floor of his sundae, snatching with painted fingers whatever best bit he had been saving for last, as if gluttony would help her come to the bottom of this problem.

"So when the kid's father had a heart attack . . ."

"*Mattie* . . . That was his grandfather. The old man was Paul Newman's father and Brandon de Wilde's grandfather. Paul Newman killed Brandon de Wilde's father in a car crash. That was the whole point of the movie: he was cursed because he killed his own brother, and that's why his old man hated him."

Mattie burst into delighted laughter, much pleased by her own stupidity and her husband's cleverness. "Sam, how did you ever get to be so *smart?* You ought to write movies yourself. You could make a fortune."

That was Mattie, no opportunity let slip for a dig at his refusal to translate his wits into bucks. And then, seeing Sam already moping, she would change the subject, knee him under the table (evenings out with Mattie left one black and blue below the belt). "I don't think the old guy should have been so mean to his own son, even if the son *did* kill his other son. He was kind of a sourpuss, didn't you think? I mean, it happened years ago. You got to let bygones be bygones." Thus Mattie, who hoarded her grudges like baseball cards, with no trading.

And Sam, snickering now, "You can say that again."

But that winter night their fun had been cut short, and during a John Wayne double bill. They both liked Westerns best, Sam because they were American but also somehow still exotic, at least to a Yankee who knew only New Hampshire lakes and pine forest and white clapboard and apple orchards, and because it seemed to him that the women were always better endowed than in police dramas or war movies; Mattie because, even a mere week after Lee Harvey Oswald and Jack Ruby had sickened everyone else of it, she liked violence.

They were an hour or so into the heart of *How the West Was Won* when Sam heard a sound as if a woodchuck were digging itself a home in the seat beside him. He glanced over, startled and annoyed. Mattie was squirming.

"What's the matter?"

"Nothing."

"You all right?"

"Uh-huh."

Then a few minutes later, just as the Law on horseback was descending vertically from all sides, the puffing and heaving began again, more insistently.

"Mattie . . ."

"Be quiet," she whispered.

He could see her face, lit up by the intermittent flicker of nocturnal gunfire, fixed with a look of locked, grim determination as she wrestled to subdue the adversary within.

"Is it coming?"

"Shut up, Sam."

"Is it coming, Mattie?" His voice shot up reedy-high and he grabbed her arm. She was rocking now, between breaths.

"*No!* It's not coming for another eight days!" she barked. And then, mercifully, the spasms ceased and she sat in peace gazing at the screen. Sam tried to watch, too, but found himself instead waiting for the next bout, listening to his wife breathe, holding his own breath, cursing that loathsome twangy banjo music that wouldn't shut up. It was almost a relief when her struggles began in earnest—but now, shamefully, he was stricken with embarrassment, wishing like a child he could sneak out of the theater, disavow any relation to this banshee beside him. People were turning around to stare.

"Mattie, let's go. I'm taking you to the hospital."

"*No.* We paid for the movie—*both* movies. I want to see what happens."

"Mattie, we're going now," he said, his puling voice ascending.

"*You* go," snarled his iron-jawed frontierswoman. "I'm not leaving till it's over."

People in front and back were shushing them now, and for a moment he thought he was going to be sick. In despair, he announced, "I'm going to get the car." ("SSSSsssshhhh," hissed his neighbors furiously.) "I'll be waiting at the curb in five minutes. We're going to the hospital *now.*"

He stumbled out of the movie theater and ran down Mechanic Street to where he'd parked the Nash, only to have the engine conk out on him in the night frost. Finally, sweating and swearing, Sam got her started and in a screech of tires tore over to the Cameo. No Mattie. For a prickly eternity he sat in his boxy frigidaire, too frightened even to talk to himself. She was going to die. For the sake of a dollar admission ticket, Mattie would be the last woman in the free world to die in childbirth. If you didn't give in to an emerging baby, would it burst, like an appendix? She would murder—yes, she would, she was going to murder his only child out of sheer stubbornness. And now guilt chimed in: his wife, racked by pain, was going to die, and it was all his fault. From one furtive poke in the dark she was going to die, and the baby would die too, but if she didn't, now the atheist was praying, he would do anything, quit smoking, see his parents regularly, finish his thesis by next summer, put half his earnings every month in their joint savings account. . . .

Amid these craven ravings, Sam's wife emerged from the movie theater, deliberately maneuvering the slippery pavement on her high heels. She was wrapped in the rabbit-fur jacket her co-workers at Bolts had given her as a wedding present and was bearing aloft, like the Ark of the Covenant seized by conquering Philistines, the great waxen trumpet of buttered popcorn he had left unfinished on the floor of the theater. On the ride to the hospital, she complained between contractions, "It's a shame we had to miss the next movie. *You* should have stayed and seen it, then you could have told me what it was about."

Mattie chattered, Sam held her hand tight. She was distracted, fighting hard to bite back the yells, but game. She was a rock, his Mattie, a continent of grit.

Just before she was taken into the delivery room she turned to Sam with her dazzling smile, dimples etched clean as a skater's blades on new ice. In a rush of wanting to forestall whatever she gleefully realized or remembered, to get there first, Sam wondered if he could tell her that he loved her, cough up the obstinate words that had stuck in his throat all the years he'd known her. No, he couldn't. He held her hand tighter, and her smile broadened: "You know, we can always get Marge to tell us what happens."

"Isaac?" Mattie repeated in puzzled disgust. She was the one with the committee of friends geared up with suggestions, and it never occurred to her that Sam might have his own, as it turned out, immutable ideas on the subject.

"Isaac," insisted Sam.

"It sounds kind of weird. It sounds like the name of an old Jewish scientist or something, or a ragpicker," she protested.

"It was my great-grandfather's name, and he wasn't any old ragpicker."

"How about Duane? Or Marlon? You know, you're not the only person in the world with grandparents." He could tell, however, that her resistance was simply for show; for with that pugnacious bargainer's view of hers that everything in their life together must be evenly divisible, that every good was a good either for him or for her, and if for him, she was owed a bigger one, Mattie subsided, insisting that the next kid *she* would get to name after one of *her* relatives. Her ratty Canuck forebears.

"There aren't going to be any Jean-Jacqueses or Marie-Claudes in *my* family," Sam muttered, but he knew there was no real danger: Mattie wasn't talking to anyone in her family, except for Sue, who had been her vassal so long she didn't have a word of her own, and Sue's husband, Jim, who worked at a garage and whom Sam called "Gentleman Jim" because it annoyed Mattie beyond reason. She came on her own, clean as an orphan: that was one of her advantages. Sam had met his parents-in-law no more than half-a-dozen times: the first when they got engaged and the last time at the wedding, when her dad, with a drunk's bent for malicious melodrama, had begun by weeping into Sam's carnation buttonhole how he'd reared his Mattie like a queen and now she was leaving him in the dirt, and ended by threatening to shut down the party and get his money back because Sam had been sticking his daughter for years. The older Hookers left shortly after, on the pretext that Sam's mother wasn't feeling well: he would never forget the mortified look on his father's face, as if he were the one who had misbehaved.

From that day forth, Roger Doucette was struck from Mattie's books. Her mom, whom she'd never had much use for, dropped dead shortly after Isaac's birth while hanging out the wash: Sue found her in the yard wrapped in wet sheets like a drip-dry shroud. Roger limped along on his 120-proof liver, a merry widower, shooting rabbits, bouncing checks, spying at undressing girls' windows, threatening the neighbors. You're a half orphan now, Mattie, Sam pointed out. I been an orphan all my life, was her rejoinder; I'd have been better off an orphan. When they passed Doucettes in a store, Mattie made him look the other way. He didn't care: it never occurred to him that his wife's quarrelsomeness was a trait that perhaps should be curbed before it ran wild.

One of the world's minor gambles is what kind of parent a person will become. To Sam, the humble rapture and perfect concentration his infant son roused in him and just as obviously didn't in Mattie were utterly unforeseeable, and the reverse of how each had approached the prospect. With all her might Mattie wanted babies. The wife part of marriage played to her material ambitions, but in itself had little hold over her imagination, compared to a hungry certainty as undeniable as a salmon's urge upstream. She had been undissuadably red-hot to reproduce and dead-set from the start that their first be a boy, and once pregnant she was boisterously happy, a woman in her element.

With her son's emergence into the world, all this concentration mysteriously ended. Was it, Isaac wondered later, because he was so marred and wretched, so inconsolable an infant?

Whatever the reason, Mattie looked upon the Living Reality with unfeigned indifference. She was as milky as Rubens's great squirting goddess of the Milky Way, she rose good-naturedly at one and three and six, she displayed a dexterity with diapers amazing in a woman to whom all other domestic skills were alien, who could make a boiled egg taste disgusting, she becalmed his fits of bawling in record time; but she had instantly taken against him. As soon as Isaac was old enough to demand his father, she handed him over for good. More like a wet nurse than a mother. She thought the baby had a discontented look about him and a nasty temper, would never be changed or put to sleep without a struggle. Smile, she commanded, and he wouldn't smile. Petey Karolis and James Earl Randall burst into crinkly unasked-for grins; Isaac Hooker cast a pall over company with his manifest unblinking misery. He was always sick: she couldn't abide sickness, it was a kind of selfishness. When she and Sam were told he couldn't see past his nose and was deaf in one ear—childhood deafness; it sometimes went away—that did it.

Sam, on the other hand, had never been keen to reproduce. His own belief was that man's best course was rapid extinction; why bring another body into a dull and mediocre world? Anyway, the Russians were about to drop the bomb so what was the point?

"How come whenever I tell you it's time we had a baby, you start up about the Russians? If I got pregnant now, it'd be born in May, just eighteen months after its cousin Sarah. If you get your way, Sue's gonna be a grandmother before we get started."

"I'm going to take you to the vet and get you altered," he threatened, only half-jokingly.

"I've got news for you, buster, it isn't the girls they alter."

"Why do you want to spoil our fun?" Sam complained, and in a last-ditch appeal to Mattie's thrift, "A child would drive us to the poorhouse."

"You could always get a job," said his wife, implacably. In fact, Sam suspected her chief motive, after keeping up with her sister, was to prevent him once and for all from ever finishing his graduate work. These were the days before he had given up on being a college professor.

And yet it was Sam who from first sight cleaved to Isaac with a sure and visceral passion, as if this boy had come out of *his* gut, and taken a part of it with him.

The Hookers had been living in Jessup County since the 1860s. Sam's great-grandfather—the first Isaac—had immigrated to the United States from one of those gray northern mill towns along the Mersey. The English Hookers had been a family of Lancashire weavers and laborers, pietists and dissenters, men with Scripture in the blood and argument in the bone, lanky and devout troublemakers, high-shouldered whey-faced sons of England's traditional revolutionary class. When the first cotton factories were cast up by the spume of Liverpool, they worked as hand-loom weavers and, with the arrival of power looms, they were out of business. They came to the New World so as not to starve.

Sam's great-grandfather was luckier than most immigrants: he had a language, religion, and skills that traveled. He docked in Boston and headed north for New Hampshire, a state bespattered with several hundred townships the size of a handkerchief, each with a Congregational church, a public library, a town hall cut from Yankee-issue white clapboard, and engirding an immaculate green.

The first Isaac Hooker settled not on dairyland or seacoast or in the mountainous remote North but in the southwestern region of mill towns clinging to the Connecticut River, and found work in the Gilboa Mill, which boasted of providing "red flannel for the forty-niners, blue for the New Orleans stevedores." His family moved into a narrow and insalubrious red-brick row house built for mill hands, and there the first American Hookers were born: twelve children, nine of whom died in infancy.

Sam and his son used to ride to the old graveyard above town and read from cracked lichen-sooty limestone their baby ancestors' legends, hefty names, somber and accusing as a crow's caw, tricked out with ribands of Scripture: Hepzibah *aetat* 3, and Rufus who departed this earth aged 1 year 2 months, Mehitabel, Asa, J.H., Nettie, Reuel, Rebekah, and Peleg.

Some of the first Isaac's mobilizing determination wore off on his only surviving son, Sam's grandfather, who left the mill as a young boy to turn up some years later as the owner of a general store in nearby Hebron. Hooker's was a spruce and polished establishment that served as post office, market, social club. It sold clothing, hardware, and household goods, farm and garden supplies. By the thirties, it had a lunch counter and soda fountain in front and a warehouse out back, where feed and grain were heaved into the beds of pickup trucks. The store was well situated and did a flourishing business, acting as a kind of covered marketplace in which farmers and townspeople congregated to talk and buy. If you didn't hear it at Hooker's, it didn't happen.

Sam's father, Ned, who worked at Hooker's as a young man and later took it over, lacked the mind for it—that detached, gregarious, canny, flexible, and tenacious commercial spirit that guesses what people want before they want it, and when they don't. A vague dreamer with no taste for business, he introduced new lines when he should have cut back, and couldn't be bothered to stock the items that proved popular. While his own father was alive, business thrived, but under Ned's care Hooker's withered slowly on the vine. Eventually only old-timers came in, mostly to talk. Everyone else bought at Aubuchon's or Agway or the new Sears in Gilboa, and hung out at the diner on Route 101. With the advent of shopping malls, Hooker's was out of business. Mr. Hooker ended up selling the store shortly before he died, at the depths of the real-estate depression; later, Mattie never stopped reminding Sam how much his father's property would now be worth.

In truth, Sam's father didn't like work; his secret love was music. As a bachelor living at home he had taught himself to read scores, installed a secondhand piano, and took lessons from a Polish lady. He had a lovely tenor, too, although he could never rise early enough to sing in the church choir. At the great age of thirty-eight, a golden-haired speckled plump and sweating giant with dimpled hands and fingers like parting sea anemones, he married Emily Bramley, the most beautiful girl in the world. As far as Sam could guess, his father was scared of the store and spent his day hiding from customers, took home too many of its goods, loved to spend money, worshiped his wife, and was sorry to the end of his days he had never gone to college.

As for Isaac, he knew his grandfather as an emphysemic old man who wore his trousers belted up high over a round belly and panted like a thirsty dog, a man with small blue eyes very far apart in his pink face, clean as a baby, with a mild high voice, a few streaks of fair hair pasted across a gleaming white forehead, cheeks smelling of soap and shyness, and fingers smelling of cigarette. He always seemed embarrassed to want to cuddle his grandsons so, and afraid he wouldn't be able to amuse them.

Ned Hooker kept a diary, which Sam discovered after his mother's death, when he was left to clear out their house. Begun when its author was a lonely, indolent nineteen-year-old, convinced he would never meet anyone who loved him, the journal ran to six volumes, a family of thick, plum-colored accounting ledgers, blue-lined, with red margins, impressed in a hand curly, long, and eager, sprayed with girlish exclamation points and underlinings.

At first Sam scanned the diary mainly to find his own name, and laughed at such items as "Samuel is now five years old and contradicts whatever anybody tells him," but as the years progressed he cropped up less frequently in his father's days, usually in connection with the delicately expressed hope that the boy would find his calling and be happy. Vanity disappointed, Sam felt guiltier than ever at not having been a more loving son to this love-starved man.

From his father's diary Sam learned that the old man called his wife "My Marigold," "My Sweetness," or "My Sunshine," that he wished his little girls would never grow up and violently loathed their suitors, that he dearly loved the sweet pensive valleys, aromatic orchards, and dark hills of his birthplace and the Ashuelot River that snaked its thrusting silver coils around Hebron, and that he worshiped God with a faith more anxious and laborious than need be, perhaps because he feared God didn't like him as much as he liked God, perhaps because he knew in truth he loved music better. Sam, whose own early stabs at diary keeping alternated "Meatloaf and blueberry pie for supper" with "Uncovered a Russian Spies Nest in cabin behind Bear Ridge," felt chastened by the transparent sincerity. More unsettling were the items in homemade code intimating that well into their sixties—how could one bear thinking such things of one's parents?—his mother and father were enjoying the heartiest of conjugal relations. "Holy Moses!" said Sam, and that's where he stopped reading.

Humility has a dank and shameful smell to the young, the scent of failure, lowliness, obscurity. Growing up, an only son, Sam had added his mother's resentment of her husband's improvidence to his own masculine anxieties. He was embarrassed by his father, and avoided him as a kind of sentimental sissy, not very clever, not very manly, certainly not very athletic, a man who had brought his wife down in the world, whose eyes fogged over at "Fairest Lord Jesus" and who was more comfortable talking dresses and hairdos with his daughters than taking his son to hockey games. Mr. Hooker had an odd and unexpected sense of humor. He wisecracked straight-faced so that no-body—especially not Sam, who didn't think jokes about himself were very funny—knew for sure when he was kidding. On the rare occasions when people understood and laughed, his father, trying valiantly not to smile, crimsoned with pleasure. For ages he pretended to have joined the Shriners and threatened to march down Union Avenue in the annual parade, sporting red velvet pantaloons and a tasseled cap, waving and blowing kisses at Sam's teachers and classmates. The boy, seething, rose to the bait every time. Only later did he realize his father was a far more serious man than he.

Sam grew up never entirely having banished from his collection of beliefs his older sister's claim that he was adopted, and determined to make his getaway at an early age. He hated, as all that was cramped and timid, their tiny house on Chestnut Street, and the special voice his mother put on when Mr. Saylor, an engineer who rented their top floor, came by. It made him want to sneeze—he was *allergic* to his own home. He hated the stifled, halting triviality of table talk every evening over supper, hated being the only boy in a family of girls and getting no help from his father, who succumbed reverently to all this tyrannical overweening femininity. He was ashamed that his father owned a store, simply because he was ashamed of everything his father did and even of having a father at all; the fact that this father demanded so little of him made those few demands insufferable. Asked to help out at Hooker's after school or over vacation, Sam complied with a churlish and sullen resentment, in terror that his friends might pass by and see him trapped and on display in that musty superannuated hole. Summers he hid behind the counter, reading and smoking, hoping nobody would come in, and enjoying in spite of himself the knowing idle town talk of the old men and the smell of loose tobacco and fresh paper.

"I wanted to be a tough guy, a big shot," Sam later confessed to his son Isaac. "You know, one of those swaggering, bowlegged loudmouths who play stickball and run the neighborhood poker club out of Bobby Garvey's basement."

"Who's Bobby Garvey?"

"*Who is Bobby Garvey?*" repeated Sam, incredulously. "You mean to say you never heard of Bobby Garvey, terror of Chestnut Street? Bobby Garvey whose mother was always in our kitchen blubbering that her son was going to land in state prison breaking stones or wake up dead at the age of twenty? Who made me walk half a mile out of my way every morning and afternoon so I wouldn't get chased with a broken bottle?"

"Where's he now?" asked Isaac, apprehensively.

"Odd jobs, sick wife. Asked me for a loan a few years ago, which I scraped up for him just for the satisfaction of feeling superior." (Sam, who was always helping people out, insisted on putting the most unbecoming construction on his kindness.)

"So you weren't a tough guy?" Isaac asked, disbelieving.

"Me? I was a *shrimp*. Much lighter and smaller than you. I didn't grow till junior year of high school, and then I could never make my pounds catch up with my inches."

"What did you want to be when you grew up?"

Sam laughed. "What does it matter? I haven't been it."

"No, really," pursued Isaac. "Tell me, Daddy."

"I didn't know. I didn't want to be anything. I wasn't like you."

"You had to want to be *something*."

"I didn't know," Sam insisted. How could he explain to his confident, overbearing Isaac what it was like to be raised by Depression-humbled parents in a community whose three or four ruling families were pious, civic-minded, thrifty, and sober, whose sons farmed and served on town councils and went overseas to fight and whose daughters kept house and raised children, in which it was taken for granted you would do what your parents had done and to draw attention to yourself in any way was considered vulgar, unfortunate? Thank God for the delinquency and rebelliousness his fellow teachers lamented in today's crop of teenagers.

"Well, if you *had* wanted to be, what would you have wanted to be?" Isaac persisted.

Sam meditated on Isaac's expectant, almost reproachful face. "A starting pitcher for the Red Sox."

Isaac didn't believe him. And funnily enough, Sam couldn't bring himself to say even or especially to his own son what he really had wanted to be when he was growing up in the late forties and early fifties. This was it: he wanted to be rich. Without having to work for it. And he wanted to be famous. Badly. But famous for what he didn't know. And he wanted women dripping off his sleeves, strewing his paths. But mostly rich. And famous. But to admit that that was what he had wanted was to admit he had once believed he was owed a special break for nothing, that it hadn't come to pass, and never would. Who could say it wouldn't? You might win the state lottery. And maybe— this was more prohibited still—fame would come to him through his son Isaac. Arab patriarchs call themselves "Father of Salah," "Father of Ahmad." Glory through children.

In the winter of 1952, Sam's inchoate yearnings were given a name when Bobby Garvey squeezed him up against the wall of the ice rink and, pretending Sam's leg was the puck, splintered his tibia with a powerful swipe of a hockey stick. It was then, that housebound February, with only his mother for company, that a fussed-over, restive, and chafing Sam began for the first time to read books. It was a fiery birth. Jack London, Joseph Conrad, Somerset Maugham—and later, when he was a conceited young man, Eliot and Joyce and Yeats—were Sam's catapult to meaning and importance, to a world of soot and salt and cities, of foreign languages and sailors' dives and loose women and saxophones and native insurrections. Sam read, picturing himself a rum-and-disease-soaked ruin sprawled in the toasty bronze lap of a Melanesian sphinx; he saw himself manager of a Congolese gold mine, staking his all at the roulette table of a cross-eyed croupier in Brazzaville; or a foreign correspondent swilling Fundador with bullfighters in a cellar in Pamplona. He wanted to grow a beard, to sleep on the beach, he wanted to ride the subway to Coney Island, to wait at the stage door for a crimson-lipped showgirl—at dawn he would lead her home to his garret with a mattress on the floor and a fire escape at the window. He longed to stow away on a freighter to Lisbon and Algiers, to sip murky coffee from tiny cups at an outside café by a harbor stinking of coconuts and grease, and he hungered after these experiences with an intensity that made his chest ache and tears steam to his eyes.

What connection such pinings had to his own life Sam could not see. Only another war could have helped him out, and that wasn't the mode of foreign travel he hankered after. From high school he went on to Gilboa State, but it was more like a second story of high school than a place where it might occur to someone you could live by literature. Then in his senior year he met an English professor named Christopher Scannon, and everything changed.

Thank God for the fortuitousness with which genius and geography combine, thought Isaac years later. Thank God not all talented men and women swarm to cities and get famous and hang out together and think the same way and preen for the world's praise. No, sometimes, whether from indolence or obstinacy or reclusiveness or poverty or dependence or accident or missionary zeal, shining and rare talents burn isolated in remote parts, sometimes a first-rate sinologist may be living in Saskatchewan, or the author of a novel unparalleled in ferocity and beauty may raise geese in Maine before migrating to a mobile home in Albuquerque—he did, too—while the tiniest town library in Arkansas, thanks to the bequest of a self-taught son, might boast a stunning collection of books on French history.

And this broad scattering of wealth, this hoarding of precious objects in remote places, is what has secured the preservation and transmission of learning. The earliest extant scrolls of Isaiah and the Psalms survived because a small community of malcontents decided to leave Roman-occupied Jerusalem and live in caves in the desert. Bishop Wulfstan lived in Yorkshire in the eleventh century and by sheer longevity and isolation is said single-handedly to have ensured that English prose outlived the Norman Conquest. You can lament the homogenization of contemporary life, with every hamlet sprouting the same franchises, and local dialects and costume melting into a bland uniformity, but look closer and see the secret richness, the ineradicable quirks.

And maybe this is because people in all serious ways have more in common with their parents than with their peers, moving through their lives as unknowing carriers of these hidden impulses and capabilities, geniuses, blots, and crotchets that only bloom in age and seclusion, leaving the ancestral bone the barer.

The price, save for those few geniuses who have pursued electrifyingly unheard-of experiments in private, is a certain old-fashionedness. So it was, at any rate, with the happy circumstance that brought an accomplished professor of English poetry to a rural state college, boasting a few hundred farmers' sons and daughters, and put him in Isaac's father's path. Sam would tell you it was sheer love of comfort that brought Christopher Scannon to Gilboa, New Hampshire: he had been teaching at Boston College but after his wife's death came to live with his sister, working out an agreeable arrangement at the college to keep him in pin money and admiring listeners.

In the fall of his senior year, Sam took Scannon's course in sixteenth- and seventeenth-century English poetry.

"*You* look like a muscular young Christian," remarked the old man briskly, fixing upon Sam his pale bop-eyed gaze. It was after class and the boy as usual was loitering about the teacher's desk, hoping to be noticed. Sam gulped. Who, him? Was he being made fun of? For an instant he considered explaining that he wasn't a Christian, let alone muscular—no way was he going to be thought a churchgoing meathead like the rest of his classmates—but instead he grinned obligingly.

"Have you got a strong back? Are you willing to cart a few books for an old man? I'll stand you a drink if you help me move my office."

Fluttered and dizzy with gratitude, Sam assented.

"*Both* offices are the size of a small latrine and just as dank," explained Scannon as they set off at a clip. "My old office, however, looks out on the parking lot; the new one looks out at the blue pinnacles of M-M-M-Mount Menasseh, so that I may lift my eyes unto the hills, while marking your classmates' m-misspelt plagiarisms."

Scannon was a tiny wizened dandy, a courtly souse with a broad New England accent who could whip a class into feeling as blessed and excitable as persecuted Christians in the catacombs of English literature. Flirtatiously, he enlisted them in the conspiracy of art, infecting a dozen youngsters with his own feel for the ivory complexity of Sidney's sonnets, for Herbert's shivery winged fevers, for the diffident glory of Marvell's flaming greens, his fruits, his ticklish aromatic hay and sweaty mowers and gelid serpentine rivers, for Donne's sinewy braggart mockeries of death and desire or Wyatt's stiff-lipped laments, whose scansion no man yet could crack.

Poets and their readers constituted an immaculate aristocracy, and the rest of the world was, in his two favorite words—he had an occasional willed stammer, the tiny, bowlegged rascal—m-mediocre and m-m-m-meretricious. How m-mischievously—like an anarchist giving instruction in the art of laying explosives—he transmitted to this unformed band the knotted essence of another man's mind and language, the historical currents that buffeted him, the inherited knowledge and allusions poets turned inside out and bounced against the wall, inverted, laughed at, and renewed, thus asserting by rebellion their own place in a tradition golden and unending. How he delighted in holding a poem like a ruby in his little monkey palm, to be turned over and admired, facet by facet, gleam by gleam.

Sam was in love, from a distance. Today he got lucky.

Fourteen cartons of books and fourteen flights of stairs later, the two men sallied forth into the clear tremulous spring sunlight, steering toward the Stateside Saloon. Sam was apprehensive but thrilled. He had never tasted hard liquor; he had never been inside a bar, let alone the infamous Stateside, and he certainly didn't know you could visit one at four o'clock in the afternoon, in broad daylight. He did somehow know that liquor and literature went together. Scannon ordered Wild Turkey; Sam followed suit.

"I'm fond of the Stateside," remarked Scannon, over their first round. "It fulfills the first and central requirement for any tavern," and pausing for effect, pronounced, eyes popping, "*It's dark.*"

It was indeed dark, although Sam could spot across the room the fathers of several classmates. The two men fastened happily upon their drinks in the sympathetic murkiness of this dive that smelled like the inside of a barrel, and bantamweight Sam let the whiskey's treacled flames slide down his throat. He sat, rolling a little, his head unaccountably heavy and his neck unaccountably frail, and his back, wrenched from the last carton of books, unaccountably healed, while Scannon held forth on women and literature and liquor and spring. And Sam soaked up the racy, sonorous talk, clutching the table, saying to himself over and over, in words that ran whirligigs in his head, "This is the *life*."

"Have you got a girl, Mr. Hooker?" inquired Scannon.

"Yes. Her name is Mattie."

"Maggie?"

"No, Mattie. Mattie's her name."

"Well, you'd better get it straight. Are you engaged?"

"I hope not!" stammered Sam, ungallantly.

"Well, watch out. Women are very forceful creatures, and a man must be sure to choose one who makes subjugation sweet. My own late wife was thirty-eight when we wed, and just coming into her own, the dear thing. You know, of course, Samuel Johnson's words: 'A woman has such power between the ages of twenty-five and forty-five that she may tie a man to a post and whip him if she will.'"

Sam got the giggles so hard the bourbon came snorting out of his nostrils. He had barely heard of Samuel Johnson. He had never heard of anybody.

Thus, in Sam's senior year of college, began a sacred and intoxicating friendship. Mattie, who had no reverence for learning, sarcastically inquired how come every time Sam saw Scannon, he came home and threw up. Your Jesus, she called him. Scannon was one of those fellows who don't do for themselves, but always manage to find a supply of people ready and eager to do for them; Sam had an as yet unsurfaced hunger to do. When he wasn't courting Mattie, he was driving Scannon to the barber or mowing his lawn or raking his leaves or trying to fix his toaster, or just sitting in the Stateside getting stewed and memorizing the man's glorious talk.

There was a creased and faded snapshot of Sam that his son Isaac half loved and half hated (well, hated, really), sitting in Scannon's backyard on a summer's day, Scannon plummy, dapper, with bulging eyes, no eyebrows, gnarled hands, Sam a skinny youngster in a T-shirt and dungarees, with a look on his face Isaac never saw, laughing open-mouthed and eyes alight with joy. And another photograph—same afternoon—of Sam hugging Mattie, dragging her down, Mattie in a sleeveless dress, buxom, a dark-skinned beauty, smirking. Was everyone happier before Isaac was born?

Escapism joined with hero worship in Sam's love for Scannon and the poetic tradition. It was senior year. All his friends seemed to know what they were doing with the rest of their lives, some already had jobs waiting for them, some guys were getting drafted (he was disqualified by asthma), and all Sam knew was that he wanted this raw, snowbound New Hampshire spring to last forever, to keep on sitting in bars and reading sonnets as long as he lived. It didn't take much doing for Scannon to sweet-talk him into graduate work.

"Go for a Ph.D. in English literature. There are worse fates. You can get a master's in a year, and become a teacher's assistant to defray your expenses."

Sam brooded over the prospect overnight. Was it possible that he could escape from Hebron and its inhibiting small-mindedness, become a college professor, teach poetry all his life, maybe even write a book someday? And even if he didn't end up an English professor, mightn't he at least buy a few extra years in which to figure out what he did want to do? He told his parents, who were at once pleased and rather scared. Sam was the first person in the family even to have ventured past high school.

As for his wife-to-be, she was less enthusiastic. She wasn't really cut out to be a professor's wife. Still, she'd get used to it, or they'd get used to her.

His life was settled; he had a career. It was a choice at once exhilarating and comforting for a lazy young man eaten up by only the least practical of longings, by ambitions enormous and ill defined. It later appeared to Sam that his interest in poetry was no natural vocation but mere impressionability: if Scannon had been a plumber, he would have fallen for pipes and drains.

When it came time to apply to graduate school, however, Mattie most unexpectedly refused to budge.

"Go to Mars, Samuel, see if I care. I'm staying right here where I got friends and family and a good job." She was the one who always called him a stick-in-the-mud!

"You never even see your family," Sam objected.

"How would you know?" was her illogical reply.

Momentarily defeated, Sam applied to the University of Massachusetts and was offered a small fellowship. For one febrile and disembodied year, still living in his parents' house in Hebron yet in his own mind already married and gone, Sam rose at dawn four days a week and drove southeast to Amherst, rushing through classes and seminars and papers so he could be home in time to pick up his girlfriend from work. Years later, the mention of Brattleboro or Greenfield or South Deerfield—the milestones along his hurtling race from girl to books down Route 5, past a whiz of blue mountains and lone red farmhouses with shiny silos—still jolted Sam's nervous system into almost unbearable anxiety and excitement.

They would hang out at Sadie's till it closed, then head back to her parents' place, where Sam, the angelic hierarchies still tripping through his brain, made love to Mattie on the couch while she between stifled moans argued the merits of live bands versus deejays, sit-down dinners versus buffets, or more sharply announced, "Get off, Sam, my dad's coming down"—her father at odd watches of the night having remembered there were still a few liquid ounces of Old Crow stowed in the glove compartment of his pickup. Sam must have been out of his mind. How did he pass his exams? Then that summer was the wedding, after which he and his bride moved into a one-room apartment above the laundromat in Gilboa, and Sam didn't go to classes any more, but hung out at the Gilboa State library, fooling around with his master's thesis, which was supposedly on Fulke Greville, an Elizabethan poet of an austere and doggedly intellectual religiosity, who was famous mostly for being Sidney's best friend. That's the epitaph he had written for his own gravestone: friend to Sir Philip Sidney, who had died forty-two years before and left a big hole in Greville's heart, which he filled with somber Calvinist sonnets. And Sam, who had begun smoking a pipe and carried in the pocket of his corduroy jacket literary rags with names from the Greek myths, and who still met Scannon at the Stateside every Friday evening, hardly noticed when the Red Sox made it to the World Series. He was learning the new virtues of the age: ambiguity, complexity, and doubt.

Marriage to Mattie made life a little less ambiguous and a little more complex.

"No good, boys. The ice ain't even froze over yet." Gabriel Hanesworth, standing on the narrow rim of shore, poked a broken branch into one viscous green-black corner of the pond. It was early December and the pond in the Hanesworths' backwoods wasn't solidly frozen: a skin of wrinkled dark ice lay around the edges like skim on boiled milk, leaving islands and peninsulas of liquid sedge in the middle.

"It's thick enough for sliding," Isaac contradicted. "You wouldn't want to ride a Mack truck over it yet, but it's thick enough." He made as if to take a step out onto the crusty surface of this slippery moon.

"No, you don't." Gabriel pulled him back. "My dad would beat us blue if he found out we'd been sliding when the ice is too thin. You want to drown?"

The other children broke through the underbrush now, panting and giggling—Isaac's cousins Sarah and Jimmy Randall; Georgie Hanesworth; Isaac's younger brother, Turner; Justin James; the Hanesworths' dog Willy. A pair of brand-new white leather skates with sheathed blades hung expectantly by their laces over Sarah's plump shoulders.

"What's the story?"

"It's kinda thin. The ice ain't froze over enough yet," repeated Gabriel.

"Oh." The children fanned out around the pond, searching, prodding for solid ice.

"Maybe we oughta send Willy out on the ice to test it," suggested Justin.

"Oh yeah? Maybe we oughta send *you.*"

Justin, a daredevil, planted one leg on the surface, and leaning his weight on it gingerly, lost his balance and, arms flailing, found himself crunching through knee-deep into arctic water before Gabriel and Georgie could hoist him back. He scrambled back up the slope, leg dripping. "Uuuggghh. What a *mother.* Jeeez, it's cold as a witch's tit in there."

"Whose stupid idea was this, anyway?"

"You want to skate, Sarah? Don't mind us."

"Let's go."

Damp snowstorm air, white sky, blackish pond, laggard restlessness as the children hung around, preparing to leave. Then Isaac spoke up. Isaac was a fat boy and bookish, but sometimes he came up with wild ideas. This was one of them.

"Well, we can't slide. So let's swim." He spoke decisively, looking from right to left with a strange smile.

Nervous giggles. He was one of those boys you could never tell if he was serious or if he was kidding.

"Now, that's a great idea." Justin snickered. "After you, Ike."

"I'm going swimming," Isaac blurted out. He was serious, it seemed. "Don't be a loon."

Isaac had already moved into action. He was bent in two now, untying his laces, shimmying his way out of his high-top sneakers, hopping a little as he shed shoes and socks. He laid his glasses in one shoe. "So why can't you go swimming just because it's winter? I don't want to be a captive to temperature. I want to go swimming now." There were patches of snow on the ground, and his naked white toes curled up in instinctive revolt. It was raw, it was damp, it was December, the pond, half-frozen over, looked like death. Isaac was undressing in the wintry air. A half-frightened solemnity seized the small group. Was he really going in? Who would stop him?

"Your brother's crazy, you know that?" Gabriel addressed Turner. "Ike, you're crazy. You can't go in the water in December: you'd go in shock. Stop showing off, put your shoes back on, and let's go home."

"You're going to freeze your balls off," warned Justin.

Isaac, frowning, paused to decide whether to go in fully clothed or stripped. Don't think about it. Just do it.

"Take 'em off, stripper," yelled Justin. Isaac pulled off his undershirt resolutely.

"He's not going to do it," someone said, maybe Georgie, maybe Jimmy. Stripped to long johns, Isaac descended the slope to the pond's muddy, leaf-embedded frozen edge, his toes kneading that muddy murk. There was an almost sickened fear mingled with fascination that gripped the watching boys and girl. His younger brother, Turner, kept glancing quickly from Isaac to the other children, chewing his lower lip.

Then Isaac waded into the water and plunged, with an enormous splash that made everyone leap back, shivering. BVDs ballooning up like life rafts, he plunged into the black menacing water bordered by floes of ice, his whole body going under, blond head ducking under its clotted surface. For a moment, he was gone. The winter had swallowed him up. Trapped under the ice. The boy was gone and dead for good, frozen, lost. Who would go in after him? Who was going to tell his parents? Sarah let out a little involuntary scream, and Gabriel with his stick rushed to the water's edge, ready to follow. Finally Isaac resurfaced, gasping like a whale, squirting water and letting out a blood-curdling "Ooooooo-eeeeeeeeh!" of sheer physical shock. Waist-deep he stood, a strange blind white-fleshed whale, pale hair smeared to his head, teeth chattering, arms and face already turning blue, grinning from ear to ear. His friends giggled in nervous relief at the strangeness of the sight, and Isaac laughed, too, drumming his ice-stiff chest with two scalded-blue trembling fists and letting out whoops loud and unearthly.

God damn him, thought Turner. There was his brother swimming in December, yelling like a werewolf, and all the other kids hanging on the shore, Justin James, Georgie and Gabriel, the Randalls, wonder wearing off. He ought to get out of the water now; it was too cold. Time to go home, before he got pneumonia or some grownup came along and caught them. The joke was over.

"Come on out," Gabriel urged.

"Anyone care to join me?"

Silence.

"We're not lunatics like you," said Jimmy Randall.

"Our dad would skin us alive," Georgie decided. "Come on out, Ike."

Teeth chattering so convulsively that the words seemed to shudder and dance from his blue lips in frozen jerks. "How about you, Turner?"

He knew this was coming. He knew Isaac was going to call on him from that frozen deep. Even in the muzzy height of August, he shrank from ponds: you never knew what you were stepping on. Salamanders, mud, broken glass. Where did the salamanders go when the pond froze over? The other kids were on his side: no one wanted to go in, no one expected him to. It had been Isaac's idea all along; no reason to drag anyone else along with him. He ducked under the water again, and leaped up, bobbing and gasping.

"I'm John the Baptist. Anybody who hasn't been baptized, come on in and I'll dunk you. Turner, you never been dunked. Come on in and be born again like Jimmy Carter!"

"I don't want to be like Jimmy Carter."

But he felt the dare claiming him irresistibly, felt its momentum propelling him along. There at his side were the Randalls and the Hanesworths and Justin James, already bored by and rather fearful of this new joke, wanting to go home, and there in the ice up to his waist was Turner's brother, who never knew when to stop, who never knew when enough was enough, but because he was fat and short-sighted and clumsy embarrassingly insisted on being more daring than the fit. And Turner's guilty heart went out to Isaac, bobbing, blue with cold, too proud to come out. Everybody watching. Had to. Yes, he had to, because he was frightened to, because he so terribly didn't want to, to keep up Hooker pride. What a pain. Turner felt himself practicing the entrance, testing the muddy, leaf-clogged water; going in would be better than coming out again, wet clothes hanging, having to make your way home in air thirty-eight degrees. But if his head hit that sheet of ice . . . Just go on, don't think about it.

"I don't want to be baptized."

"You have to be, or else you're going to hell."

Somebody said, "Okay," softly and that somebody was Turner. Somebody was taking off his shoes and laying the folded socks neatly within their warm caves, somebody was slowly stripping down to underclothes, and somebody, shivering in mute anticipation, was treading barefoot in a deliberate trance of disbelief down to the edge and not stopping there, but walking on, big step after big step down into the muddy water, water flooding his shorts, swelling up, ballooning them into buoys, and a cold so mean so intense so invasive it was an ache in the legs and the joints. Eyes fixed on his brother, who was bobbing around just before the ice began, Turner waded deeper on feet turned to knives of ice like the mermaid in the fairy tale, gashed by rocks and sharp branches on the pond's silted bottom. And now he fell into the pond, and the icy dark water, which was pure ache, smelling of mud and branches and sodden leaves and winter, swept over him, flooding his eardrums like pure pain.

Mattie Doucette showed up in fifth grade, having been kept back a year.

That was in 1950, and she and Sam had grown up together, going on to high school together in that stout brick building anchored to the Ashuelot River. When Isaac, eager to know the origins of the planetary clash that ended up producing him, used to ask his parents when and how they had met, they exchanged vague looks, shrugged unhelpfully. It wasn't a small-town question. They had never *not* known each other, although Mattie professed to have no recollection whatsoever of her future husband. Sam could readily believe it. Just as tigers move through the jungle without seeming aware that birds or monkeys exist, Mattie, whose supreme gift as a child seemed to lie partly in an unassailably confident and callous disregard, could not possibly have registered Sam—not because he was a jerk, but because he lived on a different and hence invisible plane. Another time, however, she volunteered, "Your dad was always smart. He was teacher's pet every year. Honestly, I was in awe of him he was so smart. They used to read his papers aloud, tell the other kids to try and write like Samuel Hooker. I would never have dreamt he'd give a dummy like me the time of day."

"I thought you didn't remember me," teased Sam.

"That was in grade school. I'm talking high school now." It was true Mattie had no memory of childhood. Only once she hit thirteen, fourteen, did awareness set in: from then on, every encounter, speech, gesture was socked away in her mental archives, reproduced for laughs. Memory was a weapon: Mattie became a mimic.

Did Sam remember Mattie? "With dread," and he was only half joking.

Mattie had shown up in their class the first day of the new school year, snarly and defiant as a captured Amazon. Which was not far from the case. Doucettes were notorious around Hebron and Gilboa—a warring clan of hillbilly drifters, whose daughters got pregnant before they married and whose sons got caught stealing cars. They were French Canadian, which was second worse in local hierarchy only to Polish. "Mackerel snatchers" was what Sam's otherwise tolerant father called Roman Catholics, though unlike the others Mattie wasn't carted off one afternoon a week for religious instruction. A lapsed mackerel snatcher. In fifth grade, Sam looked down on her because she couldn't spell or add or read and always gave the teacher a hard time. She had a nihilistic streak that waged a permanent war against her native canniness: she not only didn't know, but was damned if she would ever learn or let anyone else do so. Prime among Sam's childhood memories was Mattie Doucette throwing her gym shoe at Miss Walters and calling her an old witch. There was a certain amount of controversy over whether the word was in fact "witch." If they had decided it wasn't, Mattie would have been expelled, and Sam would have seen the last of her. On that *w* hung his future.

In high school Mattie was never content to rampage on her own, but insisted on corralling a herd of underlings. The fun was less in the game than in the number she could force to play. The whole class, Sam anonymously included, would be pressed into cutting history or math or hiding in the boiler room or jumping up and yelling, "Boo!" when the teacher came into the room, and if anyone resisted she went into a frightful temper. Sam, susceptible but stubborn, intensely resented these attempts to herd him into collective misdeeds. She was a bully, a female Bobby Garvey, but in female lay all the difference.

A glossy-black-haired beauty, with a raven mantle that rose from her low forehead in waves, Mattie Doucette had plump limbs sealed in an olive wax, freakishly pale blue eyes, and a nose like a hawk. She resembled one of those Assyrian kings with eagles' beaks and shaggy lions' flanks who stride in profile across limestone temple walls. By twelve she had burst into precocious bloom and was already accusingly alive, with a woman's figure almost cartoonishly exaggerated, ready to go.

By ninth or tenth grade, she had begun to assume an equally imperious but now more distant, impatient look. Also, she was flunking out. She wore tight angora sweaters and swung her hips when she moved, and she had a filthy mouth. When teachers saw her on the hockey field brandishing her stick and busting out of her school uniform, or chewing gum in the halls, their hearts sank. Yet Mattie continued to rule the class by a kind of animal majesty that once he hit pubescence made Sam grovel in his dreams at her plump little feet, though he knew that practically every older boy in town had had his hands down her pants, and that her father didn't mind.

After high school he didn't see or think of Mattie Doucette. Until one evening, walking down Union Avenue from the college library, killing time in the deepening dusk before heading back to Hebron and his parents' house, he spotted her through the window behind the counter of Bolts. Without thinking, he went in and said hello. She was working there as assistant manager. He was surprised how pleased she seemed to be to see him, and how happy he was to see her. Aggressively ebullient as ever, she cracked jokes about their former classmates, her old boyfriends.

"Those guys are going *nowhere*," she said with a scorn that made Sam wonder with genuine curiosity where she thought *she* was going. "How's college? *I* should've gone to college."

"I'm a junior," he told her.

"You don't look so junior, Junior."

He started poking around the store with the professional eye of a would-be rival, wondering what it would be like to work in a place where, unlike Hooker's, people actually came in and bought things. Mattie's boss had gone home early, she explained; it was past closing time. "If you want to hang around while I close up, maybe we can go somewhere afterwards, have a drink."

Did she mean it? Was she giving him license? How far would she let him go? Did she still live at home? *Anything* might happen. It would. Sam, tingling in the grip of an unpredictable force, watched her bring down the blinds, empty the cash registers with a slapdash command. Her hips and bottom swayed as she moved. If she were a man you would almost call it a swagger. She was small but packed and curvy. By forty all that voluptuousness would turn to waistless lard: he had seen her mother waddling from curb to car like an arthritic backcountry Buddha. But the knowledge that even now Mattie was almost past her prime for some reason excited him the more.

"Come into the back room," she said, and led him into the stockroom, where the salesgirls took their break. A dangling lightbulb on a chain revealed a stuffy windowless closet furnished with a coffee machine, a standing ashtray stuffed with butts, a rack for the girls' street clothes, and a broken-springed daybed against the wall. Sam couldn't breathe for the blood pumping fast in his chest. "I have to change out of my uniform. It makes me feel like a trained nurse," Mattie dropped casually, turning her back to him as if the maneuver made her invisible. She kicked off her pumps and hiked the checked tunic up over her wide hips. Sam watched rolling masses of olive flesh unfold like farmland seen from an airplane, bordered by black nylon, no bone or straight angle in sight. He came over to her like a sleepwalker, laid his hands on her hips, and guided by hers freed her flesh from its rosetted confines, unhooking brassière and garters. And Mattie, spreading herself out on the daybed, helped him do to her what he was quite certain many others had done before, meeting his demure entrance with an enthusiasm for which he was altogether unprepared.

It wasn't till he got home that he started wondering why they had a daybed in the back of a department store, and if it hadn't been he who looked in the window that night, would it have been Frank Olszewski or Bobby Garvey? But by then it was too late. He never figured out what she saw in him. A pushover. She told him she liked his sense of humor, that he made her laugh. You got class, she said, and this was puzzling and ludicrous since this "class" of his mainly expressed itself to her in ineptitudes—his ability to get drunk on three beers, his inability to keep track of how much he spent, his dislike of violence.

For one whole year Sam resisted marriage, humming, daydreaming, while she yelled at him. This war of the wedding became a great source of merriment between them. She would start up, "So where's the ring?" or "You want to get hitched in May or June?" and as soon as the words were out of her mouth both would be in fits of laughter. "I thought *you* were going to get *me* a ring," Sam would retort. "You're the moneybags." Or "Hitched? What do you think I am, a horse? I'm a happy bachelor, and so I'm going to remain. I'm too young to be thinking of marriage."

"You're going to be a happy bachelor in your grave if you don't get a move on. Nice corpse you'll make," and they both laughed uproariously.

Then, suddenly, Sam realized they had crossed some barrier and there was no backing down. One day he could have told her seriously he didn't want to marry her, but a month later things had gone too far, and he wasn't really sorry that they had. Judge Hurd married them at the end of Sam's first year of graduate school.

Later their union seemed to him a terrible mistake. Mattie would have had more fun with someone more outgoing, less censorious, while for him desire had gotten yoked to disgust at the start. He married a woman he looked down on, who made his parents blanch, but who somehow freed him from his inhibitions. If Sam had cherished lofty notions about marriage and the Mother of His Children, he would never have consented to a union that seemed like little more than ensuring himself a steady supply. Instead, he had, or thought he had, a terrible mocking uncertainty at heart regarding all the things other people revered—church, country, family—although this skepticism was nothing compared to his wife's jeering contempt for the sanctities. He married Mattie because he didn't want her to leave him and because he was frightened of being alone and because like many goody-goodies it pleased him to have a wicked and aggressive mate, and because getting married was what a young man did, after getting his driver's license and registering for the draft, and because maybe no one else would have him. He spent the next decade pestering her to tell him who else she'd taken to the daybed at Bolts.

The trailer was a dirty white hutch of corrugated metal propped up on concrete blocks, like an unfinished ark beached waist-deep in ragweed.

"Anybody home?"

The two boys peered through a grimy window. A witch's house. Dishes, food-encrusted, stacked high in a tin sink, piles of yellowing buckled magazines, plastic milk shake containers with straws still cocked from the spout holes, cobwebs thick as curtains. Isaac reached up and knocked boldly on the door. When it opened, both children jumped like scared rabbits. A woman climbed out groggily onto the wooden plank that served as front steps, moving through the air as if it were dense as water and she an ocean diver. She peered around with a comically dazed and candid squint that Isaac recognized with a pang of fellow feeling as the protective armor of a myopic without specs, until she caught sight of the two of them, now hiding behind each other, squirming.

"How can I help you boys?"

She was a slip of a woman, tawny, narrow boned, with a boy's slim figure. She was wearing patched and faded jeans shorn at the thigh above slender golden legs, and a tie-dyed tank top against whose purple and orange galaxies two small round bosoms pressed. She isn't wearing a bra, thought Isaac, drunk with pleasure, wondering if he might simply reach under her shirt and scoop all that ripeness into both hands, bury his head in it. Ragged blond spikes of hair, dark at the roots, stood up from a tiny monkeyish face, the face of a hard-living woman, older than her body.

"We're bringing you back your tarot cards, Mrs. Olszewski," said Isaac. "Our mom sent us. We're Mattie Hooker's sons."

Cindy Olszewski peered down at them from her rotten wooden ramp, one leg crooked around the other, hand on her chin, and then laughed in delayed recognition. She smelled deliciously of liquor; it oozed from her pores. She had only just woken up: she must have drunk so much the night before that it had become the perfume she exuded, the air she exhaled. She lit a cigarette.

"Is that Turner and Ike?"

"I'm Isaac, he's Turner."

"God, you boys are big. I haven't seen you since—Jeez, I don't know when. Hey," she was sizing Isaac up, laughing still, "you're a *monster*. It's no fair. You're too much bigger than I am. How old are you now, anyway?"

"Sixteen."

"Christ almighty, you're a man already."

"I'm thirteen," piped Turner.

She rewarded him with her sleepy smile. "Well, that's still child age, isn't it? I mean that in a *nice* way. You make me feel so *old*. I was already *married* when you were born," she told Turner. "A child bride." Both boys put on long pious faces at that, but she laughed again, scattering the sands of their solemnity.

"You look very young," Isaac volunteered gallantly.

She stubbed out her cigarette against the side of the trailer, tossed the stub into the weeds. "Aren't you sweet. Come on in and visit."

They followed her up the ramp like mismatched ark animals, grinning at each other goonishly. They didn't know women could flirt. In fact, they didn't even know they were being flirted with.

Inside reeked of stale smoke, musk oil, cats, sex, dirty laundry—the spoor of a grown-up orphan. The trailer was dark, lit only by a fat piebald candle sitting on a crate that served as a kind of altar bearing sacrificial bottles of pearly nail polish and vials of body oil. A mattress covered with purple sheets and horoscope magazines, and on the wall a poster of a chubby blue man with an elephant trunk and as many waving arms and legs as a beetle. At her invitation, they all sat down on the bed: there was nowhere else to sit.

"Who's he? Is that your boyfriend?" kidded Isaac, pointing at the elephant man. Turner frowned, shocked by his brother's disrespect.

"No, silly, that's Krishna. He's the incarnation of Vishnu. I'm really into Indian mysticism. It brings you closer to your emotions. That's what I've been talking to your mom about: she could get a lot out of meditation."

"I don't think Mom should get any closer to her emotions than she already is," replied Isaac. "Our backsides couldn't stand it."

"You're telling *me* she's got a short fuse." Cindy was momentarily roused from her dreaminess. "That's why meditation could really help her a lot."

Isaac, shrugging, handed her the pack of tarot, idling over a crimson-and-gold tower in flames, a prancing jester.

"Did your mom try the cards? Did she like it?"

"Yeah, she loved it. She found out she was going to make gobs and gobs of money and find a new love. Dad was thrilled."

"Did she tell your fortunes, too?"

"No," said Isaac, smiling kindly. "I don't go in for that hocus-pocus. How can the position of the planets influence a human life, or a flip of cards tell your destiny? It's housewife stuff."

"Hey, I know it sounds kind of kooky, but the occult is a really powerful force," said Cindy Olszewski, not in the least offended. "Maybe you just had a bad experience with someone who didn't know how to read fortunes for real. There are a lot of fakes out there, I'm warning you. When you get a good reader—well, it's out of this world. Lots of people don't believe and are, like, blown away by it. Just the other day I did Angela Molina's chart. I tell her, You're going to get an important visitor from overseas. She says, You're kidding me. The very next morning her boyfriend shows up on her doorstep unannounced on leave from the Marines and asks her to marry him. Angela nearly flips out. I thought you were in Germany, she says. She says to me, You're unreal. You must have second sight or something."

"So did she say yes?"

"Did she say yes what?"

"Did she marry him?"

"No, she tells him to get lost. I could have told her that, too. I didn't see any wedding in her immediate future. That's the kind of thing that usually shows up. Latin girls are fussy. I says to her, I can't blame you. I told her, Christ, if I had to do it again, I sure wouldn't have married a guy about to ship out to Vietnam, but I was seventeen—what did I know? You're marrying a corpse. I hate to say it, I'm almost glad Frank was killed. The boys who came back got so weirded out you almost think it would be better they didn't come back. Now, wouldn't you like me to tell your fortune and *then* you can laugh at me if it doesn't come true?"

Isaac all this time had been craning his neck to look down Mrs. Olszewski's shirt, and as she bent forward was rewarded with a glimpse of rosy buttons. She knows I'm looking at her tits and she doesn't mind, she's letting me, he thought, breathless, but when she turned around and asked him if he wanted his fortune told he wondered whether maybe she'd caught him peeking and was mad. He was beginning to wish that his little brother wasn't there, a dark stern child beside him registering intense disapproval of Mrs. Olszewski's views of Vietnam vets and glancing up at his big brother expectantly, silently demanding that he defend America's finest.

"Do you mean it about telling my fortune? I don't have any money."

"This one's on the house."

"Turner, would you like to go home now? Mom will worry."

"I'll stay," said Turner, stubbornly. "Isn't she going to tell my fortune, too?"

"Turner, you're too *little* to have a fortune."

The child blushed, lowering his head.

This was how Cindy Olszewski made skimpy ends meet, in between waitressing jobs—doing astrology charts, casting horoscopes, reading palms. Their mother said she was lazy and overcharged.

"Give me your hand." She took Isaac's big paw in hers. "Jeez, you sure got deep, deep lines in your palm for a young boy. Lines carved deep as a grown man."

Both boys grew very silent and taut as the older woman, crossed-legged, pored over Isaac's broad palm, parting its lines, tracing its creases with her chipped bitten pearly butts of fingernails, muttering to herself. Isaac felt he might almost get drunk himself off her boozy breath. "Don't tell me a marine's going to come propose to me," he joked uneasily.

"Ssssshhh," hushed Cindy, and then finally she spoke. "Well, your path isn't easy. A rolling stone, that's what you're going to be, always traveling from pillar to post, without a roof of your own. You're going to have trouble with your health—maybe you ought to try meditation. Yellow's your lucky color, remember that. See all these little daggers and crosshatchings—that's trouble. Hard times, but I see you coming out on top. If you want to come back another time, I can try and tell you from your charts . . ."

"Is that all?" demanded Isaac, impatiently. "What about fame and glory and money and the love of women?"

Cindy shook her head. "You're going to have to fight for what you want. It's, like, you weren't born with a silver spoon in your mouth. But I tell you, your own worst enemy is yourself."

Isaac withdrew his hand, obscurely nettled. "Tell Turner's, now."

Turner looked at the woman, wide-eyed, transparent in his desire to hear about himself.

Cindy laughed. "Well, what did you say you were—twelve? Thirteen's a little young. Part of your fate's not really formed yet, and I don't want to influence things one way or the other. It's like it's still all jelly."

Turner without a word held out his hand to her stiffly. She laughed. "Okay, okay, you Hookers don't take no for an answer, do you?" She pressed his white bony little hand in hers, spread out its map of dried riverbeds and estuaries, its creased deltas. There ensued the same tense silence, both boys drinking in the scent of liquor and wax candle and funk, glancing around at the blue beetly Krishna on the wall. Isaac took another peek down Mrs. Olszewski's shirt. Turner sat proudly straight, as if having his hair cut, with the kitchen towel around his shoulders and their mother pushing a scarlet ear out of the razor's way, Isaac fussing just to make sure she didn't lop one off.

"Jeez Louise, have we ever got a hard-headed customer here," Cindy pronounced at last. "Head over heart for sure. That's the head line. Look how strong it is—you oughta go into business for sure. You'll be supporting your whole family one day—a real tycoon, if you want to be." Isaac frowned, all that goofiness turning ugly.

"Is that all? What about love?" he inquired on his brother's behalf.

"Oh sure," said Cindy, without bothering to look. "Lots of love." She dropped Turner's hand and lit another cigarette, session clearly over.

The boys clambered to their feet, thanking their hostess for her trouble. At the door Isaac lingered, hoping even now to ditch his tag-along brother. "How come you live like a hermit all by yourself in the wilds? Don't you get lonely?" he asked, sentimentally.

"I'd rather be lonely than with people who don't understand me." Cindy sighed. "People around here are very cruel and gossipy. You think you've found a friend and that person goes around town bad-mouthing you behind your back."

"Who would badmouth *you*?"

"Well, some people are just jealous."

Isaac nodded sympathetically, proud at being able to hold up his end of so grown-up a conversation. His mother too was always talking about people's jealousy, yet when he asked her why in God's name anyone would be jealous of her she called him a snotty brat.

"Come back another time, and I'll tell you more. I'll give you a good price, too. Ten bucks for a full reading, horoscope, tarot, palm, but don't tell your mom: I charge her fifteen. I do past lives, too. You know, in an earlier life I was a high priestess in the temple of Cleo-patra."

As soon as they were safely in the woods, the boys burst out laughing. Isaac gave his brother a shove. "Hey, big shot, so you're going to be supporting the whole family, huh? I'm not surprised, you little tightwad. How much you got stashed away in your piggybank?"

"Never mind."

"Lend me a dollar and we can get an ice cream at the Corner Store."

"Nah."

"Why not?"

"You already owe me three seventy-five. Anyway, Mom'll be worried about us."

"Hey, did you get a whiff of her breath? Like a still. Cleopatra—I'd like to be her Antony. Jeez, is that woman ever a sexpot."

Turner looked away. "Don't talk like that. She looked to me like a very nice lady. How can you talk like that about a friend of Mom's?"

"She has an exquisite pair of calves," pronounced Isaac, on a more respectful note.

"I didn't see any cows," Turner said, suspiciously.

"Not cows—calves."

"Where?"

"Where do you think, dummy? On her legs."

"Hmmm," agreed Turner, and then a moment later, "What was so exquisite about them?"

Isaac squatted down in the dirt track. It was a loggers' road, mud caked dry with tires' checkered markings. Seizing a branch he traced deep into the dirt four long snaky squiggles, each with two little sets of bumps. Turner bent over, staring at these four strange rivulets of earth.

"There," said his brother, triumphantly. "That's a pair of dream legs. You want 'em long, slender, willowy. Not too hefty, not piano legs. Shapely."

"Huh," said Turner. "So legs are what counts?"

"Yes. Legs are definitely where it's at, somewhere on the scale of bliss just after behinds and before feet." Isaac had a scale of feminine bliss he kept in a notebook in his room.

"Feet? Give me a break. So who else has got good legs? Does Sarah?"

"Hardly."

"How come?"

"Too stalky. They don't go in and out where they should."

"What about Mom? Mom's got good legs," asserted Turner, hopefully.

"No, she doesn't. She's bowlegged as a jockey."

When they got home their mother was out in the garden weeding. She stood up when she saw them coming, planting her hands on her hips. "Well, you squirts sure took your time. Did you give Cindy back her cards?"

"She read our fortunes for us," Turner volunteered.

"I bet she did. Try any hanky-panky on you?"

"No. *Does* she?" asked Isaac.

"Wouldn't you like to know. She tell you about her life as Cleopatra's thingamajig?" Head cocked, coy finger in mouth, Mattie suddenly made her dark bulldog body snake into Cindy's languorous drapings. The boys roared.

"Is she a hippie?" Turner asked. He had never met a hippie before.

"Well, hippie is one way of putting it," concluded their mother darkly. Cindy was one of her friends she loved to hate.

"She said she doesn't like Gilboa, Mom."

"I know she don't."

"How come?"

"She don't like it because she's slept with all the men already and none of the women'll talk to her."

"So how come you talk to her?"

"Well, you don't expect me to go around doing what everybody else does all the time. Besides, anybody that hauls Jeb Hurd's and Tom Driscoll's ashes for 'em deserves a medal. That, or her head examined."

Shortly afterward Turner told Mattie that Isaac said her legs were bowed. He didn't break confidence from malice, but simply because he still told his mother everything. But it didn't turn out so well for Isaac. During supper several days after their trip to the trailer, she started up, with a ferocious glint in her eye. "So I hear you're going around town saying I got legs like a jockey. That's a fine way to talk about your mother."

Isaac, nearly choking on a frankfurter, held his ground. "You *have* got legs like a jockey, so why shouldn't I say so?"

"And what kind of legs do you think *you* have, may I ask? Go on, stand up. I want to see your legs."

The boy, trying to ignore her, kept on eating.

"Go on, show us your gorgeous legs."

Isaac finally heaved himself to his feet, smoothing his cut-off jeans. They all looked down at his bare legs in silence. Head hung in shame, ears pounding, he stood on display like a dog with a can tied to its tail, like a thief in the stocks, while his mother examined him coldly. "Huh," she snorted, finally. "You think the girls are going to go for that pair of tree trunks? You got legs like an elephant. I don't see where you get the nerve to criticize women's legs, when you got a damn ugly pair yourself."

Isaac sat down again, face burning, unmanned by this first, most unexpected intimation that men too could be judged by women for their sexual allure, and that he might be found wanting.

Chapter 2

I CAN REMEMBER being born, the little boy told everyone who would listen. He had been cast up onto his mother's shores gored, afflicted, lassoed by umbilical cord, and vociferously wretched. And, he insisted, fully conscious.

"I was born half-dead," he trumpeted at all passers-by, converting his mother's disparagement of her first-born into a medal of honor, a Purple Heart of the birth field. He had cheated death, he was a bruised and persecuted spoiler. He loved to hear the story of his coming, from his mother's first thrashings in the movie theater to his own near-asphyxiation. First of all, it was about him. Second, it was a hero's tale of adversity overcome against the odds. "How the West Was Won" was the story of Isaac's nativity.

Years later, his mother once again reminded him, just as a way of putting him in his place, "You came into this world like a drowned puppy."

"I wonder if you know what they call the mother of a puppy," he snapped back.

Foremost among his afflictions was eyesight that transmitted the world as if through a sheet of gasoline. His failed sight seemed to Isaac the central experience of these early days, weighting them with urgency, desperation, strain. He lived in fear of missing the obvious, of being left out, laughed at. Objects were shrouded in a dull mystifying haze: Isaac had to grab things to his very nose, lest they be lost to him. Or, worse still, he took his first giant pigeon-toed steps only to find that he had crushed underfoot a toy or small animal he hadn't seen; he stood up from the table and overturned board games, shattered crockery, and had to pretend it didn't matter in an effort to drown out, fortify himself against, his mother's recriminations, his father's well-intentioned teasing.

"It's nothing," insisted Isaac, towering like an all-thumbs Colossus over the shards of a broken lamp, refusing to help as his mother ostentatiously swept up the pieces.

"Do you think it can be fixed? No, I guess it's smashed beyond repair. Ikey, will you never learn?"

And his father, when his son approached, yelped, "Oh no, it's the Abominable Snowman. Hide the china, Mattie."

He was always butting against things he couldn't see, too proud to cry out at these self-inflicted bumps. At every move he made, adults were frustratingly, shamingly rushing ahead to clear his path, like the vanguard of a locust plague or an idiot king, like icebreakers before a barge. Nothing he loved went unbroken, untrodden on by its loving possessor. Cursed with a voracious and cagily despondent adoration of the beautiful and dainty, Isaac was forbidden precisely those music boxes and cuckoo clocks that most aroused his passion. As a consequence, he shunned toys, refused himself games as prospective helpless casualties, potential harbingers of disgrace, and consoled himself with stones and sticks—fortresses, irreducible, that he could pet and keep in his bed without crushing. His bed on wash day shed small avalanches of bark and grit. Sticks were like people who didn't complain when he knocked into them.

What would life be like for the eagle-sighted, Isaac wondered later, if everything were *seen*, if he could make out a picture high up on the wall or read a newspaper across a room, spy the flights of geese or cigar-puff aerial alphabets of skywriting pilots other people were always pointing out, if he could glean from the look on someone's mouth whether she was cross or tired or amused? Unimaginably easy, obvious. One could move through the world with a magnificent shrugging casualness, doze off and resurface at will, watch the landscape of social relations, politics, marriages, or sports unfold in their entirety, not reconstruct them cryptographer-style in pored-over fragments.

Instead, Isaac grabbed things to his very nose and breathed over them effortfully, compensating for his disability in a hundred tricks of heightened smell and taste, of trained concentration, memorizing his mother's wardrobe like a train schedule, counting the number of stairs from bedroom to kitchen, kitchen to cellar, studying in advance all the shaded minutiae of gesture or expression he needed to know in order to survive and understand, and yet laboring nonetheless under the hysterical anxiety of feeling himself unnaturally unequipped for life, ignorant of things everyone else knew without thinking. Memory grew superrefined; he lived like a spy without a holiday, perpetually on the qui vive. He wound up more attentive to caught detail, more discriminating as to a lady's earring, the lettering on a cigarette, the crisp fuchsia tint of a maple leaf than a man blessed with a microscope on either side of his nose.

So dire a short-sightedness demanded from daily life the kind of constantly discriminating and calculating vigilance, the total mobilization, bestirring of your faculties, required in listening to a foreign language half-learned: if you daydreamed just a moment, the thread was lost, the conversation a quickly receding mystery. For this reason the invisible realm of mathematics brought to an older Isaac respite: long accustomed to carrying large sums of information in his head, he finally had the advantage.

When Isaac told his mother, as he did weekly, "That's not a very pretty dress. Its sleeves are too long, and I don't like you wearing brown. Brown is for bears and dogs," it wasn't just sassiness but a hard-won conquest.

At four years of age, he had been fitted with a pair of thick black-rimmed spectacles that rode hard on his nose and behind his ears, leaving reddened grooves of flesh. Outlines were crisper now, letters jumped off a page, but his declining sight seemed to march just a little more briskly than the succession of lenses that struggled to keep up.

"They make him look pathetic," complained his mother to his father when the specs first appeared.

"What's pathetic?" asked Isaac, before his father, scooping him up for a hasty kiss, shushed her. His excitement at learning a new and clearly complicated, resonant word turned to horror at what it meant. Did she feel sorry for him? No, thank God, she never felt sorry for anyone, especially not him. She was only pretending she felt sorry for him. It was a way of putting him down.

His father called him "Foxy Four Eyes." After initial uncertainty, Isaac begged to be called "Foxy Four Eyes" as a permanent mode of address, and flushed with satisfaction as each repetition conjured up afresh this new and very desirable image of himself. Foxy Four Eyes, who outsmarts them all. He was a cartoon character, a Mister Magoo in the know.

Blindness; well, God made you near blind so you could listen to the heart's stirrings and promptings, so your inward sight might grow the keener. No one, not even self-lacerating Isaac, could call near-sightedness a psychological weakness or moral capitulation.

But vision wasn't all: his other apertures to the world were equally polluted. He had been born deaf in one ear, intensifying his terror of exclusion. Deafness wasn't silence but a buzz like a bee lodged in the eardrum. His mother claimed that deaf people just didn't *want* to hear, and others, too, irritatedly made fun of him for firing "What?" before they had even finished their sentences. People avoided you because it was inhibiting to have to broadcast so enunciatedly, robbing conversation of its pounce, drift, throwaway; jokes repeated loudly three times lost their carbonation. His father claimed that deafness was what lent Ike's own pronouncements their soliloquizing orotundity, made him talk like Daniel Webster.

More incriminating, more tainted were his respiratory ills—allergies, asthma worse than Sam's, bronchial woes, those afflictions of the anxiously unloved, who choke for air, swallow their tears, and fear suffocation. For his first half decade Isaac couldn't breathe three-fourths of the year, but huffed and wheezed and hacked like a dying Pekingese, choked by dust, molds, greenery, and hairy animals.

Winters his volcanoes of phlegm often erupted into full-blown diseases with harsh Latinate names like dinosaurs—bronchial pneumonia, tracheitis, pneumonitis—relegating Isaac to his bed for weeks and weeks on end, with a quilted lap full of toy soldiers and slimy green rags of decomposing Kleenex. Immobility was made more tolerable once he learned to read, but even Isaac Hooker couldn't read *Treasure Island* more than four hours at a stretch without getting fractious.

Strange things happen if you spend much time in bed: you think hard, read hard, dream hard, imagination grows riotous, luxuriant, and oceanic. You feel superior to healthy outdoor mortals, with their abbreviated, inattentive sense of time. Left to his own devices all day, except for soup-and-juice runs from his mother, bedridden Isaac became captive to the heresy of faith. It was inevitable: he could hear God walking downstairs, with much creaking of the floorboards, a child's Bible given him by his grandparents was fatter and juicier than any other reading matter handy. When his father came home in the late afternoon he would hound this rueful agnostic with questions of cosmogony and divine doings.

"Don't worry," Sam reassured his wife. "Ike's a born skeptic if I ever saw one. He asks too many questions to believe. He'll grow out of it."

Near-sightedness, deafness, and bronchitis—these were the three determining constants in his early life, darkening and thickening his impressions to a kind of panicky phlegmy soup. Sickness went in unhappy circles: a week of honking and snuffling around the house grateful to be kept indoors, two weeks of aching delirium, a week of cranky listless recovery. For the worst of it he was unconscious with wretchedness. This was Isaac's first continuous memory, not of an event but of a condition, a state of being in time: thrashing and tossing in sheets in which his exhausted burning flesh could find no comfortable position, wheezing to the moist hum and regular-as-heartbeat exhalations of the vaporizer—a small bedside furnace, a miniature deity that breathed eucalyptus and not fire; gasping, moaning, whimpering, and not knowing he was making a sound, till someone came to the rescue.

One day Dr. McCormick appeared at his bedside with black bag and icy stethoscope, his brick-red jowly cheeks frosty from outside.

"How are you feeling, Ikey?"

"Fine, thank you," said Isaac, automatically.

"Fine? What am I doing here then, if you're so well? You don't *look* fine. Why are you whimpering?"

Isaac was embarrassed: he couldn't hear himself whimpering, nor could he grasp the principle of telling a stranger how bad you felt.

The animal panic of not being able to breathe overwhelmed him: sometimes his throat stopped up altogether, before the clogged air came whistling through again. The fear of not breathing was enough to make him a kind of night watchman over his own respiration: if he fell asleep, he would surely forget to breathe and die. How these nights preyed upon him, nights that followed at the tail of days of heavy hot sleep, when fever soared, and there was no one to tend to him, and the small hours seemed to stretch like taffy. Some nights he would hack a wheezy notch into his throat, a glitch that brought on coyote yelps of coughing at every inhalation, and Isaac, pleading to be sprung from crazy solitude, howled himself into exhaustion.

This is what he remembered: head propped high by a stack of pillows, watching the dark of the house with everyone asleep but him, bellowing at the top of his glutinous aching lungs from terror at being sick and awake and alone, prey to all the phantoms of the night, the tiger under the bed, the Martians he could hear landing in a saucer on the roof, the hanged man formed by his clothes thrown over a chair, the half-open closet a vertical coffin disgorging dead people. So he howled and coughed until he could hear the slippered shuffle of his savior mother come to him, eyes scrunched up, nightgown twisted around, to plump up his pillow and make it cool, to straighten his quilt, to rub his chest gummy with aromatic Vaporub, to order him to stop coughing and crying and—these sick nights, these sleepless nights—to sit on his bed, telling him funny stories about her drunken father and the naughty tricks she played as a little girl, until Isaac fell asleep in mid-question.

One magical night that stuck in his memory it was his father who appeared at the side of his bed fully dressed although it was surely long past midnight, not after hours and hours of Isaac's baying, but just as soon as he opened his mouth in earnest.

"Don't go away."

"I'm not going anywhere."

"Stay till I fall asleep."

"I'm right here, soldier. I've got all the time in the world."

But this particular night all the usual stories of knights and scientists and presidents failed to pacify an Isaac who grew ever more agitated, more inconsolable, until finally his father spoke these unimaginable words, "How would you like to come down to the kitchen and have a midnight snack?"

He watched as his father got down on his knees on the bedroom floor, hunting in the dark for Isaac's slippers, which had been shunted far under the bed, sliding the child's bare feet into their felt innards, wrapping him in a blanket, and carrying him downstairs. There they took their respective places at the kitchen table just as if it were broad daylight. In the fluorescent night light, bluish like skim milk and cold, sat Isaac, with the blanket draped around his shoulders like an Indian chief, like a passenger on the deck of a steamship, drinking milk and eating cookies, while Sam, scooping up two or three at a time, swallowed without chewing.

Isaac remembered till the end of his days their conversation, calm, grown-up, convivial: they discussed Bob Gibson and the Cardinals, who had just wiped the floor with the Tigers in the World Series, and why certain lowly inferior states like Missouri and Michigan had baseball teams while other noble and glorious ones like New Hampshire didn't, and how many bears Davy Crockett killed in an average season, and how Apollo 8 got to the moon, and how come Saul kept on trying to kill poor David.

The next day it seemed like a dream, a surreal overturning of the grim edict that no matter how many times he clamored to join his

parents downstairs, under pretext of thirst and hunger and wakeful-
ness, nothing short of a three-alarm fire was to allow him out of bed
once put there. Was it a dream? Night after night now Isaac tested
reality, demanding a reprise. His mother was mad at her husband for
undoing all their good work. "Baby," she said balefully.

"He's been sick in bed three weeks. No wonder he can't sleep—he
needed a little motion to get himself calmed down," said Sam, and
those words fixed in Isaac's mind the permanent and fateful belief that
motion cures all ills. But it never happened again.

"Remember the time we had milk and cookies in the middle of the
night?" repeated an insomniac Isaac piteously. "Remember the midnight snack?" Midnight was a territory alien and unapproachable as
Mars—to have domesticated it with milk and cookies was almost frightening.

"*Never*," said Sam. "*Me?* Milk and cookies? Never. You dreamed it.
You must be thinking of another guy. Go to sleep, buster."

Once the crisis of pneumonia or bronchitis was passed and his fever
broken, convalescence became a frantically itching scab he was forbidden to scratch or peel off; Isaac wandered from room to room, short
of breath, crabby, disconsolate as a ghost, begging to be entertained,
waiting for his father to come home and answer his questions. It was
a kind of aggravated parody of his regular preschool condition: chronic
curiosity, chronic boredom, chronic rebellion against his own stuck
powerlessness.

The room was dark, and on the ceiling shadows cast by cars in the
street below flickered from corner to corner, like a phantom drag race.
For one dopy moment Mattie thought she'd slept through the evening
and into the middle of the night, but no Sam lay beside her. It was
eight-forty, Sam would be home any second—*should* have been home
long ago—and she still had to clean the apartment.

The room was stupefyingly hot—window closed, radiator going full
blast. She heaved herself up with a groan, smoothing her crumpled
warm housecoat over her belly (the monster inside was quiet for once—
must have corked off too) and opened the window, leaning out into a
rainy autumnal night, the smell of wet pavement and sodden leaves
rising to her nose, and even, it seemed to her, borne along the currents
of rainy western wind from the mountains, the bittersweet smoky scent
of bonfires. The smell of Halloween.

She had to pick up the week's wash fast before Sam came home. That was the law he had laid down: on Fridays you cleaned house and did a wash. The wash was a cinch since their apartment was over the laundromat, so Mattie need only dump their weekly soilings on Mrs. Buonpastore's counter, to be picked up the same evening—she usually stayed open till ten or eleven at night. Later Isaac claimed his first memory was an olfactory one, the toasty smell of starched cotton and simmering irons, sheets steamed like polyester wontons.

At school Friday was Fish Day. Now just as immutably it was Cleaning Day. Her husband's finickiness both amused and irritated her, since it seemed self-righteous and a little accusatory: she had never heard of a man who bathed three or four times a week and washed after sex and insisted that his wife wash too, who winced at crumbs though he wouldn't stoop to pick them up himself, and threw out an entire carton of tomatoes if one was found gray with mold. The princess, she called him. Her dad, who practically had to be evacuated from his clothes, would have been amazed. Sam's fussiness initially made her laugh, even gratified her, but now it was getting to be a real pain in the ass. It was his mother in him talking. She'd never met such a mamma's boy.

When she and Sam were first married, his ma had set about instructing her new daughter-in-law how to keep house, as if she were a Hottentot fresh from the bush. Mattie had put an end to this game halfway through a recipe for Sam's "favorite pie," when she looked up from her fingernails and declared in a voice bored, victorious, and final, "*I'm* Sam's favorite pie."

Sam had grown up in a house of women, coddled and pecked, and none of these ladies was too keen on his acquiring one of his own. Mattie had readied herself for an all-out war, but his sisters were smart enough to steer clear: one lived in North Carolina, the other was moving to California. In fact, Jane hadn't even come to their wedding. Which was all right with Mattie: when it came to relatives, less was more.

Imagining his prissy condescending puffed-up ma inquiring whether Mattie was taking good care of him made her want to kick that woman's face in. Let him look after himself, the big baby. She was the pregnant one; he ought to be looking after her. Instead he was out on his Friday-night soak with Scannon. Ten to nine, and not home yet.

Their apartment was one room with kitchenette: that was all they could afford since Sam was still a student, with a Ph.D. lined up if he ever finished his master's. Not that teachers ever made big bucks, anyway. The bed took up most of the apartment. Sam's mother, again, had tried to talk them into getting a more modest convertible that could be tucked away into a couch in the daytime. No doubt she'd have preferred they have separate rooms. But Mattie had insisted on a frank queen-size bed that no one could possibly mistake for a couch or for anything else.

With three people living in it, the apartment would soon be smaller still. She didn't mind—she had grown up in a house with five people in three rooms, and found the crush warm and reassuring, but it drove Sam nuts. He didn't like having to sleep in his own living room or eat supper in his bedroom, or however you wanted to look at it. He needed to be alone to think. He would lock himself in the bathroom to read or suddenly jump up in a tizzy while they were watching TV and rush for the door, muttering that he needed fresh air and was going for a walk.

Until she met Sam, Mattie had never heard of a walk. If you needed to go somewhere or pick up something you drove; you didn't just set out into the blue for no reason, and certainly not on foot. On Sunday afternoons Sam sometimes tried to persuade Mattie to come along, but she wasn't exactly wild about the idea. The only reason she could think of was to show off new clothes, and since she had a husband she no longer had the money or the need.

Sam complained that he couldn't work on his thesis at home, couldn't concentrate with her there, watching television or talking to him. To say the least, this struck Mattie as bizarre.

"What would happen if you were a bus driver and all of a sudden you said you couldn't drive with people in the bus?" But that's the way he was—nervous, fanciful, easily thrown. And since he didn't answer, she did. "You'd be out of work. Which is what you are, anyway."

Before they got married, Sam wasn't quite so unsociable. Mattie used to be able to coax him to go drinking and dancing Saturday nights with her gang—Frank, Raymond, Bobby, and their dates, her sister Sue and her husband, Jim Randall, who were the first of their set to get married. (Mattie had told her, Wait till you've seen something of the world, but Sue had no imagination.) They would pile into a couple of booths at Sadie's, drink rum and Coca-Cola, and dance slow to Frank Sinatra on the jukebox before driving home at three in the morning, sated and stewed. That is how she pictured Sam in those days of their courtship—driving home too fast along country roads in the dark before dawn, singing "One for My Baby" off key in his creaky comically mournful voice. Even though he had his baby right there under his arm he always liked those sad songs of loss.

Mattie was hellbent on having fun, he complained. It was true: she felt this heady, furious sap of vitality boiling up in her, a frenzy to let loose, dance till she dropped, exhaust all that fever of youth before childbirth and motherhood and debt and sickness laid claim to her, before she got old and gray and dead in a grave. For the first year or so they went out, Sam could be persuaded to hit the town with Mattie's friends. He would go along, protesting at having to spend six hours jammed in a booth with men whose only common point of interest was that they'd all slept with his girlfriend, sometimes bored or sulking at imaginary jibes, but compliant nonetheless. Now it was all she could do to drag him to the movies: he would rather sit at home and fret about how he wasn't getting any work done. If he went out on a spree, it was with Scannon and not her: she was pregnant, she should take it easy. Was this what being married and grown-up was about, learning to bite back your energy, waiting for your husband to come home and be unhappy?

Mattie put on her slippers and ran downstairs to the laundromat, slipping into its steamy churning bowels, lined with machines like roaring soapy aquariums. Mrs. Buonpastore was sitting behind the counter reading a comic book.

"My son gave it to me to make me read better," she apologized.

"Have you finished our wash?" Mattie demanded. "I don't want to get called on the carpet tonight just because you're too busy with Spiderman to iron Sam's shirts."

"I finished, I finished. Don't worry. You too young to worry."

"If I wait till I'm your age, I'll be dead already."

"Am I dead?" Mrs. Buonpastore demanded ironically, hands on hips. She and Mattie loved insulting each other.

"*Are* you dead? That's exactly what I want to know."

Mrs. Buonpastore heaved up the bag of laundry, pressed shirts on top. Ironed shirts were Sam's extravagance. Mattie protested but in vain. Her mother had taken in washing in the days before laundromats, and you couldn't get Mattie near an iron for love or money.

Back upstairs, fumbling in the dark for the doorknob, she sensed a movement behind her and turned around with a start to find her husband had sneaked up the stairs behind her, his step camouflaged by the muted roar from the laundromat below.

"You scared me sneaking up like that."

They walked into the lit apartment together, jostling each other play-
fully over who should go first. Sam, grabbing her laundry bag and
throwing it ahead of them into the room and setting down his own
things, jabbed his wife with an elbow to keep her back and she in
return pushed him tight against the doorway with her stomach, thrilling with a wave of excitement at the press of her hard belly against his
hip, at the easy loose soaked smell of liquor that emanated from her
young husband like steam from a hot plate, like mist rising from a
meadow. She imagined his white satiny flesh under his shirt and
reached out for it, pushing her fingers through the gaps between buttons and feeling him quiver at her touch. Once in the apartment, Sam
pushed the door closed and pinned her up against it, kissing nose and
ears and eyes, running his mouth over her neck, where little archipel-
agos of crimson had sprung up from kissing nights before. Mattie was
melting with pleasure, almost swooning as his hand moved up under
her dress and into her pants. In another moment they'd be rutting in
the fresh laundry, Sam ramming her against starchy mounds of cooked
sheets and scented underpants, the two of them falling, dripping across
a cotton-swept floor, and she was already laughing and groaning in
importunate anticipation.

And then, just as suddenly, she remembered it was nine P.M. and
she was hungry and furious, she'd been expecting him home since six,
and he only got so horny on her when he'd been out drinking with
that monkey. There he was, her husband, a long skinny rail of a boy,
pale, one hank of slicked sandy hair falling into his eye as it always did
when he was a little sloshed, face lit up by an almost unbearably vivid
excitement, a strange, half-furtive joy. He was beaming like a jack-o'-
lantern and also trying *not* to smile. What was *he* so happy about? He
bent his head to press his lips to her strong neck, finger curving in
and out achingly, other hand resting on her belly. Angrily, she pushed
him away, meaning him to spring back at her harder for the rebuff, to
coax her into amorous forgiveness, but instead he uncoiled himself and
turned stiffly away. Damn his touchiness.

Leaning against the door, Mattie watched her husband unload his
knapsack of books, peel off his windbreaker, and then haul up onto the
kitchen table a massive parcel, square and hefty, wrapped in soggy
brown paper and string. She came over, curious despite herself. Was
it for her? For the baby?

"What've you got there, buster?"

"You'll see." Sullen, Sam moved to the kitchen sink and washed his hands carefully with soap, removing all sticky trace of her. Unsheathing the knife from his belt he slit the restraining strings. Inside lay a brown surface, gold letters, which he lifted free from its swaddling and laid before her. It was a book. The biggest book she had ever seen, but a book—an expensive book, was Mattie's first thought, and her second was she would like to hit him. Scannon.

"It's an encyclopedia," Sam explained. "The new *Columbia Encyclopedia*. They don't even have this edition in the library yet!" His long narrow hands moved over the canvas surface as lovingly and alertly as a blind man's, turning the encyclopedia on its side, fingering the thumbnail indentations, opening to every entry he could think of— Fulke Greville, New Hampshire, time, Archimedes, baseball—reading aloud in his best Declamation Day delivery. Mattie said nothing, but chewed on her lip.

"Is this your book?" she asked finally.

"Mine, to have and to hold." Sam's happiness swiftly assumed a breezily defiant edge.

"You paid for it? You bought it? How much did it cost?"

"Not all *that* much."

"How much is not all that much? Two weeks' rent?" The words flew; she couldn't have stopped herself even if she wanted to. "Why did you bring this thing home? Who needs it? Who made you get it— was this your little mick Scannon's big idea?"

Sam's hands dropped abruptly. "Yes, Christopher got one, too. We both ordered them from Columbia. We got a teacher's discount. But nobody *made* me get it. An encyclopedia is one of the most useful things a person can have—we *need* one in the house. It's not just for me, it's for the baby when he grows up a little." His voice shook, but Mattie could tell he was too angry to breathe. This is it, she said to herself. The moment was going, going, gone at which this quarrel could be mended and the evening's amorousness reclaimed. Some guys you fought with and the fights always ended up in crazy love, but Sam was a sulker who never mixed anger and sex. No, now they wouldn't wind up in the pile of laundry with Sam's pants around his ankles, or even sitting over a civil supper; now he was well and truly angry past repair and it would be days before he would come around.

"Oh, it's for the *baaaaby*," she crooned. "I should have known. How much did it set us back, Sam? I don't think you told me."

Sam wasn't looking at her. He was still standing over his treasure, but his eyes were fixed downward and he had turned his face the other way, so that his words floated back to her in stilted indistinct streams of disdain. "What's all the dramatics about? That I didn't buy *you* a present? You've got no respect for anything, Mattie. You debase everything, books, people, civilization—everything is dollars and cents to you. You got a cash register for a brain."

Mattie could feel her face flushing bright red, her voice growing louder and sharper as his got fainter and wearier. "You got some nerve," she said, shaking her head. "You got some nerve coming in here at nine P.M. in the evening, feeling no pain. You come in here after *crawling* from bar to bar with that little Jesus of yours—how much money did you spend on drinks tonight, Sam? Who paid? You blow our month's savings on this load of crap—we need a carriage and a crib yet, remember?—and then you got the nerve to tell me I don't care about people."

"*I* paid," said Sam. "And I'm not drunk. You ought to know: I'm the only guy you ever met who *isn't* drunk."

"You let that little mick who's twice your age sponge off you again? It's not fair. He has no family to support, he's sponging off his own sister—I bet he doesn't pay rent in that house. If you go boozing at the end of the day, the least you could do is take turns. Especially since he's having two for your every one. He knows you're just a student," her voice grew almost conciliatory here, but she could see him flinch at the word "student." "He's taking advantage of you. And how dare he talk you into buying expensive books, when he knows we've got a baby coming . . ."

"There's something you don't understand . . ." Sam began.

"There's something *you* don't understand," she snapped back. "We don't have any money coming in. We got a baby about to pop and rent and food and bills and payments on the car, and we don't have a nickel coming in because you care too much about civilization to get a job. I guess your darling mother didn't teach you about jobs."

"Oh, now I get it," said Sam, cynically, all joy at his new acquisition fled, for he still believed a new book or even a new razor could change your life. "So it's thesis-nagging time again. Which is it? You want to know when I'm going to finish my thesis or you want to try to make me quit? You want me to ditch it? Fine."

"I never *met* anybody as allergic to work as you," said Mattie in feigned astonishment. "How are we going to feed the three of us until you decide to finish? Are we going to pass the hat or what? How come you won't let me stay at work: you can stay home and look after the baby if you're too high and mighty to get a job. An encyclopedia!"

Sam sat down at the table, straddling the chair backward with his long legs, and eased out the Gilboa *Recorder* from his knapsack, leafing through its smudgy pages to the Help Wanted section, licking his finger very deliberately before he turned each page. "Okay, Mattie, find me a job, any job. What do you think? A crane operator? Great. Security guard, like your dad once was? Let's see what we got here: maintenance man wanted; mechanic, foreman; gas-station attendant; web-press technician. Sound good?"

Mattie had a plan, which she now unfolded casually, only looking at him out of the corner of her eye. "No, you don't have to soil your pretty hands with greasy work. I was behind the counter yesterday, Mrs. Cartwright comes in and says that Elmer Hynes is in the hospital with terrible diabetes and they're looking for a substitute teacher at the high school. So I ask, What's the pay? She says, It's not bad, and the benefits are decent: they need a teacher right away, and Elmer Hynes, poor guy, won't be coming back this year or next year either."

"Elmer Hynes teaches *science*."

"Well, science and history, she said."

Sam was almost green with disbelief. "You want me to ditch my graduate work and go teach high-school science?"

"You don't have to ditch it. Plenty of guys have a job *and* go to school. You can study nights."

A sickening silence hung between them.

"Fine," said the young man tightly, as if he had agreed to walk the plank for a high principle, and grabbing his windbreaker, he stormed out again into the drizzling night, leaving his wife at the table with the encyclopedia in its nest of paper, too proud and full of an obscure dread to move. This is it, she kept on thinking, I've really done it now—and with a defiant laugh aloud, I guess he'll go home to mother.

Sam Hooker could remember, as distinctly as if it were his wedding day or the instant of hearing bad news, when he stopped reading fiction. Even the word "fiction" seemed a retroactively slighting term for what he had once unquestioningly regarded as the chief glory, the sanctifying end of human experience. For a long time after he started teaching at the Ashuelot Regional High School, Sam still read novels at night.

It was a ritual he spent the working day waiting for, an activity made possible by the purchase of a house roomy enough for him to have a study of his own. The ritual was finicky and a little crazed. Every evening as soon as Mattie cleared away his plate Sam bolted to his study, closing the door behind him. He sank into the easy chair, drew out a packet of Half & Half, padded his pipe's lacquered bowl with twigs of cherry-scented tobacco as daintily as a bird building its nest, set a lighter to his edifice, and puffed till the brown brambles glowed ruddy. Next, he poured himself a shot of Jack Daniels (he kept a pint and a shot glass in his desk drawer) and drew forth his book from its hiding place under the chair.

He read whatever he could find in the town library that had been written a hundred years ago or more, for he wasn't interested in hearing about people in circumstances similar to his own. Most happily, he gave himself over to long nights of chunky nineteenth-century novels, French and Russian mostly (the English were too stodgy, with their "Monday-morning-like sobriety," as Van Gogh put it), poring over yellow-and-black pages in small print offering themes of adultery and revolution, court politics, Napoleon. He rooted for noblemen who fought duels in wintry forests at dawn, who hunted wild boar and drank to the dancing of hired gypsy bands in distant villages or lay wounded on their backs in battlefields gazing at the grazing clouds; his heart soared and somersaulted in unison with a young girl's at her first ball. He marked his calendar by his reading as his neighbors marked time by sickness and natural disaster; they knew the winter of '68 as the year the McCormicks' house burned down and Frank Olszewski was killed in Vietnam. Sam knew it as the season he read *The Charterhouse of Parma* in a fit of such caught exultation he could hardly breathe. And then, suddenly, enough.

It was the end of a long day teaching slow-witted and distractible teen-agers how plants eat light and rats eat grain and why Americans fought a war over not paying taxes. His eyes were beginning to glaze over and he turned pages unseeingly; his stomach churned and thundered and cramped up with a sickening discontent. And then, suddenly, Sam was like a man who realizes that liquor doesn't make him happy but only quarrelsome and sick. He was no longer frightened of what might face him if he *didn't* have that world of estates and hunts and revolutions and mazurkas to which nightly he might retreat. Shortly after supper he put down the shiny rhinoceros-hided library volume of *Dead Souls* right in the middle of a chapter, and wandered out to see what his wife was up to, knowing he would never go back for more, that it wasn't worth it, and that one unhappily rich epoch in his history, a kind of double life, was ended.

Strangely, some vestigial and maniacal refusal fully to surrender made Sam incapable of returning the book to the library when it came due. For months the Hookers received reminders, and then threats, and finally bills for the lost book from the nice Miss McCormick, and Sam's heart sank with dread with each morning's mail, but he wouldn't return it and he wouldn't pay up. Instead, he simply avoided the place.

It was only when his son Isaac, who was cutting his reading teeth by systematically devouring every book from *Antarctic Adventure* to *Zsa-Zsa!* insisted on being taken there that Sam dared set foot again in those varnished mahogany entrails. Had Miss McCormick forgotten or was she too polite to bring up his criminal record in front of his son? The uncertainty made him address her with a grating jocularity that drew startled looks from Isaac, a child with no tolerance for artificiality.

The library's Gogol remained on his shelf at home, strait-jacketed between the encyclopedia and a tall schoolboy atlas like a small townhouse on a block of high-rises, condemned but still standing.

There were a slew of good reasons not to read novels any more, self-satisfied, arrogant reasons that made one's chest swell in pride to voice them. He could say to himself that fiction (that word again) no longer grabbed his fancy or satisfied his intellect, that a grown man's sitting down to invent episodes that never transpired and to rally sympathy for men and women who never existed is finally a trivial fruitless enterprise, a waste of spirit and labor; that novel reading, after a certain age, becomes a shifty nauseating habit, like downing a box of chocolates on the sly. You grow out of your sweet tooth, you have two kids who need putting to bed, and papers to grade, and a wife to wrangle with, and a mortgage to be paid, so what business have you got swooning over two young girls leaning out a window dreaming of future lovers on a summer's night?

But in truth it was the opposite; it wasn't that he didn't care but that he couldn't bear it. *Their* limitlessness pressed too brutally upon the ever-narrowing confines of his own possibilities, his burdened life, his deepening acquaintance with compromise, and daily widening knowledge of all he would never be or do or have.

Now in the evenings Sam watched television, like everyone else, or read the sports page.

On a Sunday morning shortly before Halloween, he drove the Nash over to Sturgis, where Scannon lived with his sister, Mrs. Clark.

Scannon, a late riser, was camped out in the den in a tartan flannel dressing gown and tiny leather slippers, his sandy-white hair standing up in tufts, waiting for his sister to come home from church to feed him. The den bore all the marks of a foreign occupation: where formerly Mrs. Clark's herds of china rabbits and pink jade elephants had grazed on glass shelves, now a city of battered paperbacks and textbooks rose in unsteady stacks through a malodorous fog of pipe smoke, while the late Mr. Clark's La-Z-Boy lay buried deep in yellowing newspaper and old magazines—and a brand-new *Columbia Encyclopedia*.

Scannon as usual showed no surprise at seeing him. "Have a drink, dear boy."

Sam inadvertently glanced at his watch.

"Don't mind the time: we must celebrate the Sabbath. Remember what W. C. Fields says in *My Little Chickadee*—'While traveling through Afghanistan I lost my corkscrew and was compelled to live for three days off food and water!' Well, Sturgis is no hub of civilization, but at least we have our corkscrews. How about some sherry?"

"I'd better get to work while I'm still upright," Sam said. Grabbing a rake from the shed, he marched out to Mrs. Clark's front yard, followed by Scannon still in bathrobe and slippers. It was a crisp morning in which all creation had ripened into a glory of scarlet and gold. The autumnal sky was a china blue, a blue of deep ingenuous probity scarred only by one tiny snail trail of an airplane, and the round hills about were dyed flickering crimson, fuchsia, blond, like stained glass in a gray stone cathedral. The yard lay bedded in a dry sea of beech leaves. Scannon, hopping from foot to slippered foot in the cold air, talked while Sam set to work, the green tines of his rake like a witch's fingernails clawing the leaves into broad, crackly heaps.

He loved raking leaves: it was hot work, and one of those seasonal, cyclical acts steeped in vivid, stirring memory—with his father in Hebron, at Mattie's house two years ago when they were courting— no, he didn't want to think about cursed Mattie now. Autumn was childhood's season. He remembered trick-or-treating on long-ago Halloweens—he a mustachioed pegleg pirate annoyed to be seen with his tittering princess sisters—sticky, heavily laden, they would traipse home to a front porch blazing like a party cruiser on a dark sea, carrying for passenger one strawhatted scarecrow in their father's old clothes and decked in jack-o'-lanterns, luminous, orange, gat-toothed, mysterious yet ingratiating, each with its jagged flickering grin, its blackened guts like a campsite in a cave, its pungent cannibal scent of scorched flesh; pagan martyrs who beamed while their insides burned.

Fall was the season of rebirth and fresh starts, of a new school year, whose virgin notebooks with blue lines leaping from the page were the banners of a marching army, in which everything seemed possible and the soul swelled with exultant optimism and generous ambition, and you wanted to sign up for as many courses as possible and try out for the school play and go for the football team, and wage a new campaign against all the girls you had already spurned or been spurned by. But for grown-up Sam, who just a couple of weeks ago had been determined to polish off Fulke Greville by Christmas and become a new man, all hopes were now dashed: he wasn't bound for a plummy common room; he had just consigned himself to winding up a local loser.

He rolled the wheelbarrow along the pebbly drive from one leaf-mountain to the next, heaping great fluttering orange armfuls into its rusting iron belly, and bearing them off to the compost heap. Scannon, still trotting behind, chattering as he went, stooped to pick up a fallen straggler, marmalade-colored, flame-shaped, dry as paper, and fingered its delicately ribbed spine, like the hull of a boat, like a golden sole, pan-fried on one's plate. "What kind of leaf is this?" he wondered.

Sam looked at him in astonishment. How could you not know a beech, with its mild yet spirited tenacity, its protective femininity, its dun bark, whose leaves were the first to fall and the first to turn up intact after the spring thaw in great heaped tresses like buried treasure? How could you read poetry and not know the names of trees?

The young man moved about the drive, tending to his raking and not really listening to Scannon's chatter, intent on the words he himself had to say, full with betrayal. He had to tell him now, or burst. "Are you trying to do the Cumaean sybil's work for her?" Scannon inquired, as Sam gazed dumbly at the leaves.

"I'm dropping my master's," he blurted out.

"Oh. Bored with Fulke? I can't blame you—he is a dour soul."

"It's not Fulke, it's me. I'm quitting. I'm not going for a Ph.D. after all." Sam spread his jacket over the laden barrow. On staggering legs, he pushed it back uphill to the compost heap, fighting a high wind. Once he had said it, all he wanted to do was snivel and be comforted.

"I've accepted a job, and I'm starting next week. I had to get a job—we have a baby due in eight weeks, and Mattie's going to have to leave work" (these were the kind of domestic details Sam usually spared Scannon), "so it was up to me. I know myself: I got little enough done working on the thesis full time. I'll never get it finished evenings and weekends, so I might as well face facts and quit school," he concluded in a monotonous rush, forestalling all possible protests and counter-arguments.

To his consternation, Scannon didn't argue. "A job!" he remarked brightly. "That's a very sensible idea. Education's gone to the dogs, anyway. Much better to go work in a bank or insurance company and read poetry on one's own than to waste one's time drumming learning into the skulls of semiliterate incorrigibles." He began to tell a story of a student of his who at the end of a year of Modern Literature thought Joyce was a woman.

"I'm going to teach science and history at the local high school," explained Sam, apologetically. It sounded so brazenly ignominious that surely now Scannon would say what Sam had come to hear: that's ridiculous, keep on with your studies, and don't you dare for a moment think of getting a job. Gird up your loins, man.

Scannon, bending to pick up stray leaves, made a wry little face. Sam knew what he thought about science altogether: science was for drones. You paid people to know about that sort of thing—mechanics, electricians, doctors—to free yourself for real pursuits. But instead, "Chacun à son goût. It's a shame, but I suppose the world can wait for the definitive exposition of Fulke Greville's Calvinism. When do you start?"

Sam was stunned. "Do you think it's a mistake?" he finally fished, not looking.

"My dear boy, it's a different world today from the world I grew up in. If your wife says you must get a job right now, well, of course you must. Women are always right about these things."

Sam finished up his yard work blindly, in a concentrated fury of bewilderment at his hero's indifference to his fate. Did Scannon care whether he lived or died? If he lingered or persisted, would Scannon relent and tell him not to quit his graduate work? Could he really acquiesce so merrily, so unconcernedly in Sam's ruin? No, the subject was closed, and after a few bland pleasantries about the season, in which it seemed to the stung, wretched young man that his friend was already treating him more like a yard man than a colleague, Scannon went back inside to his Sunday *Globe*. Sam left him in the sunny kitchen, fussed over by his widowed sister now returned from church, who urged Sam to stay for dinner. He couldn't—he had to be . . . not home, but somewhere, he glumly lied. Scannon didn't even look up as he left.

Back in the car, he found himself in what seemed like the geometrically impossible position of being furious simultaneously at Mattie and Scannon, like being in the North Pole and Antarctica at the same time. And now he had nowhere to go. Loss was something physical—

a hard lump in his chest, a burning, not being able to breathe, a prickling pent-up feeling of tears suppressed. Stuck. He was stuck. He replayed the conversation with Scannon in his head, wondering if he should have asked the old man more forcefully if he were any good, if he should try and keep on with his studies at any cost. No, he'd humiliated himself enough. "Showing my fall to them that scorn, see not or will not see," in Fulke Greville's words. For Scannon, he was now just another local clod. This man, whose talk he treasured and hoarded in his heart, whose record player and toaster and lawn mower he mended, whose yard he tended from season to season because he loved him and wanted to be near him, to care for him, this Scannon couldn't care less whether he ever saw Sam again.

The door had been shut in his face. He had quit that caste whose religion lay in examining the entrails of sonnets and villanelles, and now, a weak-kneed Adam, was being driven by the angel with flaming sword into the world of work and childbirth's pains.

And then something in him burst. "No," he said aloud, "I won't. I won't." He swung the car around and drove back to the Clark house, pulling up crookedly across the drive. In the kitchen sat Mrs. Clark, nicking the tiny eyes from a bowl of new potatoes the purplish sheen of Mattie's favorite nail polish. Scannon had retired once more to the den and was engulfed by a cloud of newspaper like a little tartan genie. Again he showed not the least surprise at Sam's return, but glanced up quizzically at the young man who, face working, towered over him.

"*You* got me into this."

"Into what, dear boy?"

"*You* gave me the idea of getting a Ph.D. and becoming an English professor. You talked me into it, told me I was good enough."

Scannon demurred. "Well . . . good enough? Don't romanticize. This isn't the Olympics, this is a profession of m-miserable m-mediocrities. One doesn't have to be very good to teach."

"You made me think it was something noble and I wanted to do it because *you* did it," Sam persisted, stupidly, glaring down at the dapper little gnome in pajamas and dressing gown. "So don't you even give a damn if I quit? Can't you even be bothered to tell me to keep on going and finish what I started? I thought we were friends." He didn't notice his voice rising up into those thin, plaintive registers that usually made him cringe.

"Do please stop before you make me weep," said Scannon, with a sarcasm that did indeed stop Sam in amazement. There was a moment of silence, and then Scannon continued dryly, "My, my, what a hysterical self-pitier you are. I only told you to keep on with your studies because you were so utterly blank. And in so doing I ignored a very wise precept of mine: never, never get mixed up with a man who doesn't know his own mind. This, then, is my punishment for trying to be kind to you. Am I your mother? Is it my business whether you teach high school or college? Does it really matter? What matters is the inner life. But *that* you've already renounced. You're a grown man and I assume you've sized up your own needs and I wouldn't insult you by questioning your choices. But whatever you do, *grow up*, for pity's sake, and don't come barging in on your elders whining that they don't look after you properly."

Sam was seeing his teacher as if for the first time. The purple veins in the puffy cheeks, the tufts of yellow-white hair sticking upright, the egg stain on the collar of his flannel pajamas, the belt of woolen dressing gown that was trailing on the floor. "*I'm* the one who's been looking after you," he said.

"What nonsense," replied Scannon, coolly. "You're an agreeable young man who seemed to be at loose ends. I happen to enjoy the company of young people, and I had no wish to hurt your feelings if you were eager for my friendship, but to say you've looked after me is a gross and truly bizarre delusion."

Sam deliberated. They could hear Mrs. Clark pottering around the kitchen, and the delicate clatter of china dishes, could even smell the roasting chicken and the steam off the potatoes, the sedate sunny scent of Sunday stillness. "Go rake your own fucking leaves," said Sam.

As he strode out of the room, muttering "Little fairy" under his breath, he could sense Scannon's plump shoulders gathering up and sinking back against the La-Z-Boy in a not quite audible sigh of relief. As he passed through the kitchen, Mrs. Clark, basting the portly golden capon, sang out, "Oh, Sam, have you changed your mind? Will you be joining us, after all?"

Sam stopped, riveted by the trussed bird with its self-satisfied belly and helpless little legs. "That bird—why, that bird bears an uncanny resemblance to Mr. Scannon, doesn't it, Mrs. Clark?" he said.

Have you ever dreamed that nightmare in which you, a free soul in command of your destiny, with job and family and freedom, are suddenly dumped at your childhood desk and made to understand that you will be repeating fourth, fifth, sixth grade, a school slave all over again? That is how Sam felt pulling up one Monday morning in his familiar high-school parking lot and tramping up the well-worn stairs to his old ninth-grade classroom with its clocks that jumped backward one minute before creaking forward two and its big windows facing out over the Ashuelot River and its smell of shiny carbon paper, wet hair, and turpentine. This time he had no chance of getting there early enough to nab a desk in a back-row corner farthest from the teacher's eye: he was the teacher, and on the other side of the big desk were all the familiar names, except now it was Frank Olszewski's nephew and George Hanesworth's youngest brother and a whole new gaggle of Herringshaws to be coped with. Same old school, same old cafeteria, but now they served lasagne and ravioli and chili along with the usual pot roast and Yankee beans and fish fingers on Fridays, and now he sat with the teachers and had to reprimand boys blowing spitballs through their straws. The oddest thing of all was that to his students it seemed not in the least incongruous that he should be sitting at the teachers' table. To them he was an old man, desiccated, hopelessly cut off from human conflicts and passions, who, if he ever lived, had lived long ago and now was bent single-mindedly on preventing them from living.

Thus began Sam's tenure at the Ashuelot Regional High School. One quarrel, one fit of pique, and all of a sudden Sam, chased away from the self-reproachfully slothful Eden of graduate-student life, was getting up at six-thirty in the morning (nighttime) and coming home in the afternoon with chalk on the seat of his pants and a pocketful of red ballpoint pens, bone-tired from browbeating coquettes who painted their nails in class and pit-cheeked hulks dreaming of the day they could spend the rest of their lives on their backs gazing up at car engines.

For the first few months he was too exhausted and, despite himself, too intrigued by his live material to regret Fulke Greville or mourn his thwarted university career. Besides, he had his baby son to worship. Yet if Sam, God help him, turned out to be a born teacher possessed of an ample fund of sympathetic curiosity about teen-age plights— were Danny and Marcy going to get back together, was Billy ever going to graduate from ninth grade, was Astrid Albright narcoleptic or merely the mistress of a very demanding night life?—still, this was not one bit what he had meant to do with himself. No, on the contrary, teaching high-school biology and chemistry and physics and European and American history and basketball (a sideline that redeemed him in his students' eyes) represented an unconditional collapse of his ambitions and exalted plans, an unmitigatedly humiliating surrender.

The soul revolts against such knowledge. Rather than resign himself to hating his wife and job, Sam decided the fault lay in the size of their apartment. They must find less cramped quarters before he and Mattie cut each other's throats. His teacher's salary seemed at first oceanic, and once poor Mr. Hynes kicked the bucket and Sam was hired as a permanent teacher, the Hooker family moved to a farmhouse six swollen climbing miles northwest of Gilboa.

Isaac woke up bursting with something to tell. He had figured it out while he was asleep and now basked in the speckled sunlight of his room, listening to the roar of the furnace downstairs in the cellar and playing the wrestling game with his two hands. Each bunched fist was a man with his arms folded and a hooked swan neck (the forefinger) and the two men fought by hooking each other's neck, with accompanying war whoops from Isaac. He always yelled just to egg the wrestlers on, but this time he was hoping that if he made enough of a racket his parents would wake up and come rescue him.

Hours and hours he lay bursting with this secret, and then miraculously there was the scuff of his mother's mules across the wooden floorboards and the door opened. There she was looming over his cot in the dappled early-morning light, fat and solid and smelling enticingly of motherly sweat. The sweat from her armpits smelled like chicken soup.

"Mommmmmmm . . ."

"Come on, Isaac, time to get up. Let's get you bathed and dressed quick before Daddy gets up, so I can get the house vacuumed and be on the road early."

That meant it was Saturday. Saturdays his father slept late and Isaac took his weekly bath. Saturday his dad didn't vanish early and come home drawn and harried but was at Isaac's beck and call, pleased to goof off and explore. Saturday they went to the library in Gilboa, while his mother stayed home with the baby and cleaned house.

"Why do you want to be on the road?"

"I'm going shopping with Mrs. Karolis."

"What are you shopping for?"

"A store."

"A store?!"

"Lift your arms high, Isaac." He lifted and stretched with uncustomary obedience as his mother pulled the pajama top over his head—the hole wasn't big enough for his great noggin; she nearly pulled his ears off.

"Are you buying a store, Mom?"

"Maybe. I'm looking at one."

"A bookstore?"

"No."

"A general store, like Grandpa's?"

"No."

"A dinosaur store?"

"No."

"What kind of store?"

"A dress store."

"Oh." Isaac lost interest. "Mom, guess what."

"Shush, Ikey, help me with your pajamas. No squirming now."

"But I'm ticklish . . ." He stepped obligingly out of his pajama bottoms. "Guess what, Mom."

"I don't feel like guessing today, Ikey. Come on into the bathroom. Quick. I don't want you to catch cold."

At these words, stark naked, white as a fat albino goldfish, Isaac went tearing out of the bedroom and careering around the house to escape his watery fate, peeking in on his father to make sure he really was asleep, struggling when his mother caught him and dragged him into the tub.

Baths were the bane of his existence. His mom wasn't wild about them either, that was one thing they had in common, but where he was concerned she had no pity. It was bad enough being stripped of his warm clothes, which had only just unstarched themselves into his own smell and shape, so that if you stood his pajamas on end they might look like a headless Isaac, a tarbaby Isaac to fool Brer Rabbit. On top of that, the water pressure was so low she never bothered to fill the bathtub with more than a glazing of water, so from the waist up Isaac froze. And then she scrubbed too hard, with no respect for the actual contours of his face and body, poking soap in his eye.

Once in the tub, however, busy with his flotilla of rubber toys, he refused to get out again until the sea battle taking place was won, and all the enemy ducks were dead ducks. If generals fight the last war, how much more so do children. This very morning, while the 9th

U.S. Infantry Division was laying siege to the Vietcong-infested district of Saigon, Isaac reenacted the Battle of Midway.

"That's enough, Ike. Hurry up, time to get out. If you don't get out and have your breakfast now, you won't be ready by the time Daddy wants to go." When he didn't listen, she pulled the plug. Isaac shivered on the porcelain, still agitating his battleships until the last tepid gust of water escaped with a loud slurp down the drain. He always waited, just to see whether he might not be swept down too like Alice in the song that went "Holy-Moses-Jumping-Joseph-there-went-Alice-down-the-drain."

Over breakfast he remembered the amazing discovery he had made that morning and hadn't yet told anybody. How surprised his father would be! It concerned a subject that had long preoccupied him: how come American Indians and Eskimos and Chinese people all looked alike.

"Mom, do you know . . ." He pulled at her dress, butted against her broad bottom.

"Shush, Ike. Aren't you done yet?" She swept away his bowl of cereal. "Bring me the vacuum."

"Mom, did you know—*guess* who invented America?" he yelled happily, torn between wanting to keep her in suspense and needing to get the story out fast, but she motioned him along. "Can't you do *anything* I tell you? All right, lazybones, I'll get it myself."

Isaac watched her drag the machine from a tight, overloaded closet. Every time he had something important to explain to his mother, she revved up this machine that roared him down. Not much time to get his message across.

"Mom!" he yelled, choosing terseness over drama. "You know what, it wasn't the Norse who discovered America at all."

There, he'd got her attention, but he hadn't said it all yet. Radiant sunny day outside. Good library day, thought Isaac, riding roughshod over his mother's notion that rain and books went together.

"I know."

"What do you mean you know?" Isaac was crestfallen.

"It was Christopher Columbus."

Stupid. "No, it wasn't," he cried. "Christopher Columbus only got to South America: he didn't get to North America at all. Leif Ericson was the one who landed years before Christopher Columbus was even born, before his parents or grandparents or great-great-great-grandparents were born."

"No, he didn't. Whoever heard of Leif Ericson discovering America? Just wait till you start school—is the teacher ever going to get a good laugh. It was Christopher Columbus. Everyone knows that."

"No, it wasn't."

"Yes, it was," contradicted his mother, in between vacuum blasts, not looking at him but nosing into corners with the gluttonous vacuum, a cigarette hanging from her lips. His mother and Aunt Sue were wonders at smoking with no hands. When Sarah came over to play they sneaked their parents' butts from the garbage can to practice in front of the bathroom mirror. It always fell out as soon as you laughed or tried to talk. This talent made his mother hard to kiss: you might catch fire.

"Where did I put the car keys?" she wondered aloud, patting behind the radio.

Isaac persisted. "But I know who really came first. It was the Chinese who invented America. *And* they left behind the Eskimos," he finished in a crescendo of triumph, grabbing hold of his mother by the dress and wringing its skirt so she would turn around and look at him. She wouldn't.

"Don't pull like that, Ikey. It's my best dress. Are they in my purse?"

"THE CHINESE!" yelled Isaac. "THE CHINESE!"

"What about them? Isaac, would you go look in the bedroom and bring me my pocketbook without waking Daddy up? And check on the baby while you're there. No shouting, or else it's back to bed."

Isaac didn't move. He reached down and pulled the vacuum's plug from the socket. And then he spoke, fast, before she got mad. "The Chinese invented America. It wasn't the Norse and it wasn't Christopher Columbus. And then they went home and left the Eskimos and Indians behind. That's why they all have slanty eyes. Now will you learn to shut off that machine and look at me while I'm talking? It's very rude to play the vacuum when I'm telling you something."

It was a gamble. Either she would smack him for his freshness, as she called it—or, less likely, she would listen. Isaac's mother was the least predictable woman in the world; you never knew which way she would jump.

She capitulated. "Well, it's rude of you to talk while I'm working. Anyway, who told you that?" she added, reconnecting the vacuum. "It's just not true. It was not the Chinese. You just made that up."

"Well, I did not. You're completely wrong," said Isaac, and narrowing his eyes the way his father did, added, "There are just a lot of things you don't know about, Mom, that Dad and I do know about. So maybe it would be better if you were quiet and listened for a change."

Then his mom was done vacuuming and turned off the machine. The room was suddenly quiet, and with a start they both noticed that Isaac's father had come downstairs and into the kitchen while they were arguing. He stood in his pajamas, cake-eyed, hair standing on end, hawking the morning junk out of his throat, looking cross. Isaac ran over, wrapping his legs around him as around a tall prickly tree, but his father didn't pay attention. It wasn't a great idea talking to him in the morning before he'd had a cup of coffee.

Mattie slapped down his breakfast. Sam, still snuffling and hawking, glanced up at his wife, who was standing over him impatiently, all dressed up and itching to go. He sipped at his coffee, regarded his cereal indifferently, and finally took a leisurely spoonful. Mattie eyed the kitchen clock furiously; Sam dawdled.

"Do you mind not standing over me like a prison matron while I eat? You're blocking my sunlight."

Mattie retreated a few feet without a word. Now, however, to her outraged disbelief, he laid down his spoon and stopped eating altogether. "Why don't you listen to the boy?" he continued, in a studiously polite and stilted voice.

"What?" snorted Mattie.

"You heard me. I said, Why don't you listen to the boy when he's telling you something?"

"What was he telling me?"

"About the Chinese. You should listen to him when he's talking. He's right: it's rude not to."

No matter how late she was running, Mattie couldn't resist such provocation. "Well, how do you like that. So I'm rude to Ike. Remember this, I'm the one who has to listen to Ike's chatter nonstop from six in the morning till six at night, seven days a week, when he's cranky and needs his breakfast and his lunch and his dinner and won't take a nap and won't take a bath and the baby's crying because Ikey's crying, and I have to tend to both of them throwing fits at once. *I'm* rude not to listen to Ikey?"

There was silence. Isaac wasn't looking at them, he was staring hard at the floor, playing with a little dust bunny his mother's vacuum had overlooked. Maybe his dad would walk out. Or maybe he would yell. But maybe his dad didn't want Isaac either. He tried hard not to cry.

His parents' quarrels were of one terrible piece: his mother ranted, his father stormed out, and for the next few days they didn't speak to each other and Isaac would hide in his bedroom with the door closed, his stomach tied up in knots of anxious misery. During these ice ages his father was always extra-solicitous of him, but all the same Isaac preferred lying low until his parents made up. Heart-sickening were the breakfasts and suppers when two of the three of them weren't speaking, when Isaac would bravely chatter, only to run out of steam and trail off midsentence, disheartened by the realization that neither was listening, and collapsing into the common oppressive silence. When he was alone with his mother, she badmouthed Sam to him, and his father did the same. Isaac, simultaneously flattered and distressed by these confidences, was caught in the middle. In his mind now he pictured the Chinese, descending from boats delicate as walnut-shell vessels and teeming across the shores, tea-colored, bowlegged, discreet. The Chinese, first to discover America.

"This boy—our Isaac—is a very smart boy," said Sam finally, in that same dull polite voice. "Every day in his life is like a whole lifetime. He's growing fast and he's learning the world, and he needs attention and stimulation. You ought to thank your lucky stars you have the honor of spending these precious hours with him. It doesn't seem too much to ask that you do your child the common courtesy of listening to him and answering his questions."

"What questions?" demanded Mattie. "He doesn't ask me any questions, he just bosses me around. He makes up lies and contradicts me when I try to tell him the truth. You tell *him* to treat *me* with a little respect. I'm his mother."

"He's not a liar. Don't you ever call him a liar."

"I think you're a liar," said Mattie. "You told me if I wanted to start up my own business, you'd ask your dad for the money."

"I never did. My dad doesn't have any money, and you know it. I never told you to start up a store. You pester me and pester me, and then you decide I've said something I haven't. I tell you, it's a stupid idea. And it's stupid to go look at premises you know you can't buy: you're just wasting the owner's time."

"You said your dad could get me a loan."

"I never said it."

Silence, while they both went back to staring at each other, eyes smoking.

"Who's going to look after the baby while you go gallivanting around the countryside inspecting real estate?"

"I'm going to leave him with the Randalls."

"I don't want that woman looking after my son. She's a nitwit."

"She's got more sense in her little toe than you're ever going to have. I've just about had it with you turning your nose up at my family," warned Mattie.

Isaac had a stomach ache that was kind of an important stomach ache, but still he didn't really feel like telling them about it at the moment. Maybe he was just hungry. He wondered what was for lunch, and hoped it would end in chocolate pudding and not jello, then he remembered he had just had breakfast.

"Don't be a hypocrite, Mattie, it doesn't suit. You're the one who has no use for your own flesh and blood. You do whatever you like with the child. I'm leaving," said her husband. At these words, Isaac lost it. Sam, catching sight of his son's crumpled red face, the streams spouting horizontally from his screwed-tight eyes, melted. He grabbed hold of the child as if catching a falling cup, swung him into his lap. "Now, now, sergeant-major, now, honey-darling-pie," he murmured, rubbing his face against Isaac's hair. "Everything's going to be all right. Everything will be fine. Your mom and I just don't always see eye to eye, that's all. I didn't mean I was leaving for good. Only place I'm going is to the library with you." Amidst his sobbing Isaac smelled the bitter rindy tang of orange juice on his father's breath, mixed with the stale drooly smell of people just up. And then Sam asked, not in the stilted voice he had used to his wife, but in his own voice, the voice of Isaac's father, gravelly and loving, "What about them Chinks, Isaac? They discovered America and left behind the Eskimos and Indians, is that what I hear?"

"Didn't they?" asked Isaac, doubtful now, still snuffling.

"No, they didn't. They were too busy inventing gunpowder and macaroni to discover America. You got to leave *something* for the Italians."

"Did you say hello to Miss McCormick?" he asked, as soon as they were settled down.

"Yup," said Sam.

"And what did she say back?"

"Hello."

"Why are you saying hello to me?" said Isaac, sputtering with laughter at his newborn capacity to make jokes. His father reached down and pulled him by the ear.

"Wise guy. Go pick some books."

"You don't pick books. You pick apples," Isaac corrected. "Books don't grow on trees."

"You sure? Where do they grow?"

Isaac was stumped. "On the moon?" he suggested, laughing too loud at his own joke. His clear, carrying voice made people turn around, the old ladies reading *McCall's* and *Ladies' Home Journal*, who smelled of lavender powder, and the old men reading the local papers on wooden hangers like scrolls, with creased leathery necks and mammoth ears and shirts buttoned up to the Adam's apple and large spotted hands whose square-tipped fingers had gnarled nails.

"Why are old men's ears so big, Daddy?"

"Ssshhhh, Isaac." Then, relenting, whispered unwisely, "Because the rest of them shrinks."

A moment's digestive silence, and then, "OLD MEN SHRINK?!" exclaimed Isaac, horrified, fascinated. Now all the people in the room turned around indignantly. He wondered how big they had all been before they shrank.

"Go get a book."

They were sunk deep in the dilapidated armchair, Isaac in his father's lap, in the children's corner. The library in Gilboa was a dark Victorian mansion that had once belonged to the Herringshaw family, who owned the mill. It was, to Isaac's mind, an extraordinarily beautiful and mysterious place abounding in carved mahogany banisters and stained-glass windows and white marble busts of juvenile Herringshaws, both male and female. The reading room smelled of steam heat and varnish, wet galoshes, licorice cough drops, books. In winter, its radiators hissed, rattled, and jangled like a calypso band.

Sam called the library Isaac's "office." They went to the office several afternoons a week, as often as Sam could be persuaded, and stayed almost all day Saturdays. Isaac was a tyrant for routine. Sometimes his father tried to talk him into catching tadpoles or butterflies. No dice.

"You drive a vicious bargain, Mr. Hooker."

"No bargain."

"That's just what I mean. You take no prisoners."

"Take them where?"

"Anywhere."

"Where do they want to go?"

"Well, not to the library again, for a start."

The library constituted for Isaac something of a slow road to Damascus. His father had first brought him there a year ago and watched Ike install himself in the children's corner, surrounded by bulwarks and turrets of picture books pulled down from the shelves, frenzied by the profusion of compacted delights, and determined to have consumed every book by closing time.

"We can take a few home with us," the father reassured the increasingly frantic child.

When it came time to pack up, Sam returned from the bathroom to find his son was busy transferring the entire children's section to Miss McCormick's desk. The librarian and the child were at polite loggerheads. Miss McCormick was explaining that new borrowers could check out no more than three books at a time. Isaac, who went especially deaf when words were not to his liking, red-eared and talking even louder and more deliberately than usual, replied, "Oh no, miss, it's all right to take them all home. Daddy said I could. They won't be gone long."

"Isaac," remonstrated Sam. "You have to choose. Three books, that's all. Miss McCormick doesn't want any book hogs in the library, do you, Miss McCormick?"

Isaac, betrayed, looked desperate. Miss McCormick cast him a melting glance. It was the worst thing she could have done. Born with a dread of anything that might be construed as pity, Isaac flew into a fury. "You're the wart hog, not me!" he shouted at her. "You're the one who gets to sit with them all day!"

The next day, prompted by Sam in lessons of diplomacy, Isaac returned with an apology and a matchbox containing a black-and-amber caterpillar.

"It's a yak," he explained to the librarian.

"Really? You know, it looks awfully like a caterpillar."

"No, it's a yak. It's a very little yak."

By now, more than a year later, Isaac had read all the books in the children's corner several times over and was poised on the brink of grown-up territory. He read furiously and loudly. Reading was revelation of a peculiarly urgent, blissful, violent nature, and he fought with, quarreled with, ingested these worlds upon worlds made palpable with every sentence. Here he had learned about George Washington and Benjamin Franklin and Patrick Henry and the two Thomases—Jefferson and Edison—about the invention of the steam engine and the invention of the long bow, about Marco Polo and Vasco da Gama and

Scott and Amundsen, the Trojan War, the Battle of Lepanto, the Vikings, and the Aztecs. He liked wars and heroes and was suspicious of divine intervention. He liked biographies of great men. Hardship, cleverness. The science of things—systems, structures, classification, maps, dates—satisfied him mightily.

Once he had learned to read, things had gotten more confusing because then he was distracted from story and intoxicated, driven almost to tears, by the beauty of the alphabet with its rich subtle shapes and sounds, ravished and mystified by the complex amplitude of an *a*, the woody, forested dry burr of an *r*, capital *E*'s crotchety as a garden rake, tadpole *q*'s swimming in the wet saline infancy of evolution, *b*'s blustering and blunt, capital *H*'s broad ecclesiastical pillars, playing-field high jumps in appearance but tentative in sound, a warm, silent exhalation like the breath of God in Adam's nostrils, like a horse's muzzling, *h* like heart like hot like hecatomb. Sometimes Isaac preferred his father to read aloud to him just so he could concentrate on the story and not dissolve into wild love for the black curly letters on the page, which he longed to pluck off, to hold in the palm of his hand, imprint on his heart.

Impossibly early, Sam tried to explain to him about genetics and the double helix. You, too, come in loops of encoded alphabet, each person is a one-of-a-kind Bible, a comic book, an epic poem, a geological tract, a sonnet, with nail biting or wiggly ears or near-perfect pitch a kind of coda. Everything is written; you just have to know how to read it.

Reading, of course, was power, too, self-sufficiency. Once he had learned everything in the world, he wouldn't need anyone.

Now he deposited on his father's lap a hailstorm of books. "Let's read about your least favorite character, Ferdinand Magellan."

It was true Sam was not beguiled by this desperado, who managed to shipwreck his own boats, starve off his sailors, and put down numerous well-deserved mutinies before getting himself killed by raging Filipinos. This same pig-headed lunatic, however, was Isaac's special favorite. Why? Because he stuck by his guns when nobody else believed him, and was the first to prove the world round by sailing it, though it cost him his life and three boatloads of men. Only one skipper survived to tell the tale. But he was right: there was a western passage to the South Seas. The Straits of Magellan at the bottom of South America stood testament to his obstinacy, and the Magellanic Cloud that floats north of the South Pole. He was the only person to have both earthbound and heavenly geography named for him, an uneasy posthumous sort of vindication. Isaac ground his teeth in satisfaction.

Sam read aloud the tediously familiar words of the story, trying not to look at its lurid illustrations. What crummy stuff they wrote for children these days. Isaac, breathing heavily from concentration, slipped a little in his father's angular lap and hoisted himself up again, buried his head under a less rocklike portion of chin, ducking free of the octopus arms turning pages. Isaac was imagining himself Magellan, arguing with King Manuel for his mission to the Moluccas. You bad Manuel, give me my ships or else! Then he was on the high seas in his storm-racked galleon, putting down the mutiny—a word that secretly made Isaac think of the green stuff in his nose.

"Spanish fools! I'm going to make you walk the plank if you don't behave!" His father had stopped reading and looked down, mock surprise crumpling his forehead. "Who are you telling to behave? I can hear you. Are you reading or am I?"

Isaac, embarrassed, quickly changed the subject. "So what happened to the sailors when they got home? Did they punish the sailors who mutinied him?"

"Certainly not. They were just poor slobs who thought their boss had gone crazy and was trying to kill them all. And they were right."

"He was crazy?" repeated Isaac, disbelievingly.

"Well, yes. You've got to be crazy sometimes to get things done."

"Back to Magellan, Daddy," said Isaac, his whole body and voice registering violent disapproval of this heretic idea. "He wasn't crazy. It was everyone else who was crazy."

"Whatever you say, boss."

"Don't call me boss," said Isaac, sternly. "Just keep on reading."

When they got home late that afternoon, Isaac bearing two big books about Marco Polo, Mattie still hadn't returned. He followed at a nervous trot as his father swept from room to room, incredulous.

They sat at the kitchen table in the fading light, Isaac munching on the sandwich his father assembled him for supper, while Sam, chain-smoking, bitter, railed against his wife.

"Very maternal of her, abandoning her infant for twelve hours to those dismal flit heads. Lucky if they don't let him fall into the well. And she pretends to care about the baby! Some way to bring him up— a boarder baby, more like it."

Isaac nodded in solemn agreement, rather hoping that Turner might disappear down the well. He wanted to contribute to this conversation but wasn't sure how. "You know something, Dad?"

"What, honey?"

"I don't think I like mayonnaise on tunafish."

Sam came back to earth reluctantly. "But, Ikey, you've got to have mayonnaise with tunafish, just to make it stick to the bread."

"I guess I don't like tunafish all that much."

They sat in silence, each chewing on his own thoughts.

"How come Mom wants to buy a store?" Isaac asked finally.

"Oh, I don't know," said Sam, in the same bitter undertone. "Your mother wants to get rich."

Isaac squinted at his father in surprise. "What's so bad about that?"

Sam, blowing rings, emitted something between a laugh and a sigh. "You want to be a millionaire, old man?"

"Of course I do. Don't you?"

"Maybe. But a store's sure not the way to go about it. Your grandpa's almost gone bust with his store. Anyway, it's not your mom's place. She ought to be home taking care of you and Turner."

Isaac considered. "If she doesn't want to take care of me, I can take care of myself just fine."

"Why, what will you do?"

"I don't know. I guess I'll live at the library and read," said the child, trying to make a forlorn voice sound stalwart.

"What will you eat?" Sam was curious. "You wouldn't even get tunafish in the library. You think Miss McCormick's going to take you home with her every evening in her big black handbag?"

"I don't know. I guess I'll eat bugs. Insects can be very nutritious."

"Oh, they can, can they? So you don't need your old man to take care of you?"

"I didn't say that," Isaac replied carefully. "I just don't want to get in anyone's way."

He pictured to himself with a mixture of excitement and trepidation this life of bookish survivalism. Maybe he would live in a box. There was a story his father had told him about a local eccentric long ago who lived in a piano crate by the Boston & Maine railway tracks. That would be kind of fun. You could hole up in a piano box with a flashlight and a blanket and lots of library books and live off bugs, and no one would bother you. All you had to do was find the crate, the crate that the piano came in.

Isaac was asleep when his mother came home with the baby. He only learned several days later, when he asked her about the purple smudge on her cheek, that his father had hit her for staying out. It was the only time he knew of his father hitting his mother, which was unusual for those parts, where Aunt Sue or Mrs. Karolis occasionally came over, a couple of scared-looking kids in tow, to escape their husbands' wrath; Frank Olszewski beat Cindy blind whenever he was home on leave.

Getting slugged didn't seem to bother Mattie too much, because for the next couple of weeks she was remarkably cheerful, and nobody heard anything more about her and Mrs. Karolis buying a store. But still Isaac thought from time to time about going to live by the tracks of the Boston & Maine in his piano crate—a pine cave whose fixtures he improved and embellished from time to time, now adding a tin chimney pipe, now planting it on the banks of the Ashuelot, where he would laze with a bamboo rod, catching little silvery fish to broil over a campfire at night.

Chapter 3

BEING A CHILD is largely a flux of bold and furtive guesswork, fixed ideas continually dislodged by scrambling and tentative revision. We are put on this earth like amnesiacs behind enemy lines. All our energy and cunning go into getting our bearings without letting on that we are ignorant and lost. Such was Isaac Hooker's condition the year before his brother, Turner, was born.

"Now we're going to Aubuchon's to pick up some shears," his mother would announce, and Isaac would fish around trying to figure out what "shears" were without asking. Or "Aunt Sue wants us to come by after the baptism." Who was Aunt Sue? How could a person be an ant? What was a baptism? Which was his right hand, which was his left, was Sturgis the town with the covered bridge or was that Hebron, was he a boy or was he a girl, what relation was Grandma to Sarah and Jimmy (none) and was Grandpa older than Mom or younger, who was Mrs. Karolis's husband, where did the sun go when it got dark, who was the President of the United States, where did his new teeth come from?—these were all problems Isaac was determined to solve although he was damned if he would admit he didn't already know the answers.

Of his mother, he generally refused to ask any questions and stood fast by the wrong information he fed her. With his father, a face-saving fiction prevailed that Isaac was a person so august in experience and advanced in learning that he had merely forgotten some of the more elementary items of the everything he already knew.

"I forget—what does that letter mean?" said Isaac, learning how to read.

"It's an *e*, like in 'egg.'"

"No, I don't think it's an *e*. I remember it's a *muh*."

"Well, maybe in *your* alphabet, Ikey, but not in the King's."

"Is this the King's alphabet? I forget who the King is."

Mostly, however, he was in too much of a hurry, and without any preamble unleashed questions like grapeshot splattering open grown-up paragraphs. (Who is Cindy? *How* did she get in trouble? What does "divorce" mean? No, what does it really mean? What's an MIA?)

In this manner, Isaac filled in his map of the world country by country, river by river, orienting himself by the compass of certain helpful dichotomies—day and night, good and bad, girls and boys (this one was fluid and tricky, since Grandpa looked not ungirllike and his mom looked like a boy, and he was always forgetting which he himself was). Chief among his securing divisions was indoors and out.

Near-sightedness, sickness, and a certain inborn sloth combined to make Isaac an indoor boy. Inside was his sanctuary, his wooden fun-house, graspably Isaac-sized, cozy, familiar, enclosed, and yet also positively cathedral and surprising in its proliferation of secret cubbyholes, larders, crawl spaces behind sofas and over the staircase, lairs to hide in, to set up tent, to which he might drag his favorite blanket, his flashlight, his rocks and sticks and picture books, only to forget them there, but places, too, that frightened him at nightfall, were unsafe to approach alone or to pass in the dark. An attic above, a cellar below, like heaven and hell, sweet menacing realms that, encircling the known world, left one continually conscious of the unknowable.

Inside, the house was as noisy and demanding and companionable as an only child. Doorways swelled and warped as wood wettened, sweated, and breathed, ceilings shed their paint and papering, there were ominous dark patches of damp on the walls covered in buckling paper. One afternoon Isaac peeled back the wallpaper at one seam only to discover beneath it an entrancing pewter-blue procession of shepherdesses and pagodas. *That* was worth a spanking, knowing there were people living underneath. When Isaac in three or four years discovered his own passion for ancient cities, he understood Pompeii, and Jericho whose tenth story was a thousand years older than its eleventh story, by thinking of the shepherdesses and pagodas underneath the yellow paper on his own living-room wall.

The house itself, like one of those cities, seemed perpetually on the brink of collapse. The ceiling slanted at a crazy angle, and the floorboards mimicked the ceiling's rises and dips like sea reflecting sky. If there were ever a snowstorm indoors, Isaac figured, he could toboggan very nicely from front door to back. When it rained, and it always rained, although the fall rain sounded and smelled quite different from the spring and summer rain, there was as much commotion as if God had commissioned an ark from the Hookers. Isaac and his mother rushed around the house closing windows and planting pails and buckets under all the leaks. Then he would sit at the kitchen table, with its dented aluminum top and its white curly legs, drawing pictures to the sound of water drops splattering against plastic basins. Rain—a sound half sickening, half lulling, and soporific, like a Chinese water torture. Isaac looked forward to bad weather, because it meant he could work in peace, without his mother trying to badger him out of the house.

When he wasn't practicing his alphabet with the patience of a Koranic scribe or a Puritan daughter at her sampler, he drew flame-colored and gun-metal-gray tableaux of armies at battle, besieged cities, and exploding bridges. He liked to invent new ways for legions to conquer fortresses; his battle scenes came with instructions for the weapons he had invented, for levers and cables and pulleys and giant catapults and battering rams with rockets at their flaming tips. Isaac drew against time on rainy days. When the skies cleared again, his mother was sure to urge him out of the house and there was sure to be a fight. Sam liked to repeat Isaac's furious demand, "What's so great about outdoors, anyway? What's so great about fresh air?"

Downstairs, in the dank, earthy basement, was his father's workroom, abounding in disassembled innards of radios and lawn mowers; sawed wood in moldy pyramids; Isaac's Flexible Flyer and old crib and baby carriage, broken furniture waiting to be mended; and mice. At the heart of the cellar the furnace mounted guard, square, barrel-chested, monstrous, real boss of the house, roaring like a lion as it shifted into higher gear. An immovable idea had gotten into Isaac's head, distilled from and conflated with Bible stories and sermons heard at his grandparents' church: the furnace in the cellar was God, and God was angry at Isaac. When his mother put him upstairs for his afternoon nap, Isaac would lie in bed, under the sloping eaves, waiting for the hot-breathed roar, but jumping nonetheless when it sounded. The furnace presented an interesting problem: although the jerky roar of God's wrath was bloodcurdling, equally certain it was that if the divine blaze ever went out the Hookers would become extinct, just like the dinosaurs.

·   ·   ·

Outside, the Hooker house, up a dirt road overlooking the village of Auburn, was a clapboard farmhouse built at the end of the last century. Painted the yellow of beaten yolks, merry and derelict as a carousel, it was as tall as it was wide, like a hatbox: those are the bold, comfortable proportions of many old New England farmhouses and schools and town halls, proportions that pronounce not with haughtiness but with a kind of stout optimism their inhabitants' solid grounding and just aspirations upward.

On drives down the main streets of villages more elegant than Auburn—Sturgis and Walcott, for instance—Sam pointed out to his son houses that had been restored by tender and pedantic owners to a high gleam of authenticity, with all their original grace notes preserved intact and their birthdays proclaimed in black numerals above the lintels. The Hookers' house, in contrast, was a seedy mutt of undistinguished and neglectful parentage. It knew no bull's-eye windows, no Greek Revival columns, no gingerbread moldings and latticework. In prosperity its many owners had slapped on ugly sun porches and outhouses, and in bad times patched and propped up collapse. The Hookers lived in the moldering wreckage like Bosnian shepherds squatting in a Crusaders' fort.

"We ought to put up aluminum siding," Mattie urged as wooden seams split and splayed in spring thaws. "Why bother about siding when the roof is about to fall in on us?" Sam shrugged. Conversely, whenever he proposed doing something about the roof, she said illogically, "Not till you buy me a dishwasher."

The roof was of chipped slate tiles the shimmery green-pink sheen of a pigeon's plumage. The original structure was quite sound, but the added kitchen, over which sat Isaac's bedroom, sagged in the winter like a fallen cake. Every heavy snowfall his father, dressed in his hooded parka and snow boots, clambered out Isaac's dormer window to shovel the roof. The better insulated a house, the more snowy its roof, he explained. The Hookers' house leaked heat like a punctured balloon but still was topped with snowbanks. Isaac watched from inside, enviously, as his father—soon ruddy-cheeked and stripped to shirt-sleeves—stabbed the ice with his shovel and heaved great drifts of loose snow down the roof, to dissolve into shimmering spray in the sunlight.

One day after his father had come back inside and Isaac was quite sure that both parents were safely occupied downstairs, he decided to inspect the roof himself. Standing on the top rungs of a chair, he struggled with all his might to hoist up the high window and slithered out onto the roof's sloping and crenellated slate pavement. It was his first glimpse of eternity, his first sense of creation.

From the roof Isaac saw wooded hills of a dense and smoky blue, pine and birch and maple and beech, climbing upward and westward, low-lying valleys, and even a church steeple—white and spiny—poked up its pointed nose from a town Isaac didn't recognize because he had never seen it from above. *That* was the church whose crisp clamoring bells they listened for Sunday mornings. Church was a running joke between his mother and father, an institution held in complicated contempt. "Go on, you sinner, go and confess," Sam teased his wife. "Don't you even want to see Mrs. Eldritch's new hat?"

And Mattie would launch like a wound-up toy into a harsh monotonous chant of her favorite words, "Phonies . . . fraud . . . hypocrisy . . . baloney . . ." Isaac, who went to church when he stayed with his grandparents, kept silent.

He and his mother could never agree about whether the churchbells pealing across the valley and hills came from Auburn or Sturgis. There it was now, but how funny to see it from above. Yes, he was standing higher than the church steeple. In his pajamas! Truly he was king of the castle, with all the world below his very own rascal.

Leaning way over, perilously far, on his stomach now so that his flannel pajama top got banked with snow, and the ice trickled down his front, he saw below him his own backyard with its shiny red swingset and twisted hunchbacked cherry tree, under which some months before he had buried in a shoebox coffin, with tears and prayers, a dead starling found in the fireplace—there was always something dead or dying and Isaac was a ready and enthusiastic mourner. And beyond the cherry tree, emerging from the snow like the broken masts of an arctic shipwreck, rose the metal fence posts and vagrant stalks, scrappy, straw colored, of the vegetable garden, Isaac's pride and joy, where in a rare union of interest he and his mother grew tomatoes and onions and cucumbers and string beans and potatoes and marigolds and snapdragons and sunflowers—victory gardens, people used to call them, in a usage that intrigued him. All summer his mother had dirt under her fingernails from gardening. Unsettling to come upon it in the winter, like visiting the Gilboa ice rink in June.

Strangely enough, it was the garden that had taught Isaac to read— that is, to make words of the letters he so copiously produced. Last spring, when he and his mom were planning the season's vegetable strategy (lots of quick growers, since she was as impatient as he), he made off with the Agway catalog and returned much later with this suggestion: "How about lett-uck?"

"How about what?"

"You know, lett-uck. Let's plant lett-uck."

"What's lettuck?"

Isaac pointed on the open page to a sea-green crown of Buttercrunch.

"Oh, lettuce. It's pronounced 'lett-is,' Ike. We always plant lettuce."

"But it says lett-uck. It's lett-uck. It says so. Or," he continued cunningly, "how about planting 'sed-z'?"

This time Mattie followed his laboriously moving lips and the whistle of his murmured mouthing of the syllables, and the truth dawned on her. "Ikey, you're reading! When did you start reading? You little sneak!" She gave him an affectionate push. "You don't want to be a child at all any more, do you?" Isaac crowed at the fine trick he had played on her. Now there would be no stopping him! He could hardly wait till the end of the day, when he could drag his still-overcoated father to a chair, spread the catalog across his lap, and trumpet, "*Dill! Eggplant! Seeds!*"

His Agway epiphany left Isaac convinced that the alphabet could be sown, planted, grown, and eaten. The letters were indissolubly entwined in his mind with vines and fruits and rocky soil; edible, some were wet and green-headed with crisp white hearts or prickly, warted, could grow to be immense.

Now, high above the buried garden, Isaac felt like God's spy, let in on the secrets of the universe, like a semidivine cartographer. How feathery and dovelike looked the rim of trees circling white hills, how soft and thrushy without their leaves. Below and inside were his parents, safe and oblivious, his mom in the kitchen, his dad in the study, while here was he high above their heads, on the icy pinnacle of the universe, halfway up to the clouds, in his pajamas and slippers—*that* was the joy of it.

He did a little war dance in the banked snow of the roof, scarred by his dad's shoveling. He skidded on the ice, lost his balance, and fell quite hard, knocking the wind from his chest and sliding down toward the gutter. His glasses flew in the opposite direction. Was he going to fall off the roof? No time to think. Then he hit the undisturbed powder and his slide ended in a final snowbank his father hadn't dared reach to dislodge. He was sitting in snow on the very edge of the roof. Better not look down. Anyway, without his glasses it was all a haze of gray. Isaac sat a while, trying to get his bearings and not to cry. Was he stuck? Don't say stuck yet. If he was stuck, would they ever find him? Better try and climb back up to the window and inside, before his parents missed him and there would be hell to pay. This was easier said than done. Isaac whimpered to himself a little as he kept losing his balance with nothing to grip, and sliding back down to that ultimate ledge of ice.

What if they never found him? "People freeze to death in the cold," he reminded himself aloud. First their icicle fingers like fish fingers dropped off; then their nose and toes. He had seen morning cartoons of St. Bernards trotting through the snow with barrels around their necks and frostbitten travelers between their teeth, but how did St. Bernards know where to look? Anyway, dogs don't climb roofs. What if it got dark? Was it time to start crying? Not yet. He sat a while longer, getting wetter and colder, trying to figure out in his head how to spell "Saint" and "Bernard." Then he got up again. After a few false starts, he learned a kind of splayed-foot penguin climb that worked him all the way back up to the open window. He still had no idea where his glasses had gone. How surprised his mom and dad would be if they knew where he was, and that he had almost fallen off. It was Isaac's secret; he would go in without the glasses before he got caught, and then he could always sneak out again later.

Things worked out differently: he forgot to shut the window, once inside he discovered his pajamas were half-sopping, half-frozen stiff, and his slippers had become drowned puppies, their soft suède no longer velvety. He had to find a hiding place for his ruined clothes, where his mom would never find them. He took off pajamas and slippers and rolled the drenched icy bundle under the bed, extracting a dry pair of pajamas from the bureau. Then the trouble really began: in his panic, he forgot how to dress himself! Isaac hopped up and down in frustration trying to find the right holes for his legs, pestered by impenetrable sleeves and defeated by buttons he couldn't unbutton. The long and the short of it was, when his mother came in to see why Isaac was so quiet, she found her son naked, blind, and shivering in a pool of melted sludge. This was how his dance on the rooftop ended: his ma smacked him hard across the face and his dad, with ashen face, locked the windows. "Never, never pull such pranks again or you'll be a dead boy, do you hear me?"

"I'd like to be a dead boy," said Isaac.

"You don't know what you're talking about," snapped his father, uncharacteristically, and Isaac, hurt, subsided. Still, his climb onto the roof lingered in his mind as a moment of power, majesty, autonomy, his first glimpse of nature and of his own life—house and yard and parents—not from an earthworm's perspective but from God's eyes.

"Does he like you this way?"

"He likes me any way. Well," Mattie mock-ruefully qualified, "I'm not so sure it's *me* he likes."

The women laughed.

"When Ikey was on the way, I said to myself, Finally a few months of peace and quiet. But no such luck. Let's be honest: men are *weird*. I mean, you look at yourself in the mirror at seven months, and can you imagine wanting to hump such a *whale*? A guy ought to be booked for bestiality just *thinking* about it. It's a crime against motherhood, having those kind of feelings about a woman with a belly like a submarine. But Sam doesn't think so: he just smiles and shuts his eyes and digs right in."

Margery and Sue let loose that tight, pent-up, too-loud laughter of women talking dirty. They were sprawled around the living room, smoking and quaffing Tab, watching television with the sound way down, reveling in the mess and freedom and laziness: the middle of the morning, children in school or being tended by grandparents or older brothers and sisters—a snatched moment of girl talk so unhampered and needed it made them feel giddy, boastful.

Every couple of weeks the girls got together to smoke and dish and hang out, to escape duty and this strange disguise of wifeliness and motherliness they had assumed at a still-childish age—Mattie's sister Sue, Margery, and sometimes one or two others—usually at Mattie's, since she had the biggest house.

Mattie was the ringleader, and she ran her gang with an iron fist and a certain arbitrary vengefulness that kept them on their toes. She was fickle and a brawler: she would develop a sudden passionate fondness for one of the neighborhood's rare freshbloods, someone's new wife or girlfriend, usually on the grounds that so-and-so was down to earth, not stuck-up. For a brief spell she would parade her new bosom buddy around town, repeat her witticisms at table with relish, cut her more shopworn and familiar girlfriends. But count one month or two, and she'd find herself to have been sorely betrayed: Cindy Olszewski was a prize bitch and her worst enemy, and what's more, Mattie had told her so, and if Sam ever said as much as hello to the little slut, Mattie would regard it as an act of treason.

In such a small community you can't fall out with *everybody*, at least not at once—her vendettas went in spells and enemies were sometimes rehabilitated. Moreover, Mattie had two rock-solid allies she could always fall back on—Margery Karolis, her business-partner-to-be, whom she was a little in awe of, and Sue, who was no fun to fight with because she wouldn't fight back. Mattie and Marge quarreled periodically, usually about money, and Sue reconciled them.

As a teen-ager Mattie had only wanted to run with the boys—she despised the brittleness of girlish cliques. They seemed a kind of hysterical hedge against the real business of life, which was men and women, and what they did under bridges and in haylofts and the back seats of cars. Now, lonely from living stranded and cooped-up in a house of men, she was surprised by her own hunger for this more sympathetic, raucous camaraderie. That's what marriage did to you: she could talk and laugh more freely with Marge than with her own husband, who, long-faced, sanctimonious, aggrieved, was always either scolding her or taking offense. With Sam one of them had to be in the right and it was a constant struggle over which of them it was to be. What a relief to be able to relax and vaunt her badness!

Mattie was clowning now—she never knew when to stop, that was what they liked about her—flushed, voice belted out, dimples flexed, cigarette waving. "I mean, listen, you read in the paper about burglars raping ninety-year-old ladies. If a guy can get excited about a person who's almost a corpse, why stop at a woman seven months pregnant? Let's face it, men have got no shame."

"Look who's talking," teased Margery. "How did *you* get in that interesting condition, may I ask? What have *you* been doing? Are you going to blame it on the burglar?"

"It wasn't *my* idea," protested Mattie, laughing, patently insincere.

"I sure wish I had that problem," Margery said. "I'm the one who has to do the raping in our house. Michael's always so pooped at night he corks off in front of the TV. And once I do get him upstairs, as soon as things are getting interesting, in comes Peter with a nightmare or Marie wanting help with her homework or Mikey complaining Peter's stolen his koala bear. Three kids leave your sex life kind of ragged: you get pretty quick on the draw. I tell him, let's leave 'em with Mom and go away for a weekend—go to the beach, have some fun. He says, Without the kids? I'd miss the little guys. I nearly belted him one."

"Michael's so cute."

"He's cute, but he's not aggressive enough. He likes to sit and let the world go by."

"When's the baby coming, Mat?"

"May 10. I hope it doesn't pull a Pearl Harbor on me, like Ike."

"Girl, I don't want you popping this one on the floor of the Cameo, hear?"

"I never popped one at the movies; Ike was born in the hospital just like everybody else's. 'Course, he *would*'ve been born on the movie-theater floor if Sam hadn't been such a Nervous Nellie."

"I'm glad it's you this time and not me," Margery said. "I feel like I've been pregnant ever since I was born."

"I can't *stand* being pregnant," Sue confessed. "It's the pits."

"I tell Michael, the kids are the greatest: I'd pop a baby every year, twenty more screaming little brats, if I didn't have to be pregnant."

"Oh, I kind of like it," Mattie demurred. "Even with Ikey, I never got real sick. You get kind of used to sleeping on your back and having your insides turned into some kind of football stadium. Anyway, being pregnant sure beats labor—I'm just dreading the day this little squirt decides it wants *out*."

"*Tell* me about it," her sister agreed. "I always think there's some kind of conspiracy going on. You read all these books about babies and child care—I know you don't believe in baby books, Mattie, look at that face she's pulling, but I do—and the one thing they never tell you is how goddamned much it *kills*. And *afterwards*, too. Even Mom didn't tell us."

"If they told you, you'd never be such a fool as to do it," Margery said. "Women would go on strike. Can you imagine—telling your husband, *you* have the baby this time, see how you like it."

"Anyway, as soon as it's over, you forget how bad it was. Till next time."

"I don't."

"It's men who want to have a ton of kids—"

"No wonder, they don't have to do the dirty work."

"—I would have been happy to stop after Sarah, but Jim wouldn't hear of it," Sue continued.

"Didn't you want to have a boy?" Mattie asked in surprise.

"A *boy*? No way. Quit while you're ahead. Girls are perfect—little dolls. Boys are hell."

"I don't care if it's a boy or a girl, as long as it's healthy. Sam thinks it's going to be a girl for sure—he's got a hunch. This one's so *quiet* compared to Ikey, I'm always wondering what's going on in there."

The conversation trailed off for a minute into an idle contented collective sigh, and all three women gazed at the silent blue screen.

"Want some coffee, girls?"

"No, I got to get going soon, before the little darlings eat each other alive," said Margery.

Suddenly there was a noise from behind the sofa on which Mattie and Margery were plumped, and a small stern injured voice spoke.

"What do you mean boys are hell?"

Aghast silence. The three women rolled startled guilty cow's eyes at each other; Mattie cursed herself mentally. She thought she'd heard a strange sort of snuffly breathing—Isaac was too adenoidal to be a successful eavesdropper—but figured it was Marge. People made all kinds of weird noises without knowing it, if you listened hard enough. "Isaac," she said, "come out this instant."

More silence, another scuffle, and the child awkwardly emerged on all fours, head lowered, face hiding behind those gruesome Coke-bottle specs.

"What are you doing there, hiding and spying on us like that?" Mattie demanded sharply. "If you're in a room and people come in, you're supposed to make yourself known, not eavesdrop."

"I wasn't spying. I was busy reading when you barged in. What do you mean, boys are hell?" he addressed himself to his aunt, author of the rash judgment. Already the kid had decided women weren't worth much, and Mattie was embarrassed for her sister; it was Sam's fault, teaching him not to respect her kin. Just when she'd finally half persuaded Sue that no, Sam didn't hate her, he was just tired, that was why he darted her furious looks when he came home from work to find her in his den.

"Not you, honey," replied Sue Randall in a slow sweetened baby voice. "Anyway, it's only a way of speaking. I just meant boys are rowdier than girls."

"I see," said Isaac, unconvinced. What did she mean it was just a way of talking? Why didn't people say what they meant?

"Run outside and play, Ikey," his mother said. "You shouldn't be moping around the house on a day like this. Go out to the garden and make sure the rabbits aren't getting into our lettuce."

Dragging his feet and scuffing his shoes, Isaac exited huffily. I hate it when those ladies come over, he muttered to himself. He decided not to think about the almost scary way his mother talked with those ladies—not motherlike at all—and her loud laugh. Better not think about it. Better think about the American rebels who at this very moment were digging an underground tunnel that would sneak them into the British fort for a midnight invasion. Did the British sleep with their wigs on? What if the American soldiers stole all the officers' wigs while they were asleep and ran away with them? *That* would be a good trick to play. Maybe there was a special hook you could make that would reach into the British fort and pluck them all up at once. *That* would be funny.

"Now he's going to go tell Sam we said boys are hell, and then guess who's going to be in the shithouse," Mattie said.

"He sure was quiet back there."

"He's a very quiet boy when he's quiet. He can sit by himself with a book for hours."

The women spoke now in subdued undertones, even though Isaac was gone.

"Did we say anything terrible? I can never figure out how much kids understand."

"*Everything*, in a back-assed kind of way."

"Does he know the baby's coming?"

"Oh, sure. He's so excited he's ready to go in there and pull the baby out himself."

Isaac was indeed looking forward to the new baby's arrival. He was too young for school, and time weighed upon him mightily. He was lonely and bored. His father, whom he found both infinitely desirable and strangely evasive, was away till late every day, and came home wan and irritable. That left his mother for company and his mother drove him up the wall. Either she was busy at tasks that bored him, or she was yakking with those wicked lady friends, or she was watching the soaps, which Sam wouldn't let Isaac watch because they were too dirty. In any case she didn't listen.

Both of them liked to talk, and neither had much patience for the other's interests. Isaac would tell his mother how the dinosaurs became extinct, and his mother would tell Isaac what a cheapskate Cindy Olszewski was, and somehow Isaac always wound up feeling he'd gotten the short end of the stick. It was almost worse when she did listen, for then she would contradict him—not, Isaac believed, because he was wrong, but in the arbitrary way certain larger children come along and kick over your sand castle. She would come out with the most outrageous and upsetting assertions. "Thomas Jefferson wasn't such a hero: he kept slaves."

"No, he didn't," cried Isaac, horrified.

"Well, he most certainly did. They all did, all the founding fathers. They were just a bunch of slavedrivers." Neither would budge or back down, so that either they had to argue all day or ignore each other until Sam came home to judge. Then, even when Isaac turned out to be wrong, his father would yell at Mattie for being such a fool as to get into an argument with a child not yet four. What truly flummoxed Ike, however, was that on those rare occasions when he was right his mother didn't in the least mind having made a howler. On the contrary, she found her own errors hilarious.

No wonder Isaac was eaten up by a hunger for full and true companionship. He was plagued by demons who taunted him with his terrors, and although it seemed to him he never slept at night but lay rigid and vigilant, in the morning he awoke with his confidence rattled by nightmares whose memory cast a kind of pall over the rest of the day—about invading Japanese armies and space creatures, about robots he willed himself to vanquish. Over breakfast he told his dreams, but for some reason, no matter how hair-raising they were (and perhaps occasionally Isaac embroidered, just to make sure they really were hair-raising) his parents laughed. This, it turned out, was because, unknown to him, he crooned them in a strange monotonous singsong. When they laughed too hard, he stopped, offended.

"Go on, Homer, sing us another," pleaded Sam, penitent, and Isaac couldn't resist, although as soon as he resumed his Buddhist chant his parents would start spluttering again.

Sometimes, however, his father frowned and shook his head. "No, Ike, you didn't dream that. No way." Isaac was adamant, "I did, too," although in fact he had no firm sense of whether the story had come to him in sleep or whether he was spinning it out of his waking brain as he went along. Had he really dreamed about pigs swimming across the ocean or was he making it up now? Did he know what was concretely true, confirmed in books, historical fact, from the moilings of his own hot head? One day he had woken up and told his parents a whopper, and from that time on, he lied. It was like peeing, the way these tall tales streamed forth in reaching golden arcs: you had made it, but you didn't know quite when it would stop or where it would land. The funny thing was, his mother couldn't care less whether he was lying or telling the truth, and let him ramble on till he ran out of steam, but his father, usually the softy, challenged him sternly at the first sniff of a tall tale. And Isaac, accused, indignantly denied it. There *was too* a gang of robbers that had come into the house and held a saber over his head while he was having his afternoon nap.

"There wasn't, Isaac, don't fib."

"You're the fibber! You're the only fibber in this house!" yelled Isaac in a sudden passion, and when his father shook his head warningly, bent down and butted him in the stomach like a bull, stamped his foot, and burst into wet tears of rage. "They did! They jumped away through the window when they heard you coming!"

"You're your mother's son, all right," muttered Sam.

Isaac, chest heaving, was stopped in his tracks by this cryptic statement, too abashed to ask what it meant. Years later, he remembered and worried: Was he his mother's son? Did he have to be? He wanted to deny it, but there was no one to deny it to any more.

With such an unsatisfactory or equivocal audience, it was no wonder that Isaac hankered after a warm and biddable body beside him (his mom had promised him when the baby was older it could sleep in his bed sometimes), who would never go to sleep till he had drowsed off into a clenched oblivion, who would join him in his dreams and help him lick the Japs, who wouldn't laugh at him.

Now he liked outside a little better, and rejoiced in striding through the prickly underbrush of the fields behind the house, walking stick in hand, shouting aloud, and stopping for long stretches to seize on flowers and insects, dismantling their petals and wings, and mourning when he couldn't piece them together again and make them live. Everything burst with life and meaning: walks in the fields drove him wild with desire for the secrets to nature, and he yearned for a co-discoverer to answer his questions and listen to his answers.

In less buoyant moments—Isaac had his black spells aplenty—he imagined that his new little sister would be less a colleague than a beautiful walking talking doll (dolls, girls were dolls, that's what Aunt Sue had said), whose hair wouldn't come out when he tugged. Isaac had the largest collection of bald dolls in North America: his father proposed that thanks to Isaac's diligence they should change the national symbol to the bald-headed doll. A doll who would admire and obey him, play soldiers under the bedclothes, and lose at his favorite games. It is not good for man to be alone, said God to His angels, and Isaac, tired of naming the animals, was long past ready for his Eve.

He talked to her inside his mother's stomach and sat for ages listening for her kicks and tussles, like radio signals from a distant country. Every morning now he woke up laughing, and over breakfast assaulted his parents with a torrent of new names for "my baby"—"Sassafras," "Garbage-face" ("Hush . . ." remonstrated his father), "Measles," "Hannibal," "Shipwreck," "Red Paint," and finally, with a funny pious look on his face, "Evangeline." (Sam had been reading Ike poetry.)

"That's a lovely name, Ikey," said his aunt. "What are you going to name the baby if it's a boy?"

Isaac thumped his fists on the kitchen table. "She's not going to *be* a boy. *I'm* the boy in the house. There isn't going to *be* another boy."

"But, honey," cajoled Sue, who besides Sarah had one boy of her own, "it's fifty-fifty odds the baby *might* be a boy. Boys are nice, too."

"Remember?" said Isaac, dirtily. "*Boys are hell*. No fifty-fifty. And . . . if she is a boy, I'm flushing her down the toilet."

"You can see who's the boss in this house, Sue," said his mother, rolling her eyes.

She *was* a boy. When Sam, home from the hospital, woke Isaac in the morning to tell the child he had a brother, Isaac's face crumpled tragically.

"Why didn't you tell me *before*!!"

"I didn't want to wake you, hon."

"I *was* awake! I never sleep!"

"Well, to tell you the truth, I peeked in at you after I got back home and you looked just a little bit asleep to me."

"I was *resting*," insisted Isaac, ashamed at having his own fallibility exposed before his aunt, who had come in the middle of the night and was now sitting clumsily at the foot of his bed with a condescending smile on her face. "Now you've got a little brother, Ikey, to keep you company."

Isaac glared at her. "Oh, shut up! I know that already!"

"Isaac!" snapped Sam. "Say you're sorry to Aunt Sue, and never tell *anyone* to shut up."

"Be quiet, then, Aunt Sue," Isaac corrected himself.

That day his father slept a lot, and when he woke was off again to the hospital, leaving Isaac at the Randalls'. When his mother came home a few days later, he was told he shouldn't knock her around, maul her quite as roughly as he liked to do, but ought to stay a quiet distance. With her was a skinny brick-red Indian-looking infant—looks like a cigar, said Ike—with matted black hair and slit eyes. Asleep. Always asleep. They had even gone ahead and named him without asking Isaac: Turner Hooker.

"What a NAME," said Ike. "Sounds like a machine."

His mother looked at his father. "What'd I tell you? You don't listen to a word *I* say, but if the kid tells you, you'll believe it. Anyway, I thought it was my turn to name the baby."

"Only if it was a girl."

Isaac was standing by the crib—*his* old crib—speculating with a lowering concentration. "Maybe the Iroquois will come and scalp him. Maybe he'll get hit by the atom bomb," and then, having just been told the story of President Roosevelt, "Maybe Turner will get polio." When Mattie left the room, he made cross-eyes at the infant, rattled the crib's bars like a gorilla in heat, and sang to the tune (roughly) of "Ol' Man River" "Go—away."

Sam, a little shame-faced at his own treachery in begetting the new boy (as if Ike weren't enough kid for any family), laden with debts, and convinced all over again that his wife's fecundity was going to drive them to the poorhouse, pretended to commiserate.

"Do you like your little brother, Ikey?" everyone asked. The same boring question. Isaac made cross-eyes. "Do you like *your* brother?" he retorted. The funny thing was, he sort of did, in the most involuntary way.

That summer he went to stay with his grandparents so his mother could rest up, and when he came back he found Turner was still there. He wasn't going anywhere. He was staying. And what's more, he was already a little bigger. And Isaac still liked him.

It was hard not to like Turner. He was healthy as a little horse, merry, incurious, imperturbable, and later on, full of wet kisses that Isaac ostentatiously wiped off with exclamations of brotherly revulsion. He was like one of those round, lead-bottomed ducks that can't be knocked over, no matter how you push. Isaac would punch him in the stomach, slam him against a wall, drag him around the room by the feet, and still Turner didn't cry. He could sleep through a car crash. Mornings and afternoons he woke up smiling, as much from gleeful cognizance of the pleasure he caused others as from his own delight. His father was amazedly grateful at having produced a child seemingly so free from inner demons of anxiety and dread.

"Turner's *my* boy," said his mother, triumphantly. That meant he was more biddable than Ike, more docile. She could leave him on the sofa while she cleaned house or drag him to town to check out the white sale at Bolts, and he didn't stray or complain. He was her son, to be raised as she saw fit, in the hale blistering winds of her stubborn callous jealousy, her obsessiveness, and Sam saw to his dismay that she had found what she was looking for, and that it wasn't him. The child was dark like her, and comely. Loving. Hers. "He's a little man," she said. "A regular Romeo. Look at those dimples—look at that smile."

"Am I a Romeo, too?" demanded Isaac. "What's so great about dimples?"

When Isaac got back from his grandparents' house, he found that he had been transferred to his father's care, and this arrangement, begun to make life easier for Mattie, signaled a permanent and inexorable family division. Ike was Sam's son, Turner Mattie's, although Isaac ran periodic raids on his mother just to see if he could win her over. With Turner's advent (whose import didn't fully make itself known for several years: he was like a little time bomb, a delayed threat, a slow and at first negligible invasion), Isaac was no longer an unsexed thing who played with dolls and happily went shopping with Aunt Sue and Cousin Sarah, but became a man among men, his father's chosen companion, his aide-de-camp.

Now at the end of that first summer of Turner's infancy, Isaac was drawn up into the world of chain saws and ladders, wrenches, grease, and caulking. Together he and his father sallied into the yard to chop wood or repair the lawn mower; they pruned the cherry tree and doused the grass with weed-killer; they mended the garden fence and put up screens; they wandered down to the creek to see how high the waters were and whether the day lilies were in bloom; they hung out at the diner.

His father, Isaac discovered, was a bit of an idler, promiscuously curious. He liked to stroll, son in hand, along Union Avenue on a Sunday morning in August when the library was closed and stores were safely barred against his spendthrift appetites, making covetousness theoretical. First Sam and Isaac would pause by the window of Carpenter's to argue the merits of every rod and reel, every shotgun on display, although Sam was too squeamish to be a sportsman, and then ducking past the reproachfully open doors of the Congregational Church, through which floated hymns like the smell of sugar cookies hanging on the still summer air, they glued themselves to the window of the Army Surplus Store to drool over camouflage jackets and Bowie knives, only to end up worshiping at a distance Bill Walters's powder-blue Studebaker, which its owner was polishing to a high glossy glaze, until finally Sam, forcing himself along, gave Isaac a nudge, saying, "Quit dawdling, son. The night cometh when NO man can work," a warning both ominous and comical.

All summer long Sam seemed shamelessly to lack all sense of time or direction. Or maybe he just pretended not to know where they were going or when they should head home before Mattie blew her top. He and Isaac would set off in the Dodge—son of the late Ambassador—to pick up the groceries, but as soon as they got past the driveway, it was, "How about a little rabbit hunting, General Grant?"

And Isaac, drumming his heels with happiness, shouted, "That's just fine with me, General Sherman."

Afternoons were spent thrashing through the underbrush, strolling through the Bear Ridge Reservation, chasing rabbits and Confederates—dirty rebs, said Ike—wading in the river with trouser legs rolled to the thigh in search of turtles and gold: Sam taught Isaac how to pan like a Gold Rush Californian. Lying on their backs in the meadow behind the Auburn graveyard, Isaac tickled his father's ankles with a blade of grass or turned the cleft in his chin yellow with a buttercup, to see if Sam liked butter. (Everyone did.) And chattered incessantly.

"Tell me a story, Daddy."

"I don't know any stories."

"Tell me a story about Vasco da Gama."

"I've forgotten the story of Vasco da Gama."

"Then tell me about all your favorite cars and all the cars you had when you were young."

This ploy sometimes did the trick, and Sam would unfold for his son the more exquisite points of heraldry and lineage that marked the beauties he prized, for his taste in cars was as high-flown as his own purchasing power was low. Isaac liked to hear about the cars Sam actually owned—that race of giants that died out before he was born and whose deaths, in his father's telling, were inevitably inconvenient and embarrassing.

"Tell me about the Green Lemon, Daddy," Isaac pleaded.

"You know all about the Green Lemon already."

"I've forgotten. Where did it conk out? Honest, I don't remember."

So Sam told Isaac about the Green Lemon (this was father to the Nash Ambassador), into which he had been bamboozled by his former classmate Joe Gadzack, who worked in a secondhand dealership on Route 101: a smirking and broad-hipped monstrosity, a lime-green Mercury with siren-blue plastic seats, in which Sam and Mattie had confidently set off one winter morning bound for Florida (this must have been a *long* time ago; Isaac never remembered his parents going anywhere together), only to watch their car die in the noonday heat outside Columbia, South Carolina.

The child roared with laughter. It tickled him enormously to think of his parents, not yet married and thus not yet his parents, all dressed up in their holiday clothes, suitcases stuffed in the trunk, stranded in the silent carcass of this dead beast by the side of a broiling southern highway.

"What did Mom do?"

"She cursed."

"I bet she did! How did you get home?"

"Took a bus, till we ran out of money, and then we hitched. Took us three days to get home."

By the time Isaac was conscious, the Ambassador had bit the dust, too, and after that, Sam contented himself with drab hulks that seemingly only a town sheriff would have the gall to be seen in. Isaac remembered his father saying to his brother-in-law, while waving a lordly arm toward the dun-colored '61 Dodge, "Jim, meet the new woman in my life." And Uncle Jim replying, "Why, Sam, she's got a face to stop traffic."

With such a well-developed and expansive taste for wasting time, it was no wonder that Sam liked best of all, after his secret pleasures, which he once at Isaac's request, wrote down on a piece of paper: rye, cigars, paintings of angels tooled in gold leaf, books bound in crumbly red leather (Are those really them? demanded Ike, incredulously. No, not really, Sam admitted, I was just grandstanding), to drive for the sake of driving. He scorned air-conditioning or suspension, but thrived on motion, whizzing sights, the slap of the wind, the radio crackling a country lament of failed crops and jilting women.

Once school started again in September he would sometimes quit in the middle of marking exams or reading the newspaper, scoop up Isaac, and take off for hours of nowhere, climbing narrow mountain roads carved through silent, mournful black-green forest, whose firs and birches shot up high and spindly from inching for the sun, past lakes bordered by boarded-up rotting motels laid out in miniature-golf-sized, teepee-style cabins, and over some disused sidetracks of the Boston & Maine, whose slatted iron rails hadn't suffered a train in decades. Sometimes they would leave a penny on the tracks just to make sure, and come back a week later to see if the coin had been stretched to copper taffy by a speeding locomotive.

Once (this was later on) they picked up a hitchhiker outside Hebron, a short stocky fellow with a head of flaming red hair, sly blue eyes, and a milky freckled skin, even a freckled mouth he had that turned up at the corners so that it looked as if he were perpetually smiling.

This fellow turned out to be a lay preacher from the Church of the Brethren, who had just come back from building outhouses for migrant grape-pickers in California. Isaac, who rather resented Sam's including a stranger on their ride, marveled jealously at the sympathetic intimacy, the bantering understanding, that at once sprang up between his father and any man he met. (Years later, on visits home, he was always being told by neighbors, former students, the janitor at school, Sam's fellow selectmen, the waitress at Sadie's, what a wondrous listener his father had been, how golden, quick, and knowing, what a miraculous capacity he had to draw a person out and put him at his ease, to comfort, congratulate, console. And Isaac, who knew his father at heart to be as solitary, as self-loathing, and even misanthropic a man as ever lived, thought on hearing this, Well, why didn't you ever *tell* him so? Don't tell me; you should have told him.)

So here were Sam and the young preacher talking about Mexicans, how hard they worked, how good it was to see foreigners love our country and its bounty, about the Church of the Brethren, which was the conservative branch of the German Baptists—Dunkards, they were called—and its troubles in attracting young membership, since it forbade smoking or dancing or drinking or even a cup of tea.

"Don't you miss all those dubious pleasures? Isn't it hard for a young man like you to forgo so much?" asked Sam of the preacher, who seemed old to Isaac but in retrospect couldn't have been voting age yet.

He laughed aloud now. "My dad's a farmer. There are six of us boys—I'm the runt—and one poor girl. After school, my brothers and I weren't allowed to play sports, but had to come straight on home and help out, do our chores. Passing up football, that was hard. My brothers farm yet, but you couldn't get me back on a farm for love or money. Farming's hard, but preaching's easy, and the pleasures are such that you don't think about what you *don't* have."

"There's the difference between us," said Sam. "I've got everything in the world a man could want, and all I think about is what I don't have. It's the modern disease."

"Modern as Adam and Eve," replied the hitchhiker. Why did Isaac remember that preacher's speckled-egg face forever? And brood as over a tricky but important riddle what it was his father didn't have and wanted so ceaselessly (or maybe just sometimes, when it rained, or in the spring?).

A middle-class boy with an unarticulated appetite for the high life,

Sam was drawn, by some kind of instinctual nostalgia for a world soon
to be swept away by malls and tract homes, to the poor parts of backcountry. The two of them would drive, quiet and reflective, past miles
and miles of hill shanties, of isolated broken-down firetrap houses, none
so tiny and desolate that it didn't have a porch out front cluttered with
motor intestines or the hulk of a boat, and once, on someone's porch,
someone's grandfather with red eyes and a shotgun.

"What's he gonna shoot, Daddy?"

"Raccoons. Ever had raccoon pie?"

"No, *never*," intoned Isaac glumly, as he stood up in the front seat,
pleased to have something else to feel deprived about.

"It's a little tough and stringy. And the raccoon's tail sticks out of
the pie and tickles your nose as you eat," continued Sam, tickling Isaac
now with the tail of Ike's own raccoon-tail hat, until Isaac giggled so
much he fell into the back seat. "Now, Ike, behave yourself. How do
you expect a man to drive with you rumpusing about? You sit in the
back and don't stir." So Isaac came crawling back into Sam's lap, just
as he knew his father wanted him to.

There were whole families, too, men with their heads buried in the
lifted hoods of pickups, women sitting out on the steps, children playing with sticks in the dirt or circling the road on bicycles, and once a
little girl who made a rude gesture at Ike.

"Daddy, that girl on the gate back there stuck her butt out at me,"
said Isaac, angry and humiliated.

"Don't fret, Ike. Girls don't fight fair. You'll get your own back
someday."

There were yellow snarling dogs that sprang out at the car on stiff,
hobbling legs, and made the child start.

"Don't worry, Ike, Rover here's just playing chicken with us. You
never realize how stupid animals are till you drive a car: men build
cars, dogs just chase them and get run over."

But it wasn't the dog and it wasn't the girl, it wasn't even the dirt
and poorness: it was the men who just sat there and stared, giving
Isaac the extraordinary impression that strangers might bear him ill
will.

"How come those men are sitting around all day?" he asked, half-
bewildered, half-indignant. "Don't they have anything to do?"

Sam paused. "People fall into a kind of slump sometimes, and *can't*
do for themselves, but just wait to be done by," he said at last. "Sometimes they're born in a slump and can't find the will to pull out. You

shouldn't look down on them for it, just make sure you try and help out where you can."

But that evening when they got home Sam repeated to Mattie with amusement Isaac's taking to task the rural poor. Mattie as usual took it personally: you could see the hackles rise.

"Why do they sit around all day?" she repeated in slow disbelief, fixing Sam with her pale, stary blue eyes. "Why don't they do anything? Does it ever occur to you that if one of those fellows came on a tour into *our* house one afternoon he might want to know why *you* just sit around all day and don't do anything?"

But what stuck in Isaac's mind and became to him later something between a fear and a principle, a kind of cautionary goad, was this realization that you could fall into a slump and not come out again. The economy went into a slump, and businesses and factories closed down—no one could look at downtown Gilboa and not absorb that lesson. So too a living soul could go out of business, dismiss his thoughts and ambitions and enthusiasm like so many workers laid off, and put out the lights, living on in a kind of supernumerary torment of vacancy, of dead time.

Between intelligent active life and such a fate lay only luck, the force of will, and the loving goodness of other people.

Chapter 4

THERE THEY WERE in the crystalline twilight, the two of them, sprawled by a blazing crackling campfire, up on the top of the mountain, just as he had always dreamed it. Soon there would be shooting stars. For as long as he could remember, Isaac had wanted to camp out, more from dread of cowardice than positive desire. Isaac, after all, was the boy who threw his Daffy Duck night light out the window precisely because he was scared of the dark: some children like to have fun, he was more interested in self-conquest. For months, without much success, he'd pestered his father to take him camping.

"Young man, twenty thousand years of evolution have gone into getting people out of the dirt and onto the mattress. Do you know how many millennia it was before the first human being ever slept between sheets? And now you want to undo all history's good work in one hot, buggy, sleepless night."

Isaac, adamant, knew sometimes it was best not to listen even though his brain was almost blowing a fuse over the concepts of evolution and millennia. "I've wanted all my life to go camping out," he said sadly. Isaac was not yet five years old.

Unexpectedly, it was his mother who came to his rescue and told his father she wanted the two of them out of her hair for a night. "Fine," said Sam. "In that case Isaac and I'll roll over to the Stateside Saloon and hoist a few."

So it was that early one September evening while it was still light the two of them trudged up Bear Ridge Reservation with backpacks and a cooler. Bear Ridge was a wilderness of craggy verticals studded with rocky lips, gashed by inlets, and bearded by forest, whose floor was dryly laden with brown pine needles and curling ferns. His mother had given Isaac a parting hug that took his breath away (she was a strong, muscular woman) and had said rather kindly, "If you don't like it out there, come on home."

"I won't." Isaac's first, last, and favorite word that year was "no." Besides, he was mad at her for wanting to get rid of him in the first place. Now he was polite, curiously formal as always when he had gotten his way after a struggle, and wasn't sure he knew what to do with it. "Why is this place called Bear Ridge?" he asked a little diffidently (everyone knew that bears at night ate boys) and his father replied, "Because by the time you get to the top, you're so hungry you could eat a bear. Only trouble is, all we have for supper is a pack of hot dogs. Now, Isaac, can you eat two dogs or three?"

They camped on the mountaintop itself, which was worn down to a broad, platelike plane like a burnt-out volcano, scored with charred ashes from earlier campfires and crinkled beer cans, which Sam, a former Boy Scout, made Isaac collect and dispose of decently. There was a slightly dank but romantic lean-to, with initials and interesting messages carved across it, in which they would be sleeping that night. Isaac immediately set to deciphering the graffiti. Names and spelling were his current passion: "Have you ever heard of somebody called Jean who spells her name J-e-a-n-n-e? What kind of name is Alvin?"

"Come on out of there, scout, and enjoy the view."

"What does '4-Ever' mean?"

And now, up on Bear Ridge on a crisp-edged autumn night, the sky fizzing with falling stars, father and son sat by their campfire, charring hot dogs on a skewer. Below them shrouded in darkness was the human world of cultivated fields and electricity and domestic animals. There was the Gilboa Valley (somewhere on a ridge above it was their house), pinpointed with a few sputtering bluish lights, and across the valley the intermittent red flare from the radio tower over on Mount Elmo, as if at night human life were reduced to a bowl of colored constellations twinkling back at the more densely populated bowl of stars above. Northeast of Mount Elmo and Mount Menasseh lay the ridgy furred spine of the White Mountains and beyond them Canada, spreading its icy tentacles all the way to the Arctic Circle. And then what? The North Pole, around whose pivot milk-white polar bears, paws clasped together, danced in a great circle.

Fire. A tiny burning bush on top of the silent mountain, a low-slung pyre of crackling hissing branches lit up by tendrils of white flame, a campfire shooting smoke signals up into the black September night.

"Are there any Indians around?" whispered the child, creeping a little closer to his father. What if a whole horde of ghostly Mohawks came galloping up Bear Ridge, conjured up by their smoke signals?

"No, none, except on dinky little reservations. We wiped them all out."

"How come you're whispering?"

"Because you are."

Both laughed softly, relishing their own awe at the immensity hanging above them with its gulf of cold galaxies.

My Isaac, Sam dreamed, putting his hand very lightly over the child's head and then pressing down, to make him get littler again. He was growing up too fast. "You're growing up too fast, Ike. You're getting too big."

Isaac hearkened to such parental nonsense politely. All he wanted to do in the world was grow up, make things change. Regret he didn't know yet, only frustration, terror, desire. He had got his first short haircut two weeks ago—a grown-up haircut consonant with his new role as first-grader. No more bangs, but instead blond hair cropped close as an army conscript's, duck hair that swirled and rippled and eddied in obstinate cowlicks away from a round high solemn tanned forehead. Fat ruddy cheeks, arms and legs like young oak trees (the floorboards thundered and shuddered as he trotted about the house), a big bottom, a child of a stalwart, amazing solidity that made Sam's heart melt and quiver deep inside him. How had a slinky jerk like him, a sly laggard with a mean mind ever fathered so beautifully robust, so sweet-souled and red-blooded, so generous, so true a boy? Even Isaac's afflictions—his gluey sight, his deaf ear, his seasons of pneumonia, his labored breathing—swelled Sam with the dearer pride. My Magellan.

That summer Isaac had once again gone to stay for a month with his grandparents. Sam telephoned every other night to find out if he was all right, only to discover that, far from being homesick, Isaac in fact was so absorbed in this new world that he had nothing whatsoever to say, could hardly wait to get off the phone.

"You want to go fishing when you get home?" Sam asked, guilty at his son's exile.

"Mmmm . . ." hedged a small voice at the other end of the line, the voice of a child humoring an importunate adult.

"You liked it at Grandma and Grandpa's?" Sam asked now, jealously.

"Mmmm . . ." said Isaac, once again, noncommittal. No use even trying to explain, for what he loved so much about his grandparents' house was precisely what had driven his father crazy growing up. It was a kingdom of solemn prosy certainties, of immutable routine, like the Gilboa library on a condensed and humbler scale. Where everything at home was irregular, chaotic, combative, wanting, here he rose at six and watched the agricultural shows on television while his grandmother fixed him cereal, bacon, and eggs. After breakfast, they drove Grandpa to the store and worked in the garden. After lunch at half past twelve his grandmother took a nap while Isaac read *National Geographic*s in bed, and at the end of the day they walked into Hebron to pick up his grandfather. Delicious and emboldening certainty prevailed: the only dilemmas were whether to choose Pop-Tarts or Lucky Charms for breakfast, whether to read about Portuguese fishermen or African ivory traders.

Hooker's was yet another kingdom to be reveled in and plundered, an extended larder storing his surplus toys. Amazed and gratified at there being so square, so material, and so well-provisioned a place named after him, with his own last name blazoned across it, Isaac couldn't wait to be old enough to help out behind the counter, as his father had. Every afternoon, his grandfather let him dig the scooper deep into one of the big glass jars and empty into a white paper bag two ladlefuls of candy—cinnamon red hots, caramels with bull's eyes of cream, or pink and green hearts that said "Oh Boy" or "My Girl" on them in salacious red letters. Isaac spent all day trying to decide in advance what candies he would choose. More enticing still was the aisle of fresh yellow legal pads, pencils the orange of school buses, crisp glossy notebooks pining to be filled with his bold wandering stories and flaming battle scenes, his diagrams of ancient cities. "How many notebooks do you *need?*" his grandmother intervened, with the incomprehension of the noncollector.

When he was done, they turned off all the lights and locked the front door, hung up the WINSTON TASTES GOOD LIKE A CIGARETTE SHOULD sign that said CLOSED, and walked home to supper.

Most glorious was the Fourth of July, when every white clapboard house hoisted the Stars and Stripes and Ike, clad patriotically in red-checked shirt, blue shorts, and white P.F. Flyers, marched with the other sons and daughters of Hebron around the green, brandishing crepe-paper streamers and accompanied by a brass band. "I'm a Yankee Doodle Dandy," shouted Isaac, and the trumpet and cymbals were so thunderous no one noticed he was tone deaf. That night there were public fireworks, sinuous golden dragons and Catherine wheels exploding into streams of scarlet dust, and Isaac, amidst his awe—of the same kind that engulfed him now, under the starry skies—found himself peeking in mischievous derision at the rows of open-mouthed grownups cooing "Oooooh" and "Aaaaaaaaaaaah" in unison.

At his grandparents' house he discovered Sundays, which were hushed, sugared, wheezy with organ music. At first he was as surprised to learn that churches possessed interiors as if his grandparents had proposed that they all crawl into the cuckoo clock. Yet there was Mr. Angell in the entrance, yanking the bell rope as if he might get hoisted up to the belfry. His grandmother gave him a handkerchief and, wrapped up in the handkerchief, a quarter for the collection plate; Isaac pretended the coin was a flat ridged-edged silver tank rolling along the book rail of the pew, and inevitably it had got lost by the time Mr. Angell in his blue suit and muttonchop whiskers came along, outstretched salver piled high with a salad of worn green banknotes. Then a moment's panic and confusion, everyone had to get up and hunt for the quarter, and Isaac lived in fear that next time his grandmother wouldn't entrust him with his own church money but, forgiving soul, she always did.

Isaac listened hard to the sermons and the Scripture readings, each of which rooted itself deep in his mind. He chipped in enthusiastically with the responses, and belted out the hymns. He could recite the entire service from memory and certain lines resonated, although he couldn't have said what significance they had to him. One sentence in particular embedded itself in his consciousness as a permanent refrain that later periodically exploded in his heart: "Lord, I am not worthy to receive you, but only say the word and I shall be healed."

It was that summer in Hebron that Isaac discovered a larger God, who far from being caged in the basement furnace at home turned out to be invisible and everywhere, in cups, grass, chain saws, pie. You turned on the garden hose and out came God. And once he realized that there was a book describing God's exploits written by God himself and that this book was the same book whose lessons were recited in church, there was no stopping him. At night his grandfather read him stories from the Bible, and when Isaac returned to Auburn, he bore this same child's Bible. To his father's discomfort and his mother's frank disgust, he regaled them with tales of Joseph-and-His-Brothers and David-and-Saul and the Devil-in-the-Herd-of-Swine-That-Drowned (*that* was a good joke), and demanded more where those came from.

At Isaac's pleading, Sam had even agreed that he be allowed to go to Sunday school at Hebron even though he was four or five years younger than anyone else in class, figuring that once he got home and started real school in earnest all his churchiness would be forgotten in the exultation of secular learning. (Although not many years later Isaac came out a furious atheist, his spiritual education nonetheless remained a source of contention between Sam and his parents.)

Isaac had come home a petted and more confident boy. No dummy, he knew how to play his parents and grandparents off against each other, a pastime at which his grandmother, who wore her martyrdom like a home-knitted cardigan, was an adept, and for the last couple of weeks he had been informing Sam prissily that at Grandma's he had pie every night or was allowed to watch cartoons all morning. He stopped when he caught on that his father thought this game rather sissyish, and soon Hebron's kingdom of clockwork propriety and mild golden certainty was lost and forgotten.

"How's school, Ike?"

"Fine."

"Miss Maguire treating you all right?"

"Fine," he repeated, pulling away a little, and added quickly, "You know what? Romulus and Remus were raised by a *wolf*, and when they got big they built Rome. But then Rome fell. Why'd Rome fall? Is Rome the same Rome that's around today? How come it used to be a country and now it's only a city?"

"Well, empires tend to run out of steam. Rome conquered most of the West, and then they had one weak Caesar after another, and their armies went to pieces because they hired too many Visigoth mercenaries who didn't fight right."

"Why didn't they fight right?"

"They scattered. The Romans stuck together, advanced in one mass like a cloud of locusts. The Visigoths were all over the place. Ikey, do you like Miss Maguire?"

"Why did the Visigoths scatter? What's mercenaries?"

"You know something, Ike? You're the best boy in the world. Just remember I said so."

Isaac, shivering in the autumnal chill, squeezed closer. "Why were the Caesars weak?"

He hated it, in fact, although he was too puzzled, too proud to say so. He hated school mightily. It was altogether different from how he had imagined it. A world of solitary pottering, of empty busy days about the house, had come to an end and Isaac was overcome by anxiety. Those strangers he thought would admire him didn't understand him. For such a long time he'd been anticipating his first day at school: all year he had made his mother slow down when they passed the magnificent brick elementary school so he could admire his prospective schoolmates, gloat over his future playground; his father, after all, went to school every day, and Isaac pictured it a garden of books, where tall beautiful ladies listened to your tales of war. Instead Miss Maguire was angry that Isaac could read already: the children weren't supposed to know how until second grade, and anyway Isaac had learned all wrong.

"I'm surprised at your dad—he's a teacher, he ought to know better," she said unwisely. Isaac, who had never heard anyone but his mother criticize his father, was appalled. "He didn't teach me, I taught myself."

"That's impossible." Miss Maguire smiled.

"It is not impossible: I did it," said Isaac, between clenched teeth.

"Well," condescended Miss Maguire, "you certainly have an active imagination." Isaac could have slugged her. Was he going to have to sit in a corner all year until everyone else learned how to read? A year was a lifetime.

His experiences with the other children were no more promising. He was a head and a half taller than even Mapie Williams and was teased for being deaf. Sixteen wriggling half-pints would start mouthing vociferously, miming conversations he couldn't hear, or jeer while Isaac explained to them in his loud overenunciated drone why the British soldiers in the Revolutionary War were called "lobster-backs" and how the Americans beat them because, intoned Isaac, now raising his forefinger didactically, "It's every man's *duty* to rise up against a tyrant." He was used to being contradicted; what he wasn't prepared for was people who didn't know or care what "tyrant" or "duty" meant.

Not even Miss Maguire took to him, because he corrected her in class and even when arrantly wrong refused to be quiet but, hands on his hips, red lower lip stuck out, filibustered valiantly or, worse yet, extended to his benighted opponent that charitable patience that was Isaac's by nature. Also he cried easily and unabashedly, and the boys mocked him as a blubbermouth, and girls stared as at a circus exhibit. Equal parts curious and scared, avid and clumsy, he was the first to crack his head falling off the playground slide and the loudest to cry.

Now he lay propped against his father's chest, while Sam swigged a can of beer and smoked with narrowed eyes, staring into the red embers.

"How come Abraham sacrificed his son Isaac?" the child piped up suddenly, out there in the stillness and the dark and the stars. He felt his father's body stiffen beneath him. "What are you talking about?" The voice came out too sharply.

"I'm talking about the sacrifice of Isaac."

"Where did you hear about that?"

"You know where."

"In Sunday school?"

"Yup."

"Well, he didn't sacrifice his son."

"So why don't you tell me what he did do?" Isaac persisted.

Christ, the Bible is barbaric, Sam thought in resistance. "Why don't I tell you a different kind of story—about the Knights of the Round Table or George Washington."

"I'd rather hear about Abraham and Isaac," Isaac said, firm.

"I think it's kind of scary for a camping-out-in-the-middle-of-the-wilderness story."

"I don't, so why don't you just tell it."

Sam threw his cigarette into the fire and lit another from the embers, dislodging Isaac a little as he did so. He drew out his jackknife, impaling another tin Schlitz on one triangular prong—the beer sighed a little under his branding—and cleared his throat. "I've forgotten it."

"I'll help you remember."

He had heard the story that summer in Hebron and couldn't have said for the life of him why he liked it so—better even than David and Goliath (in which he felt for Goliath), far better than the ten plagues of Egypt, and almost as well as Hannibal crossing the Alps with his elephants. It wasn't just that it was about a boy named Isaac, or even because of the *frisson* at death narrowly averted. Perhaps it was Abraham he felt for, Abraham with his strange and almost incomprehensibly difficult sense of justice, his taste for unpopular causes—half Lincoln, half Chaldean, a President who fought a war to free the Negro slaves and got shot in a theater and walked to the Land of Canaan on God's marching orders and entertained angels at the door of his tent with roast lamb and curds and sent his nephew Lot to Sodom and spirited him away before the city got blasted sky high in fire and soot. Pillar of salt, that was Lot's wife. Because she looked back. Had she been told not to? If she hadn't been told not to, then it would hardly have been fair.

He pictured Lot's wife like the little girl on the Morton's salt box with her umbrella and rain boots, skipping through the puddles and accompanied by the mystifying legend "It never rains but it pours." How could it pour but not rain? Did Lot's wife pour raining salt? What would his mother look like turned to salt? What if he and his dad, staring down into the valley, saw Auburn and Gilboa explode, flame sky high, vanish in a pillar of smoke, like a Fourth of July grand finale, bright and crackly, impaled against a moonless sky. No more Turner, no more Mom, just him and his father, spared for great deeds.

"So—so—so why did Abraham sacrifice Isaac, anyhow?" He snuggled up, craning his neck back so he could see his father's expression as he narrated. Sam was a fine dramatic storyteller, who rolled his eyes drolly and pitched his voice to a low shivery whisper, pushing the echoey words into the darkness like pebbles into a deep pond. But Isaac could feel his resistance to the story, like a donkey that had to be kicked at each step of this burdened journey, spurred by God's command that Abraham take his only son, Isaac, whom he loved, to the top of Mount Moriah and sacrifice him. Maybe, Sam was hoping, Isaac didn't know what sacrifice meant.

"What about Ishmael—didn't he love Ishmael, too?"

"Of course he did, but he knew that Ishmael wasn't really where it was at, dynasty wise. He knew Ishmael's hand would be against every man's, that he would be a spoiler for trouble and live in the desert, a lonesome archer. Isaac was a good boy."

Prodded, Sam told reluctantly the tale of the sad tense three-day journey to the mountain, of the steady and remorseless ascent, father and son leaving behind donkey and servant boys, of Isaac, heartbreakingly trustful, having gathered the wood for the fire, asking his father where the sacrificial lamb was, and Abraham, words surely sticking in his gullet, answering in truth, "God will provide."

"Then what?"

Abraham bound the boy, said Sam quailing, he bound him and placed him on the pyre and was just bringing down the knife to his sweet throat—"What was the knife made of?" Isaac interrupted.

"You tell me."

"Maybe stone. They didn't have steel back then"—when just in the nick of time the angel of the Lord stopped him and brought instead a thrashing ram fettered by the tangled mountain undergrowth, sparing Isaac from his father's slaughtering.

His New Hampshire namesake, nestled in his own father's arms on the dark mountaintop, snickered uneasily. "Whew. That was a close call. Why did Abraham *almost* do it?"

"To show God the transcendent love that dwells in trustful obedience, and for that love-that-doesn't-question-or-rebel God made Abraham the father of nations innumerable as the stars and countless as the sands of the sea," said Sam, insincerely. "All right? Are you satisfied?"

The boy didn't answer. He was busy rehashing the earlier Isaac's part in this story, nettled by his curious passivity. "You know what I would do if God told Abraham to sacrifice me?"

"What?"

"I'd turn right around and sacrifice Abraham. Bind him and serve him up for Sunday dinner."

"You'd eat your poor old dad?"

"Sure thing. And if God came to kill me because I didn't do what he told me to, you know what I'd do? I'd build a rocket and fly away to another planet."

"I don't think it works like that."

"How come?"

"Well, the idea is, if you believe in God, that is, that God is boss on the other ones, too. Anyway, you can't breathe on the other planets."

There they lay, stretched out on top of each other and all intertwined in the electric night air, Isaac whispering in a low grumbling voice as he reenacted the drama, trying to devise ways to breathe on alien planets, Sam poking at the dying fire, staring down into the valley and up at the great milky canopy of stars above. A nip in the air, a cold glary moon rising, harvest almost in.

"Do you think it's bad I said I'd kill Abraham?" The small voice was at once timid and defiant.

"No, just realistic."

The fire was down to scarlet coals. Maybe he should throw on a few more branches before they zipped themselves like mummies into the quilted flannel straitness of their sleeping bags, and stretched out on the fresh pine boughs lining the floor of the lean-to like rushes in a feudal dining hall, mixing their dry herbal scent with the fire's smoky pungence. He wondered whether Isaac would fall asleep easily or want to ask questions all night. What a funny darling was his parricide-cannibal son. How merciless and violent children were, unforgiving in their imaginations, helpless in practice. How nice it was to be out in the nocturnal wilds under this vast black starry sky alone with his boy, and how thrilling it would be to wake up next morning in a cold gray dawn, to force himself barefoot from his warm sleeping bag to bring more wood to the fire, to watch Isaac's blue eyes widen in astonishment to find himself not in his own bed but on a mountaintop. He was almost asleep when two hands suddenly clawed in desperation at his face and two round arms swung throttle-tight around his neck.

"Honey, what's wrong?" remonstrated Sam, hugging his son tight.

"Can we go home now?" shrilled Isaac's small voice, muzzy with incipient tears. "I didn't mean it about eating Abraham."

The child clung to his father wildly in the dark, seeing in his heart's eye the knife coming down and no angel there to intervene, no ram in the underbrush, no reprieve out in the wilds.

"You are home," murmured Sam into Isaac's quivering peachy cheek, pulling him up into his arms in instant readiness to pack up quickly, for a nimble descent, a swift journey back to the house. "Don't be frightened, my darling, this is home."

BOOK
TWO

Chapter 1

MRS. CARTWRIGHT neatly sealed the V of an envelope and laid it in the wire Out box, ignoring the pounding on her office door. Thump-thump-thump-THUMP. The threatening rhythm of a Harrowing of Hell, the syncopated drumbeat of a cannibal feast. Whoever was knocking wanted less to be admitted than to register his fury at being kept waiting. When she was done with her morning's correspondence, she lifted her head.

"Come in."

The door burst open and a young man charged into the room like a bull let into the ring. Head lowered, high-tops pawing the floor, plucking at his jeans, the intruder glanced around wildly as if searching for all exits. He was a fat ungainly raw-boned hulk, with coarse blond horsehair cropped in a shag that stood up in spikes from an enormous head. Someone had given him a black eye that engulfed in livid purple one side of his ruddy baby face, and his ragged jeans, covered with patches, insignia, and inscriptions in ballpoint pen, had split at the knee, revealing a dirty ace bandage beneath. Mrs. Cartwright, swamped by a distaste amounting to revulsion, had to steel herself to look the teen-ager in the eye.

"Is that your idea of knocking?"

"Are you *deaf*?" he retorted.

A showdown, that's what he was looking for: a clash of wills. Well, she could play hardball, too. "Get out of this office, young man, close the door behind you, and knock like a human being this time."

Isaac Hooker rocketed out of the room again, slamming the door behind him, and evidently took off on a short rampage through the halls. It was a good eight minutes before Mrs. Cartwright, irritatedly waiting, heard another sharp rap on the door. She let him knock a few more times, sounding all the percussive songs of impatience and resentment that knuckles and wood could combine to express.

Once allowed in, Isaac demanded rudely, "Didn't you hear the first time?"

"Your tone, young man, is utterly unacceptable in this school. Please speak to me with the proper courtesy."

"Where's my dad?" Isaac's eyes were rolling about the room, as if he suspected his father might be hidden under the brown corduroy sofa or up a lampshade. He looks a little bit insane, Mrs. Cartwright thought, watching with a new wariness how he veered about the room in great perplexity, refusing to sit down. Sometimes the most gifted people went completely mad—just look at Van Gogh.

"We decided it would be better if you and I discussed this situation alone, without putting your father in an awkward position. After all, you're a grown boy and shouldn't need your father to sort out all your troubles for you. Do sit down, Isaac."

He wasn't listening, but still paced about the room, a bruised and livid Cyclops, plucking at the seat of his pants, muttering to himself, grimacing.

Mrs. Cartwright was running out of patience. "*Sit down*, Isaac. You know very well why you're here: You struck Mrs. Ailes without provocation. Is that correct?"

"I punched her in the stomach," Isaac agreed, almost amiably. "She wouldn't leave me alone." He was looking at the print of Breughel's summer harvest on her wall: a field of mown hay, parched sunbaked stubble, paunchy peasants slumbering and cavorting under the haycocks' blond shade, a lad up a tree shaking apple-heavy boughs—a scene of wholesome heat and sweat, animal satiety, abundance. In the distance, a looking-glass sea. He was staring so closely his nose almost touched the picture.

Mrs. Cartwright lost her temper. "You punched her in the stomach! You *punched* an older woman—your own teacher—because she wouldn't leave you alone? What the hell do you mean by that?"

"DON'T say 'hell' at ME!" bellowed back Isaac, in a sudden seizure of indignation, even distress, flinging himself on top of her desk, and leaning over so that, spit flying, he was shouting right into her face. "Don't you DARE curse at me with such foul language—you're a principal of a school! SHAME on you!" And heaving himself from her desk, he set to pacing the room again. "This is a farce," he threw back over his shoulder. "I win a school prize—you gave it to me, remember? Three thugs—your students—lie in wait for me after school, destroying my prize book, beating me to a pulp—you see?" he thrust his purpled cheek at her. "You think I was born with a baboon's rear end for a face? And you've got the—the *shamelessness* to haul *me* in here for a scolding!"

"Lower your voice, Isaac, and sit down. I will not be shouted at."

"You raised yours first."

"I don't think that's true."

"You yelled 'hell' at me."

"Let's both calm down, then," managed Mrs. Cartwright, her tone unnaturally even. "The boys who assaulted you have also been reprimanded, let me assure you. We do not allow violence of any kind in this school. What I want to know is why you hit Mrs. Ailes when she came to your assistance."

"I told you already," said Isaac, low. "I didn't need any *assistance*. She was in the way. I told her to go away and she wouldn't listen. She was interfering in my business." And wandering over to the picture again, he asked over his shoulder, "Who painted this picture? What a merry, raucous bunch of mowers. You can almost smell the mown hay, can't you? How I wish it were August and I were out of this pit."

Sam had butterflies in his stomach. There he was, bisected and crunched up in a metal folding chair on the lacquered oak floor of the auditorium, one eye glued to an empty stage, the other morosely skimming a row of squirming gum-chewing whispering fourteen-year-olds—his son's classmates, his own students—while his stomach felt as if it were being spilled down the stairs like a Slinky, drop after precipitous drop.

In a matter of seconds Mrs. Cartwright would come out on stage to introduce the three finalists in Ashuelot's annual Composition Contest, and then Sam would see his son, aloft, illuminated, his growly-squeaky adolescent voice cast before a crowd of hundreds, saying his piece. Let my boy be calm and steady, let him talk loud and slow, preserve him from the terrors of the crowd, the fear of a sea of faces, willed Sam, wiping his palms on his pants. Stupid to be nervous—Isaac by now was a veteran orator, a professional prize-seeker. He had begun plying his trade at the age of ten or eleven, scouring local newspapers and library bulletin boards and cereal box tops for contests to enter. He by now had won hundreds of dollars for rhymes about baking soda and for solving riddles on detergent boxes, and in fifth grade Sam had taken him to Boston, where Isaac won a *National Geographic* geography award, getting his picture in the paper. He mopped up New England spelling bees with the greatest aplomb—it was the irregularity of English spelling that enchanted him—and to competitions sponsored by the Veterans of Foreign Wars submitted essays on "Why I Love My Country" so sappy and heartfelt they would make a draft dodger weep.

Sam teased Isaac mercilessly for such preening and attention grabbing—a publicity hound, he called him—and was in truth mawkishly proud of his successes. He checked his watch. Get your scrawny butt out here, Mrs. Cartwright. Get this show *moving*.

Seated directly ahead of Sam was Caroline Ailes, indifferent as a calf. "Richie, leave Dawn alone," he heard her whisper to an oversized baby who was tweaking his wiry little neighbor by the nose and squeaking, "Heeeere, little piggy. EEEEEeee-eeeee . . ." In twenty years, sunk in debt and matrimony, this Richie would recollect Dawn as the only love of his life.

What an amphibious age high school was, Sam thought, surveying his sons' classmates. Most of the girls in ninth grade were already land animals, self-assured, socialized, demonstrably mammalian in their angora sweaters, bell-bottoms, and wedgies: the ones who knew Sam not just from school but from play dates with Isaac back in those single-digit years before boys only talked to boys and girls to girls, now smiled at him, waggling their fingers conspiratorially. A lot of good this early social avidity and finesse did them, too, Sam thought: utterly wasted on their male cohorts, it kept girls flunking math and science. As for the boys, they were on the whole still hopelessly seabound, most of them shorter than the girls, plump or runty, immature, clustering in tight, goggle-eyed schools, gawkily blind to everything but math and basketball. When Sam locked eyes with Billy and Paul and Clement, they ducked and glanced away glumly without a nod.

Those ninth-grade boys who had breached pubescence stood out like sore thumbs—a couple of wiry-thighed acned hulks with smudgy upper lips, cracked voices, and bulging biceps, bullies or potheads who had been held back several grades, boys who exhausted their mental energy trying to lure females under the town bridge and who made his son blank-eyed with despair. Of Isaac's friends, only Peter Karolis, a year older and already needing to shave, was sufficiently dexterous to spend his weekends dunking basketballs in the Hookers' garage-door hoop and his evenings on the telephone with Christina Molina and JoAnne Krowalski—a smooth operator, that kid. Otherwise, only one or two of Isaac's friends, Sam suspected, were beginning to get hot and furious about sex, but it was still an untried alliance forged between the hormones and the pinup magazines, secret, abstract, utterly divorced either from the living curves and scents of their more grown-up and knowing female classmates (who in turn only had eyes for seniors) or from the really important things in life.

Up to this point at least, Isaac had been remarkably successful in laying down the line about what exactly the important things in life *were*—that is, in interesting them in matters quite far from what Sam imagined to be their own natural tastes. Just as a small or ill-situated nation manages by the power of an organizing principle to rule half the earth, so Isaac by fury of imagination had won his friends' fealty. It had been a slow chancy process requiring the patience and determination sometimes of a general, sometimes of a nurseryman persuading his apple branches to grow espaliered.

Not that Isaac had always been interested in other children, or people at all. Sam had watched Isaac charge through elementary school oblivious to the presence in the classroom of sixteen persons rather smaller and quieter than himself. Every evening Isaac regaled them with his latest battle with Mrs. Baldwin, who knew diddly-squat about the American Revolution and had never even read Benjamin Franklin's autobiography.

"You have to give the teacher a chance to talk, too," Sam chided. "She *is* getting paid to do this. And you never know, maybe she's read something you haven't." But Isaac could tell his father was amused.

"What about the other children?" The boy looked evasive, or maybe just blank. If they made fun of him or wouldn't play with him, he wasn't telling. Anyway, people went to school to learn, not to play.

In fifth grade all this had changed and Isaac had become rambunctiously social. Now he was passionately and rather protectively enamored of various boys in his class and older, boastful about their characters and abilities, moved almost to tears by their accidents, illnesses, family sorrows. All you heard about now was Billy and Paul and Peter and Clement and Raymond. "Ray's aunt got run over by a tractor when she was a little girl," he confided in hushed tones.

"What happened to the tractor?"

Most of his friends were quite different from Isaac, and it was this very thing that won his heart. Paul Chen's father worked at a Chinese restaurant in the Teasdale Mall, as did the younger Chens after school. Isaac would recount the high drama of the Chens' escape from mainland China, their travails in Hong Kong and eventual apotheosis as managers of the Phoenix Garden. Sam, clod that he was, liked to make fun of Mr. Chen's egg rolls in a cartoon-Oriental accent, and whenever Mattie turned his undershirts pink or shrank his long johns to mouse size would mutter dolefully, "This wouldn't happen if we'd sent out the laundry to Paul." Isaac turned scarlet and yelled. Paul's Chineseness, like his neat handwriting and his talent at math and science and chess, was something delicate, precious, to be wondered at and sheltered. Only *he* was allowed to make fun of his friends. Sam would never have guessed that his son might possess such reserves of tact and tenderness.

Isaac, overweight, near-sighted, bad-tempered, and deaf, couldn't play outfield or shoot a basket, but sat by the side of the school playing fields, reading and smiling self-deprecatingly if he got hit in the head with a ball. He forgot the name of his own school's football team and stayed away when they trounced the Wendell Warriors and the Brattleboro Braves and made it to the New England High School Superbowl. He had no interest in cars (except to humor his father)—eyesight too bad to tell a Maverick from a Vega—and didn't much care for rock 'n' roll—trouble enough hearing without the intervening amps of an electric guitar. Nonetheless, he had succeeded in gaining and exerting absolute dominance over a band of intelligent attractive athletic boys, whom over the years he had managed to persuade that they would rather play chess after school than hockey and that Greek epic was cooler than heavy metal. Isaac read aloud to his friends from Homer. They played Civil War games, talked in secret languages, corresponded in a kind of cuneiform of Isaac's devising. Sam listened to them arguing politics in Isaac's room, although they fell silent as soon as he approached. Let it last, he wished hard, haunted as always by the worry that Isaac might somehow go wrong, that his internal clockwork was so peculiar that certain blows might knock it awry, derange its balance, bring on those fits of blackness and self-loathing that were his paternal legacy. That superstitious dread a father feels on counting his newborn baby's fingers and toes had survived discreetly in the back of Sam's mind, accompanied Isaac through his teen years. If these days he breathed a little easier, it was only by thinking that just such a phalanx of hale affectionate friends would shield his son from whatever harm he might do himself. Billy and Paul would do anything for Isaac; Sam wasn't quite sure how girls would change the equation.

Isaac's happy band of brothers weren't the only ones to fall under his sway. Strangers he didn't even know were beginning to come up to Sam to tell him what a character his son was. He couldn't figure out how the boy got about so much—he seemed to know more people than Sam did, and spent a great deal of his time paying calls on Dr. McCormick or the Driscolls. Sam hoped he didn't wear people out talking too much: the one thing he hadn't learned was when to give in and let his listeners either get a word in edgewise or go to bed.

Mrs. Ailes had a fat back and russet ears, glossy as a Northern Spy or a Paula Red. Though her hair came down to her shoulders, Sam (concentrating hard to master his nerves) was sure he could make out the three wrinkly puppy rolls of fat that marked the sunburnt neck of every farmer and mechanic in Jessup County. A redneck, then, with a touching appetite for verbal flair. Isaac came home laughing over her misbegotten efforts to convert her ninth-grade ruffians into men of letters. Tired of grading stories that read, "says Mary, says Joe," one day she covered the blackboard in two columns, one of juicy verbs of speech (chuckled, replied, shouted, growled, stammered, announced), the other of snappy adverbs (angrily, lazily, stupidly, menacingly) and ordered her nines to produce a dramatic dialogue from this mix-and-match. Surprise me, she pleaded.

"So half the students *totally* ignore her and write, 'Time to go sledding,' says Joe. 'Yes, it is,' says Mary," recounted Isaac, hilarious with contempt for teacher and classmates alike. "And everybody *else* writes—" here he was almost suffocated by laughter—"'Time to go sledding,' retorts Joe, stupidly. 'Yes, it is,' yells Mary, lazily." Sam's professional sympathies surged for this still ambitious and optimistic woman. Thank God he'd been spared teaching those subjects that might lead one into the disaster of expecting any glimmer of originality or wit.

Mrs. Ailes had gotten all het up about the Composition Contest, which this year was on the topic "What I Did on My Summer Vacation." Inspired. What did kids do on their summer vacations but ride their bicycles, play brain-destroying music, help their dads with the harvest, swim in Auburn Lake, and whine at their parents that they had nothing to do?

Except for Isaac. Isaac had read books about Napoleon. *Every* book about Napoleon, first in the town library, then at the college, to which Sam—fear of bumping into Scannon overridden by Isaac's merciless pestering—had secured him a summer pass. He wasn't allowed to take books home, so every morning from June to September he had risen at ten and bicycled out to Gilboa State, only to return, like a weary businessman, at nightfall, silent and preoccupied. His interest in the Emperor was as much sentimental as military or political: Sam once caught Isaac lying on the floor reading over and over again the story of Napoleon's last days at St. Helena, weeping over the royal captive's humiliation at the petty-minded English governor's hands and brushing away his tears so that he might read on unblinded. Unless you had news for him about the Duc d'Enghien or the Peninsular War, Isaac was best left alone. When school started again he spent nights and weekends hammering away at an essay that while purporting to be about how he had spent his summer vacation was actually about Bonaparte. Sam helped him think it out, pruned his high-flown language. He didn't need much correction: Isaac could *write*.

"Who do you think is greater, Dad, Napoleon or Alexander the Great?" Isaac was still, miraculously, not quite grown out of that father worship in which nothing he heard or saw or thought was wholly real or true until he had laid it at Sam's feet, like a bone or a broken-necked mouse, for approbation, explanation, comment, delectation. It wouldn't last. Sam's own chronic, crippling uncertainty was no match for Isaac's waxing authority. Sometimes Sam could see a disappointed or more skeptical look meet his jokes and shrugging-off of his son's oppressive seriousness, disgust when he responded as usual, "I don't know." How could you not know? Isaac was like a self-made man flummoxed by passive poverty. If you didn't *know*, you guessed. But it wasn't exactly information Isaac wanted from him: long ago he had realized that he had exhausted his father's fund of knowledge and must be content merely to share his own. It was approbation.

Every time Sam spoke to his son these days he felt his reputation at stake. The more he felt Isaac's impatience for him to be serious, the more he was inclined to kid.

"Well, that's a tricky one. I'd say Alexander," he mused. "Alexander conquered most of the globe by the age most guys are trying to decide whether to buy their first new car. He died unbeaten; Napoleon lost it all. Why? What do you think?"

"Napoleon was a greater man," said Isaac.

"Why do you say that?"

"*Because* he lost, and they thought they'd polished him off for good when they sent him to Elba, but he snuck back fighting, and was emperor another hundred days. He knew how to come back from defeat. He shouldn't have made himself emperor, that's all. *That* was his tragic flaw, vanity. The whole point of being Napoleon is that you don't have to be upper-class to be great, all you got to have is talent and *nerve*."

Sam was amused. What was a late twentieth-century New Hampshire boy raised on Thomas Jefferson and Thomas Paine doing worshiping a half-pint Corsican dictator from whose red lips had flowed such pretty sentiments as "Men who do not believe in God—one does not govern them, one shoots them"?

"An *emperor*, Ike? Are you sweet on an emperor? Don't you think that's a little un-American?"

"An enlightened dictator," countered Isaac, puffing out his lower lip pompously. "Napoleon preserved the Revolution's ideals of liberty and equality, the rights of man, without its more murderous and coercive aspects; without him, the Directory would have been toppled by a Lenin."

"That's all very well, but what about the poor Poles and Austrians and Spaniards and Dutch? They didn't need rescuing from any Terror."

"Napoleon freed them from their rotten benighted absolutisms, and imposed his Code wherever he went. It was the conquest of liberalism under law: he was the first invader since Rome to conquer in the name of an ideal, a propagandist-emperor."

"Oh, come off it. His rights of man were just a front for French nationalism," retorted Sam. "He wasn't interested in making Poles free: he sold them to the Russians in the Treaty of Tilsit, just like Ribbentrop did, a hundred and thirty years later. He made his brother Louis abdicate the Dutch throne for the crime of putting Dutch interests before French, and annexed Holland. He was just a French warlord with a lot of big words."

"No, that's not true. He was a genuine universalist, and the Napoleonic Code is the greatest legal document since the Ten Commandments. It's too bad it had to be introduced by invading armies, but that's life. It would have been nice too if the Allies could have restored democracy to Germany without having to level the country first."

"What kind of a comparison is that? Napoleon started his wars; we just fought back. You think if Napoleon had been given the choice between Code and conquest he would have sat peaceably within his borders, rejoicing to see Alexander I or the Bourbons get enlightened all by themselves?"

"No, of course not," Isaac rejoined. "He was a military man with a genius for power, and made no bones about it. That's what I like about him: no cant. But he also taught the world the transcendent nature of greatness—greatness of imagination, daring, flexibility, execution— and showed hundreds and thousands of people in other situations, poets, musicians, too, that you can conquer your own limitations and change the fates of nations."

"Yeah, like Hitler," said Sam.

Isaac, annoyed by this diversion, retorted, "Just because greatness can be perverted doesn't mean people should abandon ambition and set their sights low."

Sam, taking this as a personal rebuke, subsided.

Last night, as Isaac practiced for his big day, Sam had noticed something. As Isaac stood before him, belting out his composition, he kept jerking at the seat of his pants with one hand. A nervous tic. Isaac was exaggeratedly sensitive to remarks about his strange habits, but Sam didn't want people laughing at him in school.

"Leave your pants alone, Ike," he interrupted. Isaac gave him a dirty look.

"Are your trousers too tight?" Isaac was very shy about his chubbiness. Sam didn't think he was too bad, baby fat, but it tormented his son.

"My underpants are too big—they keep falling down," he said in stifled surly tones.

"What do you mean—how can underpants be too big? You mean the elastic's gone?"

"Mmmmmm . . ." Isaac assented. "Can we please get back to Napoleon?"

"We'll get you some new ones."

Sam had thought no more of the falling underpants till the next morning, when Ike had come down groggy with sleep, decked out in his usual patched faded jeans and dirty red sweatshirt. Sam was annoyed. It reminded him of Mattie, this slovenliness: it was an affront to his elders. Three teachers would be judging the contest that day, and teachers noticed these things. They heard Jena and Marengo, but they saw the red flag of Isaac's grimy shirt.

Trying not to let his irritation show, he suggested, "Why don't you put on a clean pair of pants?"

"These are all I got."

"That's impossible. What about that pair of Arbees I bought you at the Army Surplus Store?"

"That was years ago, Dad. Turner had them, now Mom uses them for cleaning."

Rummaging through the boy's bureau, Sam discovered it was true: not only did Isaac's three pairs of underpants seem to have been manufactured for giants in the Pleistocene Age, but he only owned two shirts, one sweatshirt, and the Wranglers he was wearing. Hadn't Sam ever noticed his son wore the same shirt and jeans every day? Sort of, but he knew Isaac's hatred of change and figured those were the only clothes he liked. On a sudden impulse, he pulled Turner over to him and looked at his fingernails. Dirty.

At breakfast Sam confronted Mattie with his discovery. Why the hell did his two sons go around town like paupers with only the clothes on their back?

"It's about time you noticed. They're growing so fast there's no point getting them more than one pair of jeans at a time," Mattie retorted. "Anyway, I don't have time any more. Why don't you take them shopping? You got afternoons free." The boys slunk low in their chairs, rolling their eyes at each other and pretending to be invisible. It was the last straw.

Last spring, after a tantrum-spent Sam had run out of objections and given sullen consent to what could no longer be prevented, Mattie had finally gone into business. Taking advantage of the energy crisis, she had started up a taxi service and hired Danny Olszewski and Tom Driscoll as full-time drivers to run people between Gilboa and the outlying towns, sometimes even as far as Rockingham, Ulster, or Pittsfield. They worked in three shifts. She fitted her new Matador with a CB radio and Turner painted MATTIE'S CAB SERVICE in curly white script on its broad scarlet flank (Sam didn't know whether to be offended or relieved that she had refrained from dragging the Hooker name through the mud). Next she kidnapped his basement workshop— he had the study to himself, was the argument—and converted it into company headquarters, replete with a blaring two-way radio that drove them all nuts. It was like being married to a doctor—a doctor who lost money. This was inevitable the first year or two, Mattie argued, what with starting-up costs, the price of gas, insurance on Danny's and Tom's cars, and the native conservatism of their neighbors, who never liked a new thing till it was a little bit old. Already, however, she had a couple of regular commuters to Rockingham, and plans to expand.

In the old days she had nagged him. Now she had no use for him, and he and the boys scarcely laid eyes on her. Either she was on the road or she was in her office, and if she sat still long enough for you to tell her your thoughts, she would stare above your head, brow carved in a terrible frown. You might be confiding in her about a pain in your chest or about Jay Thibodeaux, whom you were going to have to flunk for the second year running, she was adding up insurance premiums or the cost and efficacy of flyers versus ads placed in the *Recorder*. "How much of a discount should I offer for each coupon?" she would interrupt, unaware that someone else had been talking. "I wonder whether these gimmicks really work . . ." Sam didn't mind for his own sake: he never told her anything anyway; but didn't she remember she had two young sons who needed her?

In fact, Isaac and Turner proved remarkably keen on the business. Ike helped her keep her books when he should have been doing his homework, Turner was trying to talk her into a computer. Sam's prayer to the god of the highways was that Mattie's Cabs would go bust by the time the two of them got their drivers' licenses. His only demand was that Mattie keep up her end of the housekeeping—a hot supper every night and the weekly vacuum—but even this niggling minimum she reneged on, spending more and more evenings on the road. She would come home at midnight, exhausted, met by a fuming Sam. It was like being married to your sixteen-year-old daughter. "I thought we agreed no night driving. That's what you're paying those two young punks for."

"The guy wanted to go to Manchester. What am I to do, pull over to the side of the highway, tell him sorry, it's sundown, my husband keeps me on a curfew, you're going to have to hitch the rest of the way?"

It worried him to think of her driving around alone at night with strangers, although Sam pitied the poor lunatic who dared give his wife a hard time. Mattie solved this problem by applying for a handgun license and buying a Beretta to stash in the glove compartment. New worries: Turner, who had grown into a rather cool and uncommunicative child, went wild over the sleek little pistol, implored his parents to let him learn how to use it. Sam put his foot down. An absentee mother, a trigger-happy son.

"How come Turner's dirty?" Sam demanded now. "Don't you make him wash any more? He's not old enough to decide for himself when he needs a bath. An *animal* has the loving decency to keep its children clean."

"Why don't you give him a bath? You got nothing to do all afternoon," Mattie threw back over her shoulder.

"Dad," interjected Isaac, now standing at the door with Turner, knapsacks over their shoulders, Turner's face assuming that shuttered, absent look it took on when things were not to his liking. "Can you people please continue this conversation later? Turny and I have to get to school."

It was more than negligence that kept Mattie from providing her sons with a change of clothes; it was her pathological stinginess. True, they were harder up than ever with the bank loan for the cab company on top of the mortgage; but this red-eyed gleaner existence was inhuman. They lived off coupons and beet greens the local farm stands dumped as garbage; they ate meat once a month, plucked from the special-sale freezer at Stop & Shop; Mattie refused to keep the pilot burning because it wasted gas; they hadn't been to the movies since the kids were born. Such scrimpings were laughable, just barely. But to make their children wander around dirty like beggars—*that* was unforgivable.

Look at how spruce and glossy Paul Chen was. The Chens didn't have any more money than the Hookers, but their kids dressed as if off to a job interview. The Hooker boys would get rickets or fleas if their mother had her way, and people would laugh at Ike in his scarecrow pants. Why hadn't Sam noticed?

She should have come to Isaac's Prize Day, but of course she wouldn't. She was on the road to Rockingham. She wouldn't take the afternoon off because it was Isaac's day and Isaac was Sam's responsibility and Sam spoiled him rotten so he didn't need any more spoiling from her. Isaac hadn't even asked her: he shielded himself against such rebuffs, expecting nothing.

Now Mrs. Cartwright stepped out on stage to introduce the finalists: Isaac Hooker, ninth grade; Warren Chen, a senior; and Johnny Bruschetti, a senior—Johnny a burly youngster, big-headed; Warren, older brother of the famous Paul, long-boned, skin like sanded cedar, dressed as soberly as a Mormon in a white button-down shirt and pressed pants. But where was Isaac? Mrs. Cartwright beckoned to the sidelines encouragingly, and now Isaac Hooker came galloping out on stage like a frolicsome horse, the floorboards thudding beneath him. For a moment it looked as if he might just go cantering off and out the other side of the stage, but then he clattered to a stop. "I lost my essay," he explained to Mrs. Cartwright, in a voice loud enough for the whole auditorium to hear. "But I found it!" He waved the crumpled pages at her reassuringly, as everyone laughed.

Isaac, who was reading first, at Mrs. Cartwright's direction moved to the very edge of the stage, so close it looked as if he were going to tumble off into the pond of spectators. Isaac at fifteen was a sight at once comical and a little alarming. Blond shag standing on end, mouth a crimson popsicle, fat knees popping through his dungarees, he looked like a baby swelled up to man size, a parade-day float—a rubescent child-giant whose bobbing head and gesticulating limbs expressed a kind of runny, overflowing, ludicrously hopeful joy, self-importance, a desperation both to dominate and to be loved. The expressions on his face were almost unbearably fluid and unguarded, his sunny beams, his grimaces, his hurt, crushed disappointments and tantrums so exaggerated that one wished he had a few thicker layers of skin to him. It seemed to his father that Isaac looked altogether very absurd and very adorable, like a happy idiot, and he wondered if anyone else looking up at his boy was swept by the same wave of exultant love he seemed to exude and also to elicit. Not, Sam added, that he wasn't also frequently a frightful pain in the ass.

Isaac, beaming out at his audience, wasn't in the least bit nervous. On the contrary, the hushed and expectant silence and the bright footlights of the gym, whose radiance made him feel like a chicken in an incubator, the sea of bobbing faces spread out beneath him acted as a warming stimulant, encouraging him to sound forth, knowing that he had enthralling and immensely important things to impart and that no one might interrupt him until he was done. It was only a question of holding back a minute, catching the natural rhythm, like a little girl about to plunge into a game of skip rope.

Thus it had been ever since he first rose to his feet before a crowded hall: a preliminary rush of blood to the head that made his stout legs tremble, his ears roar with his heart's terrified pounding, and then, miraculously, as soon as he gained the pulpit, a commanding clarity— yes, this was what he had been put on earth to do, to rock on his heels and wave his arms and hold forth before hundreds, pitching his voice like a choirboy aiming at the limestone vault. And as soon as he was done, he wished he could do it all over again.

This one was a cinch, pure pleasure—he liked his essay, and hoped they would laugh at the funny parts, even though they never did. He only wished he weren't competing against Paul Chen's brother, who was going to MIT next year and who would take it very hard if he lost, yet the outcome seemed to Isaac a foregone conclusion. For prizes they gave out books with the date and occasion inscribed in dainty calligraphy on the school seal, which bore the same sententious saw that was carved across the school's brick façade—"What sculpture is to a block of marble, education is to a human soul." Yuck. Addison, or was it Diogenes? Isaac only hoped it wouldn't be a book he had already read. Last year Macy Driscoll won Blake's *Songs of Innocence and Experience*. Isaac asked if he could borrow it; the mingy girl refused, so he borrowed it from the library, memorized half those eerie childish chants. Sometimes he was scared that by the time he grew up he would have read every book ever written—famine!—just as a few years ago he had felt desolate when he finally finished reading his father's encyclopedia. "What do I do now? I know everything."

"W-why don't you take up basket weaving?" Sam mimicked his son's pinched hypochondriacal quaver. "Don't let it sweat you, brother, you'll forget it all."

As soon as his broad-voweled peremptory voice sounded out, Isaac was once again caught up in the lambent mystery of the tale, and he unloaded with growing excitement into this glassy ocean of listeners his hero's military genius, his rise to power, conquests, overreachings, fall, brief comeback, and sour and cancerous last exile.

The audience, which because he couldn't see it very well or hear its murmurings and disruptions seemed to Isaac wonderfully receptive and acquiescent, was engaged in many different sorts of pursuits. Very few people were listening. Some of the students were picking their noses, or whispering, or writing notes to each other, or fiddling with each other's pigtails and ponytails, or daydreaming about the weekend before and the weekend to come. The teachers for their part were thinking about what they were going to make for dinner and should they go to the beach this summer or next. Even Isaac's advocate, Mrs. Ailes, was worrying about her father-in-law, who was having a gallbladder operation that week, and thinking that if he died she and her husband would have to take in her mother-in-law, and that would be the end of the world. Of the three teachers who were judging, one leaned over to another and whispered with facetious relish, "A red!" The other tried to remember that saying about how anyone who wasn't a socialist at twenty had no heart and a conservative at fifty no brain, but garbled it and gave up, pleased with himself nonetheless.

Isaac, done, sat down on one of three chairs on stage and listened quite hard to Warren Chen's essay about his butterfly collection. A pretty, stilted, and rather vapid job, he thought pityingly, not up to his brother Paul's caliber. He hasn't managed at all to convey the rather mineral beauty of butterflies, a species created a hundred million years before men and which converts its own shit to pure pigment. It isn't just their speckles that beguile—their maculations, that's a fine word, they use it of saints' wounds—it's that mysterious process of self-transformation. The Greeks saw it as an emblem of the progress of the soul, Coleridge used it as a metaphor for the philosophic imagination. Isaac, bouncing up and down on his seat, chanted to himself fervently the words from the *Biographia Literaria* he had pounded into his mind: "They and they only can acquire the philosophic imagination, the sacred power of self-intuition," yes, that was it, "who within themselves can interpret and understand the symbol, that the wings of the air-sylph are forming within the skin of the caterpillar; those only, who feel in their own spirits the same instinct, which impels the chrysalis of the horned fly to leave room in its involucrum for antennae yet to come. They know and feel," Isaac belted out, quite loud now, "that the potential works in them, even as the actual works on them!" How he had labored and struggled with the hope, the determination, that he who had left so much room for his wings and antennae would yet burst forth into horned flower, into flight, that this groaning straining potential might become actual. But how mammoth the wings that could bear his grievous clownish weight! The image of himself exploding from the chrysalis of Wrangler jeans and sweatshirt to sail above Mrs. Cartwright's head, over the astonished audience, filled him with exultation.

Warren concluded and sat down. Isaac and Johnny Bruschetti exchanged inexpressive looks—Johnny, too, thought the lepidopterist was dead meat—and then Johnny got up and delivered in an aggressive, challenging voice with a slight stammer his rendition of a family trip to the White Mountains. Isaac knew that Johnny had been chosen chiefly because he was struggling with a bad case of dyslexia. Boring. Nature was boring. It rained, it snowed, it got dark, the earth moved, the sun didn't, so what? It was human beings, those wingless over-reaching makers, who mastered nature or devastated it, who raised granite cities on swampland and changed the direction of a river's flow and *named* the butterflies and knew how long they'd been on earth and what their ancestors looked like and how they breathed, that commanded one's awe; it was the atom splitter and not the atom.

And was there a God who had set this all in motion, Isaac wondered for the millionth time. When he was little, he had pictured God like the Jolly Green Giant on a packet of frozen peas, lurking merrily with arms folded across his chest just beyond the horizon, just behind Mount Elmo. How far beyond the black stars of outer space was the creamy white of heaven? Beyond the Milky Way? But beyond the horizon were Hebron and Wendell and Walcott and Sturgis all coiled around Route 101, with the Teasdale Mall, from whose ashes rose the Chen family's Phoenix Garden, and beyond Mount Elmo was no smiling giant in a leafy doublet, but lakes haunted by ratty boarded-up motels and trailer camps, and beyond them those White Mountains in which the Bruschettis were so fond of romping, and before long you had come back to where you started. And beyond the stars, there were more stars, all floating in a kind of sack, an envelope folded in on itself.

Where was there room for God, in all this emptiness? To Isaac it had seemed sometimes that his own sense of sin, his bad conscience at not believing proved the existence of The One he was ignoring, but maybe that sense of sin was merely the dog tag separating man from the other warm-blooded mutts—not the animal created in the divine image, but the animal that invents and worships gods, and feels guilty for neglecting them. Anyway, could God possibly have made Johnny Bruschetti? What for? No, only Mr. and Mrs. Bruschetti could have made Johnny, and seen their handiwork and found it good.

As he read about the American and French revolutions it struck Isaac that his own times were dismally petty, mediocre, insipid. All the great political ideas had been formulated in the eighteenth century, and then there were Napoleon and the rise of industry, the invention of the steam engine, cotton mill, novel, airplane, skyscraper, equality, and from then on it was all downhill. Nothing left, except the expansion of baby slave states, a growing uniformity. I was born too late, he decided. An age of heroism and daring and discovery was past, he was absurdly out of step with the times, he knew things and cared about things that no one else knew or believed. Will I go through my whole life finding Ulysses more real than I am? Could Homer make a hero of Billy Ostrich? Does everyone else prefer books to his friends, dead battles to flesh and blood? His own family seemed to Isaac so fixed and rutted that nothing he could do would ever make his mother change her gray sweatshirt for blue or serve supper at six instead of half past, and yet so intensely had he pored over Napoleon's battles that he almost believed he might reach back to delay Blücher, reinvigorate Marshal Ney, and bring forth Bonaparte the victor at Waterloo.

His sense of power took his breath away: the private certainty that he, Isaac, was born to change all this traduced dullness, to transfigure America in some vague huge way he didn't yet understand. He wished he could tell someone about this destiny of his—Isaac of Arc—but even his father would feel left out to know that Isaac was bound somewhere he couldn't follow.

The judges were conferring. Isaac leaned over. "Hey, Warren, are you a Democrat or a Republican?" He had been told that for some strange reason you weren't supposed to ask if you didn't already know the answer, like asking how much money someone makes, but this reticence didn't make any sense. Warren made as if he weren't even going to grace this pink pipsqueak with a reply, but then "Democrat," he said, indicating by the exaggerated whisper that he didn't believe in talking in assembly, especially not when the fate of his own composition was being decided.

Isaac was surprised, impressed. There weren't many Democrats in Jessup County. "Does that mean you actually like Jimmy Carter?" he asked, incredulously. "I didn't know anyone liked Carter."

Warren shrugged. Johnny Bruschetti was listening too now. "I can't believe this Panama Canal business," Isaac continued. "Why should we give it to a little warlord who is going to close it off every time he wants some more money from us? Let's hope Congress has got the sense to kill the treaty this time around."

"It's their country," whispered back Warren.

"We built it. Look what happened with the Suez Canal: they'll shut it to ships and there'll be another war, and we'll retreat, just like England did, and not dare set foot in the world south of San Antonio. Jimmy Carter wants to make the United States into a kind of King Lear. Nobody forgives you if you have power and property and give it all away."

Mrs. Cartwright hushed them. The judges had handed in their verdict, and she stood up now, and Isaac could feel Warren beside him growing rigid, clearing his throat.

I don't care whether or not I win, he thought suddenly, as if in response to the tensing of Warren's narrow bony shoulder. After all, Napoleon will still be there, and there's so much more left to read. I'm not finished with him yet. And in a sudden access of diffidence, it seemed to him that his version of the man had been too wooden, had missed his hero's gay playfulness, flexibility, self-mockery. I hope Warren wins, with his Red Admirals and his white shirt and his scholarship to MIT. But why *do* people hunt butterflies? If I asked, Warren wouldn't be able to tell me. Something atavistic, from the days when little Chinese boys kept crickets in boxes and bred goldfish with tail fins so long they couldn't swim. Mao Tse-tung outlawed songbirds. Better let Warren win. If he doesn't, who knows? He may have to commit hara-kiri, Isaac thought, giggling. No, that's the Japs. What's the matter with those Chinks—don't they believe in honor too?

Mrs. Cartwright complimented the three boys on their lovely compositions and explained to the audience that Ashuelot Regional held such contests because it believed in encouraging good writing and independence of mind. "Like hell," Isaac muttered. Warren gave him a dirty look—Warren who had no inkling of the generous thoughts that were coursing through his neighbor's brain. What if he won and abdicated in favor of Warren? Would people think it weird? Hard to imagine Napoleon forfeiting a territory in favor of a worthier candidate. No, I really don't deserve Prussia—let the Russians have it. But then Isaac remembered the prize book, with its gold-star-edged school stamp inside Macy Driscoll's Blake and inscribed on the stamp those letters in calligraphy that looked like cast-iron fretwork, and he imagined showing the book over supper to Turner. His dad would laugh at him if he offered the book to Warren Chen, accuse him of grandstanding; his dad was a bit cynical about altruistic gestures, especially Isaac's.

There was Mrs. Cartwright still blathering on, but suddenly she'd stopped and was waiting pointedly. Johnny Bruschetti reached over Warren and gave Isaac a shove. "Hey, deafie, go get your prize."

"I won?" breathed Isaac. "Did she say I won?" So proud, so bursting he felt like dancing a furious solitary little war dance right on stage.

"Yes, you won. Go get it, dork," repeated a no longer so friendly Johnny. "Doncha even know your own name?"

So Isaac rose, smiling, incredulous, and crossed the stage in a flushed dream of success, Napoleon vindicated, and all thoughts of self-sacrifice fled. Mrs. Cartwright, who usually struck him as a chilly prune, with her smile that was merely thin painted lines turned up at the corners, like the pained fake lips-up smile Turner gave when he really wasn't in the least amused but instead wary and disgusted, this Mrs. Cartwright, Ike now realized without surprise, was in fact a warm and charming woman, whose every poky blistered joint expressed affection for him, welcoming pride. She was holding the book in one hand and the other hand was extended, blue-veined. What's the book? Isaac wanted to ask, the way going to his grandparents' for Sunday dinner he always used to ask as soon as he was in the door, "What's for dessert? Not fruit, I hope," and be hushed by his father.

In his curiosity, confusion, Isaac ignored the outstretched hand and made for the one holding the book. He tried to pry it away from her, but she wouldn't give it up. A furtive little tug-of-war ensued, until Isaac succeeded in wresting it from Mrs. Cartwright, who, smiling no longer, hissed at him, "Shake HANDS, Isaac." Isaac looked dubious. He wasn't used to shaking hands, and it didn't seem festive enough a seal to this ceremony. He paused. How would Napoleon welcome a victorious general? Smiling, Ike reached out and pulled Mrs. Cartwright's astonished ear. He remembered to say, "Thank you"—he wasn't a *total* savage—and then, not knowing where to sit, trotted back down the stairs leading up to the stage, and confused by all the faces and seeing no seat free, left the auditorium before the concluding hymn.

The book was *Bulfinch's Mythology.* And no, he hadn't read it. God be praised: virgin territory. He wouldn't even allow himself the pleasure of looking at the title page and table of contents right then and there, but bestowing on the slipcased cover a timid caress, stowed it in his knapsack so that he might savor the moment in private and at his leisure. His. Rather than wait for the school bus he would walk home across the fields so he could look at the book slowly and all by himself, without his nosy bus mates wanting to maul it, hand it around the aisles. Such unveilings called for a little privacy.

It was early summer. In two weeks school would be out and he could sleep till noon, spend his days lying in fields speckled with the dusky crimson of Indian paintbrush, reading till nightfall. After the spring thaw the meadows and hills were already thickening to a heavy lunacy of green, new-spawned mosquitoes haunted the woods and ponds, and nights thrummed with crickets and cicadas. Summer, summer, summer.

Isaac forged a shortcut across the underbrush behind the school, swinging his knapsack like a lasso over his head and singing to himself as he plunged through the jungly waist-high vegetation—and then, WHAM. With a jolt, he almost fell on top of a cluster of boys crouched in a small clearing in the brambles. Like startling a covey of grouse or woodcock except that these birds didn't run for cover, but stood up threateningly. They were seniors. They were bigger than he, though skinny, and there were three of them, but it wasn't just their size or number: it was their tribe. They belonged to the caste of "freaks," that was what these guys called themselves, and they wore the freak uniform: straggly shoulder-length hair, bleached sleeveless blue-jean vests studded with Def Leppard and Harley Davidson badges, square-toed boots, thick-studded belts. They rode motorcycles and souped-up Mustangs, Saturday nights they parked outside the pizzeria at the mall smoking dope, dropping acid, blasting heavy metal, hooting at girls, and they regarded school not quite as Addison or Diogenes did, but as a setting for weird initiation rites and for romances almost suicidal in their doomed intensity, and they lived to pick on people like Isaac. Their fathers worked in factories or had disappeared, and if they survived high school, they would grow pot bellies and dote on their kids—there is nothing sappier, his dad once said, than a forty-year-old biker with his baby daughter—but in the meantime they made life nervous and humiliating.

Isaac recognized the faces. That was Jay Thibodeaux, with the purpled zitty cheeks and rabbity teeth, and John Pulaski, and the third, whose name he didn't know. What a pain, too late to retreat. They had been smoking pot: he smelled the sweet odor, like burnt squash. Mostly he felt foolish. Instinctively, he hid his knapsack behind his back.

"What's happening, man?" asked Jay Thibodeaux.

"Nothing much," returned Isaac, politely. "Just got out of assembly. You missed an awfully nice hymn." His kidding escaped them.

"Oh, assembly," bleated John Pulaski. "Ain't it a shame we missed assembly. What did we miss in assembly? I hope that old whore said a prayer for us."

Isaac knew that he ought to get moving, but it was a long stretch of tall grass, about thirty feet, back to the school yard and safety, and his natural courtesy and sociability rebelled: if people wanted to talk, you talked. Also, he had to admit it, freaks or no freaks, they were older boys and he was flattered by their attention, anxious to win their esteem. So, beaming at the gang, "There was a composition contest today. Didn't you hear? Three boys read their compositions. And as a matter of fact, I won."

"You won?" the three boys exchanged looks.

"You won a trophy?" inquired no-name.

"Well, no, not exactly a trophy—a kind of prize." He realized he'd made a big mistake even raising this subject. It was menacing, the way they kept exchanging glances and inching in.

"What kind of prize, asshole?" demanded John Pulaski.

Isaac froze. He knew he had to say something back, and he suspected that if he told them it was a book they might leave him alone, but after being called a name like that, he couldn't speak. Bad language offended him, it was lazy the way his friends used "fucking" as filler. Such words were termites devouring language's springy innards, contracting its vastness to a carcass. Instead of answering he found himself reciting in his head the names of Napoleon's battles. Toulon, Jena, Wagram, Sedan, Austerlitz . . .

No escape. "Hand over your prize, fatso," said Jay Thibodeaux.

"What did you say?"

"You hear me. Give us your frigging prize."

Abrupt and unsettling physiological changes were occurring in Isaac. His heart was hammering and his legs felt wobbly. Ten minutes ago he had been standing on the school stage before a warm admiring crowd, and now here he was in an empty field surrounded by three thugs who had formed a phalanx and were advancing on him. Tilsit, Borodino, Moscow, Waterloo . . . I weigh thirty pounds too much, he realized. I don't know how to run, and I haven't a muscle in my body. Rooted to the spot in the shoulder-high weeds, and his head felt muddy, the only thing he could be sure of was that soon it would feel worse.

He found himself looking up at the sky as if for escape. Powdery shreds of cloud hurried overhead. He was frightened of pain, and of losing his glasses. "No," said a voice from inside Isaac's throat, but the "no" was too little to fend off the coming onslaught. As he backed away, clutching his knapsack hard, Jay Thibodeaux grabbed him around the waist like a partner in a country dance and jumped him, and now everything happened very fast. Falling backward, glasses flying, wind knocked out of him by the heavy body lunging onto his, head hitting something sharp. For a moment or two he couldn't breathe. Someone was sitting on his chest and someone—that same someone—was punching him in the face and head, and someone else had grabbed his knapsack and was emptying it.

"So where's the trophy?"

"There is no frigging trophy—he must have been making it up." And then, in disgust, "Oh shit, it's a *book*. It's just a fucking book."

The vindictively heavy person sitting on his chest, who was now squeezing his throat with one hand and punching him with the other, let go and got up, but Isaac still couldn't breathe. "Here's your prize book, fatso. Have a nice assembly," honked John Pulaski in a donkey hee-haw, and with the sound of tearing, rending, a flurry of crumpled pages came fluttering down from the sky.

There was a scrambling crackly whish of bodies moving away and a parting voice complaining, "What a bunch of cheapskates—they don't even give trophies any more."

Alone now. The prickly brambles made quite a cozy nest, as long as the freaks didn't come back, and for a moment or two he must have dozed off, sunk into a kind of unconsciousness of pain. When he resurfaced, his head throbbed and he could only see through one eye, and his face had turned to a palpitating, twitching jelly of pain. The pain was so large and overpowering it had become corporeal, an element like air or water. For a while he lay staring up at the clouds, thinking how happy he might be if he never had to get up and explore his losses but could lie there, summer and winter, daydreaming. But he didn't want any of his schoolmates to find him in this unmanly position, so, groaning, Isaac raised himself, sat up, moved a hand over body and face. Something wet on the back of his head: blood. Nothing else injured, so far as he could tell. Not dead or dying after all, more's the pity. As he sat up, crumpled fists of paper slid off him. Isaac uncreased a page, to disclose a glowing watercolor of two men flying with waxen wings above the burnished sea. Then he understood for the first time what had happened and a great wave of dread and hopelessness overcame him. Let it not be true. Let it not be his prize book, his Bulfinch, not that. Heaving to his feet, he thrashed blindly around the encampment for the strewn scattered feathers that had been plucked from the breast of his book, its covers and cracked binding lying open in the grass like a bird's carcass, like a woman torn limb from limb. His prize book, his Bulfinch, raped and disemboweled.

Even the flyleaf, with its gilded school stamp bearing in script like iron fretwork the date and occasion, was gone before he'd even seen it. He had been robbed and violated. Sighing, he clutched his cut head, rocked back and forth on his knees. "I'll KILL them. I'll KILL them. I'll murder them, the Goths, the lousy thieving stupid bullies . . ." They'd sworn at him, worse still they called him fatso, they'd torn apart his book because it wasn't a gilt statuette, and he'd let them. He would never be able to hold up his head again.

He was kneeling in the brambles blinded, weeping without knowing he was weeping, as he crawled about the clearing, gathering the strewn pages. He didn't hear the underbrush parting until suddenly someone was moving toward him, standing right over him. Caught unawares,

Isaac lunged forward and flung himself on the intruding figure, yelling and beating with his fists against a solid and unresistant body.

"Isaac, Isaac . . ." a female voice remonstrated, but Isaac didn't, wouldn't hear, kept butting, flailing, until the person fell back. "Isaac," repeated the voice. "It's me, Mrs. Ailes. What's happened to you?"

Isaac lost his balance and sat down hard, head lowered, breathing fast. He hated her. "Get AWAY from me! Get OUT of here! Leave me ALONE!" he yelled, brandishing his fist in the woman's direction, but instead of going away, the hateful interfering busybody advanced. Isaac hit her.

"Who did it? Who beat you up? Who did it, Ikey, tell me right now. We're going to fix *them* good."

Turner was standing in the bathroom doorway watching. Mattie had her older son standing in his baggy underpants in the bathtub, and while she questioned him, was scrubbing hard at his face and the back of his head and his legs with a washcloth, as if he were a horse and she a groom. His mother had remarkably strong arms for a woman, stronger than some men's. Her brown forearms were bowed with sinew and muscle, curved like an archer's bow—the same powerful curved forearms one sees on a baker who spends his days kneading dough or a laundress pounding clothes clean in the river. For her last birthday Turner had gotten her a subscription to *Women Wrestlers*: she had screamed with laughter, but he noticed, when she showed the first issue to Margery, a naïve proud curiosity at the sight of so many women who could clearly take care of themselves. "You wouldn't want to meet *her* in a dark alley," she said, laughing defiantly, pointing to Sheba the She-Bear. Now all his mother's muscle and elbow grease were being applied to uncaking the dirt from portions of his brother's body that looked so tender and inflamed they might explode. Turner had never seen his mother so angry before. She kept asking Isaac the same questions over and over, but Isaac wouldn't answer. "The little snot-nosed shits—we'll get them all right. Who were they, Ikey? How many of them?"

"Three," mumbled the swollen mouth.

"Did you see their faces? Who was it?"

"Couldn't see."

"What do you mean, you couldn't see. Don't give me that shit, Ikey. Didn't you just tell me you were chattering away to them about the assembly? Don't you want to get these little bastards?"

"Don't swear at me, and no, I didn't recognize them."

"Ikey, you go to a school with four hundred kids in it. Don't tell me you don't recognize anybody."

Isaac was silent a long time. Turner felt embarrassed for him. He was frightened Isaac was going to cry, and that would be the end of the world.

"It was Jay Thibodeaux and John Pulaski and some other guy I don't know," he said finally, in a cold muffled voice.

"Come on, get dressed. We're going over to the Thibodeauxes right now."

"I don't want to."

"Don't talk crazy, Isaac. Are you a coward?"

Turner watched his big brother step out of the tub, still dripping, make his way slowly back to his bedroom, followed by their hectoring mother.

The Thibodeaux family lived in a mustard-colored mobile home, with the shell of a small motorboat hauled across the front steps and an assortment of rusting motors scattered across what passed for a front yard; hanging up to dry was a parade of pink nylon slips, tiny blue jeans, and bibs. Mattie pushed a buzzer, which obviously no one ever used, and a teen-aged girl came to the door, her face keyed up with the suspicious wary excitement that greets traveling salesmen or strangers out of gas or needing directions in rural parts. Inside was a knot of dirty children, none of them Jay, congregated in front of a television game show, a bag of Fritos emptied across the floor, and a scrawny black-haired lady in a housecoat to whom Mattie marched up and gave a hard push. Afterward Isaac could remember nothing of what happened, except that the two ladies in a kind of screechy opera of anger called each other liars and sluts, Mrs. Thibodeaux denying that her son, who was a good boy and worked after school, would waste his time on such a feeble specimen as Mrs. Hooker's son, and Mattie retorting that *her* son had won national prizes, including this extremely valuable book Mrs. Thibodeaux's illiterate spawn had trashed in a fit of brutish jealousy, and that she was going to sue Mrs. Thibodeaux for vandalism and for the doctor's bills from the injuries done her Isaac, to which Mrs. Thibodeaux replied that *she* would sue Mrs. Hooker for trespassing and assault and that nobody could prove her boy had done *nothing*.

Nobody was home at the Pulaskis'; Mattie contented herself with scrawling "Butcher" in lipstick across their window. On the drive home, wound up tight like a boxer still flailing after the match is over, she replayed line by line her duet with Mrs. Thibodeaux, laughing at her particularly devastating insults, and so preoccupied that she didn't even answer the calls coming in on the CB to pick up a customer from the Peter Pan stop, switching it off impatiently.

"Did you see the look on her face when I called her precious son a dope dealer? You got to hit back hard with these lowlifes—force is the only thing they understand," she advised, as if otherwise she might have employed gentle suasion or moral reasoning.

And finally, in a fleeting outbreak of fastidiousness, "What a pigpen that dump was. That whole runty litter of hers ought to be put down. People that dirty and mean don't deserve to live."

Isaac was silent. He wasn't talking to her, and he felt as if he might never talk to her again. The gash in the back of his head where he had landed was making him sick to his stomach, and he had to hold on to the handle of the car hard so as not to pass out.

"Don't you even *want* to get back at those scum bags?" his mother repeated. He grunted.

By the time they got back, Mattie a little put out by her son's ungratefulness, Sam was home and Isaac could see from his father's pinched grave face that Turner had filled him in on the afternoon's events. But that very solemn long-faced look, expressing grief, commiseration, and guilt (it seemed to Sam all his fault for not having sought out his son after assembly to congratulate him, drive him home), was enough to send Isaac charging up the stairs without a word, head averted in blind fury.

Sam and his sons were sitting in the den in the dark, watching television with the sound off. Out the window were velvety hills, the pulsating red Morse Code twinkle of the radio tower on Mount Elmo. Stillness except for a dog howling down in the valley and howling again when no one answered. From time to time Sam dipped a washcloth in a saucepan filled with ice water and pressed it to his son's feverish head. It had taken him only a moment to see that the gash needed stitches, and that Mattie ought to have taken him straight to the clinic.

It seemed to Sam that it was all his fault for not looking after Isaac better, and it seemed to him a criminal act of folly to bring children into the world for other people's children to pulverize, and he was surprised by his own murderous rage against John Pulaski and Jay

Thibodeaux and all his other students who had mush between their ears and hatred in their fists. He longed to kiss his son's dear sewn-up head, but as soon as he moved closer to Isaac, who was sprawled on the couch with Turner—in times of trouble they still snuggled together for animal comfort—a surly voice fended him off.

"Don't tell me about Bobby Garvey and all the bullies who beat you up when you were a boy."

"I wasn't going to," said Sam, offended. "I was going to offer you another book."

"I don't want it."

"Wouldn't you like my *Columbia Encyclopedia* for your very own?"

"No."

The next morning he would go to Ellen Cartwright and complain (although the prospect of explaining why his son had pulled her by the ear was a little daunting). What kind of war zone was this where children were robbed and beaten? If she couldn't ensure her charges' safety, Sam had every right to bring his children to school armed with shotguns and Mace. "I want to tell you something about today, son," he ventured.

Isaac, leaning back against Turner in the reeling dark, eyes shut, wasn't listening. It wasn't that he didn't want vengeance, rather that the wrong done him was so deep that no punishment short of death was thinkable. If he were to unleash his fury nothing would suffice, short of borrowing Billy Ostrich's father's twelve-gauge shotgun, lining up the three goons in the schoolyard, and blowing their grinning heads off one by one. Anything short of mass murder was impossible, unsatisfying, *more* shameful still. And to have let his mother go to battle for him was as unbearable as the thought of how Jay Thibodeaux would gloat when he heard.

He pictured himself strolling into the senior homeroom at the beginning of their first class of the day, walking up to Mr. Ellsworth, standing by the blackboard.

"Mr. Ellsworth, I'm afraid there is a mad dog in your class."

"What are you talking about, Isaac?"

Isaac would hold up the scratched and crumpled nest of paper that was the remains of *Bulfinch's Mythology.* "He tried to eat my book, and I'm afraid he isn't paper-trained." Then he would cram that wad of paper down John Pulaski's throat, until the boy choked and gave up the ghost right there—suffocated in his senior homeroom.

But why did I hit Mrs. Ailes and why did I keep on slugging her even after I knew it wasn't one of those lummoxes come back again? Why did I hate her worse than them? In the Old Testament you're put to death for striking your mother—imagine what you get for hitting a teacher. What a loathsome contemptible worm I am. But Isaac, even as he berated himself for cravenness, once again felt boiling up within his breast irritable fury at the woman who saw him crawling around on his knees like a crazed mole, blubbing and whimpering. Could she see him thus exposed and live? And he, could he face her? After having punched her in the stomach, could he go into class tomorrow and answer her questions on the use of the gerund? Was it possible after all that he was not the smart and lovable boy adored by his father, idolized by his kid brother, respected by friends, but instead a gutless slime who shouldn't associate with decent people?

When the Goths sacked Athens in the third century and were about to burn down the Great Library, one commander protested. "Take heed what you do, for while they are busy about these toys, we shall with more leisure conquer their countries."

This story had amused Isaac vastly when he first read it, but now it appeared to him in a different light. For as long as he could remember, the Greeks had been the men for him. Philosophers, mathematicians, architects, explorers, not only did they write odes and tragedies, they conquered the known world and invented democracy; they sculpted red and black vases detailing in comic strips the doings of their gladiators, gods, and clowns; above all, they were the first people in history to be interested in alien races, to catalog from pure curiosity the origins and customs and religions of foreign nations. They gave the English language all its abstract words, so that if you wanted to say "chair" or "letter" or "table" or "meat" you could stick to Latin or Anglo-Saxon, but as soon as you talked ideas and science, you strode ineluctably into Greek. And yet this great city of Athens had stood by while the Goths, jabbering meatheads with bones through their noses, laid waste their theaters and temples and hippodromes and argued about whether or not they felt like burning down the Great Library while they were at it. What was wrong with them, anyway? The Goths, muttered Isaac aloud, picturing to himself pimply straggle-haired hordes descending from their ski-mobiles and Harley Davidsons. No, it didn't matter how much you knew about how Austerlitz was won and Waterloo lost if you didn't have the strong arm to fight for your ideas, if your body was flabby lard the color of tadpole's flesh and if the only person you had the guts to hit was the gallant lady who had come to bail you out. The Greeks had held sway for seven hundred years before the Goths picked them off. Isaac was fifteen years old and already a geek, a vicious loser.

The bottom of a deep black pit whose walls were covered in slippery slime, and high above him, impossibly high, a tiny chink of lit blue heaven. Yet every time he tried to scrabble up the sides, down again he slithered into its dank bowels.

Chapter 2

TURNER AWOKE with a shuddering jolt as if he'd been kicked through sleep's door by a brutal bouncer. It was 5 A.M. and the room was cold and blue. He had been having a nightmare he was sure he had dreamed before: his brother, Ike, standing waist-high in a frozen pond, and Turner among a ring of jeering spectators watching this polar gladiator flail in the water. Then Ike suddenly yelled for Turner to join him, and he, hideously, was too chicken not to obey. Waded into water so cold it seemed to him that he would go into shock before he reached his brother—for now it seemed Isaac was drowning—but the farther he waded, the farther Isaac receded, until suddenly out of nowhere he felt his brother's hand on his head, pushing him down below the ice. He tried to scream, but water flooded his mouth and lungs.

He woke up in a cold sweat, teeth chattering, so relieved to be alive and awake that these first twilit moments were bathed in a kind of grateful charity, before he started to worry again, before the cogs and little wheels in his stomach tightened and ground into gear. Stop worrying, his mother always told him; you'll be gray before you're twenty. With a peculiar satisfaction, he imagined himself with coarse, iron-gray hair like his mother's mane. He longed to be ancient, patriarchal, out of the fray, for already he felt burdened by unspeakable responsibilities yet with none of the freedom or respect responsibility is supposed to bring, Atlas disguised as a shrimpy eighth-grader. Sometimes he dreamed sights that later happened—his mother in the doorway, evening sun flooding her figure to pink sherbet, Isaac announcing over supper he was going to learn to play the banjo—the picayuneness of these vouchsafed anticipations was almost insulting. Knowing they would come true left you cautious, weary: forewarned is helpless.

For those few moments (he had beat the alarm clock by ten minutes) it was sneaky bliss to lie half-frozen under the shrunken quilt, toes staring out bare and petrified at the other end, to watch the darkness rustling behind the window shade and listen to the blue jays, the blackbirds, robins, and harsh crows brag, caterwaul, and squabble in their morning market. His room was drafty for so small a box; pinpoints and corridors of chill air came seeping, racing across the floor from leaky windows, forming a kind of wind tunnel.

In the wall behind his bed's headboard lived a mouse. He hadn't yet told his father, who was supposedly responsible for all unwanted indoor wildlife. Daddy the mighty hunter, Isaac called him. The mouse kept the same hours as he, made a scrabbly to-do about midnight and then subsided. It was small potatoes, the mouse to his south, compared to the more volcanic tumult of his brother to his west—groans, loud energetic monologues, clamorous tone-deaf songs. All that week it had been a Gregorian dirge Turner was sure that Isaac thought was the tune to "I Been Wukkin' on the Railroad."

Isaac, a nocturnal animal, a stentorian layabed, talked, sang, sometimes laughed to himself long into the night, while Turner, who needed silence the way others need their three square meals or seven hours, lay rigid next door, not daring even to think of sleep. For the baying and bellowing were so erratic you would think the creep had finally corked off and would at last sink unsuspectingly into slumber only to be jerked awake in horrid fear by a sneak attack, by the revived enemy's new fit of pacing or—this was Thursday, the night before Turner's math test—a stern voice demanding, "Is there such a thing as history in America? No, there's too much space." And then, once Turner had been asleep and jolted awake again, sleep was gone, and the next day's math test would surely be shot, one more C and now he would never get into any decent college, and Turner tossed, rigid with resentment, aghast at how the half-hours and hours hurtled past in precipitate panic, the small hours, that's why they called them the small hours because they passed so quickly.

It was lunatic to talk to yourself aloud all night, lunatic to be deciding at two in the morning that there was no history in America or that you had been working on the railroad all the livelong day, and unpardonable to din these discoveries into your sleeping neighbor's ear. Turner was sorry for Isaac's being such a weirdo, but despised his incontinence. Red-eyed, raw-nerved, he'd finally complained about the singing but Isaac kept forgetting, paced and galumphed about next door, arguing with himself at full holler. If Ike could hear the mouse above his own racket, he never mentioned it; if not, it was Turner's secret. As soon as he had saved up $700 (he had $275 in his savings account already from his paper route) he was going to send away for one of those mail-order log cabins you assemble yourself and set it up in the backwoods, live on cold cereal and silence.

Five o'clock on a black November morning. Too cold to put bare feet to the wooden floor, too cold to go pee, let alone wash, but Turner forced himself to do *all* of the above, seeking a kind of pleasure in shocking his body. Water cold as his nightmare coming out in sparse trickles, bald towels, their Marvel Comics heroes' springy legs and powerful fists and eyeless helmet-masks almost effaced by age, the linoleum slippery, more leaky windows trailing gray putty ribbons of caulking. Jeez, he noticed, it's frozen *inside* the goddamned window, too.

The farmers said it promised to be a brutal winter. Early frost had already nearly wiped out September's apple crop, turned McIntosh to mush, Halloween's pumpkins had looked yellowish and peaky. Every time nature diddled New Hampshire, every time it rained too hard in the spring, froze too early in the fall, his father would go all stricken for the neighbors' sake, grieve guilty as if *he'd* set the winds and hail loose by accident, forgotten to lock up the snow. "Promise me, boys, you won't even *dream* of making a living off the weather. Go learn accounting, sell insurance."

When Georgie Hanesworth fell into the combine Sam didn't speak for a week. Isaac too nearly bawled his eyes out although Georgie had been Turner's friend. Suspicious of so instant and ostentatious an access to grief, he reminded his brother, "You didn't hardly know Georgie. What's it to you?"

Ike brushed him aside with an impatient gesture. "So, he's dead, he's fifteen years old. So what? Doesn't know what he's missing. It's his *parents*—how can the heart *bear* it?" And he'd begun to snuffle all over again. Theatrics. Turner couldn't imagine crying for anyone's parents. Worse, Ike had headed right over to the Hanesworths, who you'd think would want to be left alone, practically moved in with them. He still went to pay his respects once a week; my other son, the otherwise taciturn Mrs. Hanesworth called him. How did Gabriel like having a brand-new brother? Had Isaac no pride, that he went roaming around the countryside like a stray cat appearing at the kitchen door every evening at suppertime? The trouble was, it made Turner act grumpier in reaction. He watched Ike and their dad hold hands, pummel, mess each other's hair, exchange sweethearts' insults; they joked smugly about Turner's loathing of being touched. Such family legends are carved in granite: he could spend the next forty years bouncing in his daddy's lap and still Sam would call him "The Untouchable." Only his mother knew him truly; she, too, thought Isaac a phony—to the point where Turner himself sometimes felt uneasy at the freshness of her contempt.

Now, having dressed in the half-darkness, he could hear his mother and father breathing as he crept past their bedroom door like an Indian scout, knowing and shunning all the noisy floorboards—could hear his mom snoring a little, the whistle of a fat, full animal obliviousness.

Increasingly these days Turner couldn't bear the grossness of sleep, revolted against all the body's prosy stolid constraints, all the things one had to do regularly or bust, like a union of workers who without their negotiated core of rest and meals went on strike, stomach roaring, saboteur eyes seeing double. If only one could take a pill and never have to eat, sleep, relieve oneself, what freedom, twelve extra hours to the day, what conquest over the stupidity of need, the mindless cycle of animal hunger, animal satiety, animal evacuation, the bondage of the fleshly vats, crammed and emptied, crammed and emptied.

At the front door Turner pulled on his boots, his father's army jacket (his own down jacket was warmer, but the nylon was so noisy you couldn't hear a sound above your own rustle and squeak). Above his head, suddenly, he heard a thump, a double thump, then creaks as his mom, no, his dad, a catnapper, got out of bed, straggled to the head of the stairs, and called down to the kitchen, hesitantly, "Turner?"

In his mind Turner could see his father already groping his way downstairs, sandy hair standing on end like a golliwog, mouth and eyes caked with night drool, pajamas twisted around his body, long bony feet and naked white ankles (it was fairyish not to have any hair on your body like that), and yet sublimely unaware of his own ridiculousness at that moment, solely possessed by eagerness to see his son off, to keep him in the house a while longer, enchain him with orange juice and cereal, or "at least a doughnut for the road." Ugh! So Turner, with another plaintive sleepy "Turner?" on his heels, pretended he didn't hear, and fled.

Outside was still dark, blades of grass stiff and gunmetal gray from frost, leaves underfoot crunching like Rice Krispies. Nippy—that's what Isaac always said when it was cold, and the two of them would giggle because they knew it was also an ethnic slur. Turner hung around at the end of the drive, shifting from foot to foot. Five-twenty-two. Listening hard until he heard the truck's motor all the way across in the next valley, and finally came Preston's snot-green pickup, with his dog and his equipment in the bed; door swung open, Stash got out, so Turner—the shrimp—could sit in the middle, between him and Preston. Turner hopped inside, gratefully clutching cold metal and slippery Leatherette.

Stash was Preston's partner, a big fellow, dark, amiable, eyes squinted shut when he laughed, broad and hulky as Preston but longer. Turner felt like a tadpole between them. He half wished Preston hadn't brought Stash along, but at least Stash would keep the conversation going so he could listen without having to think about what to say back.

"She didn't want to wake up this morning," Preston explained in his slow voice with a jagged laugh, always a moment after the wisecrack, bringing up the rear. "Tell the truth, neither did I. Sunday mornings are for lying in bed, flipping the channels and fucking your wife."

"Thus speaks a man with no kids," said Stash, who had two little girls. No matter what you talked about—bird dogs, college basketball, the Vietnam War, cars, Clint Eastwood—Stash always managed to drag the conversation round to his two daughters.

Preston ignored him. "She conked out on me three times this morning—truck, not wife. I thought we'd have to walk to Walcott."

"But here we are," remarked Turner. (Everything he said these days sounded trite, either naïve or schoolgirl prissy compared to his friend's dark cynicism, especially when he had to shout over the motor's rumble and the roar of open windows.)

"Yes, here we are," Preston agreed. "Boys, it's gonna be a black day for the ruffed grouse."

Starting on an air rifle and a target out at Preston's place that fall, Turner had become a fairly decent marksman. (Preston had recently bought forty acres below Bear Ridge, no house yet, just a trailer. That's the way with builders, he said, always the last ones to have a roof over their own heads.) Turner had keen sight and a steady grip, and for as long as he could remember had been gun crazy, wild for the mahogany sleekness of a rifle's body, the bracing click of the bolt, the sulfury tang of burnt powder. Enviously, he watched hunters, flushed, bone-tired, jubilant, working their way noisily through a full breakfast at

Sadie's, their camouflage tribal and festive as a medieval knight's colors, their carcass-laden pickups out front; he devoured *Soldier of Fortune*, hoarded spent ammo, memorized the vital statistics of Smith & Wessons, Remingtons. Only time his dad ever hit him was for sneaking the Beretta from his mom's glove compartment and shooting it off in the woods—'course, he couldn't let on that she'd told him he could.

That year, when Turner found Preston, his dad finally relented. It was right after he'd decided not to try out for football or basketball, because his grades were slipping, and anyway, Turner didn't like team sports. (And anyway, said an unwelcome voice located somewhere in his stomach, he was five feet four and *not growing*.) In any case, in no time flat he had learned to enmesh the bull's eye in a snare of copper pellets at twenty yards easy, then fifty.

Under Preston's tutelage, he moved on to blackbirds on the bough, picked off with a shotgun whose kick bruised and deafened you even with earplugs, and then to skeets, orange saucers launched by a fierce metal trap. Head down, eye on the bird, keep swinging, follow through, Preston intoned, and Turner nodded, cheek to the stock, not sure he knew what he was being told to do. His heart went after moving targets in an uneasy sort of way: you *rooted* for things on the wing, and at first something in him had quailed even at shattering a skeet in its clay flight. The gun's kick was like the recoil of conscience, but somehow exciting, too, as if it were you that was flying.

In September came doves. On his first day out Turner had missed and missed, willfully almost, and then, God forgive him, *grazed* a bird, and watched her drag, flail, and fall live to the ground. It had taken ages for Preston's bird dog to nose her out, caught in a tornado of brambles, eyes dewy red. Preston held the small thrashing body in one hand, wrung her neck with the other.

"Makes you want to burst out crying, don't it?" he said, sympathetically.

Turner was too furious with himself to answer. After that grief of learning incompetence's damage, he overcame his qualms and took to wing shooting with a passion. He no longer even minded the din much. People who weren't sportsmen thought it had to do with the landscape, the beauty of plain, of thicket, of gray salt marsh in a chilly dawn, a good bird dog's intuitive genius, but it wasn't just the scenery, it was the kill. His brother, of course, couldn't shoot, blind as a bat, and a little deaf (earwax, Daddy insisted), and begrudged this new love that took Turner farther away from his managing, couldn't decide whether to be curious or act supercilious when Turner came home at night with a couple of woodcocks for his mom, already plucked.

When Aunt Sue had declared hunting was cruel, Isaac had treated her to a derisive lecture on the inanity of ladies who thought animals—not even mammals, mind you—superior or equal to people.

When she left, Isaac concluded in a dark triumphant finale, "Next blackbird Turny shoots we'll save the brain and perform a transplant on Sue: her husband will be amazed by the improvement." Mattie, who loved to make fun of her sister but wasn't going to have anyone else do it, had set on Ike with a vengeance.

Another time, he had said wistfully, "I guess they won't call you Turnip at school any more."

"Why not?"

"Well, if they tried, you could take out your Remington 1100 and blow their heads off." After that, he used to hear Isaac boasting to his friends about Turner's deadeye. Whenever they ran into trouble with a teacher, Isaac said, "We'll get my kid brother to *obliterate* old Ellsworth with his Magnum at one hundred yards blindfold."

"I don't *have* a Magnum," said Turner, who didn't like being reduced, colonized to "my kid brother," or, for that matter, having his talent co-opted for such infantile use. Isaac, who didn't take anything seriously, always got things wrong, just like their mother, but in her it was forgivable: he loved her and expected nothing of her. Isaac was a man.

Preston had a mug of milky coffee in the drinks holster that slopped over his knees whenever the truck hit potholes where spring floods' depredations had washed away the macadam and the road hadn't yet been repaired. "Hey, Turner, tell your dad to scare up more money from the state to fix the goddamn road." His dad had just become a town selectman.

They were heading east to a great brown plain past Walcott, a knotted thicket of prairie land where grouse and woodcocks congregated. Preston slugged coffee, sang back to *Tannhäuser* on the tape deck, and chattered—if you can call the conversation of a man of two hundred pounds with a pitted face covered with black beard "chatter": he loved to sound off, and better even than sound off he loved to be listened to. Turner, though close-mouthed, was not always a very responsive listener, but Preston's talk he relished.

They had met the year before, when Preston was building a new barn for the Karolises. Mike Karolis and Turner hung around every day after school, watching the pine skeleton rise and soaking in the builders' talk of the weekend's sport. When Turner confessed to the older man that he wanted in the worst way to learn to shoot, their friendship was cemented.

The next weekend Preston telephoned Turner. "You want to come on over and exercise your constitutional rights?"

"Huh?"

"The right of the people to keep and bear arms shall not be infringed. I'll pick you up in an hour."

Turner was grateful. Once he quit school sports, it seemed as if time would never end.

That first day fooling around with the air rifle, Preston pronounced him a natural. The rest of the afternoon was spent sitting out on the back step of the trailer in the Indian summer heat, talking. Preston, swigging beer from the can, showed him the plans for the new house, replete with many rooms for the babies he was planning to spawn off his wife, Suzanne, and then told the boy a little about his own history and how he came by his ideas about the world, how as a young radical in the sixties he'd dropped out of school in Boston and come to Jessup County to be a carpenter and live off the land.

"And look what happened: ten years later I got my own construction business, me and Stash employ three men, I got a wife and two mortgages, I make a bucket of money, and I'm still up to my neck in debt. An American story."

He found himself getting more and more conservative as the government got increasingly "yellow abroad and confiscatory at home." "If you want to see action, learn Spanish," he advised. "Next battleground is America del Sur for sure. Or the Philippines. Geostrategically, the Philippines are where it's at: lose them, and between Cam Ranh Bay and Clark and Subic, the Soviets got the Indian Ocean tied up in red knots, no help till South Africa, which the Sovs are bound to get sooner or later. Might as well float our subs in the bathtub. If Ronald Reagan wants to make forty million people very happy, first thing he'll do in office is declare the Philippines a U.S. colony again."

"Do you think he'll win?"

"You think the American people want four more years of inflation and gas lines and hostages? National malaise, bullshit. Only national malaise we got is sitting in the Oval Office. I can't wait to send that smarmy constipated Bible thumper back to Plains, Georgia. I'm all for the rights of the unborn, but when it comes to the born-again, forget it."

Two things had changed Preston's mind. One was paying taxes, the other was what happened in Vietnam after the Americans left. "I was against the war," he explained. "I still would be, since we didn't have the balls to help our boys win it. But if you have a party in someone else's house, you clean up afterward, and you lock the door after you: you don't let in the thundering hordes. They trusted us, we left 'em genocide, a bloodbath.

"This steams me: you get these Vietnamese who've been ten years in the *gulag*, orphans, widows, starving men, they set sail in a leaky boat, get savaged on the high seas by Thai pirates, finally land half-dead on our American shores and what happens? They work, they save, and then they get their skulls bashed in by some inner-city dead-head whose feelings are hurt because the Asians have it so easy. If it were up to me we'd open our borders and let everyone in who wants to enjoy our blessed liberty and opportunity. Like Stash."

Stash's family had come from Yugoslavia when Stash was a little boy. He grinned. "*Everybody*? No way. After me, a closed door. I don't want to let in all the riffraff, to come sniffing after my daughters."

Preston was seized by a few great passions: for guns and hunting and Nietzsche and Wagner. He read voraciously, everything all mixed up together, *The Twilight of the Gods* spliced with *Guns and Ammo*. Turner in an unguarded moment had confided to Isaac his friend's intellectual interests. Isaac snorted. "Nietzsche and Wagner! That's like saying you like hot dogs and—and—*wallpaper*. Not only are they utter frauds, they're utter opposites. You know how Nietzsche described Wagner? As one of the great charlatans of a moralistically mendacious age."

To Turner, maintaining you couldn't have two heroes just because they didn't like each other was like saying your pants had to match your sweater. But that was Isaac, who would sooner die than let anyone else look good. Everything (and Isaac sure had everything) wasn't enough for him; he had to be sure nobody else had anything.

From then on Turner made all the surer to keep his hero and his home life separate. Preston didn't know Isaac looked down on him; he thought Isaac a wonder boy, always asked after him. *All* the town asked after Isaac. People were always coming up to Turner and his mom with plans to put Ike on game shows and win big bucks, make them all famous. Last big deal who had come out of Gilboa was Mike O'Riordan, who'd opened up a steakhouse on Route 101 after being dropped by the Redskins. People only came back home if they bottomed out.

With Ike around, it seemed like nothing was left for Turner to be

good at. Nothing but those more masculine pursuits and responsibilities Ike belittled—hunting, saving money, looking after their mother;
and even in these Turner was no better than indifferent. His only
chance was in remaining invisible, lying low.

And yet he was proud of his smart brother, too, who brought honor
to the Hookers—something Isaac, egotistical, who seemed to think he'd
sprung to earth fully fledged and self-created, owing nobody, would
never be able to understand.

It was lighter out now, light enough to tell it was going to be a raw
dreary day. A listless dawn, fog smothering the naked brown furrowed
fields, a sulfurous sun just hinted at, too weak yet to cut a swath
through the clouds, and the hills all around plump, rotund, the rusty
gray-brown of a grouse's breast. As they drove east, mountains flattened out to the broad dreamy lows of the Connecticut Valley, cultivated land. They passed reeky farms, by whose fences lumbering
sour-mouthed cows bumped each other's bums in the fog, udders swollen and swinging, waiting to be milked. Turner spotted another hunter,
in his orange blaze, rooting among rows of dead corn stalks, looking
lonely and purposeful.

Stash and Preston were discussing the talk afoot to regulate lead
shot, and switch hunters over to steel. Both had tried steel shot. Preston
was bitching: nothing sacred. Stash was more philosophical: "You get
used to it. You just load different, that's all: No. 2 steel for No. 4 lead-
shot loads."

"I don't like getting used. Anyway, steel's got no velocity. You might
as well shoot peas, or rubber bands."

"It'll get better, once they develop powder that burns even. I tell you
the advantage: real extra-deep penetration, like little missiles. Steel
don't flatten out like lead when it hits the bird. I tried steel shot last
weekend with Randy: got the goose deader than dead, clean hole front
and back—you could see where the shot went *outa* him."

"Nothing sacred," Preston repeated. "No lead in your tank, no lead
in your shot, no smoking in movie theaters, no muddy feet in the house.
What's left?"

They had reached Walcott now. Preston pulled the truck over, parked
sideways up a dirt road, made them sit while he finished his cold gray
coffee ("rocket fuel"), loaded the guns. They dismounted, the three of
them and Isolde, Preston's bird dog, a butter-yellow animal, rangy,

long-legged, with a perpetually guilty grin on her sweet mug. Preston called her a setter, but she was the daughter of a generous and popular mother. If she were a painting you would have called her "School of English Setter" or "Workshop of English Setter" at best.

It was a widish covert, a tangle of dry bristly underbrush of juniper and weeds and blasted blackberry bushes, bordered by forest and brook, with a broken-down barn in the middle (birds like ruins). Preston boasted of days when he'd bagged four grouse and a woodcock in five shots.

They strode into the underbrush, Isolde off and slashing ahead, doubling back, gorgeous and tentative, quivery. When she pointed, Preston warned, "She don't mean it: she's just being polite."

Most guys used electric shocks to teach dogs not to flush too soon, but Preston held out tenderly: if he couldn't teach her himself, he might as well give up the game. It meant an edgier shoot and they missed more birds than need be. It was an hour before she pointed in earnest, holding the grouse until it flushed right under Stash's feet, with a whir like a helicopter taking off, doubling back for cover, rising dappled, delicious against a dull sky. Turner watched as Preston leveled his shotgun, pinned the bird, and then stood back, waiting for one prolonged and lordly moment till it climbed. He fired, and missed, and fired again, and it fell, catapulted from the sky with a surprising velocity, a cloud of sharp-smelling thunder, landing somewhere in the brush.

"Dead bird, dead bird," he nudged his mutt, and Isolde took off, leaping through the grasses, whining, came to a wiggling halt, dived, nosed, and finally, plumed tail waving frantically, bounded back to them, bird in her slobbery jagged maw.

"Sweet girl, what a gentle mouth you have," cooed Preston, extracting the grouse, which, heartbeatless, wings fanned out, was reduced to an ornament, an artifact, like an Indian headdress, a medicine bag of dappled feathers and pin-thin bone.

It was another stretch of vain starts before Isolde froze once more to signal the men forward. Three steps and the grouse's mate jumped out suddenly, scurrying through the underbrush and breaking cover only toward the end of the run, a little far for comfort, with a loud terrified clamor of wing beat.

"She's yours, take her," Stash ordered Turner, or at least that's what Turner through the earplugs thought Stash might have said, but he wasn't sure. But Stash was standing back, so, flustered, he went after the rising bird, Preston's litany drumming in his ears: "Wait. Aim over, hold above, swing, follow through." Oh, he dearly loved that climbing winger and wanted to bring her down, but he waited too long, drinking in her jerky gait, her muted beauty, until she'd climbed above his holding point, and *then* he fired. At least he thought he fired, but no kick, no bruising recoil, no smoky powder from an open barrel, no empty. Just two men standing thigh-high in the brambles, grinning at him, and a busy dog. "The widow flew the coop," said Preston.

Turner rubbed his face, dazed. "What happened?" he asked.

The two men burst out laughing. "I guess she got away." Turner cursed himself silently, wanting to die. Had he really? Could he have? Just let her go, open-mouthed? Not even shot, worse than missing. *Much* worse. And he'd hogged the bird, so no one else could get it, either! Weren't they angry at him, really? So few grouse—just to let one go like that, what a dope.

"I never knew you were such a preservationist." And, winking at Stash, "You know, most young guys shoot too soon. Boy, are the girls ever gonna eat you up."

It was cold, it was raw, it was raining, and Turner's boots leaked. They followed Isolde's wavering, frantic, doubling-up lead, west, east, southwest, east, springing off after a whole flock's stale feeding trail. Turner hadn't fired, but still there was something so keen and exciting in the air and his lungs were flooded by gratitude at the men's good nature. Jeez, how tactful they were, what great guys, not only to forgive him but to put him at ease after spoiling their sport, what large souls. He was almost glad he'd done such a dumb thing, just to learn the extent of their goodness. They weren't just smart and knowledge-able, first-rate builders, but kind-hearted men too, and he wished he hadn't ever underestimated Stash, thought him a bit boring. And here they were all together, the three of them, out in the thicketed wilds, tramping.

Grouse were hiding somewhere—where?—underfoot, somewhere in that thicket, tiny hearts racing. They knew a scenting predator was onto them, they were cunning birds, but they had a shorter sense of time than humans, they would wait what seemed to them forever and then break and run, dart for yards, under brush, zigzag. Or Isolde would scent them out, and then a loud startled flurry of wing beating, a rise, a wait, a fire, a fall.

Turner hung back behind the others, reveling in the chill, in a wind so fierce it sucked the tears from your eyes up your nostrils, so cold it made your toes swell up and wish they could die. He felt almost sick to his stomach with suspense, tasting the prospect of infernal din and smoke, the prickliness under his feet, the glory of brown bird against gray sky. He hoped—he trusted—he would shoot that day, hating the roar and recoil and loving it, wanting more, hoped (he was too old to pray) he would hit his bird that day, would bag one of his own. Maybe two.

Already in his head the shoot was over, they were driving home wet and bushed, to Preston's house, not the trailer, the one he lived in now off Barton Road. There, in its tight, stoop-ceilinged kitchen, they would pluck and breast the grouse, and Suzanne would down them in a pan. They would eat them just like that, pan-fried, except Turner, who wasn't much of an eater. Grouse and fried potatoes and beer, a movie on the VCR. Suzanne liked war movies, too. When women were bloodthirsty, they were bloodthirstier than men, Preston pointed out. Aw, come on, Suzanne, I know you wouldn't hurt a grasshopper. And after the movie—Preston and Stash always talked through it, and Suzanne would hit her husband with a pillow to shut him up—he would run Turner home, motor idling in the Hookers' drive while he wound up what he was saying about *Rheingold* or the war in Angola.

Already in Turner's mind it was Sunday night, and he was back in his cold narrow bed listening to the mouse behind the baseboard, dreading the school week to come, dopey kids, work he didn't understand, Mrs. Ailes who complained he didn't write with feeling. But what did she want? What kind of feeling?

So he clung fiercely to this moment, while the grouse were still hiding, still lying low, not yet routed, not yet rising and scattering in fast panicky loops. *This* moment, this one, let it not move, not pass away, and his knees faltered, and he nearly swooned from the desperation of secret joy. Let it always be him and Preston and Stash and the eager bitch, always a black November morning, always eight o'clock on a cold frostbitten Walcott plain.

Chapter 3

"HAVE ANY OF YOU ever seen an angel? *I* have," he said. The minister had a moon face with a chalky pallor to it, as if the moon really were made of green cheese. His eyes were perfectly round globes with much rolling white encircling a velvety brown. He was young but balding, and the retreat of his wispy hair presented another pale globe to match the two in his eye sockets. His head reminded Isaac of the grandfather clock in the town library, a moon from whose gold-notched cheeks were cut blue swatches of stars that told the progress of the lunar cycle. His high sweet voice, impatiently inflected, articulated a kind of syncopated tune that Isaac found catchy despite himself. The minister seemed by turns wound tight with the tension of conviction (as if faith were a jerky-taut length of string) and then suddenly limp, boneless, like a stuntman easing into a long fall. Isaac was sitting so close he could see the pearls of sweat standing out on his forehead. Why do bald men sweat more? he wondered.

"Yes, I've seen an angel. And what's more, so have you, whether you knew it or not. I say 'angel,' and you think of a dimpled rosy tot with wings and halo. But that's not who wrestled with Jacob till daybreak at Jabbok, spraining his thigh, and that's not who Mary Magdalene and Mary, mother of James, and Salome saw sitting on Jesus' sundered tomb. And those pink-and-gold Pillsbury doughboys wouldn't have done Lot much good in Sodom. 'Angelos' means messenger, someone sent by God. I believe we all of us have angels appear at different crossroads in our lives. I believe I might be an angel, and you might at times be an angel, and we all know Mrs. Hurd is an angel." (The judge's wife who provided punch and cookies after the service and organized church dinners and bazaars ducked her head, brown eyes blinking shyly behind pearly harlequin spectacles as everyone else laughed and applauded.)

"An angel," continued Mr. Popper, "doesn't always come down from on high in flaming raiments. An angel can be humble and modest, self-effacing, an angel can be a regular Sumo wrestler, for so Jacob found, an angel can be your wife on an icy highway telling you you're driving too fast, slow down. Of course, we don't always appreciate our angels." He got another laugh for that. Condescending twit, muttered Isaac.

"I want to tell you about a harrowing night which, to me, brought forcefully the lesson of how we might act angelically, sent by God, in each other's lives. You all remember my father, minister of St. Andrew's thirty-five years, and you know he passed away two summers ago, but I don't think you know the circumstances.

"My father and mother were vacationing in the White Mountains, staying at the Conway Inn. After dinner their second night my father collapsed in the hall. My mother, a fragile woman, was frantic. Suddenly, the door opposite opened, and a fellow guest appeared—a pleasant, inconspicuous person who came to my mother's aid with the most gentle and womanly dispatch, searching out a doctor staying at the inn, telephoning my sister and me and telling us to come straightaway, sitting by my mother's side, comforting her, strengthening her, persuading her to seize an hour or two's sleep while she waited for us to complete that six-hour drive—the wildest and most agonizing drive of my life, with every slow-moving truck, every stop sign seeming a malicious, diabolic obstacle against our ever seeing Daddy alive. Who knew what awaited us at that Conway Inn?

"When we got there, my father was already dead. And at my mother's side was this stranger, who offered us words of comfort and withdrew, leaving us alone with our strange new grief. When later I asked her name, she told me, saying, 'My husband is a friend of your father's.' Funny, I thought, my father has many friends, but I had never heard him mention that man. She went her way, after helping me embark on that gruesome mechanical procedure one undergoes whenever a human soul leaves its body. And when I took my mother home, and tiptoed into my father's study to sit alone at that desk where he had sat so many years, reading and thinking and writing and receiving you, his parishioners, there on his typewriter was an unfinished letter. And who was it addressed to but this woman's husband of whom I had never heard, to the husband of this angel with gray hair and sensible shoes, whom God sent to help my mother bear in a strange and public place the loss of all that was dearest and most familiar to her.

"I never saw my mother's angel again, the wife of my father's unknown friend, but I know we remember each other in our prayers. And so let us, too, try to be angels to our fellow wayfarers in their dark nights of the soul. And, angels, let us pray, now in the light of common day, and every day of our lives."

The pale moon-faced young man paused, and in the pause before the prayers took up again Isaac leaped to his feet and shoved his way along the pew, down the short aisle, and out the door, into a dark and grisly November noon. He glanced right and left to make sure no one had caught him visiting the house of prayer, and hurried off along Church Street and down to the bridge.

Angel . . . angel . . . angel . . . well, that wasn't very inspiring. No, that's not what an angel is at all. But to think of one's father dying in a strange place . . .

Dead Sunday: it was enough to make you dislike God, the way he'd chopped up the week, and canceled out one day from seven. A day of rest, indeed: people rested too much already as it was. No one abroad. Everyone locked up behind doors, watching television. "It's Protestantism," pronounced Isaac, aloud. "That killjoy censoriousness. I bet in Catholic countries they don't mope at home on their day off—no, they sit in cafés in the sunshine and watch the girls go by. I think I'll go live in Madrid or Lisbon. Angels . . . messengers . . . I wonder who my angel is. Will I ever be an angel to anyone? Doesn't seem likely."

He had reached the river now. Across the Ashuelot from Gilboa's massive red-brick textile mill was the satellite town where in its boom days mill hands, among them his great-grandfather, once lived in tiny row houses, which even now had a bellicose and unsavory reputation. Isaac crossed the oxidized green suspension bridge that held at steely arm's length Gilboa proper from its thrusting western brother, and stopped midway to lean over and stare at the river below. The molten sky was reflected in the dull metallic water, and on its mudbank shores, just by the foot of the bridge—which served as motel for the young, desperate, and hardy—lurked a few town toughs, one in Day-Glo orange earmuffs, stamping their feet to keep warm. Orange earmuffs waved at Isaac in great calisthenic sweeps like a signalman, and Isaac, recognizing John Pulaski's gorilla arms, saluted. He hated waving, made him feel like a fool. What if they weren't waving at you—then you looked pretty stupid. Smoking dope probably, better move on before they asked him to join them, and he would have to pass the time of day awhile before making his excuses, avoid explaining where he was going.

And that was quite funny, really: three, four years ago if he'd run into that gang of bully boys, he'd be sure they'd pick on him, taunt him, steal his hat. In ninth grade John Pulaski's ambushing had sent Ike into such a fury at the brutality of the world and his own craven impotence that he had almost gotten himself suspended—the outbreak of his war with Mrs. Cartwright, his first realization that nothing was fair and that he had to learn to fend for himself. Now, at almost eighteen, he got a little respect from those clods, if only because he was bigger than most of them and strong, which made life simpler, and also disgusted him. What was John Pulaski, now a crane operator at the quarry, but a lobotomized brute, a gormless steer soon to be saddened by the discovery that, once past high school, size doesn't count for much.

By now he had crossed over into the western side of Gilboa, with its low houses covered in yellow asbestos siding, through whose net curtains blue images flickered depressingly. They should ban television, that's what; it made people forget how to talk. Take his mother: addicted to the hum of bright, tinny voices, resentful if you dared interrupt the singing salesmen's blandishments, she watched the screen as fixedly as a cat guards a mousehole. *You* watch B thrillers at 3:40 A.M., she countered, what's the difference? You're not trying to have a serious conversation with me at 3:40 A.M., Ike insisted, that's the difference.

He lolloped up Franklin Street almost at a skip, turned into the yellow linoleum-floored vestibule of a shabby house.

"Who is it?" piped a sharp voice through the door, one flight up.

"Hooker, Isaac," bellowed our hero, and a second later he was wiping his muddy sneakers on a ruby-red Oriental carpet that covered the floorboards of a one-room studio-apartment.

"Isaac! Take off your shoes!"

He did, reluctantly: one sock was gray, one was a mangy green, one had no heel, and from the other a big toe rudely stuck out, red, wet, and embarrassed. She would notice. She noticed everything.

Sure enough, "Doesn't your mother even *clothe* you? What can she be thinking of, letting her sons run around in the winter half-naked?" And just as Isaac had forgotten his embarrassment in amusement at her unfailing ability to find any excuse to insult his mother, she leaped up from the sofa where she had been stretched out, reading, and before he could stop her, grabbed his stinky sneakers and deposited them beneath the radiator to dry.

"Who needs socks?" Isaac objected. "The Red Army conquered Hitler with rags wrapped around their ankles."

"Yeah, and they all died of disease before—"

"You have to die some—"

"*Infectious* disease."

When Isaac first laid eyes on that apartment, he felt a great wave of sentimental pity at its doll-sized tininess—a spinster's quarters in miniature—mixed with wonder at Miss Urquhart's handiness and the profusion of beautiful things tucked away.

But why did she live there? Nobody lived in Gilboa, especially not West Gilboa. You lived in one of the outlying villages or in the country. Downtown had gone into a dangerous slump once the mill closed down; boarded-up department stores, the library, one lone pizza parlor specializing in subs and grinders. Even doctors' offices had moved out to Route 101. Lifeless and dangerous, too. The Urquharts, a prosperous landowning family of lawyers, farmers, ministers, owned a red-brick Federal farmhouse near Sturgis, in which she had grown up; her younger brother, Joe, and his family now lived there. But Miss Urquhart lived in town, on the 200 block of Franklin Street on whose ramshackle roofs lit-up reindeers and Santas danced six months of the year, a block that figured prominently in the Gilboa *Recorder*'s police blotter, home territory for any number of youths arrested for stealing stereos or hot-rodding cars or beating up their girlfriends' fathers. These hoods were her neighbors, and he'd seen her chattering gaily to fellows who looked like they ought to be making license plates. When he thought about her coming home alone at night, it made him blanch.

The apartment was one room fourteen by eighteen (Isaac had measured), with a stove, sink, and refrigerator on one side, along with a closet containing a toilet. You used the kitchen sink to brush your teeth, and there was a tin claw-footed tub beside it. Miss Urquhart had done a job: stripped the floors of linoleum, the doors and window sashes of cheap paint jobs, and had whitewashed the room into a tall-ceilinged luminous square, put down her rich Oriental carpet, encased all the walls in whitewashed bookshelves—she even slept against a wall of books, on a plump brocade sofa of a dusty pink that unfolded into a bed at night. Long billowy rosy-gold curtains framed her bay windows, which looked out on tangled backyards deep in rusty bicycles and coffee cans and discarded spare parts; in front of the windows stood a kitchen table, where Miss Urquhart worked and ate. The room looked like a ship's cabin; so snug and compact and workmanlike was Miss Urquhart's room that whenever Isaac visited he thought to himself with a pang, "If *I* lived in a room like this, just think how much I'd get done!"

"Why weren't you at church?" he said now, accusingly.

"I was playing hooky," replied Miss Urquhart.

"Well, you missed a doozy of a sermon. Your young man was in fine fettle."

"Are you being sarcastic?" she asked. "What was it about?"

"It was about angels. Now, angels is an electrifying subject as far as I'm concerned, but your Mr. Popper's idea is not of Rilke's 'Creation's pampered favorites,/mountain-ranges, peaks growing red in the dawn/ of all Beginning,—pollen of the flowering godhead,/joints of pure light, corridors, stairways, thrones,/space formed from essence, shields made of ecstasy,' but of some gray-haired lady in flat shoes who came and held his mom's hand when his dad croaked. That's not just sappy, it's harmful to be so *willfully* prosaic, so demystifying. There's no transcendence whatsoever in this stone pit of yours, nothing hair-raising. Serves 'em right everybody's defecting to the fundamentalists. It's all milk and cookies. In fact, it makes me sick. If Mrs. Hurd's an angel, I'm voting for hell," he fretted, pacing up and down, wiggling his wet feet.

"Hmmmmm," said Miss Urquhart, disapprovingly. "Well, you see, that's just the point. Religion is supposed to be prosaic, ordinary. Like life."

"My life isn't prosaic," Isaac objected.

"No, your life is just a mess," retorted Miss Urquhart. "I'm trying to *make* your life prosaic, and as you can see, I'm doing a pretty good job. But you know what I mean. When the Reverend Popper tells you an angel is an old lady sitting with his mother when his dad died, he isn't saying there's no mystery in the world, but that holiness consists of small routine kindnesses done day after day."

"No, I'm sorry, but for daily routine, ordinary goodness, you don't need a God," said Isaac, decisively. "I know plenty of atheists who are much kinder than Catholics."

"You need faith and its legalisms to make kindness adequate and consistent. Your atheists may give the poor tons of money, spontaneously, out of the fullness of their hearts, but only by tithing—by something as automatic and mechanical as ten percent of your income, yearly—does charity become something that actually feeds and clothes the—"

"Oh, that's a total washout, Miss Urquhart. If tithing is what religion is about, it's been thoroughly supplanted by a much more equitable system called the progressive income tax. No, don't try and tell me the point of religion is it makes people good. Either it's good for you like jogging or yogurt, and the government imposes it on you just like it puts fluoride in our water, and I'm not having *any* of it, I'm going to decide for myself what's good, or whether or not I want to be good at all. Or it's true: there is a God, and he did create the world in seven days—"

"Six."

"—and he did send his only son down to die for our sins, and that's it. Truth. So which will it be, Miss Urquhart, am I to be a Christian because it's revealed truth or because Miss Urquhart thinks it'll keep me quiet?"

"Oh, I've given up hopes of *that* long ago." She stared at him hard as she laughed her high nervous laugh. "It's true. There is a God, and he created the world in six days, and he gave us certain laws and ideas to help keep us honest, and to remember and formalize that truth. That's all."

"Sounds like the Constitution of the United States to me. Can we vote in a new God every four years?"

"I think you better find someone more challenging than me to sharpen your wits on," Miss Urquhart replied. "Have you got an application for me?"

"It's the Sabbath. I'm resting. What's for lunch, anyway?"

"College," replied Miss Urquhart. "Do you want Harvard, Williams, Swarthmore, or Yale?"

"I guess I'm not so hungry after all. I haven't decided whether I'm going to graduate from high school or not."

"Well, I guess that's up to me, isn't it?"

God and college: these were the twin poles of Isaac's friendship with Miss Urquhart, around which they danced, fastening upon these set topics for conversation, meetings, jokes, as people do who are shy of each other or clumsy or fearful of rebuff. Not that each wasn't deadly serious.

Their friendship had begun over the question of religion, a question that had agitated Isaac since he could remember. Long gone were the days when he trotted avidly to Hebron's Church of Christ with

Grandpa and Grandma Hooker: by the age of eleven he had already rebelled like a red devil against even this thin broth of observance, deploying against the minister all his stockpiled artillery of aggressive disbelief. At thirteen he discovered quantum physics and told anyone who would listen that the world was an accident taking place in the suburb of an undistinguished galaxy, an imperceptible shrug of an unconscious shoulder, and human civilization an instant's random spasm. He had stoked up on scientific rebuttals of divine intent and gloomily cherished the utter awfulness of life without redemption, law, or meaning: there was, in fact, something dreadfully satisfying in all this negation, something noble in his refusal to be conned or consoled. And yet somewhere in him he harbored the understanding that all his talk was blasphemy, uttered with a fearful, hopeful eye cocked for thunderbolts, and he knew that without this sense of blasphemy, which is the obverse of a bowed knee, a bared head, of taking one's shoes off before the burning bush, no other kind of belief was possible, and that from it, eventually, a more positive faith despite himself might rise. Lord, I am not worthy to receive you, but only say the word and I shall be healed. In the meantime he bragged and ranted, hoping someone would stop him.

That someone was Miss Urquhart, and now he *still* didn't believe but he found church interesting.

Miss Urquhart was a redhead, with a milky skin daubed with freckles distinct and shocked-looking as raindrops. Her hair was a bobbed crown of a rich and brilliant auburn that stood out from her small skull in electric waves. She was tall and straight-backed as a lead soldier and so skinny you could pass her waist through a napkin ring, and she dressed expensively, in suits and silk dresses and high-heeled shoes, all of which made her quite unlike most of the other teachers at Ashuelot, who tended toward the stout and dowdy. She was also different in another way: many of Isaac's teachers cultivated a sort of canned bedside manner that gradually got more strained over the course of a day or week, as if they were social workers dispatched to mollify cranky incurables, and though some kids warmed to this false sunlight, well, Isaac was revolted by it.

But Miss Urquhart, who taught math, French, art history, was bristly and she yelled a lot, although she also commanded a sarcasm so piercing in its acoustics and import it sent shivers through the school. Perhaps it was this made Isaac for once relax, knowing he would never have to strain to catch her words or irritate her with his litany of "What?" Everyone else, however, thought her a harpy and a shrew.

She was one of those teachers who are bored by most of their students, and teach by making an example of an especially egregious case, and she fastened extra fiercely on those few who had brains but left them behind with their homework.

It was inattention she couldn't abide (though she was no lover either of outright stupidity), and when Isaac had asked why, she'd explained that inattention, like cowardice, seemed to her a kind of primer-coat vice without which the more colorful vices couldn't stick.

Isaac and Miss Urquhart were an accident in the making, for by senior year even Isaac was forced to agree that he had grown into something of a disaster, a swaggering rabble-rouser, an awkward and boastful misfit. He couldn't really blame his teachers for not liking him, for teachers quite naturally take no pride where they can take no credit. (Sam, who got wind of Isaac's reputation as a lazy wise guy, grieved that no one yet had cottoned onto his boy, but could do nothing: the more he talked him up to his colleagues, the frostier the looks he got.) And Isaac, in turn, who did his homework between telling stories on the school bus in the mornings, made it abundantly clear to them that his real work, his serious reading, was done elsewhere and for his own pleasure, and that as a consequence he regarded school as a social club in which to relax with his friends, let off steam. There were days when six of the class's term papers on American history or *Julius Caesar* had obviously been composed by Isaac Hooker, trying out different attitudes.

What was one to do? As Mr. Ellsworth complained to his pal Sam, "I don't know whether to give him an A or an F. I don't know whether to give everyone else in the class an A or an F. I'd like to suspend them *all*. Anyway, any kid who's got six different ideas about *Julius Caesar* is psychotic. I don't even have one idea about it: it's a boring play."

At recess and between classes, Isaac sat rocking and slump-backed, dictating homework while ten smaller boys eagerly scribbled. He was strong, too; it was his favorite habit to play Gulliver to a crowd who would jump on him from behind only to be shaken off again, as Isaac arose from flailing arms and legs like a dog emerging from the water.

And yet this was the terrible fact: that all his foolery, all his learning were in vain, because inside he was eaten up, wretched, aflame, because he could think these days of only one thing, and that thing was a torment to him. It was girls, and girls, and then girls again, and try as he might to think of *real* things, all he could think about was legs and stomachs and behinds, about ramming them, burying himself in them; he hated, worshiped, was going crazy for female curves, guile, gamesomeness; he wanted horribly to make a girl submit to his vicious, bestial, unspeakable desires, to bind and fetter all that flesh, hair, laughter, to engorge and be engorged by it.

Even an atheist had no choice but to believe in the devil who made men's bodies an itchy furnace to them and made them turn other human beings—women—in their minds into animals. It was not much consolation knowing that all his friends suffered from the same problem: it was something to his mind private, too urgent, too violent, too degrading to be discussed; it was worse (unbelievable) hearing as his father had told him that lust subsides, blood quiets down, that someday he'd have as much of them as he could bear, and not care much one way or the other. "You'll be begging them to leave you alone," Sam assured him, but this was no subject to kid about.

When? How long, O Lord? And in the meantime he clowned (they weren't interested) and hated them and longed for them and wished he were gelded or dead. That was where Miss Urquhart had come in, a prim Presbyterian spinster with a tart tongue. Not that she'd cured his female problem, but that she'd shown him, for all her mocking, that standards and self-respect must be kept up, that there were important things to be done in the world, and maybe even behind it all, when he felt presumptuous enough to imagine something else in her insults and needling, that he wasn't such a misfit after all.

She was his senior-year homeroom teacher. Sinewy freckled arms folded, she watched him roughhouse with the boys, boast and clown before Suzie and Emily and Shawn and Elise, or on a bad day hide in the corner reading two books at once and picking his nose. She eavesdropped on his talk, sometimes pretending to be busy, sometimes openly, shaking her head and making faces of disbelief, or joining in with a scathing refutation of his wild claims. She was like that: passionately nosy, wanted to know what everyone was up to, but also made no bones about finding it quite babyish. He could tell she knew what was driving him crazy, and felt ashamed. When he saw her, he wanted to act sober, like a man, but the blood rebelled.

Now in class she swooped down upon him with a sarcasm like talons, drilling and ribbing him mercilessly.

"No flashy footwork, Mr. Hooker, just the answer" was her refrain.

"Let's keep Euclid out of this one," but Isaac could tell she sort of liked his talk. When explaining theorems she would say with an almost flirtatious glance at Isaac, "Mr. Hooker here would say that *x* can never be *pi* because after the Peloponnesian Wars the Greeks swore off *pi*, but the textbook says . . ." and the class would laugh appreciatively.

Even Sam learned—from the horse's mouth—that the terrible Miss Urquhart was sort of sweet on his boy, because one day she came up to him in the teachers' lounge, and said, with her awkward laugh (this was the funny thing about Miss Urquhart, that though she came from a good family she singularly lacked the social graces), "You know, your son's in my class this year."

"Well, good." Sam had never much taken to Agnes Urquhart, known her since she was fourteen, when she used to tag along after her older brother, always thought her stringy and uptight.

"He's a big boy, and he's got big ideas," continued Miss Urquhart, "but there's nothing *bullying* about him."

And though it had never occurred to Sam that any child of his *might* be a bully, he was all at once ludicrously happy that Isaac wasn't one. When he got home that night, he gave Isaac an extra-wet kiss on the head. "You know, I always thought Agnes Urquhart had a rod up her ass," he told Mattie. "But she's not such a pill, after all. Just a bit shy."

It was some time, though, before Isaac and Miss Urquhart became friends. One afternoon after school, he was hanging around her desk, snapping her rubber bands, unwinding her paper clips while she snatched away her hardware before his blind advancing grasp. He was wishing all the girls were like her—ladies, that is—and waiting, really, for her to tell him to get going, for Isaac could hardly get himself from one place to another without a kick in the pants.

Instead, she asked in sudden seriousness, "Why were you telling your friends just now that religion is a 'mug's game'? Where do you even get such a silly expression? Do you believe what you say?"

Isaac looked up at the clock. The bus had already gone; his father would be leaving any minute. He weighed the possibilities—a six-mile hike, unless he thumbed a ride—and answered a little hesitantly, thinking—hoping—she would be shocked, "I don't believe in God."

"Obviously. But has it ever occurred to you you might have got things backwards?" said Miss Urquhart. "Maybe God doesn't believe in *you*."

Isaac was surprised.

"After all, there are five billion people in the world, and only one God—why should he believe in you?"

Isaac for once was at a loss for words, and then they both began to laugh.

"You know, I tell you what I don't like about you atheists: you're all so dogmatic and closed-minded," Miss Urquhart pursued. "My profession is math, and math is a hard science, or so they *say*, but even I feel science has got its limits, and that's where faith begins. There's nothing hard and fast in science, at all. It's all contingency and slipperiness: as soon as you say something, it begins not to be so true after all. I spend a week a year drumming into your heads the axiom that parallel lines never meet, and is it true? Not in the least. The universe is full of jokes: those jokes are God."

Isaac looked at her with a new interest. He had never heard her say so many words all at once; she usually just asked questions. Nasty ones.

"What do you mean, atheists are closed-minded?" he asked, a little stung.

"Well, I keep up with the latest books on genetics and quantum physics, but I don't see too many of you fellows who have even *read* the Bible, which teaches you a lot more about what makes man man than Biology 101."

"The *Bible*?" aped Isaac, scratching his head. "Is it any good? Who wrote it? Isn't it just a bunch of 'begats'?"

"I read somewhere once that W. H. Auden wrote that poets live off those 'begats.' Anyway, you ought to like them: that's where your genetic codings come from. If I thought you were capable of getting up by nine A.M. on a Sunday morning, I'd make you come to church with me, just so you'd know a little more about what you were denouncing. Anyway, what have you got against mugs?"

"I have no problem *whatsoever* rising at nine on a Sunday morning, Miss Urquhart," replied Isaac, with dignity. "It just takes a hand grenade to do the trick, that's all. How many pieces do you want me in?"

It was their first date. "Where are you off to, anyway, you sneak?" wondered Sam, who drove a sleep-bound Isaac into town next Sunday morning early. He was devoured by curiosity at the sight of his son, up at the crack of dawn, his hair slicked back, wearing clean pants and stuffed unhappily into a buttondown shirt of his grandfather's. "Are you joining the Army?"

"Ummpph," said Isaac, which was about as much hard information as one could expect to elicit from a teenage son, and added cryptically, "It's sort of a dare."

The two of them met at the Civil War monument in Central Square and climbed the hill to St. Andrew's. Miss Urquhart strode briskly and scolded. "What a *dawdler* you are. Didn't anyone ever tell you to pick up your feet when you walk?"

"When I pick up my feet, I only put 'em in my mouth," Isaac retorted.

Miss Urquhart cast him a loving look. "I wonder whether you'll like the minister at all. We were at school together, and I always expected he'd go on and be a lawyer or something—anything to get out of his dad's way. You're a teacher's son, so you know what it's like having things *expected* of you, just because of who you are, but it's ten times worse having your daddy a minister: all the ministers' children I ever knew wound up either goody-goodies or utter basket cases, and once in a while both. But Duncan's all right."

Congregationalists build in clapboard, Episcopalians and Presbyterians in stone. St. Andrew's was a mossy stone church, eyed in ruby-red windows, and to Ike's surprise packed to the gills with young couples and babies and teen-agers. After they seated themselves, Isaac whispered to Miss Urquhart, "I have read it."

"Read *what*?"

"*It*."

"*What*?"

"Holy Writ."

"I should hope so. And quit whispering, young man, you've got plenty to pray for." When Isaac was done muttering inconsolably to the aspect of himself, projected high, that he imagined to be God, she added, in a sharp whisper, "Well, read it again. Properly, this time. You know, there's a right and a wrong way of reading."

The service began. Isaac was at once repelled and fascinated by a certain sly knowingness in the young minister's bearing and by his familiarity with God, whom he seemed to regard as a vast warm shoulder, a sympathetic ear, someone always ready for a chat. "Easy, vulgar, and therefore disgusting," he muttered, distractingly conscious of the woman at his side, sitting closer to him than he was used to with anyone but his mother: he could hear the even intake of her breath, which smelled like an infant's—she sucked wintergreen Lifesavers—and the rustle of her silk dress, could see her white-boned knees protruding from the pleats, knees knobby as umbrella handles, and the long curve of her thighs sprung like an archer's bow beneath the false liveliness of the silk. She was a jock, he knew, and her body, like a good dog told to sit, was waiting patiently until once more it could dive into motion. How different was this consonance between spirit and limbs from his own loathsome disjunctions!

This new way of thinking about his teacher was so forbidden and yet, once it had begun, so natural and persuasive that Isaac found himself all knotted up in a painful dialogue between mind and body, in which the mind almost wept from frustration at the perverse, un-governable grossness of the beast to which it was yoked. Yes, God is a joker, all right. Why else store human wit and conscience in a house with *this* on its door? A house run by its doorbell, hostage to every passing trick-or-treater. I'm going to become a monk. Yes, I will. A Trappist monk. That'll show 'em. And when Isaac thought of how his mother would react, he chuckled aloud.

"Well?" They were walking down the hill after church.

"Well, what?" said Isaac, grudgingly, not looking at her, humming to himself. When they had lined up after the service to greet the minister, Mr. Popper at the sight of Miss Urquhart let out a great whoop of delight, enveloping her in a hug and two kisses right there on the church steps, as if she were his goddamned bride-in-Christ. It sort of spoiled Isaac's idea of her, to say the least: Miss Urquhart, whose tin-soldier figure instinctively reeled back from you as you talked, smartly avoiding contact, blushing with pleasure at that pouter pigeon's hamhock embrace.

"What did you think?" she pursued.

"He didn't exactly invent gunpowder, your Mr. Popper," he said in what was intended to be a withering tone. "I don't like this service of yours: it all seems a little crimped and bland. I mean, on one hand you've got this God who makes the hills leap like gazelles and hurls his thunderbolts at malefactors and sends us all to hell for denying his butchered son, and on the other hand what does he want you to do but turn around and give the guy in the pew behind you a nice friendly handshake and line up to nibble at that tasteless little wafer. Where's the blood and guts to it all? It's desiccated. It's not lifelike."

And yet, mysteriously, several weeks later Isaac found himself walk-ing into Gilboa early one Sunday to squeeze his large bottom once more into a narrow pew, to stare balefully up at the angular glass angel bending over the altar. Why not? His father was asleep, his mother was out, his friend Billy worked Sundays, Turner had sneaked off at dawn to go hunting with that blowhard behemoth contractor. Isaac went to church from curiosity, and just to show her he wasn't so closed-minded after all. He didn't believe, he still thought Christianity was moronic and Protestantism its prissiest subsect, and that if there *were* a God he must be splitting his sides laughing at the simpering, priggish way people talked about him. But there was something about standing up in a crowd of people most of whom he had never seen before and singing at the top of his lungs that pleased him enormously, and sometimes, praying, Isaac felt he was getting somewhere, a kind of taut and happy concentration. Anyway, he had thought he might find Miss Urquhart there.

After the service (Popper remembered him, and gave him a moist plump handshake and wise-guy smile), cross that Miss Urquhart wasn't there and unwilling to go home, he decided to try her apartment. There's no reason I shouldn't stop by and see her. She might be sick, and who would know? It would be rude not to, he told himself defiantly, circling round and round for a more clinching pretext for searching out Miss Urquhart in her own apartment, a place which was not only unthinkably off bounds to students but which, as far as he knew, *no one* had ever seen, except maybe for her brothers and sisters-in-law. For Miss Urquhart, again as far as anyone knew, had no boyfriends. (She was a little old for that, thirty or thirty-two at the very least.)

This question was often debated by her homeroom class. Just as Isaac remembered as a little boy wondering with a snicker if God went to the bathroom, in much the same way, Billy and Jason and Christina and Shawn and Suzie Hanesworth and even Macy Driscoll would crowd around Miss Urquhart's desk, begging her to tell them where she lived (they soon looked it up in the telephone book) and whether or not she had a boyfriend. Gilboa was a town of 22,000: you knew these things about people, yet Miss Urquhart was so stringent in her privacy, so prickly in her refusal to divulge the most impersonal biographical facts, that for a while it became a class game to spy on her, find out how old she was and whether she had ever slept with anyone— most people believed she was a virgin. It seemed only fair—she knew *everything* about them, and acted as confessor and judge (hanging judge, Isaac thought) to a class turbulent in its family tragedies and spats, its romances.

"I think Miss Urquhart's getting it on with Mr. Ellsworth," Christina Molina confided to Isaac and Billy.

"Uggh! With that fruitcake?" grimaced Billy. "Impossible. Anyway, he's got a wife and two kids."

"That never stopped anybody, you dork. Anyway, I saw them . . ."

"I don't care what you saw," interrupted Isaac, looking ugly. It offended him, this prying, and when he saw his classmates thronging around Miss Urquhart's desk, wheedling, he stayed away, half-fearful that enjoying the attention she might give in, reward their intrusiveness. It wasn't right: she was their teacher, you had to respect *something*, thought Isaac, hating his own prurience about this acerbic solitary woman. Besides, she was his.

He needn't have feared that she would give way to badgering. When teasing didn't deter them, Miss Urquhart repulsed their snooping with such haughty and indignant contempt that any student who wanted to be thought higher on the chain of life than the warthog learned to respect what the teacher regarded as her absolute and unassailable right to privacy. Isaac sighed in relief.

And so what demon propelled him across the bridge that Sunday to the lowdown bedraggled neighborhood of West Gilboa, which led him to her street, made him stare up at what he imagined to be her window. After three or four ambles around the block, Isaac summoned up courage, mounted the staircase, and knocked. When she opened the door a crack and saw his hot embarrassed face, Miss Urquhart was livid.

"What do you mean, showing up on my doorstep without any warning? Have you ever heard of common courtesy? Don't you know how to use a telephone?" Her long neck peered around the door like an irate crane.

Isaac sighed. "No, I've never heard of common courtesy," he said. "But only . . . say . . . the . . . word . . . and I shall be healed."

She stared at him a moment, exasperated, and it occurred to Isaac that she was wondering whether maybe he wasn't all there and that if she asked, which she was capable of doing, he wouldn't know what to say. No, not completely cracked, not all the time at any rate, but sometimes very close to it. Finally she ordered him to take a walk around the block while she straightened up, and then, still burning with resentment and clearly regretting her capitulation, she let him in. "Just for ten *minutes*, mind you: I've got work to do, and so do you, according to all your *other* teachers."

Once in the door, such was the transparent vehemence of Isaac's rapture at her apartment, his frank envy at its coziness, his insistence on examining and admiring every lamp and telephone jack, inquiring what kilim was and what the patterns on the carpet *meant* (even lifting a corner to see what the backstitching looked like), that Miss Urquhart was disarmed.

What the boy was responding to, she realized, was not only the room's airy shipshapeness, but its revelation of a world whose habits and encumberments he had never before seen. The heavy tobacco-smokened damask curtains falling in pleats linear and yet voluptuous as the Mother of God's draperies on the portal of a Romanesque church, the crumbling row of Waverley novels, the oriental carpet, the wooden chess set, all imported from her family's farmhouse and condensed, fitted like false teeth, into the new apartment's small square mouth, spoke to Isaac, in however modest and countrified a dialect, a new and delectable language—the language of money. Miss Urquhart was still embarrassed by the money, but this boy, loudly contrasting her brand of luxury to Preston's chrome-and-black-leather sofas, built-in stereo system, and glassed-in hot tub—the fanciest place he had seen to date—made such inhibitions impossible.

"I'm glad you can't see what *my* house looks like," he confessed naïvely, suddenly ashamed.

She brewed him a pot of strong tea, and though she still kept scolding him for having shown up uninvited, she forgot for a full hour to kick him out.

From that day forth, Isaac saw Miss Urquhart every Sunday. Some days he met her at church, mostly he came by her house afterward. He never called first, he just showed up, but she was always there and no longer surprised or displeased to see him. At home she wore blue jeans like everyone else, and without her heels she seemed smaller than she did in the classroom. Sometimes he would head straight for the bookshelf without even saying hello, grab three or four volumes, and plump himself down in her ladderback rocker. "You ought to get a more comfortable chair."

He did his homework at her kitchen table while she marked papers on the sofa. It was weird seeing his friends' scribblings whiz along her lap and hearing her exclaim in exasperation. He was used to it from his dad, but whereas Sam would look up from time to time to tell him, "Your friend Jason is a prize dunce." Or "Will you please tell your girlfriend Miss Molina that if she misspells Germany one more time I'm going *personally* to take her lavender lipstick and break it over her frizzed-out head," Miss Urquhart kept everyone's homework to herself, and when he asked her if she got satisfaction from her work or whether she really thought Macy Driscoll was all that smart, she would only smirk and say, "Wouldn't you like to know?" Which was in Isaac's opinion the dumbest answer known to man.

If he got there in time and she was in the mood, she served him lunch. Isaac would keep on writing, moving his work to his lap as she laid the table, put out the food. He talked all through lunch with his mouth full and his fork waving, torn between greed and expansiveness. "Don't worry," she chided, "that chicken's not going anywhere."

He wasn't accustomed to hot meals in the middle of the day, except at school, and it made him feel as if it were his birthday or Christmas. She was a good cook gone rusty from want of interest: the first time he'd come over he'd headed straight for the icebox, to be greeted only by four steel shelves and a waterlogged bag of browning celery. But though she made fun of his appetite, it became a kind of competition to see if she could cook him a larger potpie than he could polish off— it made her proud to feed him. Isaac ate anything—food was love. When she baked him a chocolate cake, he nearly died of joy.

"Does your mother starve you?"

Isaac just rolled his eyes; he never talked about his mother, and the more Miss Urquhart piqued him on the subject, the more he laughed, amused by how it pleased her to believe that their mother neglected them. If this was common wisdom around town, and not just an excuse to spoil him, well, too bad. For all her sharp eyes as a teacher, she didn't seem to know a lot about young people, and in her anxiety not to appear naïve she would ask him outlandish questions, determined to outguess the worst. Did he take a lot of drugs? Did all his friends? Did those heavy-metal bands the kids listened to really advocate devil worship? She asked him about his love life too; again he wouldn't answer, and he suspected that she was relieved he wouldn't, though she kept after him. Sam, on the other side, kidded him about "courting" his homeroom teacher ("Miss McCormick will be jealous," he warned —Isaac still visited the now-retired librarian), but even Sam didn't know it was Miss Urquhart Isaac haunted every Sunday. Well, not *every* Sunday, but almost, the way a dog returns to the same savory curb. It comforted him, it fortified him, he doted on her scolding, and besides she was quick-witted as a fox and intriguingly contrary; he wondered at her clever, independent way of thinking, and at the timidity behind her brashness. They argued a good deal, Miss Urquhart getting high-pitched, pink-faced, and indignant, Isaac patiently, immovably refuting her. Something odd was in the air: she would ask him what kind of insurance she should get for her car, which she rarely drove, or should she sell it, whether she should go to her brother's for Christmas or stay in town (for one wild moment he considered bringing her home); she would tell him that she thought she was paying too much in taxes, but couldn't be bothered to find herself an accountant. And without even noticing, Isaac had begun bossing her. In school she still kept him in the front row, where she could watch him, still called on him, but in a more respectful sort of way, as if he were a colleague, and when he roughhoused with younger boys sometimes he caught her looking at him in a funny sort of way.

Now, this Sunday after lunch she told him that he had to be going because she was expecting her brother and sister-in-law and their children to come by that afternoon.

"Can't I meet your family?"

"*No!*"

"Don't you like them?"

"It's you I don't like."

So here was Isaac back where he started, on the corner of Franklin Street, feeling unaccountably mournful and abandoned. He headed south, all at once eager to be out of town as fast as he could and feeling so blue it was enough to make him want to *hang* himself, the loneliness of life, this clever interesting woman who had money of her own and family, and yet *no one.* And yet she stayed so cheerful. Once, exasperated by her refusal to join in his general despair, he had asked her, "How come you're so damn *cheery* all the time? What's there to be so insufferably happy about?"

And Miss Urquhart had replied very seriously, as if she were letting him in on a big secret, "Well, every morning I get up at six and I stick my head out the window, and breathe in the fresh air and I thank God that I'm not seventeen any more." And Isaac, purposely ignoring this jibe, only muttered that he didn't believe she was really as self-satisfied as she made out.

He passed Domino's, which also served as a bus terminal for Peter Pan. In the doorway, hopping and jittering, were a hard-bitten peroxide-haired woman with a few dark teeth and a bottle of Thunderbird, screaming at a tiny child, and Wilson, everyone knew Wilson, a handsome, knew-he-was-handsome black man, very springy on his feet, poker-backed, but always looking at you as if he thought you might be looking at him, who spent much of his life making important business calls from the pay phone in Domino's while Isaac and his friends played video games. Now the woman was haranguing Wilson, who, narrow-eyed, responded from time to time, "Is that a fact?" And what was the point, how could they go on, Wilson or that lady or Miss Urquhart, or anyone.

Isaac cleared out of town at a gallop, not quite sure why he felt so blue, except that the world was going to rack and ruin, and hungry to be cheered up. "Who, if I cried out, would hear me among the angels'/ hierarchies?" he intoned mournfully as he loped. What did the Reverend Popper know about such despair? Almost without meaning to, he wound up down by the river again, this time farther upstream by the dam, where waters smooth as combed wet hair teased their way over the concrete, and roared into a liquid hurricane forty feet below.

> *For beauty is nothing*
> *but the beginning of terror, which we still are just able to endure,*
> *and we are so awed because it serenely disdains*
> *to annihilate us. Every angel is terrifying.*

So he declaimed to the howling watery chasm, whose spittle gleamed iridescent even under that molten sky. Every angel is terrifying: so much for family friends in flat shoes. Do angels wear high heels? Dreaming of Rilke's legendary women abandoned by their lovers, with their Italianate gasping names, guttural breaths of air—well, why couldn't Isaac too profess disdain of fleshly coupling, of the pathetic grabbiness of earthly raptures that evaporate like steam from a hot dish, and making his loneliness a matter of principle, forge a faith of the "soaring, objectless love." But Rilke, you who were *glutted* with beautiful passionate women, you could afford to deprecate such bliss. A filthy maid Isaac was, and doomed to remain so—forever? unless he could one day—when?—find someone so merciful as to accept his adoration and his person.

Unbearable, staring down into that white-water abyss, that hellish and lonely alliance of natural and human engineering: it made you want to jump. And yet he couldn't stop either. When he was done staring, and done wishing that poets still wrote so sublimely, and that Christina Molina, a girl he privately had named The Anti-Christ, would either emigrate to Tierra del Fuego or climb into his lonesome bed that very night, Isaac turned his back on the chasm and headed over to Route 4, where the Ostriches had recently moved their tire store.

"I might just look in, inspect the new premises, give Billy a hand," he said aloud, although in truth he was more bent on persuading Billy to go again to see the new Cassavetes movie, which was playing at the Marquis and which made Isaac wish he could lay down his life for that foul-mouthed honeyed empress, that frank loving moll, Gena Rowlands. A goddess, even Billy who was fairly phlegmatic on these issues agreed, way up there with Angie Dickinson, although Billy left to his own devices preferred them less mature. Billy Ostrich was Isaac's favorite friend since second grade. Whenever Isaac fought with his mother, it was Billy's house he ran to. The Ostriches all lived under one roof—grandparents, mother and father, Billy and his brothers and sister. He was a short boy with even shorter legs and a large head of duckling-silver hair that stood up straight as if he'd just woken up, a boy possessed of an imperturbably even temper and a certain modest confidence that made him very hard to aggravate, try as Isaac might.

The Ostriches ran the only garage that was open Sundays, and there was a long line of cars waiting outside. Inside, Billy and his brother Ted were busy changing tires. Isaac hung around, watching Billy sling a studded snow on the balancing machine and smartly hammer down the lead cleats once the balancer's tiny bubble floated to the center.

"Want to go see *Gloria*, Billy?"

"We seen it six times already." Billy, on his heels, grunted between bursts of the air wrench.

"Four."

"Too much business today, Ike."

"You like your new place?"

"Grandpa was glad to get out of Sturgis—property taxes too high." Until this week, the Ostriches had run the tire shop from a barn in their front yard. "Great location here on the road: we get a lot of cars going by, but it's all concrete and I don't like the bustle. When I get a moment to myself, no place to go except that field across the road. Back home, when business was slow, I could go out to the cow barn to think."

This was the funny thing about Billy: no matter what he was saying, he smiled. He would tell you with the same wide grin that his grandmother had just broken her hip and all the cows had jumped into the river. Billy was a swimmer. Tuesdays and Thursdays the two friends went over to Gilboa State, Ike to take a philosophy survey taught by a frightening lady with dyed black hair, penciled-in eyebrows, and a boozy breath, named Mrs. Duranty, Billy to use the pool. After class, Isaac would sprawl on the chlorine-steamy tiles, doing his homework and watching Billy swim laps, head down, begoggled, arrow-straight. Afterward Isaac's father would pick them up, take them for a milk shake and cheeseburger at McDonald's; Ike and Billy were perpetually starving. Sam liked Billy almost as much as Isaac did; he would sure get a kick out of Billy's having to go out to the cow barn to think.

"You sure you mean *thinking* and not *ruminating*, you old cud eater?" Isaac teased. "You know what happened to Nebuchadnezzar, the tyrant of Babylon? He spent seven years crazy, eating grass in the field like an ox. I suspect it was Daniel and the Israelites pushed him over the brink with their vegetarianism. Do you know there's a distinct link between vegetarianism and *flaccidity* of the brain?"

"Don't look at me, I gone back to beef eating years ago," said Billy, who recently had had his eye on a girl too spiritual to give carnivores the time of day.

The garage was busy, and Ted was giving Isaac dirty looks, and what with one thing and another it was gradually becoming clear to Isaac that he couldn't hang around much longer, holding up the boys' work. "I guess I oughta be going," he said mournfully, as a sort of question.

"Here, take a calendar," said Billy, handing him an "Ostrich Tire Co." calendar for 1980: its logo was an ostrich burying its head in a tire. "Take two, let your mom know what day of the week it is."

"My mom—" Isaac began, but Billy was already jacking up a Corolla. Back out on the road, he remembered he had meant to ask Billy whether Peter Karolis and Christina Molina were busted up for good and should he call her up for a date or would Peter take it amiss. But strangely enough, although Christina had his most sincere lust, what Isaac secretly was dying to find out was what Billy thought of Macy Driscoll and whether he agreed that there was a kind of creepy necrophiliac allure to her, which had to do with her spindliness. If you lay on her, you'd likely crack her little bones or smother her. Nothing would fit. She was so clever and so prudish it was tempting to humiliate her in public, as Miss Urquhart once had. Had she ever been kissed? Her teeth were tiny, close-jammed as a china doll's—she'd worn a retainer for years—and the thought of sneaking his tongue between these crocodile rows was physically unsettling. Don't think about it. Think about . . . logical positivism. Or a cheeseburger. These days excitement had become so chronic and insatiable that it occurred to him maybe he had bubonic plague or had caught airborne syphilis. That'd teach him a lesson.

It was dark by the time Isaac emerged from the Marquis, it was dark and he was hungry again, even after a king-sized cone of popcorn. "I could eat a *bear*," he said aloud with great conviction. And come to think of it, how dare it be dark already, how could it be so soon, one might as well live in Sweden, if the sun was going to conk out at 5 P.M., and at least have a pretext to drink grain alcohol and hang oneself at an early age. A mushy drizzle plummeting from the skies again, rain as big as freckles, and sticking out his tongue to catch the drops he wondered why the darkness of a misspent Sunday afternoon in November, the onset of winter, made him want to burst out crying, why the muddy violet of twilight pitching into nightfall stabbed him with dismay, with such a *woeful* wretchedness.

When darkness fell in the winters, and he lingered outside, anywhere, not wanting yet to be cooped up at home for the night—"Home is where the hatred is," sang the heartrending hoarse Esther Phillips, a black woman he'd read was too far-gone a junkie to sing live, how he wished he could save her—well, at such hours, winter fives and sixes, summer sevens, sometimes summer worse even than winter because one felt cheerful during the day so the plummet was more abrupt and unforgiving, what a smarting defeat and woeful sense of exclusion possessed Isaac, what a hopeless acrid longing to be elsewhere, to be *there*, and not wallowing in his own rutted nowhere.

At such hours, at such deepening, quickening twilights, all over the world, men and women were setting out into bright nights to attend symphonies and operas in golden palaces bedecked with crystal lamps and red velvet chairs, were starting off to lavish noisy balls and banquets; college students—not at Gilboa State, but at real universities, at the great ancient centers of learning—were carousing with their boon companions, arguing in cafés and beer halls; grown men, writers, scientists, were drinking in hotel bars in big cities, sinking into featherbeds with their mistresses, catching trains, planes, roaring in stickshift sports cars—Isaac couldn't even drive—in all the capitals of America and Europe and Asia, oh, Milan and Genoa and Lyons and Barcelona and Chicago and Munich and Hong Kong and Toronto in hotel rooms and bars.

Life is elsewhere, and *elsewhere* they were getting on with the business of living, they were central, men and women were composing symphonies and epics, designing fighter planes, staging plays, receiving prizes—the Nobel Prize, which Isaac had first read about so long ago— working out theorems, inventing vaccines against diseases Isaac had never heard of, and studying the chemical processes of thought, and making, and doing, and steaming ahead, and *not* skulking in a tepid morass of self-pity, not having headaches, not slave to the arid febrile spasms of solitary sins, not wondering if perhaps they were going mad. And with all this bustling massing tidal wave of huge Olympian striving genius flooding the world, in a universe bursting with possibility and greatness and mirth and invention, was it possible that one man at the age of seventeen should already have come a cropper, shipwrecked, gone astray, and petered out, that life should slip and slither away like a tiny garter snake?

Franks and beans and white bread at six-thirty at a table of dour shifty speechless relatives, themselves bloodcurdling exemplars of wasted opportunity, illustrated lessons in how the veins and arteries of appetite and wit can contract and shrivel, and after the beans, never hot enough and, in fact, never enough, after supper, seven hours locked up in his bedroom, like a caged bear, seven hours alone with a body grotesque and importunate, a mind that drove him mad, seven hours of pretending to read, pretending to study, pretending to stare at the stars, seven hours was enough to go mad in.

"Infectious," he concluded, aloud. And in a sudden leap Isaac felt quite merry again, agreeably wet and frozen. "I will reform," he announced, reinfused with the happiness of plans. "I'll get up at six in the morning, I won't stay up so late, I'll get up at six, that makes seventy-five minutes before breakfast. I'll read fifty lines of Latin every morning, fifty lines of Virgil before breakfast, that ought to do it, all right. And didn't Cindy Olszewski see in my palm that I'd roam the world, visit all kinds of foreign places?" There, he thought to himself triumphantly, there is a purpose, I won't despair, I will be good.

Ahead of him was Turner, whom he hadn't seen but who had obviously seen him, slinking ferret-quick up the drive, head ducked down.

"Hey, brother, wait up," cried Isaac, puffing up to the boy, who shot him a sideways glance expressing who knew what—confusion? dislike?

"Hey, yourself."

"What's happening?"

"Nothing," said Turner, thinking of the dead grouse and of the grouse's widow.

"Same here. It's always the same old nothing around here, isn't it?" pronounced Isaac, thinking of the altar and the stained-glass angels whose egret-feathered wings met at the tips like praying hands, and of Miss Urquhart's nose, the bony bridge of which went white when she was angry, and Macy Driscoll's teeth, and Gena Rowlands's honey-colored bouffant.

"I guess so."

"Well, are you going in? Ready for some fine cuisine?"

"Mmmmm . . ."

"Think we should pack Mom off to Cordon Bleu Cooking School?"

"Mmmmm . . ." muttered Turner, who didn't like Mother jokes.

They lingered on the doorstep, and then Isaac pushed Turner ahead of him into the leaky heat of the house.

Chapter 4

JUST AS ONE NOTICES in surprise that things are sailing along quite peacefully and thinks how pleasant it would be to stick out one's finger and slow down time, pitch tent forever in this very week—for sometimes Isaac really did feel all these imaginary burdens to be a satisfaction, some weeks he did get up at six and even sometimes in his Jesuitical temperature takings decided he wasn't going mad or brain dead or astray, but that this troublesome fate of his would work itself out—well, just then, things change, like a troublesome sitter blinking his eyes or wriggling just as the camera clicks.

"Isn't that your teacher, Ike?"

Isaac and his mother were at Sears buying a new battery for the Matador. Naturally, it had been no joke persuading her: every morning the car conked out, and they got out the cables and boosted it off Sam's Dart, and every morning she said, "It's this cold snap. Nothing wrong with the battery." Finally the boys took the car to their uncle's garage and got an official verdict, which was a little like being told George Washington too was no longer among the living, but their mother still insisted on doing some comparison shopping, waiting till they went on sale. "Mom, relent. Just buy a new one *now*," Isaac pleaded.

This was the difference between his parents: if the Dodge wouldn't start Sam considered it a personal failure, confirmation of his own inferiority; to Mattie, car trouble was a government plot, with the repairman as chief conspirator.

"Look at the receipt: I bought it from you in June 1977. A dud. I expect a free replacement," she threatened the man at Sears.

"Well, ma'am, I'm afraid the warranty on this particular model expires after two years."

"That's a lot of shit. Where do they make these pieces of junk, Japan?"

"No, ma'am, this battery was made in the U.S.A."

"We're living in a second-rate country," Mattie told anyone who would listen. "If you can't make a battery that lasts three years, where do you get the nerve to boss around countries half our size? I mean, why send in the Marines—just ship Lebanon a few tons of these god-damned batteries, they'll be dead on their feet in no time. And this store sucks, too. Let me see the manager," she wound up.

"You get what you pay for" was the fed-up salesman's rejoinder. They were sitting in the Sears waiting room doing just that—waiting. Until the manager got back from his lunch break, until the mechanic installed a new battery, who knows what. Mattie was telling Isaac all about Cindy Olszewski's new boyfriend who must be half her age. "It's embarrassing. She goes out on the town with him, I bet the bartender cards him. Some people have no shame. Of course, Cindy's a notorious souse, and this kid—his face is purple and he's not even thirty."

"You don't approve of tippling, Mom?" His mother only got sanc-timonious if a grudge was at stake.

"I'm not talking tippling, Ike, I'm talking *sick*. The boy at the State Store tells me they come in every week, pick up two gallon jugs of Old Crow. Two gallons a *week*. Be cheaper to open up their own still. Marge and Mike took Cindy out for her birthday last week and said she was dashing up to the bar ordering herself an extra drink *in between* every round. Of course, Frank drank himself to death," concluded Mattie with a certain grim satisfaction.

"I thought he died in Vietnam."

"No, he didn't. He drank himself to death. Isn't that your teacher over there, Ike?" Mattie repeated, maybe a little abashed to be caught out. Of course Frank Olszewski had died in Vietnam. But if he hadn't, he *would* have drunk himself to death. No doubt about it. A wet grave.

"Not so loud, Mom."

It was true. Right across from them was Agnes Urquhart. She was reading a magazine. When they had come into the waiting room, first thing he saw, with a leap in his stomach, was Miss Urquhart, who blushed painfully and cast him one of those artificial, lips-up smiles she must have picked up from Mrs. Cartwright.

"Well, isn't it?"

"Yes, it is."

"Did you say hello to her? I thought you two were like Siamese twins." And looking over every inch of Miss Urquhart, who was hiding behind *Popular Mechanics*, Mattie pronounced, "She sure is skinny. It looks disgusting, being that thin when you're older. Looks like a plucked chicken. You think she's got that disease where people make themselves upchuck after they eat? It's selfish, being that scrawny. You're just trying to get attention, make people worry about you. If a woman lives by herself, she's got a duty to make it clear to everyone that she can look after herself okay. Does she dye her hair or is it that color naturally?"

Isaac got up. Now he was blushing, too. "Mom, I'm gonna . . . I'm going to go see if I can find some . . . Mom, I'm going to *throttle* you if you don't stop it immediately."

Mattie was unperturbed. "Isaac, I don't know what you're talking about. Sit down a moment. I want to have a serious talk with you."

She started complaining about Turner, who was so unfriendly to everyone these days and so uncommunicative—"Not at all his old self. Remember how cute and cuddly he used to be, so open and confiding? You can't put a finger to him these days without his jumping a foot in the air. All he talks about now is joining the Marines. He works too hard, unlike some people I know. And I don't think all this body-building business is healthy."

That was a reproach. Isaac himself had started lifting weights after his Prize Day ambush. Turner as usual seemed indifferent, but once Isaac lost interest, the silent copycat inherited his brother's barbells and converted his cubbyhole of a room into a torture chamber. He ran five miles a day before breakfast after finishing his newspaper route, he played basketball after school, and when he wasn't working at his computer or helping out at the Army Surplus Store, he lifted weights. Plus he didn't eat.

"Turner's fine, Mom. Don't fret."

"Does he tell you anything? Does he confide in you?" Mattie persisted.

"Is the Pope a Jew? That's just Turner. He doesn't talk."

"That's not the old Turner. He always talked to me." But Isaac was only listening with half an ear. With all his might he was trying to keep his eyes fixed on his mother or on the floor, but, willy-nilly, they kept creeping over to Miss Urquhart. When her number was called and she left with a parting nod to the Hookers—"Stuck-up," growled Mattie—Isaac felt as if he had just swallowed a gallon of liquid bleach. It was all he could do not to go running after her. God, what a wretched

state of affairs. He got up, went over to the picture window that overlooked the garage area, and stared dumbly down, watching her trip
over to the car in her high heels, talk to the mechanic. She had dressed
up to go to Sears, he thought with a lump of amused affection in his
throat. Who was she expecting to meet, or was it just self-respect?
Would she turn and look at him? No, she wouldn't. She got into her
car and drove off. She was gone.

Isaac and Miss Urquhart had had a falling-out. As soon as he said
these words to himself, he felt what a crazy and unnecessary state of
affairs it was, and yet when he retraced their quarrel the same keen
indignation boiled up involuntarily. It was awful being angry precisely
for this reason—you couldn't control it, like some pill that once swallowed ran its chemical course. If you bit it back, it only burned your
guts. Getting along with people was so tricky, such a fragile interplay
of vanity and blind faith, that certain things, once said, could never
be taken back and never be forgiven. Anger, harsh and vulgarizing in
its alchemy, transmuted all the other person's decency and charm into
malign calculation, piggishness. He knew this and was angry all the
same. Forgiveness wasn't a motion of the will as religion would have
you believe, but something involuntary, physiological: you woke up one
day and weren't mad any more, like getting over a cold. There was no
virtue in it, any more than two weeks were more virtuous than one.
It was simply a matter of healing.

Just before Thanksgiving Miss Urquhart had called him over at the
end of class and asked with studied casualness, "Do you want to show
me your applications?"

He sat on her desk, and she shrank a bit.

"What applications?"

"Why, your college applications. I don't need to tell you once more
they're due in six weeks. Six weeks. You hear me? I don't know why
you didn't have the sense to go for early action. . . . Anyway, I'd like
to write you a reference, if you don't mind, since I seem to be the only
teacher in this school except for your dad who's still speaking to you.
Of course, I like to think it's because the rest of them don't know you
so well." She grinned. "They haven't heard you sing 'Onward, Christian Soldiers.'"

Isaac was silent.

"So?"

"So what, Miss Urquhart?"

"So would you like to show me your applications? And who else are you asking for a reference?" Miss Urquhart had not only decided that he was going to college: she had decided that he should apply to Harvard. She had made him take the advanced-placement tests in practically every subject offered—miraculously, she even thought he was halfway good at art history—and had so arranged it that Isaac would hardly have to take any freshman courses at all. She had an orderly, even an obsessive mind, and Isaac found himself avoiding her because of this tiresome bee in her bonnet. Yet he said nothing outright to dissuade her, either. In fact, he said nothing at all, except not to worry, he'd take care of it all in good time, which made her extremely suspicious.

"You have to write essays, Isaac. Do you understand? You need to get references from your teachers. It's not like the Michelangelo paper you owe me from last month: if you miss this deadline, you're a goner. It's *now.* Do you hear me?"

"You're not my mother," he reminded her. "What's it to you?"

"You don't have a mother, as far as I can tell," Miss Urquhart snapped back. "If you had a mother, she'd be making you do this, since you clearly haven't got the sense you were born with." This time she seemed genuinely fed up with him.

He had been staring at the booklet almost an hour. That night's supper like the waking dead in his stomach, panic rising acridly. Print, questions, boxes, language gone menacingly, incomprehensibly awry. What did it mean and what had happened? Panic. Don't panic. He got up, coughed, yawned, cracked his knuckles, mopped the sweat from his forehead, sang a little tune, paced, sweated some more, locked his bedroom door, made sure the bedroom door was really locked. Damn the quiet mouselike tapping of his brother at the keyboard. Finally, he unlocked the door and barged through to Turner's room.

"Stop making so much goddamned noise!" Turner, astonished, looked up from the computer, but Ike had already flung himself back into his lair, slammed and locked the door. Too late; concentration was fled. Now the sound of Turner's watchful silence became oppressive. Turner was listening to him do nothing. He could do nothing with Turner guarding him, eavesdropping.

Spread across his desk was the Harvard application, glossy, amiable, hip as a fashion magazine. Here it was, Isaac's future. Each page was emblazoned at the top with the stingray heraldry of Harvard's Ve-Ri-Tas and Radcliffe's barbed wire, but below these familiar markers lay a wilderness of terrifying demands, a clamoring desert of acronyms, codes, numbers, formulas, each with its own distracting, bossy type-face. Personal Data Form, Family Educational Rights and Privacy Act of 1974, Test Results in CB, IQ, NMSQT, ACT; defaults or refunds owed Pell, SEOG, or SSIG. He felt like a prisoner in the dock too dumb to understand his crime.

The questions loomed threatening, befuddling: Are any partnerships listed on Schedule E of your parents' most recent tax return? Your visa status? Alien registration number? Have you ever incurred serious or repeated disciplinary action? Which two college activities interest you most? Ethnic groups, Golf, Skiing, Water polo, Other? V? JV? In-tramural? Rate applicant for sense of humor, growth potential. Make and year of family automobiles. List cities and countries where you have lived; an oceanic space provided beneath. I've never lived any-where, realized Isaac. No cities, no countries. Where have *they* all lived? No parental partnerships, no Schedule E whatever that meant, no sense of humor, no growth potential, no skiing. If English is not the primary language spoken in your home, which language is? Com-plete the FAF and mail it to the CSS with the appropriate fee by January 1. IMMEDIATELY. IMMEDIATELY. Do not delay. What are your impressions of the applicant's character, aims, and values? Send $50. We hope this provides an occasion for fruitful reflection. Good luck.

Then there was a still more bewildering tome solicitously informing New Hampshire residents what state scholarships were available to them—a whole new obstacle course of GSLs and PLUSs and SLSs and GAPs and ALPs, scholarships for orphans of Veterans and Nurs-ing Education, Rural Rehabilitation Corporation Grants. Am I a cor-poration? Do I—yes, I do—need rural rehabilitation? Live free or die, proclaimed the granite rock profile on the cover. Die. Maybe if he were lucky he might take sick, very sick, crawl into bed, and be absolved of this terror.

It was his third night poring over the applications, and at each read-ing, the harder he tried to understand what they were asking of him, the more unmanageable and opaque the questions became. The pros-pect of finding a second teacher for a reference, of making his father itemize the family's mortgages and loans and paltry revenues, of even attempting to harness the pages in Sam's typewriter and accommodate its big wandering alphabet into Harvard's minute answer boxes, undid him. Isaac fell asleep at his desk, waking up chilly and cramped at dawn.

The next night, crouched over the page, head drumming, clammy with sweat, his sight crossed so that the words hopped and gavotted like frogs. Couldn't read, couldn't stay awake. Nothing made any sense. No sooner had he settled down to the page, desk and person and time arranged according to his secret superstitious compulsions—certainly couldn't attend to the applications unless his two favorite toothmark-riddled pencils were ground to the perfect lead pinniness, upright in their jar, unless his trousers were hiked up so that they didn't rub against the backs of his knees, his elbows just so, his glasses not pressing too hard against the skull, the clock hand not a hair's breadth past nine else all was lost—than he fell straight into bed fully clothed and sank into the death sleep of the guilty, only to awake twelve hours later, sick with dread and lassitude. He wondered if he had a poison in the blood. He hoped so. Dreaded night's coming. I can't cope, I can't do it. He was panicked by the deadline, by the menace of those unwritten essays meant to display to best advantage his character, interests, accomplishments. But who was he? What had he ever done? All his Isaacness seemed to have slipped away, leaving a trail of invisible snaily slime. I can't do what is expected of me. And what goddamned business is it of theirs anyway what kind of car or sense of humor I have?

Sam innocently asked to see the "literature," and the two of them scanned it, Ike trying to hide the fact that before his eyes the simple English sentences were being monstrified into unrecognizable gobbledygook. "Do you understand it?" he finally fished. Sam, thinking as usual that Ike was doubting his intelligence, replied dryly, "More or less. The usual shit."

What were they talking about here? He pointed to a question about hobbies and extracurricular activities. What was a hobby? 4-H Club, for example, it said. 4-H Club, he repeated, and the harder he concentrated on the phrase the more unfamiliar and frightening it became. What could the four *H*'s be? All he could think of was his own early passion for the letter *h*. *H* was hot breath, steamy exhalations in wintry air, hecatomb, hospital, hortatory, haruspication. *H* was God. Help. H_2O. Was 4-H a chemical formula, an army discharge?

"You know, they want to know what you do after school," said Sam. What he did after school, repeated Isaac to himself. After school. He talked to his friends, he played Pac-Man and Donkey Kong, he ate supper, did his homework. What more? The question was a dagger at the heart, baring the utter emptiness and futility of his life. What did he do? Nothing. What did he deserve? Even less. Turner should be going to college, not him. Turner was the one who had afterschool jobs and hobbies and sports; he just sat around.

"You just tell 'em about the chess club and the debating club and about the stories you write and all the college courses you've taken," nudged Sam, seeing his son look unwontedly blank.

Isaac hung his head, knowing he couldn't. These pursuits, most of which he'd abandoned in the last year or so, all of a sudden seemed crushingly pointless and puny. Chess club, he scribbled on the back of his hand, just so he would remember. But he didn't think he felt like telling strangers, as if he'd engineered these pastimes to impress some dean. Why should he play their stupid game, suck up, doctor his doings to make them sound enterprising, civic-minded, virtuous? Who were they to rate the value of what he did in his free time? There were times when he knew he'd learned most from downing a fifth of Jack Daniels at one sitting.

Imagining himself inside an admissions office, all plush carpets and hunting prints on the wall, crammed into a chair too small for his globby bulk, being interrogated by some self-satisfied geek in a striped tie and shoes with little dots and spangles cut out of their toes, Isaac was disgusted by his own now-vanished hunger for acceptance, his opportunism.

Why pretend? He'd never lived in any foreign cities or countries, never lifted a civic finger, slept till noon every chance he could get, was devoid of warmth of personality or potential academic growth, was one big backwoods zero, no, not even a big one, a very little one. He knew it and Harvard too would soon know it if he could ever get it together to fill out these forms. Why wouldn't his dad and Miss Urquhart accept his unsuitability and leave him be?

"I'm going to sleep now, Dad."

Sam looked at his night owl in surprise. "It's only nine o'clock."

"I'm very tired." And indeed he could hardly keep his eyes open.

Meanwhile, Isaac's friends were jumping out of their skins. It was only November, but they were already killing time until the morning of June 27 when they would stand on stage in their best clothes with boards on their heads and silly grins on their faces, listening to Mrs. Cartwright's chill pieties. Kiss their slide rules goodbye, say hello to real life. Isaac wouldn't let his friends talk about next year. He didn't want to graduate from high school at all, but mooned wistfully over Turner's homework. Wouldn't it be neat to be in ninth grade and only just learning algebra and American history? If only he could go to sleep for forty years and wake up when everyone who had ever expected anything of him was senile or dead. Why couldn't he be fourteen again, regress to that aerated dream time when nothing counted and all his accomplishments were freaks of nature knocked off for his own pleasure? But there was Billy chattering about how he couldn't wait to get out of this dump, see the last of Mrs. Cartwright.

"I'm gonna make a bonfire and burn my books." Where was his future fright? How was it that Billy just assumed he would turn out a happy, useful man, that technical school would be fun, that he would find a nice girl who loved him and have swarms of kids and live on the farm and feel pleased with himself? Why couldn't he be Billy, pretend he didn't feel squirming within him the tapeworm of ambition? I should be a farmer, he thought. How fitting and fine to rise at dawn to cultivate the earth, plant an orchard, and in the spring prune my trees so they bow their heavy branches to the ground, pick my apples in late summer and in fall press them into cider. I could set up a wooden stand, baskets piled high with round ruddy Macouns and crisp Northern Spies, golden gallons of cider. I could sit by the side of the road all day, and in the spring lie hidden under the papery white garlands of blossom. Well, and if I didn't find a wife to marry me, too bad. Get more read in the evenings. How good to read a book without feeling one day you had to write a better one, without regarding everyone else's words and thoughts as either ammunition or competition for your own.

And yet even in midflight he knew he'd make a lousy farmer, the work too hard and not the right work for him. Better to make time stop. In the olden days when he wished to shrug off burdensome demands and expectations, or convince himself he wasn't falling behind, Isaac would compare himself with friends and schoolmates. Peter Karolis was shrewd but lazy, Paul Chen was a math whiz but ignorant about life, Macy Driscoll was a human A-plus machine driven only by competition—you couldn't imagine her reading a book just out of curiosity, wanting to know anything that wasn't going to be in next week's quiz. By these standards Isaac was still doing pretty well—though sometimes he remembered that the correct canon wasn't these kids but Goethe and Thomas Jefferson and Newton. As far as college went, most Ashuelot seniors either stopped at graduation or went on to two-year trade and technical schools. Except for Peter Karolis, who was already a freshman at Amherst, the McCormick girls, Macy, Paul's older brother, nobody he knew had been or was going to a real college. Even Paul was just applying to Gilboa State, where he could study business administration. More was expected of Isaac, but Isaac's mind now clammed up at the thought. Better not think about it.

So the weeks crawled by in stupefied, greedy binges of sleep and morning terrors. How long before Miss Urquhart found out he had been cheating her, wasn't doing his duty, because he couldn't?

He sprawled across the battle-scarred desk, playing with his teacher's rubber bands, leaning closer than made her comfortable and drinking in her tidy innocent smell. She was asking him about the applications and references and essays, and Isaac, clearing his throat, afraid his hands were visibly shaking, wished she wouldn't.

Could he confess to her, he wondered for one brazen instant, explain about this uncanny physical paralysis, this cerebral scrambling, this psychic dread? No, of course not, how could you. He had no sense that language or friendship covered such nightmare territory. She'd shy away, shocked. Besides, he didn't want to tell, he didn't know what there was to tell, and even if she was willing to help he didn't want her to. He would take care of it himself or perish, and if he perished it would be in privacy. And yet it wasn't right to put her off any longer. He was her baby, she was banking on him; he should tell her now, so she could be helping some other kid who really was intending to go to Harvard.

"Listen, Miss Urquhart, I don't want to go to any of these places," he finally blurted. "In fact, I don't want to go to college at all."

"I see," she said, but not exactly sounding surprised. Isaac got the distinct impression she knew this would be coming. "Well, that's very interesting news. A judicious, well-considered move, you might say." (He hated it when she talked schoolmarm talk.) "After all, who needs college?"

"Exactly."

"I mean, you know everything already, don't you?"

"Well, not everything . . ."

"And modest, too. Really, when it comes down to it, they ought to be hiring you to teach *them*."

Isaac glared.

"Have you got plans for an alternative career?"

"No, I don't."

"Maybe you might like to pump gas? There's always room for another mechanic in the Gilboa area, though I never noticed you were all that *handy*," she pursued, in the voice that could be heard down halls. " 'Course, you might be a truckdriver, if only you knew how to drive. You see, the truth is I always thought you were cut out to be a college boy just because there was nothing useful you're fit for. Now it's a pity I spent so much time teaching you the future tense since you seem determined not to *have* one. And don't tell me about all the famous people who didn't go to college. That was then . . ."

"You don't need to go to college to have a future," asserted Isaac, nonetheless.

"These days you need a college degree to change a lightbulb. Don't pretend any different. I *know.*"

"That's just it. It's a total scam, and I refuse to be blackmailed. Colleges don't stand for anything any more—they don't believe in learning, they don't teach you anything. It's all faddishness, avarice, and cant."

"Don't recite your father to me, Isaac. I expect more of you than—"

"I wasn't!" Isaac bridled.

"Not that I would want you to stoop, or compromise your principles in any way," she continued, cheeks stamped with red spots of indignation, and blue eyes blazing. "What do you propose to do with yourself instead?"

"I *don't know,*" he confessed, "I don't *know* what I want to do, but I *refuse* to be asked to pay fifty thousand dollars to tread water till I find out."

"Isaac, I'm sure you could get a scholarship . . ."

"Like hell."

"Well, you can always try. If you don't get a scholarship, you'll get a loan. Why don't you try and find out?"

"I don't want to."

The two of them were glaring now, Miss Urquhart with her arms folded across her chest, Isaac still making slingshots out of her pile of rubber bands. One went rocketing across the room, and they watched it fall.

"I think you're scared."

For an electrifying moment he thought she understood and that everything would be all right, but then she went on. "Here you are, the smartest person ever to pass through this school. Not that *that* says much. It doesn't take much work to outshine Ray Doucette or Billy Ostrich or to bask in the admiration of gullible country dimwits like me. In fact, you've gotten pretty well used to resting on your laurels. *You* don't need to prove anything: you won the *National Geographic* award. About time to retire already. No wonder you don't want to get out into the world and meet your competition."

"Who's my competition?"

"Why, kids from Boston and New York and Los Angeles and Chicago and St. Louis who were the smartest kids in *their* schools. You'd much rather spend the rest of your life playing those silly video games than having to contend with equals. How many times did you tell me you've seen that movie about the gangster's moll and the little boy? You're too young to let your brain rot."

"That's enough," interrupted Isaac, in a tone that silenced her. "So you think I'm a coward?"

"No," she said, tartly. "Just prudent."

She was about to add that there was nothing cowardly in fear, only in giving fear a permanent right of way, but Isaac had risen from her desk.

"I'm not done with you yet," she yelled after him. "Where's the paper on the Sistine Chapel you owe me?"

He was gone, slamming the door after him.

"Damn that brat," muttered Miss Urquhart. "What do I care whether he goes to college or not?"

That was almost a month ago. The next morning in French she'd called on him, and Isaac replied in a tone of arctic indifference that he didn't know. She was like everybody else. A real bitch. He should put a match to her stiff pleated dress. The fact that she didn't seem any too pleased with him, either, only made him the sorer.

From then on things just seemed to get worse. The applications remained secreted under the bed between piles of girlie magazines; his brain lay befogged. Nothing was clear, just guilt and dread and the desire to sleep, to disappear. I'm not the same boy I used to be, Isaac told himself. I'm not so smart as I used to be. I've turned out a mess. She's got the wrong guy. Why doesn't she make Paul go to a good school?

Isaac spent all his waking moments at Domino's playing Pac-Man, and when Domino's closed he would go home with Billy and play the same silly games they had played since fifth grade, talk the secret code language only the two of them understood. When Billy had to do his chores or work in the garage Isaac hung around Turner or Mattie, who certainly saw no reason why anyone should go to college. His father he avoided.

Conversation was desultory over lunch, weighted by the weekend gloom that descended over the Hooker house when nobody wanted a cab, the kids were at home with nothing to do, and Sam was biding his time until he could sneak off for his afternoon nap.

Isaac watched his younger brother first unravel the rind from his baloney slices and then remove the meat from the sandwich altogether, eating the mayonnaise-laden bread with dainty distaste and leaving white picture frames of crust on his plate.

"I cut the crusts off already, hon," Mattie reassured him. Turner looked evasive. It didn't matter. Every day Mattie cut the crusts off his sandwich and every day he still refused to eat the milk-white edges where, if there *had been* crusts left, crusts would be. "What's the matter, you don't like baloney any more?"

"Mmmmmmm . . ." Turner was noncommittal. Isaac looked glum: this was no joke. If baloney was off Turner's single-digit list of permitted foods, that meant the rest of the Hookers were stuck with Spaghetti-Os *every* day of the week.

Ever since Turner was little the edible world had been divided for him into clean and unclean beasts, the clean a narrow and ever-dwindling realm, the unclean, like the ocean, covering most of his earth's surface. Milk, eggs, meat (except processed meat), fish, vegetables were forbidden foods. Sometimes there were pleasant surprises, like the day he ventured on creamed corn in the can and found it passable. Clean beasts were baloney, canned spaghetti, Cheerios, and for three happy boring years franks and beans. One of the more infuriating spectacles Isaac knew was his younger brother nibbling the sugar cream off an Oreo, leaving the black chalky patterned bark untouched.

These revulsions and abstentions of Turner's loomed so large in family life that Isaac tended to picture his brother as an averted head, a picked-at plate. Suggest going out for supper, and Mattie would reproachfully veto the idea with "But what will Turner eat?" Sometimes Ike thought Mattie's little prince needed his head flushed in the toilet bowl. Then there was the famous evening the boys had supper at the Randalls'. At table, Aunt Sue helped everyone to hamburgers and carrots and French fries. As Isaac wolfed his down, Turner slyly rearranged the orange and beige vegetables on his plate to make the quantity appear smaller, mutilated his burger to look half-eaten.

"Turner, finish what's on your plate," ordered the eagle-eyed Sue.

Did she mean it? Yes, she meant it.

"Turner doesn't eat meat and vegetables, Aunt Sue," Isaac explained, surprised she didn't know: Turner's eating habits were legendary.

"In my house, everybody eats what's put before him. It's good food, and I'm not having it go to waste." Sue's revenge for years of her big sister's bullying. General silence as Turner, chalk-white, glassy-eyed, gagging, chewed everything to mush (he was scared of choking, on top of everything else). It was like seeing pork being forced down a Muslim's throat. Something vindictive in Isaac gloated, "Serves him right," even as pity surged.

When they got home Turner locked himself in the upstairs toilet and didn't come out, while Isaac sat on the floor outside. "Are you all right?" No answer. "Want some more hamburger?" Jeez, did their mother ever trounce Aunt Sue: it took Uncle Jim and Sam to reconcile the two women, although Sue never quite forgave Mattie for calling little Jimmy a chinless retard.

With his ever-more-stringent dietary prohibitions Turner had become a kind of high priest in a cult of which his mother was sole and uncharacteristically obedient lay servant. Isaac knew if he became President of the United States or manned a shuttle to Mars his mother would not be half so proud as the day Turner took to canned corn, or as astonished and amused as when, after picking at the sugary yellow glop every night for six months, the boy decided he didn't like it any more.

"Is it true your brother only eats raspberry ice cream?" Isaac was asked at school, as if Turner were an imported panda who had to be fed bamboo shoots or die.

"Black raspberry," clarified Isaac. "But he spits out the pits."

"You don't like baloney any more?" repeated Mattie.

Turner, eyes on the floor, said, "Ummmmm . . . guess not."

"Hrumph," scowled Sam. "I'm glad you're not *my* son."

"We saw Agnes Urquhart at Sears," Mattie said.

"Oh yeah? Ike's sweetheart?"

"Well, they didn't look too sweet to me, but I guess Ike felt he had to play cool in front of his mom. What a bag of bones. Tell your teacher to put on a little weight, Ikey. She must be on the same diet as Turner."

"Mmmmmm . . ." Now it was Isaac's turn.

"You know what else, Sam? George Hanesworth is selling off another parcel of land."

"Where?"

"By the foot of Bear Ridge. The backwoods, near Preston's house."

"Doesn't Preston want to buy it?"

"Looks like not. A forty-acre plot, asking forty grand."

"Land's going a grand an acre now?"

"This land is. 'Course, it was going for two hundred, ten years ago, but that was then. This is prime real estate, next to a state park. Protected. You could get ten little plots out of it, make a killing."

"That's nice. Have you got forty thousand in your mattress?"

"We could raise it."

"There's only one thing we're raising forty grand for, and that's sending Isaac to college," said Sam.

From Auburn to Bear Ridge was a high straight road flanked by a double escort of stalwart maple trees, a kingly avenue that in summer provided a pale green, rustling canopy above. On either side stretched brown potato fields, now half-encrusted in a speckled beard of snow. Isaac ambled along the road, veering off at times into the potato field, talking aloud and occasionally waving his arms just to make a point.

"I didn't have to write that paper on the Sistine Chapel: it was voluntary. Nobody else wrote one." In his pocket was stuffed the Harvard application. He was going to burn or bury it, or watch it float down the stream, or he was going to burn or bury or drown himself. He wasn't sure which.

All his life it had seemed to Isaac a done deal that crack at the age of sixteen he would leave his parents' house and his hometown and his brother and his friends and go to a land that God would show him. See the world, play a great part in it. The world meant big cities. Just as it was perfectly obvious to Isaac that his own life had not yet begun, that he was subsisting in a state of unhatched hibernation that didn't yet count, so too it seemed apparent that what his parents and neighbors did wasn't living—that there was some essential juice, some pith and rind to the business of life besides grading papers and watching *Hill Street Blues*, attending selectmen's meetings about accepting bids for a new contractor to maintain the Auburn cemetery, taking a nap Saturday afternoon. Although his father knew the subjects he taught fairly well, if you asked him what price a barrel of crude oil was fetching, who won the Nobel Prize for literature last year, or the name of the Iranian Speaker of Parliament, he not only didn't know but didn't want to know. "How can you be a teacher if you don't know what day it is!?" Thus Isaac at the age of fourteen or fifteen; but with that congenital refusal to justify himself, Sam said mildly, "I don't teach days of the week. That's extra."

Don't you even want to try to make me proud of you, was Isaac's secret question. No, I won't try. As I am, or not at all, Sam answered silently.

His mother for all her grossness addressed life with a certain ardor— life international, life in the backyard. She could tell you why in her opinion we didn't need a six-hundred-ship navy, why the Tamils were making war, why Phil Donahue's ratings were falling, why Joe Urquhart would be well advised not to build a swimming pool, and why Mrs. Hurd wasn't speaking to the Ellsworths. Sam had no such punch or address to him.

Was everyone else's family happier, more purposeful? Isaac had asked his friends what their parents did in their free time, and though the routine varied—Billy's and Paul's and Gabriel's parents worked harder, and didn't have weekends, but managed to watch even more TV than Sam and Mattie—it also didn't constitute Life. On the contrary, all these activities were not only stifling, fustian, empty, they were some-how positively inimical to real life.

Some of this, Isaac used to suspect, had to do with money: rich people must surely lead more arid lives. But much as he loved hanging out at Dr. McCormick's house, it wasn't exactly the mental life that kept him there but three pretty girls, deep armchairs, and a well-stocked liquor cabinet. The difference was purely material: the McCormicks had steak or roast beef a couple of times a week, they dined at restau-rants, and owned a summer cottage in Gloucester. Even Isaac didn't believe that the line between real life and walking death lay in four pounds of sirloin or a house at the beach. Maybe they were happy, in a bovine vegetative way, but that was because they didn't know any better. Happiness wasn't enough. Only changing the world sufficed, making your mark against oblivion.

Just as you had to go to the kitchen to boil an egg or to the bathroom to take a bath, so it seemed to Isaac that you had to go elsewhere to embark on life. Where was elsewhere? Well, elsewhere was just as it sounded—somewhere besides that fresh-faced archaic self-respecting ignorant northern square of hilly pine-forested snowbound-from-December-to-March acreage that embraced Gilboa, Auburn, Sturgis, Walcott, Hebron, and Wendell, where the big news was someone's dog getting lost or someone's granddaughter breaking a wrist, and where every guy in town wore a lumber jacket and construction boots and a visored hat from Prestash Contractors and drove a pickup truck plas-tered with stickers saluting American veterans and wondering when our POWs and MIAs were coming home. Well, all that was nice, but irrelevant.

Or so it had seemed to Isaac until recently, and so it had seemed to him, off and on, ever since the day he had first run away from home with a compass and a pocketful of Fig Newtons only to be picked up five miles later by his dad, who had said mournfully—Isaac would never forget this—"Come now, Ike, Mom's cooking ain't *that* bad."

And what had Isaac replied? "Don't say 'ain't.'"

If he hadn't, Sam would have known his case was desperate.

Now everything had changed, and this trivial bustle, these anchored routines had taken on an almost desperate value. If living meant going away, maybe Isaac didn't want to live; and there was sweetness, too, in a preemptive relinquishing of claims on the world. Over breakfast he gazed at his brother's dark crewcut head, fastidiously bent over his Cheerios as in prayer, and, wondering what Turner was thinking about—shotguns and Pershings, rowing machines, modems, old cars, duty—he was filled by a tenderness so mushy it made him want to kiss him or weep, not let him out of his sight. Proud deadeye Turner. Maybe Turner inside was scared and lonely and uncertain. Maybe Turner thought he too was meant for great things. Did Turner still believe in God? Did he fall in love with girls? He must get to know his tall little brother, from whom he had been divided in the war between their parents, must reclaim him, know him, help him. How hard it was to know another soul, but how could you call yourself a man without trying with all your might?

He listened to the indignant monotone of his mother's litany—her lowdown friends, the iniquity of the government, Turner's unresponsiveness, the shoddiness of goods, the fecklessness of her drivers. He got caught in the same absurd fruitless arguments that used to frustrate him beyond endurance, but now he found himself adoring her illogic, her attack, though when he stopped fighting back she got suspicious. How come he was hanging around underfoot all the time? Why did he want to come along to the garage and Sears and the Stop & Shop? He could see her mind working. Was he in trouble at school? Had he got into some kind of jam and was he trying to soften her up for a loan? What did he want from her? Whatever it was, he couldn't have it.

It seemed such a brief moment in time that they would all be together.

. . .

As he walked along the high road Isaac gazed up at the serene milky-gold immensity of the afternoon sky, the broad sun darting its flaming beams through the piled mountains of pink bruised-looking clouds, casting a lustrous glaze over the fields and trees and purple hills, lighting them meltingly from within. All around he saw rise and fall the mild earthy brown furrows of potato fields—if he reached over, he could scoop out a withered frozen little spud the harvester had missed. He was walking now past Hurd Farms, which raised Holsteins, a brick-red farmhouse with smoke trickling from its chimney.

Surely, Isaac thought, nothing in the world could be nicer than to spend the rest of one's life walking along this same avenue of broad tall maples, past this same glowing clapboard farmhouse with the smoke trailing from the chimney and a green John Deere tractor still out in the field and the aluminum silo and the tumbledown barn chock-full of black-and-white cows packed tight as milk bottles in a crate, and a black dog sleeping on the drive, next to a child's abandoned bicycle, and the afternoon paper in the tin mailbox.

In a couple of months, after a long snowbound winter of circumscribed night-haunted days when all the woods and hills became inaccessible, and life was reduced to the fireplace and the television set and a few salted highways, spring would begin to reassert its claim over the land and each of these maples would be pierced by tubing or bear its own tin bucket of extracted sap.

Have you ever seen farmers sugaring off? demanded Isaac, accusingly—not of himself, of course he had—but of the imaginary interlocutor pressuring him to leave behind all this rural splendor and move to Cambridge, Massachusetts. I mean, seen a sugarhouse at night, at the height of the season? You drive by on a frosty March night, midnight, one in the morning, everything still, the black sky crackling with stars, blue sparkly snow round about, and there's a light on in the sugarhouse. You go in, almost knocked flat by the suffocatingly sweet steam rising from the vat. Isaac pictured now to himself Billy Ostrich and his father and his grandfather standing around the furnace, rapt faces glowing orange, like shepherds in a manger, like devils stoking up hell's fire. How much boiling and boiling it took to reduce all that flavorless water to a syrup thick, dark, and powerful as rum! A funny campfire of heat and watchful sweetness in the mountain blackness, a few men watching and tending the flames in a practice as solemn as hilarious as magical as timeless as the birth of a baby or a lamb.

And you want me to go off to college and leave Billy and his grandfather and hang out with a bunch of smartass rich kids from New York City and Fairfax, Virginia, with constipated accents, whose dads give them BMWs and who go to Barbados for Christmas and snort cocaine and are going to be investment bankers in no time flat? Not me. I'd rather be a bum in the gutter than condescended to by spoiled brats who don't believe in anything. And how's Turner going to manage without me to look after him?

"Hop in, Ike. Which way you going?" He was too engrossed to have noticed the truck pulling over. It was John Preston, and Isaac, to his own surprise, was delighted to see him. "Nowhere: I'll go wherever you're headed."

"Free and easy, huh? That's youth. So how's the world treating you, Mr. Hooker?"

"Oh, tolerably." Isaac, itching to get onto the subject that was bothering him, to sound Preston out, didn't know how to introduce it. Have you seen any hateful rich kids lately? Don't you think Cambridge, Mass., is hell on wheels? Is there any reason why an intelligent person should go to college? Should I hang myself or drown myself?

"You coming hunting with me while the season's good?"

"I doubt it."

Preston laughed hard. He laughed at everything Isaac said, especially the rude things. "Well, the offer stands. I've harvested six deer this season. Just last weekend I got an eight-point buck. Maybe you'd rather wait and come grouse shooting with me next fall: it's more challenging."

"You see the specs on me?" inquired Isaac, good-naturedly. "I'm so blind I can hardly see the pot to piss in, and you expect me to aim at a flying object the size of my fist? Anyway, where do you get off calling it a harvest? Deers aren't potatoes. It's slaughter."

Preston began telling a long bizarre story about the Gilboa police chief, for whom he had been building a house out beyond Sturgis. "Gooooor-geous, I'm telling you. No expense spared. And tasteful, too. Cedar outside, unpainted—just your natural weathered look. Cherry floors inside, marble in the master bathroom, and a hot tub out back. I'm wondering, Is this guy on the take or what? Ask your dad what he knows, if you think of it. But I'm not complaining. So we'd just sunk the foundations when I hear his wife's splitting. You know what happened? Wait till you hear this. One day she gets a package in the mail from Sears, husband's name on it, she opens it up. Inside, there's one of those remote-control gadgets for opening a garage door. Only trouble is theirs is manual. She calls Sears, no mistake, your husband came in himself two weeks ago and ordered it, and she gets suspicious. So she drives around town with the gadget, zapping every door in the neighborhood, till she reaches her babysitter's house, and Open Sesame! Parked inside the garage is her husband's patrol car and parked inside the babysitter is her husband. How do you like them apples?"

Isaac laughed.

"You laugh. What I want to know is, does a guy whose wife would like to chop him up in the Cuisinart want to go on building a $250,000 dream house or not? You're the expert in human psychology, you tell me. Am I out of a job or not?"

"I think he definitely owes his wife a hot tub," replied Isaac.

"You know, that's the one thing about fooling around I could never figure out," said Preston with the meditative smugness of a man contemplating a vice that doesn't happen to be his. "It's so much goddamned *trouble*. Who needs all that running around? How do you keep straight which lies you've told which one? Who's got the stomach for it? You know what I'm saying?"

"Don't look at me," said Isaac. "I haven't gone on a first date yet, let alone adultery."

"Well, let me tell you: it's hard enough breaking in *one* woman without having to break in two or three of 'em."

Isaac cleared his throat. "How *do* you break in a woman?" he inquired, hoping Preston was too enamored of the sound of his own voice to notice what a strange question he was being asked.

"Oh, I just mean getting someone used to your ways and you to theirs. Suzanne and I are lucky—we tend to see pretty much eye-to-eye on the important stuff. I know some guys can't talk to their wives about anything that matters. If Stash has a problem he comes to me about it. That's because he comes from a different culture, where women are more subservient and men are supposed to make all the decisions. Me, I'm a big baby: I'm a mess without that woman. Except there's one thing about her I can't understand: she hates pizza. How can you hate pizza?"

"Maybe she's Italian."

"No, she's not Italian."

Talking about women made Isaac feel left out and lonely, and it also made him think about Miss Urquhart. "What would you do," he asked Preston, casually, "if you knew a woman you respected immensely who saw the opposite of eye-to-eye with you on a matter of great importance?"

"Is that a trick question? Is this about politics?"

"No, it's about my—one's future."

"Oh, well, as long as it's not about politics, I'd say go along with her. Women are usually right about the important stuff. That's because they're on the outside—they got perspective. Women and artists. Of course, artists' perspectives can sometimes be real wacky: I wouldn't want to take Richard Wagner's advice about what I should do with my life. But if you want to talk to a real sensible woman, ask Suzanne. She knows what's what. Any time I got a problem with the business, I go to her." He brightened, paused. "Hey, why don't you come home with me now and have some supper? We'll defrost a couple of venison chops, have a feast. I just picked up a tape of *Every Which Way But Loose* at the store—you seen it?"

Preston was a happy man, you could tell. Did happiness matter? Was it a proper aim? And if so—no, it wasn't—it surely wasn't achieved by conscious effort. Was it a matter of temperament, was Preston simply born cheerful, in which case Isaac, being genetically disinclined, was out of luck, or had he arrived at this irritating self-satisfaction only after a struggle? For all you knew, he too cheated on his wife: it made you wonder, when people harped on a subject. In any case, he was quite sure that Preston would be amazed by the idea of a bright boy wanting to hang himself because he couldn't fill out his college applications.

"Nah, I got to . . ."

"Come on, you haven't seen the new house. Come over for an early supper. I'll drive you home afterward."

Isaac relented. "But I don't want anyone's advice."

"Relax. No one's offering it."

It was nighttime when he reached West Gilboa. Each row house along Franklin Street was aglow with the same flickering blue-and-white fire from the electronic hearth within. Was she home, was she home, please, please let her be home. He thundered up the stairs and pounded on the door, and when she opened, he burst into the room almost weeping with gratitude.

She was in blue jeans, barefoot, and she was startled, a little scared to see him. It made her look older, worn. "Are you all right? Why are you shaking?"

"No, not all right, but yes I am all right, I will be if you forgive me," Isaac stuttered, gasping. "There's no time for all this nonsense, for our not being friends, I mean."

Those last words hung in the air, daring. She paused. "Are we friends?" She sounded surprised.

He took a deep breath. "You're my best friend." He didn't know it was true till he said it. He reached into his pocket, handed her the mangled application, stood over her as she sat down, smoothing it on her lap.

"I can't do it."

"Do you want to go?"

"God, yes. But I won't get in. And . . . um . . . the words won't come. . . . I don't understand anything any more. I think my head's gone dead," he said, trying to speak matter-of-factly. "And it's due Monday."

She knew instinctively what must be done. To Isaac, it was as if he had foreseen her swift, unsentimental readiness. She wrapped him in a man's sweater, sat him down at the pine table by the window, brewed a pot of tea, and brought out her manual typewriter.

"What's your name?"

"I don't know any more," he said, laughing. "Oh, I guess it's Isaac."

"What else?"

"Hooker."

"That's a pretty comical name. Do you have a date of birth, or did someone just turn over a stone and find you?"

"I wish they hadn't."

"No use crying over spilt milk."

Isaac, like a tickled child, giggled. When she had teased him tired his brain started working, and at her prompting he dictated while Miss Urquhart typed at a machine like a tiny clattering piano.

It was ten when he arrived, and the next moment the bells struck midnight in a clamoring peal that made them both jump, and after that he lost count. Together, in the tense vivacity of conspiracy, they worked through the night, laying out in abbreviated chronological prose the history of Isaac's life, composing a memoir of his grandparents, an essay on general knowledge, and one on Magellan, who was the only historical figure Isaac could resurrect from his parched memory. And Isaac sat, gulping down black Irish tea so hot it scorched his throat, moved by the sight of his teacher's bare feet curled around the rung of her chair, their long elegant toes, their haughty blue-veined arches, round pink heels. He stared at her feet and talked. They finished at four-thirty in the morning, and all of a sudden noticed they had begun whispering.

Miss Urquhart put on shoes and sweater and coat and they went downstairs into the chilly air. She drove him home through Gilboa, with its shuttered stores and deserted streets, past dim silent fields and sleeping farmhouses, one yellow-lit window in the Hanesworths' house where people were already rising, and dropped him at the end of his drive. "Now, be sure and take a sober look at it before you send it off," she reminded the boy as he climbed out of the car, reassuming her brisk schoolteacher voice. "It may be utter babble we wrote, but I think it's all right. Mind you check for typos."

Isaac leaned back through the window, unsteady but beaming. He touched her hair, and she drew back. "You're my savior," he said, loudly.

"Oh, nonsense. And mind you don't crumple all those pages again."

He stood in the drive until the rumble of the car and the red of its twin rear lights had melted into the valley, hugging his arms tight across his chest and digging his shoes into the gravel.

"Oh God, she is so so good I could burst."

BOOK
THREE

Chapter 1

DAMN THE KNOCK that brings bad news. Damn its woodpecker hammer, its sepulchral toll.

"Don't get it," he warned. It would only be some forty-inch-high panhandler from the Girl Scouts, or maybe Joe's wife, dropping by to spy on their ménage and natter up a storm about her own busy affairs (that was the bitch about having no phone: people came by) while Agnes nodded and tutted agreeably, that sharp tongue magically held in abeyance where family was concerned. The strain told. After the woman left, Agnes would be down in the dumps for a day, not even snappish, just mopey, needing a squeeze, needing to be assured of her own sublime worth: spawning children wasn't everything. There are people like that can make you wretched at the very thought of them, who by their aggressive and exhibitionist self-satisfaction make your own life seem pathetic. It was a pity the person who had this effect on Agnes was her beloved Joe's wife. Family is family, said Isaac, but not even blood is as thick as envy.

"I'm not envious of her one bit," protested Agnes. "What's to envy? We made different choices, that's all. Even as a little girl Becky Hume was always tossing her golden curls, shooing away dirty boys, telling you how many more dolls she had than you. She wanted a husband and home and children to manage, and I wanted to be independent. She's got a perfectly satisfactory life, it's just not for me."

They argued fiercely about whether or not Becky Urquhart was a happy woman, Agnes insisting she was, in the blind belief that any woman with a husband and five children *had* to be. "Anyway, Joe's happy enough. He's put on forty pounds since his wedding day."

Isaac retorted, "If she were happy, she wouldn't be such a bitch.

And if a woman with no looks and no brains and no sense and no education and nothing to occupy her soul from the time she drives her kids to playschool till she picks 'em up again, if such a preening, crowing *facsimile* of a human being can be happy, well, one might as well be a sea cow and have done with it."

"Shush, Isaac."

The rapping was now being joined by an angry holler, and Isaac was telling Agnes not to get it. Or he would have been, except that it was one-thirty in the afternoon and he was alone in bed with the pillow over his head. Half into the next dream, his darling's voice like a radio news flash intervened, "Wake up, honey, your mom's here."

"Hunh?" he started.

"Your dad's taken sick, and your mom's come to get you."

Unseating the tam-o'-shanter pillow from his head, he cracked a reluctant eye. "Wha-at?"

"He's in the hospital, lovey-dove. You'd better get dressed quick."

For the longest time this news (news, he thought; in as news-saturated a language as ours there ought to be different words for good news and bad news, novelty surely isn't half so salient as *import*, but are there in any language? *Bonnes nouvelles*, glad tidings, and always plural, too, why?) was inextricably entangled with Isaac's dream, which also had involved his father. The two of them in a big blackened church, a Gothic cathedral, no, it was a building bombed in the Blitz, and Sam, holding his son's hand, was explaining that this was where he had fought in the war, while an awed Isaac nodded, not remembering until he woke up that his father hadn't fought in any war. He was awake, after all, and Agnes was still there, peering down at him anxiously, hands on hips, as if he were the sick one.

"What happened?"

"They think it's something with his heart."

For a moment, still wriggling to reinsinuate his body into the burnt black cathedral, his hand into Sam's, Isaac acknowledged that he had always known his father had a weak heart, that he was a marked man. I knew it. I always knew it. "Pity an old man's bum ticker," Sam would kid the boys on the rare occasions he was allowed up at bat and they insisted that he run all the bases. An instant later, fully awake, he shed the knowledge.

"Isaac darling, wake up, honey, you've got to get up. Your mother's waiting."

"She's *here*? In the house?"

Agnes peeked out the window.

"She's sitting in the car. With the engine running."

Isaac couldn't find his shoes or socks. Anywhere. Oh dear Christ, the horror of it. His dad sick. His dad in the hospital. Lord, let it not be. Don't let it be true. Let him live and live to be a hoary old geezer, underfoot, forgetful, captious. Like Achilles hearing the news of Patroclus's slaughter, arming, weeping, cursing, Isaac sniveled and hunted for his socks. He could *feel* his father's disease right here in his chest, as if one arrow had simultaneously pierced both hearts in a misbegotten Valentine's Day massacre, oh dear Christ, let it not be so, let him live. He could see his father's gaunt face, and he knew again he was a marked man—no, don't even *think* it—a goner—no, don't—and Agnes meanwhile was pulling on his blue jeans for him, trying to dig out a decent shirt with all its buttons on, a long-sleeved shirt that buttoned. Oh dear, I was going to do all the sewing this afternoon, she muttered, anxious that Isaac, her handiwork, be presentable even at death's door, appear healthy and well cared for, his family mustn't think she was letting him go to seed.

"Don't bother, leave it alone." Isaac grabbed a shirt from the drawer.

"Oh, not that one, the elbows are out," pleaded Agnes vainly, cramming his big feet into sneakers. Was it possible he really had no proper street shoes? Next time they went shopping she would drag him for sure to the Bass outlet. Isaac, fending off the proffered jacket—his going-to-Harvard jacket—seized a hooded sweatshirt, and snuffling, sobbing, tumbled through the door. "Don't worry about me," she called after him. "I'll be here." And God keep you, darling heart, she added under her breath.

Certain kinds of fear make you groggy. Fear for your life conscripts every nerve and muscle into clarity, but dread clouds them in self-protective stupidity. Half-asleep, half-dreaming when his true love pushed him out the door, Isaac stared down at his dragging feet, trying hard not to step on any cracks. The garden path was brimming with muddy spring puddles; he could smell the quick pungence of glorious earth reviving. How strange, and sickness and mortality were waiting at the other end. If only he could get back into his dream, wander hand in hand with his dad under that pitchy vault like the ghosts of antique lovers, if only he could sleep another hour. At the bottom of the drive his mother's gigantic red Matador was waiting, engine rumbling. Rusty holes in the rear. How in hell did she expect to pass inspection in April? And how had she found her way to their mountain safe house? Ostrichlike, he had assumed he and Agnes were living so far off the map that nobody could ferret them out. But that was ridiculous: civilization lay in the valley below, Auburn was forty minutes away. It was myopic to think you could set up house in Jessup County so far out nowhere that people didn't know exactly where you were. Not that he and Agnes were hiding.

Drumming her stubby fingers on the wheel, Mattie wouldn't look at him, gazed straight ahead. Even before he shut the door she'd jammed her foot on the accelerator. The car roared off with a screech, bouncing along the ruts in the dirt road.

"You know," she opened, "I think next time you might find yourself a concubine who comes with electricity and telephone."

"Don't use that word. You don't even know what it means, you ignorant old sow."

"It means slut, and it doesn't take a college degree to know what to call a woman who sleeps with a boy half her age."

"Shut your filthy mouth."

"Anyway, all I was saying is you oughta get your schoolmarm hooked up to a telephone. With your dad in the hospital, I'm in no mood to come hunting you down in the boondocks. And what is this no-telephone shit, anyway? She can certainly afford it. Are you ever going to get your driver's license, Isaac?"

"What's with Dad? What happened?"

"Well, he just collapsed. They won't know for another twenty-four hours if he had a heart attack or what. He's a sick man, your dad, and it's all his own stubborn fault, too. He won't go to the doctor, he nearly bites your head off if you even mention the word, tells me I'm nagging him to an early grave so's I can collect the insurance money."

"Is he all right? What happened, Mom?"

"What do you mean is he all right? He's in the hospital. It's his own damn fault," she repeated. "He doesn't eat much more than Turny. And when he eats, he gobbles: terrible indigestion. That's what kills you, gobbling." And she looked at him for the first time. "I hope *you're* chewing your food properly, Isaac. They say you're supposed to chew ten times before you swallow."

"Go on with your story, Mom."

"Well, he's been looking pretty pukey lately. I thought vacation would do him some good. Yesterday he wasn't feeling well, gas and pains all over, so I say, Sam, I want you to call Dr. McCormick, and he says, Nothing doing, and I say, Sam, you've got to: you owe it to us. I don't want a sicky on my hands. And he goes, Yeah, yeah, very sarcastic, as usual. He lays down in the afternoon and finally I get him to say he'll call Dr. McCormick in the morning if he still feels punk. Well, in the morning, he's changed his mind: too embarrassed, doesn't want to bother the doctor over nothing. Anyway, he says, we can't afford it. You walk into the office, say, Hello, Miss Franklin, that's ten dollars. You hang up your coat, another ten. The doctor comes out, says, Hey Sam, how you like them Red Sox? and there goes another ten-spot. By the time you're done, you're out forty dollars and the doctor tells you to take some Tums after meals. And the school health-care plan eats shit. If we're going to blow forty dollars, he says, I'd rather blow it on a trip to the coast, go look at the submarines in Portsmouth. I'm sure it's better for your health, he says, to go look at the Navy Yard, see the subs, than have some guy in a white dress poking metal in your ears. It's visiting the doctor that makes you sick, he says. You know your dad—the only time he thinks twice about spending money is on something he doesn't want to do. Something useful."

A fool for stories, Isaac laughed too loud. Such was the lure of narrative he forgot he already knew where it ended, with Sam not sailing off in rebel triumph to take a gander at the submarines in Portsmouth harbor but lying captive in a hospital ward.

"So the only thing wrong with him, he says, is a nagging wife, anyway, he's feeling better. And then, after breakfast, he faints, so I run him over to the hospital, and they take him into the emergency room, and then the cardio unit, pump him up a bit, say he'll have to stay awhile. Turner's waiting for him to come out. I wanted to stay, but Turner said I'd better come get you, just in case. Nice place you're living. *Central.* When you lived at home with us, you were always complaining we lived in the sticks. But I guess it's the company makes the difference."

"Who's his doctor? What did the doctor say? That he'd had a heart attack?"

"Yes. Doc is some Greek hotshot. Says they can't tell yet, but it looks like he might have had a heart attack. Or whatever fancy name they call it so you don't know what they're talking about. A cardio-what-do-you-call-it episode."

"A bad one?"

"I couldn't understand a word he was saying. Anyway, I told you, they can't tell yet."

They were on Route 101 now, Mattie all over the road, heavy on the horn, tailgating a slowpoke in the fast lane, passing on the right, and then swooping in to cut him off sharp. "Damn slope."

"He wasn't a slope."

"Driving a Corolla, isn't he? Aiding and abetting the slopes, then."

Isaac, unable to summon up his chronic filial fury, gazed with something close to adoration at his mother's strange arrowhead face, like a profile cut from Mount Rushmore, green-brown, lipless, all beaked nose and craggy jutting chin. Every word she uttered revealed a bigotry and pig ignorance that took your breath away, a deformity of the soul, really: blacks were thieving, stuck-up Jews wanted to take over the world, Asians of all description were sly torturers, slavemasters, sneaks—*Bridge Over the River Kwai* summed up their plans nicely—the sick, the deaf, the dumb, the crippled did it to impose on the healthy, she used "intellectual" as a dirty word and trusted only what she saw on television, she thought men were up to no good and women were put-upon saps, she didn't believe in God but did believe in aliens, reincarnation, and tarot, and somewhere along the way she had taken on board a strange cargo of left-wing opinions about the wickedness of the United States and its military buildup, perhaps just to irritate her husband and sons, for Isaac knew at heart she was a born know-nothing reactionary.

Everything she said and thought disgusted him, or would have if he really thought she meant it—just like a woman, she expected to get away with murder because she knew you didn't suppose she meant it seriously—and yet there was something so hard and gritty, so alive in her attack—nothing tired her, nothing daunted her, much that upset the rest of the world amused her—that Isaac suspected she would be around after all higher life had been extinguished, quarrelsome, cannibal, triumphantly astride the wreckage. And then, with her cross-eyed logic she would surprise you with a sudden burst of horse sense, or her apparent deafness would be gainsaid by reels and reels of conversation reproduced verbatim.

"Don't undervalue your mother," Sam once told his son. "That's where you get your brains from, not from any Hookers. She's got one of the cannier minds in the West just sitting there idling." It was true: she had all the equipment yet willfully chose to misconstrue, to think a kind of nasty Jabberwocky about the world, forcing the most venal and bizarre interpretations upon events. You put your arm around her and she sniffed, "Trying to warm up, are you? Well, don't get *me* cold." Every time Sue dropped by, she had to make it plain to Mattie she hadn't come for a loan. Suspiciousness. As if noble ideals had never been thought and acted on, or kingdoms founded and conquered by a mere idea, a dream. An old man plants an olive grove knowing it will bear fruit years after he and his are gone; overburdened mothers take in other people's orphans. You could argue that the impulse to sacrifice for strangers is so much genetic coding, that insects do as much to preserve and enrich their species, but whenever he heard the word "genes" he knew someone was about to try and strip human life of its divine intimations, its freedoms. His mother luckily didn't talk of genetic coding but neither would she acknowledge those piebald patches of unsought generosity: everything was greed and machinations. Sometimes, aghast, he caught himself talking back ugly: that's what she did, provoked you to be as hog mean as she and then laughed as, exhausted and ashamed, you realized you'd just proved her point.

Did he respect her? Was it necessary to respect your mother? Did he still hope hopelessly to edge Turner out of her affections? Sometimes he caught shocked glimpses of her animosity toward him, frank, unhalted by motherly compunctions. Him? Her first-born Isaac? How could she? Forced to acknowledge that she honestly wanted him to be taken down a peg, sat on, denied, Isaac periodically lurched at the edge of blurting out his great whys, not quite wanting to hear the answers. What did I ever do to you? Is it just that you don't like my face?

His mother turned to him now, pale pebble-blue eyes that never blinked, relentless as a noonday sun and equally expressionless, as if not eyes at all but mere instruments of measurement and calculation, as impersonal as an abacus, an adding machine.

"You've made a fine mess of your life, haven't you, Ike?" He pulled a face.

"I'm glad you think it's funny. I think it's kind of sad," his mother pursued. "Here you are, twenty years old and strong as a horse. You got no limbs missing or injured parts or flat feet as far as I can see. When my old man was your age, he was a foreman at the brickworks already. Why don't you get a job? Or go back to school. You know I always thought this college shit was a total ripoff, but you whined and badgered us into it, we took out a loan. So why drop out now? Your dad is worried sick about you. Why don't you finish up, make your old man happy. I met Mrs. Cartwright the other day who told me you were the smartest kid ever went through Ashuelot. If you're so smart, how come you sit around on your butt, sleeping all day, and playing tin-pot Romeo with Miss Marple? Either fish or cut bait, get a job or go back to school. Or both. Turner's still in high school yet *he* manages to earn good money."

Isaac, heart pumping, stared hard at his feet. Should he tell? No, he was damned if he'd tell her that in fact he'd found himself a job setting type in Bellows Falls. He wished he hadn't, just to spite her money-grubbing one-track-mindedness. Spite. Her spite. Don't say a word. Just let her rail. Silence was what really drove her wild. Let her make a fool of herself. She was like that, a barnyard bully. Would go as far as you let her.

Daddy . . . Daddy . . . Daddy . . . What would happen without his dad as shield and intercessor, to care for him, to see the point of him? She didn't believe in him, that was it; that was worse even than not liking him. She didn't believe that his work was important, that his ideas and projects mattered. If he told her one day he was going to write books and that these yet-unborn children of his mind were of such overriding moment that he should be paid to lie in bed and dream them out, she would laugh him to scorn. With Sam laid up a mere day, Isaac had lost his license to become himself.

"And another thing, Isaac," she continued. "I don't know whether you're ashamed of her or ashamed of us, but don't hide. Stop by and see your dad, even just once a week would do nicely. It's not as if you got anything else to do. The truth is, I can get along without you— your kids grow up, you don't *expect* them to be around much any more—but it kills him not to see you."

"Are you done?"

"No, I'm not," and she drew her words out even slower now, just to make them last. "I want to know what you're living off. Your dad doesn't think about these things, he thinks people can live like birds off the air, but I know what it takes to get by in these parts, even without electricity. Are you on welfare, or are you living off that old maid's earnings, or what?"

"None of your business."

"Are you on drugs? Or are you just a regular, old-fashioned good-for-nothing bum?"

Isaac practiced his breathing. In and out, in and out he huffed and puffed. The harder he concentrated, the more shallow and wheezy his inhalations became. I can't hit her, he thought. I mustn't hit her, not even for insulting Aggie. I can't say anything. But the more he smothered his fury, the more irresistible the urge to lean over, grab the wheel, cuff his mother across the ear. How many years would a guy burn in hell for punching out his mother? Come to think of it, she was probably stronger than he, arm and leg muscles as well developed as a kangaroo's.

She was laughing now, her harangue forgotten.

"What's so funny?"

"I'm remembering the last time I was on this road. I took a customer just the other day to Rockingham." She warmed up, shaking her head. "Well, I wasn't paying attention—sailing along 101, missed the exit, got all turned around, made him late for his appointment. We pull up, I'd already told him twenty bucks. He goes, I'm not paying twenty. You fucked up, I'll give you fifteen. I say, The price is fixed, twenty to Rockingham like I told you. He says, No way. I say, Hand it over. He goes, Make me. So," she was grinning hard now, dimples ditch-deep, "I pull out the Beretta, turn around, stick him between the ribs. I go, Mister, I'm too old to play tag. Either it's your twenty like I said, or it's your liver. Your choice. You should've seen the silly look on his rabbit face. I tell you, he threw the money at me and *ran*."

"Are you *crazy*, Mom? What's the matter with you, pulling a gun on a customer? They'll lock you up."

Her face went stony. "Isaac, you got some nerve telling me how to run my business. If you want to drive this cab, fine. Otherwise, just stay out of it; you don't know diddly-squat. People see a woman behind the wheel and think they can take advantage. You got to show 'em who's boss."

Isaac pondered. "Would you have blown him away if he only gave you fifteen?"

"I don't back down, Ike."

"You'd kill a guy for five dollars?"

"It's the principle. It was mine."

Isaac subsided, fixing his eyes once again on his sneakers. Mine, mine, mine, he whispered to himself, trying to hold on to the solidity of the word with its two greedy meanings—mine like secreted ore, mine like not-yours—in all the hurtling matter that was rocketing around his brain. His mother was a lunatic.

"You think Daddy'll be all right, Mom?"

"If he wants to be."

"How long do you think they'll keep him in the hospital?"

"I don't know."

"You think they'll let him out in a day or so?"

"Don't be a retard, Ike, I already told you I don't know. Okay?"

Pressing his nose against the windowpane, clutching himself tight around the waist, Isaac rocked back and forth in a pendulum of misery. "I was just wondering," he muttered, but it came out in a pathetic little hum.

Turner was in the waiting room. Sickly neon light, a pile of magazines about cooking and motorboats, a dusty plastic plant standing guard in the corner. Turner was squashed against an unhealthily fat young woman who was crocheting a sweater; he looked very white.

As soon as Isaac laid eyes on him, he could see that his brother was already in his martyrdom mode, that strange hypnotic trance he entered in times of trouble, a kind of hibernation, as if the blood's temperature had sunk way down, his heartbeat slowed to moribund, as if his body were storing nourishment for a long winter's sleep, his energies turned inward. Don't bother me, seemed to say each hunched shoulder blade and turned-in ankle.

"Hey, Turner."

"Hey."

"You seen a doctor? They expecting Dad out of the cardiac unit soon?"

"I don't know," said Turner, just like their mother, but wearier.

"I hate it when people say they don't know," Isaac remarked aloud, sinking into a corner, sighing and groaning to himself.

"I'm using that ashtray, too," announced their neighbor as Mattie made a swipe for a little tin plate that looked as if it were meant for baking pies the size of a baby's fist.

Mattie ignored her. "People are very pushy around here," she observed to Turner. "You know, I notice that *heavy girls* are especially obnoxious. It's like they're compensating for something." Satisfied, she leaned back, drawing long and deep on her smoke, with narrowed eyes and a little smile.

"Want to play chess?" Isaac asked Turner. He always carried a pocket set, in the hopes of rustling up a customer.

"No, thank you."

"Want to play checkers?"

"Nah."

"Want to play hangman?"

This elicited an unwilling smile from Turner, so Isaac drew a crumpled liquor-store bill from his pocket, scrawled a hasty gallows on the back, and plotted out the blanks for his sentence. Hangman is an easy game: in the old days when the brothers were still inseparable, sometimes one would only have to plot out the blanks for the other to chime in with the answer. That at least was Isaac's view; Turner would tell you he only pretended to be interested in all the things his brother carried on about.

Turner couldn't spell. In fact, spelling was one realm where he let his imagination run riot, which gave him an advantage in playing hangman: you never knew how Turner would get it into his head to spell "guinea" or "Europe." You might guess *e*'s and he, having decided on *gini* or *Urup*, would draw you a leg for your pains.

Now it took him almost a whole man, balloon body, encephalitic head, pin arms, a crooked leg, to figure out Isaac's sentence, though it was an easy one: Ike always lobbed him military phrases. He sat hunched over the creased sheet that on one side bore the legend "State Liquor Store, Teasdale Shopping Plaza, Route 101; 750 ml. Jack Daniel's, $12.99, 750 ml. Wild Turkey, $10.99, Total, $23.98," and on the other side read, D __ M N   T __ E   T __ R __ E D __ E S.

"I don't know." He pushed the paper away. He refused to guess until he was absolutely sure.

"Well, guess," persisted Isaac. Turner stared, impatient, not really paying attention, and then with a grimace of recognition muttered, "Very clever, Admiral Farragut."

Neatly and thoroughly blotting out Isaac's handiwork, he drew on the back of a library call slip, shading in the perspective of the scaffold's base. When it came to composing a sentence, however, all the boy could do was stare at the page, chewing on his lip. Stuck. Long minutes passed; it got unnerving. Is he trying not to cry, Isaac wondered, and this made him feel sorry for Turner, who didn't really know whether or not he loved their father or how much their father loved him but was going to have to figure it all out fast.

"I can't think of one," he said, finally, and Isaac knew not to press him. So Isaac thought of a couple more, Turner narrowly escaped a hanging, but neither was attending, and the lull between Turner's rehearsals of the alphabet grew awkwardly long, and the boys caught each other's eyes leaping to the door expectantly at every noise, and Isaac wondered why he'd started this silly game to begin with, instead of letting the two of them worry in peace.

Isn't it funny how Turny clenches up like a fist when things go wrong? Isaac thought to himself. First glimpse of a cloud in the sky, Mom attacks and Turny clams up. Always did clam up: you'd get ready to hit him and find he was already screwed up in a ball, white-faced, eyes closed, pretending to be elsewhere. Other kid brothers and sisters ran screaming to their parents, giving you the satisfaction of proving them sissies; Turner just went dead and silent. Somehow it took all the fun out of persecuting him. *That's* the secret of martyrs, *that's* where they get their victory. How can you triumph over the guy you're beating to a pulp when you know he is thinking about fly fishing or God or whether the Cardinals are going to make it to the World Series. When you know that his mind is a kind of chalice whose surface your fingerprints will never so much as fog.

And yet the martyr nonetheless comes up short, too. Unless he's Jesus (and maybe not even then) he doesn't *love* his persecutor truly, maybe his persecutor is the one who truly loves, and the one who loves is the one who wins, either the Kingdom of Heaven or whatever hot sweaty laughing sublunar happiness we know. Isn't martyrdom then a kind of narcissism, with its isolating sense of superiority? Isn't it in danger of selfishness? If the martyr really loved his enemy he wouldn't encourage him in evil by offering the other cheek, no more than you would incite your own child or friend to wickedness but would tell him why he shouldn't hit the defenseless. That's Jesus' fault, too: it's egotistical to turn the other cheek, to allow a man to sin against you and then encourage him to redouble his sin. Unless, thought Isaac suddenly, unless it was all an object lesson: by experiencing his own sense of sin upon sinning, man exercises free will and freely learns to choose good. But what an uppity and cold-blooded way to teach a lesson, and one that sinners never learn.

But what did Jesus have to do with Turner, who was now a high-school senior and ten years past the age when Isaac used to throw him down the stairs and practice rabbit punches and half nelsons on him? Did Turner still want to be a saint? He looked it, in a strange contemporary sort of way—a modern-day martyr to fitness. He worked out to the point where his body had become a rack of wiry muscles, and his clothes—starched button-down shirt, knife-pleat chinos (he must iron them himself; Isaac pictured him rising in the dark, bent over the ironing board, steamrollering each cuff and collar cardboard-stiff)—sat oddly on him, like a dancer's street clothes. In this waiting room littered with female mammoths who smelled, the immaculate uniform set him apart, as if he were a doctor.

Contradicting all this trendy fitness and well-being were Turner's hunched shoulders, the muscles chewing away in his flat cheeks, and that look of locked withdrawal, oblique eyes on ball bearings that never met yours. What if it weren't some bully punching him out but life itself against whose press and overtures Turner was buttressing himself? Then this withdrawal was a mistake he would pay for later. If Daddy dies, Turner will never get over it. But what Isaac meant by "get over it" was become human.

Time passes by other measures in a windowless room. Another young hippo joined the first, trailed by two tow-headed children with dirty chins; several yards of parti-colored wool had been converted into several inches of sweater; if you marked time by cigarettes, as Mattie did, half a pack passed; Isaac, studiously ignoring his mother and having gone through eighty pages of magazines, was reduced to memorizing ads; ten Turnerine fingernails were munched to the nub; and no news of Sam. It was Turner who thought of asking Dr. McCormick to come to the hospital and find out what was going on.

Every few minutes Isaac's pacing led him to the nurses' station, where a pale sister was on duty. "Any news? When can I talk to my dad's doctor? Is he still in the cardiac unit? When is he coming down?"

"I don't know, and asking me every five minutes isn't gonna make me know any faster," she snapped.

He leaned over, glasses fogging up, silenced. God, you could put your fist through a wall at the unfair odds of this class war waged between a patient's family and the bored nurses, hurrying doctors; even the orderlies rolling their trollies past the waiting room seemed to be out to neglect, imprison, torture patients and confuse and fleece their kin.

Floating somewhere in the milky-blue ether was his rock, his refuge, his fiery-haired ineffable one. If he wished, prayed, chanted her name hard enough, could he will his father into safety, propel himself into the shattering tranquillity of her embrace? Agnes, Agnes, Agnes. How long before he saw her again, squeezed, kissed, sucked, stared at, ingested her from haughty copper head to long elegant toe with arms sinewy tight around him. Agnes who would laugh off, defend him against his mother's undermining. His mind ran in tedious obsessive circles, plotting alternate routes of quick escape. If Sam was released that very day, Isaac would be duty-bound to spend the night in Auburn. And not get back to Agnes until the next day, or even speak to her on the phone? But if his father was kept in the hospital for the night, then could he race home to Aggie? If he offered his mother twenty dollars, would she drive him?

Please God let me return to my beloved darling tonight. He rehearsed what he would say and she would say, savored the smell of her, her intonations, fretted at the obstacles separating them. Kept apart when I only just found her. Stay calm, he told himself, but he was trembling with adolescent violence, heart knocking, breath rabbit-shallow. Breathe, Isaac reminded himself. He made whistling noises through his nostrils. Sit. He tried to pin himself down to the molded plastic chair, but flung loose, jumped up. "I can't bear it!" To his own surprise, the words had come out in a shout. Faces in the waiting room blinked shut. Throwing down the hangman sheet, greasy from his clutching, and stomping on it, he rushed out into the corridor, flinging open doors right and left.

"You can't go into rooms like that," pursued the nurse. "Stop it, or else I'll have to make you leave."

"I want to see a doctor. I want to know where my father is."

One flight up, Isaac bumped into Dr. McCormick trotting down the hall after a high-flying white coat topped by a pompadour like combed slate.

"My boy . . ." said Dr. McCormick cheerfully, putting an arm around Isaac and propelling him toward the other man. "This is Dr. Mavropoulos."

"We've been stuck in that room two hours and nobody will tell us what's going on and what's wrong with my dad. Are you going to let him die in there? I want to know what happened and when he's coming home."

The two exchanged looks. "Calm down, lad," shushed Dr. McCormick, patting his shoulder.

Sam had had a heart attack, he explained, not all that major but the arteries were very clogged for such a young fellow, and they strongly advised that he have a by-pass operation to reroute the blood's flow, make him as good as new. In the meantime he would be staying here for a few days just so they could monitor him, see that he'd recovered fully. Once you had one, you were likely to have another.

"Why don't you come around and visit my daughters any more?" Dr. McCormick concluded, again encircling Isaac and giving him a tight squeeze. "You always make them laugh. Lindy never stops talking about the time you declaimed Greek poetry to her in the kitchen."

"When can I see him?" interrupted Isaac. "It wasn't Greek, it was Catullus. It was the only way I could think to talk dirty to her. When can I see my dad?"

The patient had just been transferred from intensive care to a regular ward, Dr. Mavropoulos said, running a hand preeningly across the surface of his hairdo. He would be groggy from sedation, but they could go see him now.

Mattie and her sons passed rows of narrow bodies in shrouds of sheet, shrines attended by awkward pilgrims, low murmurings, yellow hands, votive flowers, piety, wasting, grief. Isaac didn't recognize his father. Sam's face was tallow colored, creased with crow's feet, his eyes were shut, their lids stained brownish lavender from a permanent fatigue, and he looked dead except for the expression on his face of intense and petulant disgust, which Isaac realized only afterward was pain. Plugged into his arm was a drip attached to a massive tank. The sight of him was quieting.

The family drew up chairs. You couldn't tell whether he was sleeping or simply waiting for them to go away and leave him be. They stayed.

The hospital window faced west onto a splendid icy sunset. Hungry for light and air, the two boys straggled over to the window, which looked over a parking lot, and beyond that, rolling hills and a smokestack along the river, puffing airy dust like a toy cannon into a marbly pink sky. The waning of a clear March day. Against that transparent pinkness dark ducks flew overhead in a diluted flock, dribs and drabs returning North from a southern winter. The brothers gazed in silent complicity at the long bullet bodies, with wings set way back on their hinges, pumping fast, like rowers on a skiff.

"O for the wings of a duck . . . You still shoot, Turner?" Isaac's voice was too loud.

"Yeah. Ducks are different: you need decoys and blinds." And a moment later, "Wild turkeys are best of all. Wily like you wouldn't believe: they got eyes that move three hundred sixty degrees and they can run like the wind. I caught a turkey with seven-eighth spurs last season. Trickiest hunt of my life . . ." Surprised by this burst of nervous loquacity, they glanced guiltily at their father. Other visitors, too, Isaac had picked up, veered between long faces and hushed tones and a sudden, inappropriate perkiness.

While it was still light the nurse brought in supper trays with their funny preserved stink. Sam didn't get any, but Isaac noticed he cocked open an eye at the commotion and made a little grimace before closing shop again. The boy moved over, gazing down anxiously, beseechingly, at a pained yellowish face that, eyeless, all light fled, seemed made of wax. El Greco's dead Count Orgaz, thought Ike, all concavities, bone and cartilage, carved to express suffering, silence, endurance. It seemed journeys, centuries away from the sly, clever, restless, sardonic mug he knew. How can something so particular, so dense with life, become in sleep and sickness a mere mask, a puckered ball of bone and flesh, like those fanned grouse corpses Turner brings home for Mom? Where was his father now? Had he already come unglued from the body Isaac was praying to? Was he off somewhere, looking down at them? It was becoming as difficult not to cry as holding his breath underwater; the tears were building up in a great tidal wave in his chest and throat.

His father's eyes opened, weary, leaden, mere strips of glazed and patterned grayish green beneath dome-shaped lids. His gaze swiveled around to Isaac, then to Turner, and on, unsatisfied. He was looking for his wife, who had gone into the hall for a smoke. When he spoke, the words were too low to catch, but the irritation was unmistakable.

"What are you staring at?"

"What?" said Isaac. "I didn't hear you, Daddy. What did you say?"

Sam shut his eyes again.

It was midnight before Isaac got back to Agnes. All those hours of conjuring her up in the waiting room had paid off, they were together again. Hallelujah.

There they sat in their crooked gaslit kitchen, Agnes heating his supper at the stove while he recounted the day's harrowings, its sour revelations, Mattie and the gun, Mattie and the fat lady in the waiting room, Turner tight as a clam, the doctors with their neglectful tyranny, his own desolation at the sight of his dead-looking father. And Agnes, listening, held his beefy hand and kissed it. Midflood, hearing the sound of his own voice, Isaac stuttered to a stop.

Agnes squeezed encouragingly. "What, dove?"

He waved his head from side to side. "Christ, the maudlin posturing of me! And how could I have deserted Turner and Mom to come prancing home to you? Oh Lord, what's going to *be* with my poor Dad? Don't I feel anything real?"

Agnes hauled him to his feet. "Quit your self-indulgence. Main thing is, you've got long days ahead of you, lover-boy, and no more rising at three P.M. Do you hear? That's what's real: five hours' sleep, coffee, and a shave. And being nice to your lousy mother."

Worry had roused in Isaac a fearsome lust, yet when Agnes led him to bed and slid her long freckly limbs under the covers, instead of doing what all day he'd dreamed of, Isaac went to the window and sat down at his desk. Outside, the tarry-black horizontal scales of the cedar tree shuffled in the wind like a slow tyrannosaurus, like the shifting of tectonic plates, staining the moonlit starkness of the grass. Above the cedar, Swiss dots of stars were pinned across the black sky and a shocked-looking moon scudded from behind fast-moving clouds. Then both moon and stars were blotted out by looming gray.

For an hour or two, Isaac sat thinking of the Jessup County Hospital, those aisles of cots, the ghoulish fluorescent light emanating from the nurses' station, his father's long narrow frame wrapped in its night-gown-shroud under the sheets, hooked up to the drip, awake perhaps, frightened, and wondering why for this first night in twenty-two years he was lying alone in a strange bed.

Chapter 2

THERE WERE TWO other men in the ward, which was painted a cheerful eggshell blue, more befitting a nursery than a sick bay.

On one side of Sam was Mr. Janssen (everybody called each other Mister), a quiet steady-eyed nurseryman with a fine ruddy-flushed northern complexion that promised diabetes and early heart failure. He dozed all day and only came to life when his bright shrewlike wife visited, or when you quizzed him about trees and shrubs. Ike would sit by his bed for ages, discussing pear thrip, which was not a dessert but a blight infesting New England's maple trees. Mr. Janssen had been born in one of those Scandinavian kingdoms of blue-black pine, frozen sea, silver light. Although he had come to the United States as a small boy, he still sang his words low in the throat. When Sam confessed to some vagueness about Mr. Janssen's native country, Isaac stared at him in astonishment. "He's from Göteborg," chewing a little on his lower lip as if to collect and savor all the associations that name conjured up, before delivering his father a brief history of this Swedish seaport, its destruction by the Danes in the Kalmar War, its part in the East India trade.

"You've heard of the Göteborg licensing laws, of course."

"Of course," said Sam. "Isaac, stop lecturing me."

"Well, they were the earliest government restrictions on the liquor business," continued his son, undeterred. "In the industrial age, that is. The Babylonians, who could have taught the modern world a lesson in state coercion, had a whole gob of licensing laws but those, thank God, weren't so Sunday school in intent."

"Isaac, will you please stop lecturing? I'm the history teacher, remember?"

Isaac, now deliberately torturing him, shouted merrily, "But, Daddy, we're just getting to the interesting part—don't you want to hear about the Code of Hammurabi's restrictions on wineshops, and how a nun who walks into a bar gets burned at the stake, and a wine seller caught charging more than the government rate is thrown in the water?"

"What the fuck has a Babylonian nun got to do with Sweden, which I didn't want to hear about anyway?"

"I was only telling you where Mr. Janssen comes from." Isaac was *always* big on history and geography. When he and Billy Ostrich first fell in, Sam used to tease him by calling his best friend Billy Toucan or Billy Pelican or asking him why his friend always hid his head in the sand. Isaac, casting his father that same look of astonishment, had said pityingly, "It doesn't mean that, Daddy. It means *Austria* in German. Österreich—kingdom of the East. It's a corruption." This, Sam discovered, was not even a piece of Ostrich lore, but something Isaac had figured out and decided for himself. Now when Billy came over Sam would start humming Viennese waltzes and inquire of Isaac when his school friend was returning to his fatherland, but secretly he was quite impressed.

Across from Sam was Mr. Horton, irascible, barrel-chested, a veteran of World War II and retired businessman. Isaac and Mr. Horton, who had been stationed in the Pacific at the time of the Japanese surrender, had so much to talk about that it seemed as if now till Doomsday wasn't time enough for them even to warm up. Such was the guilty intensity of the affinity between these two that sometimes Sam had to remind his son that he was here to visit him, not Mr. Horton. Not that Sam felt like talking.

Once you were in the hospital, properly immersed in the very bowels of it, you no longer noticed the pickled smell of bed-weary flesh, of bandages and casts, of hospital food with its formaldehyde taint, of disease, plastic tubes, misery. You weren't so distressed by the groans and racking coughs from down the hall, punctuating a nocturnal quiet so intense that only the ticking of the clock on the wall by the nurses' station disturbed it (the clock, Sam guessed, was the same make as the clocks in school, with a minute hand that jumped back a stroke before advancing), or unsettled by the sight of shrunken yellow crones who had lost their memory and didn't know where they were and frightened men with blue legs in ankle socks creeping like unshriven souls past the door on a nurse's arm.

A hospital, he realized as the days crawled by, with its harsh light, its prison paint job, its institutional stench, is a place where you learn to relinquish life slowly, living like an animal by the sun's rising and setting, low to the ground, self-absorbed, incurious, dependent upon the ministrations of people in uniform, who seem malevolently neglectful though they never leave you alone. It amazed him, when he felt well enough to notice, how quickly he had become a man who wore a nightgown and slippers, who "got up" when the nurses served breakfast and medication at six and "went to bed" at nine when lights went out, and who was never fully awake and yet never truly asleep either, but remained in a black stupor of weakness, self-pity, crabbiness, and—when the nurses were stupid—fury.

Was it hell or was it purgatory or was it a taste of existence without a divine soul, a mockery of mere survival? And the creepy truth was that much as Sam revolted against the cravenness induced by pain, much as he resented being carted around by orderlies on a metal tray, or reduced to an assiduously monitored seismograph, a trembling line on a chart, much as he hated watching a grown man, flesh dropping from his spindly shanks, being lifted by two young women to pee in a pot, still, something in him welcomed the suspension of freedom, care dissolved into a sea of sleep, pillows, daydreams, medication. If only he could smoke, if only the television stopped yakkety-yakking through all the daytime soaps with their tales of incest and abortion, if only he were strong enough to read a book, it would be a gas lying in bed all day being waited on by big-breasted country girls.

"Freedom is all we have," he heard Isaac declaiming to Mr. Horton, and yet freedom, Sam was finding, meant constant strife. Some mushy center of him was quite grateful to give it up, sink into the humble yet semihallowed profession of the "patient."

They wanted him to get better and their very health was a rebuke; he in contrast was discovering that living might require more of a struggle than he had bargained for. Did Mr. Janssen and Mr. Horton feel the same way? Were they too secretly relieved to be sick, irreproachably out of responsibility's way? Certainly Mr. Horton appeared to be every bit as irritated and depressed by *his* family's visits as was Sam.

Pain makes you captive; captives don't like free men. Sam didn't feel up to acting healthy, but neither was he willing for his many visitors, relatives, colleagues, students, past and present, to witness his surrender to churlish impotence.

And when he wasn't in pain or sleeping, he wondered what was in store. What had happened? He had suffered a serious heart attack. It was a bluff and a warning. In this brief time of truce, Sam had to decide: would he give his assent to life, and bid his faltering muscle heal and strengthen? Did he want passionately to pay off his mortgages, get the roof fixed, retire and take his wife to Florida, live to see his sons' children, or did these wayward organs, fed up with his cowardly indifference, have other plans? You don't love life; well, then, give it up.

Dr. Mavropoulos said he was going to have to have a by-pass, reroute his arteries' liquid traffic, a horrid, violent operation yet a routine one. Amazing, the things that become routine. Of course, it was Sam's decision. He had automatically said no, it wasn't worth it; Isaac had said yes. Looked like the ayes were going to have it. They had to break your chest open. They said it depressed you for ages after, and also that its good effects lasted ten years at the most, though ten years at the moment sounded an eternity's drudgery. He would have to go to a bigger hospital, of course, to Rockingham or Brattleboro. Where was he going to get the money? He was a little vague about the school health plan. Isaac assured him it covered such operations, but to Sam's mind it seemed as likely to cough up for a sex change or a face-lift as for so extravagant and minute a rehauling.

Ike (of course) had become an expert, and spouted all kinds of technical jargon; he was in cahoots with McCormick and Mavropoulos. Since Turner had no opinion, one way or the other, Sam was obliged to take refuge in Mattie, who, to his surprise, informed him that he was going to get carved up and by-passed, or else.

At the crack of visiting hour, Isaac turned up. Turner wasn't with him; Turner stayed away. This grieved Sam mightily. He understood the boy was embarrassed by his father's being sick, publicly sick, and resented the fuss. Really, Sam couldn't blame him; fathers weren't supposed to make themselves conspicuous. School had started again, but Turner had been playing hooky. Every day now Sam told Isaac his brother should get his skinny ass back into the classroom where he belonged, but Turner wouldn't. Wouldn't come to the hospital, either, except last Sunday with Mattie, when he refused to meet his father's eyes and Sam was too exhausted to coax and woo. Between his mute intransigence and Isaac's manic gabbiness it was enough to make you long for the parental equivalent of orphanhood.

"What does he do with himself all day?" he asked Isaac.

"Oh, this and that."

"What's this and what's that?"

"He's been figuring out new computer programs." A tightwad and provident, like his mother, Turner had hoarded enough money to buy himself a used Leading Edge, upgrading its hardware byte by byte. "Sometimes he plays basketball with his friends."

"Tell him to go back to school if he intends to graduate. Tell him I don't want two dropouts in the family. At least you made it out of high school. I'm not planning to kick the bucket just yet, and this death-watch makes me nervous."

Yesterday Sam had asked Mattie who was filling in for her while she was at the hospital, and when she didn't answer he realized it was Turner. Ordinarily the idea that his son was missing school to work for Mattie's Cabs would have made him bust a gasket, but these days he was seized by so primitive a need for his wife he said nothing.

Today Isaac came bounding in like a pink-and-gold baby elephant, giant head rolling a little on its bearings, blind eyes dancing behind three-inch-thick glasses, plump dimpled fingers spread and waving like underwater plants, beaming and laughing before he'd even got his foot in the door. A bumpkin, a village idiot in high-top sneakers and baggy patched trousers, pockets bulging with books, magazines, pipe, to-bacco, chess set. Ragged flannel shirt missing so many buttons it showed the golden hair on his pot belly.

Did a man ever get used to having a child two inches taller than he, thirty pounds heavier, and with far more hair on his chest? Shrink, Isaac, he ordered mentally, beating back pride. Nor could he under-stand this chronic slovenliness. It seemed to him a self-inflicted illness, an invitation to contempt. If you grew up as broke as Sam the only thing that separated you from the honest-to-God poor and that com-mended you to superiors was your appearance: anyone who looked at Isaac would conclude he ought to be institutionalized at the state's expense.

"You've been a civil servant too long, Dad," Isaac bellowed, much amused. "Don't you know the world needs more hobos?"

"Shush, Ike, not so loud. Don't be sentimental. Box-car days are over. Anyway, you need rich parents for that."

Slob though Isaac was, anyone who looked past the grime and tatters couldn't help seeing that the young man was drunk with joy. In this house of death, in whose precincts he respectfully tried to suppress it, there was something almost hysterical, unhinged in Isaac's exultation. Calm down, Sam wanted to warn his wild, moody son, calm down or you'll crash. The cause he knew, and wished he didn't.

Sam, who felt himself spectral and transparently insubstantial, often wondered how his boy could get so filthy blue. Depression as he understood it was the recognition of one's own unreality; Isaac need only look at his own big toe to be flooded by the knowledge that this was a toe among toes, a toe of undeniable and superabundant reality. I don't know who I am, he thought in a clutch of self-pity, as Isaac, done teasing the other patients and dispensing presents, gave his father a pat on the head and a great smacking kiss on the cheek. Tears surged as he wiped the saliva off with a great show of disgust.

Down the aisle Mr. Horton and even Mr. Janssen had inched up in their beds, craning necks to hear. The nurse came in and turned down the television. "This one," she nodded, "is better than *Another World*."

"Hello, nursey. Have these rascals been giving you a hard time?"

"You can say that again. I can't get your dad to eat for love or money. I tell him, You're payin' for it anyway, so don't be bashful. I go, It's good food, makes your bones strong, but he's not having any."

"It's the only grub I ever tasted that's worse than my wife's."

"I've got a present for you," interrupted Isaac.

"If you've been carrying it around in those pockets of yours, it's going to be a doozy," Sam grumbled.

Isaac drew forth a small headset and a fistful of tapes. "This wasn't my idea, you know I'm not very musical. But Agnes *is*: it was her idea. She's even infected *me* with her intolerable high-mindedness; I sit there grinning away at poor deaf Beethoven on the radio. After all, the deaf have got to stick together, and now that I've begun listening to these guys, I find they all were, Smetana too. You know him, Daddy? A stone-deaf Czech. He wrote an autobiographical quartet I've brought for you, wrote it in three days in Spillville, Iowa. The first violin's whistle is supposed to symbolize his growing deafness—that's what the booklet says, anyway. So here's some deaf music for you: lots of thunderous Beethoven all about the brotherhood of man, and liberty and excess, and Smetana about his childhood."

"You're not deaf any more," objected Sam, who hated Isaac's parading his defects. "Those guys got deaf as they grew older; you had childhood deafness." It was true that the early blight had lifted, leaving sounds nearly clarion as trumpets on Judgment Day. "Thanks anyway."

"Don't thank me; it was Agnes's idea."

If only Ike would stop mentioning that woman, whose existence he was doing his best to forget. But since Isaac knew better than to talk her up to his mother, clearly he was working to soften up his dad, the way children do: if they can't get in at the front door, round they run to the back. If he kept it up, Sam would be forced to have a talk with him about his future; for all he knew this was Isaac's secret purpose. Not yet, O Lord.

"Here's the Sturgis *Gazette*, and the *Recorder*, and the *New York Times*, and here's that English magazine I was telling you about that has an interminable article on dictionary making. Here's another very fine rag for you, Daddy, called *Aurora*. It's published in New York, and it's got a piece on child sacrifice in ancient Carthage—for or against—and an article on Eastern Europe. And there's a piece I want you to read on the Mexican Revolution, and why people should read Herodotus, and Herbert von Karajan's early years, and some mediocre poetry."

"Sounds a little bossy to me. I don't feel like reading, anyway."

"And here's a potted plant from your beloved eighth grade—if they knew the snotty way you speak of them, they would send you a tank of piranhas. And your reading glasses, as requested."

"Those aren't mine; they're Mom's."

"Don't be so fussy; glasses are glasses." Sam glanced back unsmiling (he hadn't smiled since the heart attack), wondering where Mattie *was*, anyway. These days he couldn't bear having her out of his sight.

"Is she still not smoking?"

"No, thank God, she went back to it. Turny and I begged her to, we couldn't take it any more."

Isaac chattered away high speed, about town gossip, how anxious everyone was to have Sam back home, about national and international news, about the Solidarity trade-union movement in Poland, and—resuming his hectoring tone—why the United States should certainly not reschedule Poland's debts.

"Everybody knows every penny they borrow goes straight to the Soviet Union, like a beggar child slipping alms to its drunken father. Anyway, the whole justification of making loans to a foreign government—that it might invest the money profitably and pay you back on its returns—simply doesn't apply under communism, which isn't after profit but the *unprofitable* consolidation of power.

"The trouble with America is we think the rest of the world is moved by our own rational concerns, like getting rich and spreading the wealth. You know, like every country's fondest dream is that all its people get to own their own homes. But it's not: totalitarian regimes are interested in real things, like ideas, terror, and conquest, in whose pursuit they've proved themselves again and again quite happy to starve and murder their own citizens."

"I see," said Sam, and then since Isaac seemed to expect more, added, "I don't really know much about the Polish economy," which was the point at which he'd stopped listening.

Isaac gave him one of his looks. "You may feel you don't know much about automobiles or about the human cranium, but if a man deliberately runs over an infant, you know what you think. In this case, we happen to be offering to pick up the tab for the killer's car insurance."

But Sam had already gone back to looking hard at his son's flushed face as he spoke, the way you stare at someone speaking a foreign language in the dumb hope that if you concentrate with all your might the strange sounds will become intelligible.

They pulled into the Teasdale Mall, Billy Ostrich and Justin James, the Karolis boys, Macy Driscoll, and Ray Doucette, all jammed together in Ray's father's Chevy. Isaac was waiting. He stood alone in the dark of the parking lot, waving an arm in lassos over his head, dancing a little reel, singing, pretending not to see them, droning his little song, clutching his waist in a peculiar way, running in funny darting scurries. The Chevy, like a bull charging a toreador, zoomed up; Isaac, whooping, darted away. Then he charged. "Go, on, scram, Jamesy," he shouted, pulling open the door and yanking Justin out of the back seat by a leg. "Hop up front. I demand to sit by Macy."

It was Ike's last night home. In the morning, he was leaving for Harvard. What do you want to do for a last blow-out? Peter had asked. I want to go to the Walcott Fair with you guys and Macy Driscoll, Ike replied promptly. Peter was surprised. Christina Molina, he would have understood. But Macy? Ike and the pale straitlaced little Macy enjoyed a taut snappish classroom rivalry. Peter wasn't even sure Macy would go along on an evening that included Ike, who was weird with women, frightening almost. He had never had a girlfriend, yet just this entitled him in his own eyes to any and all nubiles at large. Certain shameless little she-devils, loving the attention, let him paw them, pretending it didn't mean anything or that they were just being nice. Hothands Ike.

Justin, amazingly, obliged by moving up front, and Isaac squeezed in. He flung his loose arm around the girl; the other still clutched his stomach. She removed it firmly. Driscolls kept to themselves, and didn't touch before marriage—Macy's gawky rich parents were first cousins.

"What's with your stomach, Ike? You pregnant? Maybe he's got cramps," Justin teased.

Isaac, hugging his bulky sweatshirt, spluttered. As they drove off he drew forth his prize: a quart of Southern Comfort, half full.

"Southern Comfort!?" the boys were disgusted. "Cough syrup! Yuck!"

"Have a slug, Macy darling. Let's toast the unintended beneficence of Teasdale's own State Liquor Store."

Macy, lowering dark-lashed Driscoll peepers, declined. Isaac liked girls on the prissy side. Kept him in order.

"Go on, Macy, just a nip. I stole it for you. I want to get you so plastered you'll forget all about higher mathematics and the Corn Laws and do anything I want. Won't you be my sex slave for the night?"

"You *stole* it?" Peter Karolis, shocked, stopped midslug.

"Well, dummy, he wouldn't sell it to me, would he?" Isaac passed the bottle. "You never stole anything or any*body*, Pete?" Peter, famous for pirating other people's girlfriends, was silenced. "You won't squeal on me, will you, Mace? I just wanted a little comfort, that's all. It would be too *wretched* going to the damn fair stone sober, don't you agree? You know how much comfort costs, Macy? Ten quick fingers, that's all. Isn't that comforting?"

"Go on, Ike, keep those quick fingers to yourself," Peter warned, "Or we'll shunt Justin back between you."

The Walcott Fair was the same this year as always: the Moon Walk, silver-floored, billowed and tumbled you up out of gravity's reach, the rifle range with its angelic hierarchy of pink felt teddy bears, dodge 'em cars, a tinkly illuminated Ferris wheel. A lit field jagged with screams and music, livid with the smell of French fries and spun sugar. No ox pull, no prize sheep. The animals, it seemed, went home at night. But that was when Isaac started up. "I want to see the sows!" he yelled. "And the *coooowws*!"

Billy Ostrich had him by the arm. "Hey dude, pipe down. The animals need a rest too. Want to try shooting?"

Not such a good idea. Blind Isaac happily paid his quarter, seized the air rifle, and swiveled it point-blank at Billy's nose. Deliberately. It happened so quick, one moment Billy was gazing dreamily at hurdles of cotton candy like the terraced hairdos of Restoration cocottes, whirligigging go-carts, Dan Herringshaw with a cute baby granddaughter dribbling over his plaid shoulder, the next moment he was staring down a rifle barrel, too surprised to be scared, conscious only of the shocked murmurs of the other marksmen. Before he'd altogether registered the danger, the attendant had bullfrogged the counter and grabbed the gun from Ike's hands. An uproar arose. Everyone was furious.

"What the hey did you think you were doing?" Mr. Herringshaw berated Ike. "Doncha have any sense at all? Didn't your dad ever tell you not to point a firearm in someone's face unless you mean business?"

"I do mean business, you maundering fool," said Isaac, stroking the bottle in his pocket. "Business is exactly what I mean. Look at that hideous baby, Billy, spitting up all over its senile granddaddy's shoulder."

"Get your friend away from these grounds, son," the gallery attendant warned Billy. "Can't have people flying off the handle like that. He looks a little stewed."

Billy led him away. It was only once they started walking that his legs got a little trembly. "Want to go home, Ike?"

"Not on your life," roared his companion. "It's my last night among you hicks and I'm de-ter-mined to milk it for all it's worth. Hey, where are those prize cows, anyway?"

"Told you, Ike. Cows gone home. Hope you don't mind my asking why you stuck a gun at my face? Anything in mind?"

"Anyway, I never told him before . . ." Isaac was saying loudly to himself. "I never told him in all these years—and it's *bothered* me. Billy, I never told you in all these years how I don't like your face. It's not that your expression isn't very jovial and willing: it's the nose. All squashed in somehow. I only meant to rearrange it, give it substance."

"I'm no so wild about your beak either, brother, but I never thought to do anything about it."

"There's the difference between us. How come you never want to change things, Bill? Don't you just hate the world the way it is? You know what I mean? Too many days in the week, too many years to the century. It's not just your nose—it's everything."

"Let's go home, Ike."

"Noooooo . . ." he yelled again, leaning heavily against Billy. "I want to ride the Ferris wheel with Macy Driscoll. And I want to lie down in the grass and look at the stars. Do you think she'd lie with me?"

"I sure don't, dude."

They had wandered off into a corner of the field, Billy gently propelling him away from danger spots, and now Isaac did indeed flop onto his back in the wet grass, legs in the air like a dead sheep. Billy sat beside him.

"The goddamned stars . . . they don't know a thing. Little blind eyes in the sky. We see them, they see us. Do they give a damn? They're dead already. 'The stars be hid that led me to this pain.' That's Thomas Wyatt. D'you know any Wyatt, Billy? A courtier poet—Ann Boleyn jilted him; Henry VIII beheaded him on a trumped-up conspiracy charge. The guy had no luck, but he understood disgust through and through. See the Bear? Do you ever think of killing yourself, Billy?"

"Yes."

Isaac, surprised, flopped up on one elbow, stuck his fingers into Billy's face to see if he was serious. "I don't believe it."

"Why not? Doesn't everybody?"

"Why don't they *do* it then?"

"Too much else to do. And you think better of it."

"I don't," said Isaac, rolling up a sleeve and thrusting in Billy's face a fat white arm blistered with purple searings like a steak's charcoaled cross-hatches. "I'd poke my own eyes out soon as go on living sometimes. I did that with a pen-knife, night after night. Homemade tattoos. Just from boredom, really."

"Come on, Ike, let's go home."

But Isaac was back on his feet and tearing across the fairground like a child escaping its mother. Nimble, for someone so fat and drunk, though Billy's hunch was that Ike was feigning.

Nobody should have let him on the Ferris wheel but he barged to the head of the line, shoving a couple out of the way. Billy, way behind, saw with a sinking feeling that Ike had somehow succeeded in seizing Macy along the way, a doll-sized hostage, and now plumped himself and his prisoner down on the little swinging chair. It would have taken an ox to dislodge him. The chair lurched skyward, Isaac and Macy sailed to the stars; no sooner had they reached the top faltering pinnacle of the wheel's pivot than the machine ground to a halt. Their little chariot tipped in the wind, the village of Walcott counterpaned beneath them, Billy and Justin and Peter and Mike milling specks in the crowd.

It was there, at the faltering pinnacle of the wheel's pivot, two hundred feet up, bared to the stars, that Isaac made an indecent proposal. Afterward, nobody seemed quite sure what had happened.

Macy, scared of heights, clutching the bar, went white. "Isaac, stop it."

"You're my bride-in-the-sky, my straight-A Macy. Open up, now. Want to see how much I want you?"

"No . . . Isaac . . . Please stop it . . ."

But he had already crossed a boundary and rocking the chair, laughing maniacally, put his hand where he shouldn't have.

Macy, trapped, petrified with fear, flattened like a bird. "Don't . . ." she finally uttered between clenched teeth, pushing his hand away. "You've got no right."

Hand suspended in air, Isaac paused. His face darkened, looked suddenly hideous with anger. Was he going to force her? She knew she would slip through the railing and fall, but better to fall than remain trapped with this beast. He didn't. He put his fingers into his mouth, then withdrew them. It was over.

"I have no right?" he rolled out the words inquiringly before crashing down hard. "You and your family!" The metal chair flew, she leaned away from his spit. "You puffed-up, putrefied, smug, eviscerated Driscolls who never did anything for a hundred years but keep your skinny lips and crotches and wallets pinched tight, you mean-hearted prudes who marry your own snivelly kin like fucking Ptolemies, you frigid insipid limp little puppet of a girl."

He paused, grinding his teeth, puffing, glowering. Her rigid-with-hate stare only made him explode all over again. "You think you're a treat, Macy, just because you get good grades, because you're going to a nice girl's college, and you got an allowance bigger than my dad's salary and a maid to wipe your pitiful ass? You're not even smart. You know what it means to live life like a report card, only out for grades and teachers' smiles, venturing nothing, not minding you know nothing so long as your hand is up with the answer in the book? There are no more teachers, you silly rich girl," he bellowed, shaking her by the shoulder. "All that's done with. All that matters is what you do with your heart, what you make your own. No more grades, Macy. Understand? Ride's over, Macy, get off."

They had returned to earth with a wallop. A burly boy lifted the rail. Isaac, without a look back, lumbered off to his friends at the rifle range. Macy, sprung, wandered toward the parking lot on tottering legs. Gabriel Hanesworth found her there, leaning against the hood of someone's pick-up truck, trembling and white-faced. On the ride home, she wouldn't say what was wrong.

"You have fun last night, Ike?"

"Mmmmmmph."

"What did you say?"

A resentful sigh.

"You and your buddies paint the town red? Where did you go?"

Long pause. "Don't bother me, Dad."

His father stared at him hard, sideways, from behind the wheel until finally the boy recited, "Walcott Fair. After the fair shut down, we went to the drive-in. You satisfied? May I please go back to sleep?"

"Good movie?"

"*Texas Chainsaw Massacre*. It's been playing at the midnight show a year already. Seen it three times."

"Grows on you, huh?"

"I wouldn't know," Isaac said. "I was puking popcorn all over the deluxe interior of Ray Doucette's dad's car."

"Who cleaned up?"

"I don't know."

Sam cleared his throat. "You should have said goodbye to Turner properly."

"Don't bother me, I said."

"You still should have. It wasn't right just to yell up the stairs at him like that."

"He could have come down."

"He did come down. You'd already hightailed it out to the car and wouldn't look at him."

The boy mashed his nose against the car window. "Jeez, am I going to be glad to get *out* of here," he intoned, barely audible. That put his father in a sulk for the next twenty miles.

Isaac, too, for once was silent. He didn't toss and thrash about in the confined space as was his wont but slumped against the window, stuffed into the jacket and tie Sam had forced upon him. His first tie. An egg-catcher, Isaac had called it, a skinny napkin. True, it was already slop-encrusted from his farewell breakfast. What had gotten into the boy? He could be a real pain. Ungovernable, callous, nasty. Seeing the stricken look on Turner's face as he came running out to the car to say goodbye and Isaac, through glass, turning a mountainous shoulder, you almost hated him. For his last few hours, he could have tried, not left the stay-at-homes feeling burned, cast off.

And then, melting, Sam reminded himself that this was Isaac's first solitary trip into the world. Except for visits to his grandparents and the *National Geographic* contest, his boy had never been away from home. Nerves, that's all.

Isaac hummed. He was thinking about Macy Driscoll's crotch. That was a mingy unfeeling word for it—he recited sweeter names to himself, hoping he wasn't talking aloud. It hadn't felt cold and calcified like her, but a toasty, fragrant pouch, exasperatingly alive. How might he get back there? He'd burned his bridges for sure. Not that he cared for the rest of her. Rich brat. Would there be others? It wasn't a prideful debut, Isaac realized, but could he now go legit? Desire stirred, mixing with the remains of popcorn, Southern Comfort, fear, and self-loathing already sloshing around in his stomach, making him sick all over again. *Twat,* Sam caught Isaac muttering in a deliberate burry whisper, and felt helpless. How little he knew his boy now, and how much he guessed. If only he could keep him at home a little longer, send him into the world stronger and perfect.

"Do you absolutely insist on going away to college and leaving your poor ol' dad behind?" Sam said aloud. "*Must* you go to this repulsive school? What's wrong with Rockingham Tech? You too snooty to stay at home like everyone else? Will you still talk to us once you're a Harvard man?" Isaac, irked by the pleading clinginess in his father's voice, didn't bother to look around. Was he already bored by the enormity of his triumph?

It was another galaxy, worlds and oceans away, Sam reflected. He himself had never even met anybody who'd gone to Harvard. No Driscolls, no Herringshaws, no Urquharts had come close. Isaac had shot for the moon, and what's more, it had always been clear to all who knew him, to everyone but Isaac, that this particular moon must surely drop into his lap. He was a Latinist, he was good at math and science, he worshiped language and wrote like an angel, he loved to ask questions and loved to argue, and his mind was never still but always grinding away as indomitably as most people's large intestine, and his memory was staunch, he knew reams and reams of poetry by heart. Higher education was invented for children like Isaac, who never troubled themselves with thoughts of careers or utility but learned like swimmers, long-breathed, thrashing, arrow-straight, with every muscle of the body.

Harvard agreed; Ike was in. The only question was who would pay. Full scholarships were no longer so easily come by for middle-class white boys from New England, even sons of a family of four whose combined income (not that Mattie would throw in a dime) was twenty-seven thousand dollars a year and that not taking into account their debts. Two other colleges, including Boston University, offered to pay his way. No money from Harvard. For one wretched enervating month he moped around the house driving his father berserk pretending he didn't want to go anyway, in fact didn't want to go to college at all.

"What do you want to do instead?" Sam was cursed with the fatal flaw of taking his children's declarations at face value.

"Sleep."

"You boys," said Sam, darkly—he was having trouble with Turner, too. "I told your mother we ought to have got her spayed, raised chickens instead."

After a few dressings-down from the ferocious Miss Urquhart, Isaac had relented and allowed his father to take out a loan from the state. It grieved Sam sorely to teach so young a boy the life of debts; if only he could have played Polonius to his college-bound prodigy, instead of saddling him with decade-long installments of anxiety.

"You're going to have a lot less money than other kids," Sam fretted now. "It's not going to bother you, is it?" This was the moment for Isaac to *stop* feeling like a freak, to unlearn ostracism, to quit trying so furiously to dominate, to meet likemindedness and unbend. God keep poverty or a hard New Hampshire accent from being obstacles to his success, his assimilation.

Isaac frowned. This wasn't just a question of food and clothes, he realized, but of a world of allusion. "I wish I'd learned Greek."

"You can study it there . . ."

"I already know what I'm taking," he cut his father off.

"Oh? You decided already, without telling me?" Sam, still in love with the limitless possibility, the new starts offered by course catalogues, couldn't hide his hurt at having been denied the chance to advise, to compare Harvard's history courses with his own, to gloat a little over how well he'd prepared his boy for this expensive future. "What are you taking?" he asked in a small, jealous voice.

"Not interesting."

"Oh."

They dawdled on the journey to Moriah. At a Sears, Sam pulled in to buy Isaac extension cords and a desk lamp, at Arthur Treacher's they devoured fish and chips. Sam let Isaac play a little Pac-Man and even played a little himself. Bloop-bloop-bloop-bloop-bloop, gurgled the merry shark mouth as it swallowed dots. Sam made it all the way to Stage Three. Isaac wasn't looking. Funny how you crave confirmation not just from your elders but from your own children.

"We should have bought hangers," said Sam.

So they went and bought hangers at a mall, and Sam to his own surprise insisted on wooden ones, and even special hangers that clasped one's trousers at the ankles, although Isaac had no clothes to hang up and what clothes he had would reside in a tight fetid knot on the floor.

"Have you got a pencil sharpener? Have you got enough towels?"

Isaac looked fed up.

Back in the car Sam found his foot lighter and lighter on the accelerator. Sore as the boy made him, he would die just to keep skimming by inches down 101, never reaching Harvard Yard. He shrunk a little inside when they got to Nashua and turned onto the interstate, with the border only minutes away.

"Ever been to Benson's Wild Animal Farm?" he inquired, hopefully. "See the sign? I haven't seen many wild animals in my life. Except for your mother."

Despite the foot-dragging they reached Cambridge by three. Sam sailed through Johnston Gate and anchored his shabby Dodge amid a navy of Mercedes and Volvo station wagons smeared with wildlife stickers and laden with electronics. Together they unloaded Isaac's pitiful sack of belongings—books, sneakers, jeans—plus the wooden hangers. "I should've bought you a record player," chafed Sam, offended by the gleaming stereo systems, computers, television sets, ascending staircase by staircase in the arms of ruddy fathers in heather-colored Shetland sweaters, glossy olive corduroys, mothers with hairdos—why hadn't Mattie come? Turner had volunteered, but Isaac refused. "As you know, I don't like noise," Isaac said. All this petted splendor was being decanted into closet-sized suites, Isaac's inhabited by four other callow youths who hadn't the wits to say hello to a man of Sam's advanced years. Indeed, that whole weekend Sam was destined to be continually astonished at how juvenile college students were these days, and how unmannered. Isaac was the only boy in a jacket and tie. Why, not one of these pukey little runts had half the manliness of Peter Karolis or the panache of Christina Molina. The girls did look a bit older, and were better at bossing their parents. Sam tried not to embarrass his son by ogling too ravenously these proud beauties in black leggings—Christ, think what the boy might bring home for Thanksgiving—before realizing that to Isaac he had become invisible, although nonetheless microscopically irritating. Ike was busy choosing bunks with his roommate, Casey, a worldly-wise bruiser with a blue angel tattooed on his brawny arm and who looked like a Pict the Romans hadn't yet gotten around to beating the shit out of. Isaac innocently ingratiated himself by insisting on taking the bottom bed: he'd be sure to fall out of the top one.

Sam, just so this blue-armed mick wouldn't get into the habit of pushing around his favorite son, protested. "Ike, you'll always be hitting your head in the bottom bunk; there isn't room for you down below. Why don't you take the top?"

Once again Isaac silenced him with a look, and then suggested, as a very special favor to his father, that having done everything needful, they might now go and look at the Boston aquarium.

It was a giddy, disquieting night. After the aquarium they cruised the harborside and Faneuil Hall, gawking at the people abroad on a balmy September evening, and then Sam treated Isaac to a lavish surf-and-turf supper at a restaurant recommended by Donald Mroczek, who kept a summer house in Sturgis and was one of Mattie's prize customers.

Released from home, adrift in a strange city for one last night of his boy Sam felt prodigal as a sailor on pay day, raring to burn money and see the sights and make the hours last, avidity sharpened by dread of tomorrow's return to a house without Isaac, to which his son would not return till November and then only for a week, a young man changed, under foreign influences, eyes opened to visions Sam would know nothing of. When college kids came home on vacations they slept all day and only got up to eat and no longer had a word to say to their parents, which didn't stop them from being filled with contempt for all they saw: this Sam knew, he'd seen it happen to the McCormicks, and now God help him it was going to happen to him. Four times that evening he must have asked Isaac if he wouldn't change his mind and come home. Isaac, who at the third whisky-and-soda emerged from temper into chattiness, smiled tolerantly.

Both men got pie-eyed; Isaac, allowing Sam to hold his hand, explained how the United States should have fought the Vietnam War, and how Germany had recovered not because of the Marshall Plan but in spite of it. At two in the morning in Sam's motel room he confided to his father his guess as to how the universe would come to an end, which was quite different from most physicists' suppositions, although even they didn't agree. Sam, talked down to, felt small and very sad.

"Do you remember the night we camped out on Bear Ridge?" he interrupted suddenly. "You were just a little squirt, but you begged me to go. Then you got scared up there on the dark mountain, us all by our lonesomes, and I had to take you home quick. Remember?

That's when I taught you your constellations. You'd just started school, and didn't like it a bit."

Isaac, smelling campfire, hearing thrashing ram, shied away. "No, I don't remember." Then, "I wasn't scared. I was testing you." Suddenly, he turned black, rocked his head in his hands, wouldn't speak. "Bedtime, buster," said Sam as brisk as he could manage.

It was three A.M. when he dumped Isaac at the gate to Harvard Yard and watched him reel into a maze of shrubbery and glowering brick. He didn't drive off at once, but sat in the car, motor idling, picturing his son, his only son, even Isaac, whom he loved, settling down to sleep in a room of 18-year-olds.

Until now, he's been mine, a Hooker and a Doucette, God help him, a member of our tribe tattooed with that tribe's tastes and prejudices. And he's been his own man too, a world to himself. He didn't talk like other kids at school, or like people on television, or like Mattie, and he thinks for himself too. He doesn't even belong to this day and age especially, he's been too busy eyeing the dead greats. Now what? He won't be my firstborn, my Magellan, the wonder-boy of Jessup County, won't be the child of our family, now he'll be a son of his goddamned generation, a squirmy amoeba in a sea of goddamned baby-boomers who don't live by who their grandparents were but by what they watch on TV and what health club they belong to, by flaccid egotistical pop songs. Now his professors are going to teach him to look down on all the ignorant rednecks who live in this country and die for it, and he's going to follow suit, or spend his life lonely and insulted and out of step with his wonderful, warm, caring scum bag of a generation.

I should have kept him at home and taught him myself. He'd be better off going to work for Farmer Ostrich pitching hay and studying on his own at night than paying fourteen grand a year to join this warren of sanctimonious conformity. He'd have been better off driving his mother's cab. And who will he be after four years of learning closed-minded arrogance? Will his red ears still stick out? Will his hair still look like he cut it with the lawn mower? Will he still talk to himself and sing songs at the top of his lungs and not know he's singing? Will he want to hold hands with his old man when no one's looking? Will they help him iron out his moods, achieve his equilibrium, tame his violence?

Are you jealous? Mattie had asked him that morning, hearing Sam rail. What do you mean? Jealous that he's getting to go where you didn't. Sam was offended. You're the jealous one in this house, he reminded her. Now he felt like throwing a rock through the dean's window, who with so much pomp and self-satisfaction and so little trouble to himself was taking charge of this young man's soul, farming him out to two dozen indolent conceited professors and advisers and teachers' assistants. The great universities of Europe did it right, entrusting a student to one tutor for all his undergraduate years and not casting him adrift in a kind of out-patient clinic manned by a hundred malpractitioners and tenured frauds. Shit, he muttered to himself, shit on a shingle. I should've . . . but he couldn't think what he should have done, so he drove away.

Late in the morning he showed up at Ike's new digs. The boy, already ashamed of his tag-along dad, was eager to get back to exploring and making friends. "Can I see the catalogue?" Sam begged.

Together they pored over the courses Isaac had chosen, Greek historians, Italian Neoplatonists, German philosophers, twice as many as one was supposed or even allowed to take. Isaac had done his homework, read up on the professors, picked the champs.

To Sam, most of the subjects seemed frivolously narrow, strange kickshaws and bizarre canapes designed to keep instructors amused at little effort and not a square meal of learning in sight. What a breeze to teach a class a week on "Ideas of Self-Fashioning in Renaissance Discourse" instead of six a day in chemistry, physics, and biology, and European and American history. And everything was scheduled so that it overlapped with everything else!

"It's a scam," he said, rather pleased. "You want my advice? More modern literature, less classics, and get some fresh air."

Did Isaac want his advice? Isaac looked like a Presbyterian minister being told to try saying Hail Marys. There was nothing to do but buy him lunch and drive back to New Hampshire, very fast and very wretched, leaving his Only Delight to the mercies of the tattooed Pict.

It was almost midnight when Sam got back to Auburn. It seemed fifteen degrees colder in his house than in Boston. No one around, Turner probably working at the computer, Mattie maybe asleep already. The thought of teaching the next morning felt like going back ten spaces into drudgery, rote, provincial isolation. Pouring a gigantic glass of Jack Daniel's, Sam sat down at the kitchen table, treated himself to a Romeo y Juliet bought at a Boston tobacconist. Blue smoke, sweet savor. Silence. Where did cicadas go in the fall? House felt empty. Sipping, puffing at his cigar, he was almost asleep.

"James Driscoll came by while you were gone." It was Mattie, come up from her basement office.

"What's *he* want?" Sam drew her to him, kissed what middle parts his mouth could reach, tried to corral her into his lap.

"He says Ike tried to rape his daughter two nights ago."

Sam choked, pushed Mattie away. Bourbon down the windpipe. "Oh God. Are you *serious*, Mat? What are you saying?"

"That."

"Start again. Slow."

"He says Ike tried to force Macy at the fair—molested her, and when she fought him off, he got abusive. The girl's been having fits ever since. Her dad, too—he's threatening to bring charges."

Sam couldn't speak. "Ike . . . It can't be true. Ike . . . I'll . . . I'll call him up right now." Grotesque. Ike didn't even like her. But scattered violences came unbidden into his head, the time he nearly drowned Turner, the time he threatened Mrs. Cartwright, punched Mrs. Ailes in the stomach—no, that was different, he'd been provoked—his weirdness about girls. Ike's surliness on the drive to Harvard, his unwillingness to talk about the night before. Was it possible? He heard again the whispered litany of female parts. What had he done wrong? Mattie's fault for not loving him enough. And just when he'd sailed off in triumph for Harvard, to be roped back. Rape, molest? Such harsh words, at once too vague and too specific to limn what might only have been an unwelcome pass. Rape. Calm down, you've only heard third-hand that prissy girl's version of things, you don't know what happened. If anything. He looked up finally, met her flat pale gaze. "So what are we going to do?"

"Do?" she shrugged. "Those fancy-pants Driscolls got it coming. I says to him, the girl's got a rod up her ass, probably wishful thinking. Why doncha buy her a boyfriend so she'll stop accusing innocent people? Believe me, Sam, when it comes down to it, they won't want to drag her through the mud, make a federal case of it. A little hanky-panky at the fair. Big deal."

Money piled up in Sam's head. Charges. Driscoll fortune stacked up against his insolvency, bringing his firstborn to early shame. Helpless. The boy should talk to someone. But who? "I'll call Ike," he muttered, but he didn't move. Thank God he's away, he needs getting away from home bad. But what Sam really meant was, home needed getting away from Ike.

Mr. Horton pocketed Isaac's queen. He had a way of glowering extra-ferociously, eyebrows like furry precipices, to hide his pleasure. He was glowering now, tiny painted prisoners all stowed in his pockets like a squirrel's bulging cheek of nuts.

"We fought the wrong war," Isaac was insisting, happy to have lost half his plastic army to Mr. Horton's concentration. "We should have fought Stalin, too. You were there—why did you let the Red Army snatch the Kirile Islands?" It's very nice of the kid to spend so much time shooting the breeze with old codgers, Sam thought, but must he always be so aggressive with men three and a half times his age? Just the other day, after one especially fierce bout, Sam jokingly apologized to Mr. Horton for Isaac's rambunctiousness.

"Get away with you," the old man replied. "All the other youngsters, mine included, are too damn polite. They smile, they nod, they say, Sure, Grandpa, cool, Grandpa. But do they listen? No sir. They figure the old man's senile, might as well butter him up. You're a teacher, you'll appreciate this: my sixteen-year-old grandson had never heard of Pearl Harbor. Thought maybe it was some rock 'n' roll group from before his time. I told him, It's your war, too. We fought and died so you could wear your hair like a girl's and walk around with that idiot music plugged into your ears."

But now Sam listened a little closer, and discovered that Isaac and Mr. Horton were in fact in perfect agreement: America should have fought a three-front war, and chased the Red Army out of Europe and Japan. He swiveled around, and there was Mattie standing by the side of his bed, staring down at him. That was the outrageous thing about being sick in a hospital: people felt they could just creep up and look at you when you weren't looking. Even other patients' visitors came and gave you a brazen once-over. Sam stared back, offended. From this supine perspective he could see the few black hairs that sprouted under Mattie's chin wobble as she breathed. A witch. He'd married a witch.

"I guess I must have dozed off on him," Sam nodded toward Isaac, who was now telling a less-interested Mr. Horton about the political inconsistencies of his Harvard teachers. "It's a kind of arrogant narcissism to insist that America and America alone be better than any country that ever existed," he was holding forth. "Is human nature so perfectible? Or only the portion of it born somewhere between the Rio Grande and the Bay of Fundy? Saudi Arabia didn't outlaw slavery until 1964, Mauritania and Somalia still revel in it. In Burundi the Hutu regularly slaughter the Tutsis by the tens of thousands and no one murmurs, China forces mothers to abort at the ninth month. Why does it only matter what we do?

"American intellectuals are weird. Can you imagine a Frenchman declaring France a terrorist nation the way my politics professor does of us? What would you think of a Bostonian who went around rooting for the Mets? Italians laugh at their motherland, with good reason. Yet my professor honestly believes America is evil because it wiretaps people who aid terrorists in Northern Ireland, or doesn't give enough money to Marxist-Leninist dictatorships that hate us."

"America isn't perfect," interjected Mr. Horton.

"No, America's not perfect. If America were perfect, we'd have nowhere to go when we died."

The slant of the sunlight against the wall said it was late afternoon, and from the way she twiddled an ankle Mattie was clearly itching to leave. God forbid I ever get old on her, Sam thought; she's going to join the Jessup County chapter of the Euthanasia Society and wheel my wheelchair right into Bellows Falls to see if I float.

"You all right?" inquired Mattie. "Can I bring you anything?"

"Yeah, a rope ladder, and a set of street clothes. You know, pants with *flies* on them like a grown person's, shirts with buttons, shoes with laces, that kind of thing. I'm gonna make my getaway."

And when Mattie stared back blankly, he added, in a resentful quaver, "Think I'll get out of here alive, Mat?"

"You better, or I'll kill you."

Mr. Driscoll calmed down; Sam never spoke to his son about the episode. Meanwhile, Harvard Ike got homey on them. Twice, three times a week freshman year he telephoned, jabbering for an hour or two at a time. A newfangled habit. Even as a grown man Sam had never telephoned his parents, except on birthdays or Christmas, and certainly not just to pass the time of day. Isaac would get on the line and want to know about Cindy's broken arm, had Mom planted the garden yet, what new programs was Turner figuring out on the computer, and how did Sam like them Celtics? Itchy to escape this crackly tyrant buzzing in his ear, Sam thought about his phone bill and to-morrow's history test, still unwritten.

He dropped by unexpectedly, too, hitchhiked back to Auburn every few weekends mostly to sleep and eat. While home, he insisted on riding around in the cab with his mother, or helping Sam swaddle the attic in fiberglass insulation, tacked tight with a staple gun. To Sam's satisfaction, he even made up with his brother, who was having trouble at school. Out in the backyard when it got warm, he set up a table and chairs and there the two boys reclined in the afternoon sun, working at English assignments concocted by Ike.

Turner wanted to go to college. All he knew was he wanted to go far away, and where they had good computer training. If he couldn't hike up his grades, he was tempted to go straight into the Marines OTC. In the meantime, he ran six miles a day uphill and down. Isaac rode a bicycle alongside, chattering while Turner puffed. Leaning out the window, Sam watched his two sons vanish down the sun-sluiced road, the runner long-legged, intense, lean as a rake, sooty crewcut skull bent low, the other mandarin fat, golden, slovenly, veering wildly on a bicycle too small for him. Don't go away, he wished hard, don't come back only to leave me again.

He paid calls on his old high-school teachers, on the doctor and his daughters, on Mrs. Hurd and the judge, on the Hanesworths and Miss McCormick. Even old Mr. Herringshaw, whom he'd insulted at the Walcott Fair, got befriended by Ike, though what Sam's son and this good old boy, who lived for hunting, fishing, and poker, had to talk about was anybody's guess. "The good dead old days when youngsters weren't too big for their three-cornered britches and didn't play bone-head football," Isaac mimicked, almost Mattie-like.

More disturbing, without telling Sam, Isaac had gone and looked up Christopher Scannon. "I knew he'd been such a hero of yours, I wanted to see him."

Unfair. Sneaky. "You knew we had a falling-out. You should have asked me first. Did he say anything about me?"

"He's awfully old, Dad. Mostly we talked Pope and Dryden. He said you were a lovely fellow, too bad about Mom."

Sam, half-mollified, grinned. "Is he still kicking? Not sick?"

"No, just repeats himself a bit. Merciless to his poor sister, who waits on him hand and foot."

"You shouldn't have gone without telling me," Sam repeated, in the next breath pressing, "Did you tell him what you're studying? Did you tell him about your writing?"

Everyone in town wanted a handful of Isaac, and he was happy to be dragged off to Elks lunches and Boy Scout benefits at the Masonic Lodge, to be sounded off at by old men sick of each other's company, and to eat indigestible batches of sugar cookies brought by widows eager to pet him.

Even more, Isaac thrived on the company of younger boys, and whiled away his vacation time walking in the fields with fourteen-year-olds. His father's son, said Mattie, but Sam was troubled by Ike's hungry idleness; he couldn't bear to be alone even to sleep. When the Hurds or the McCormicks or Mr. Herringshaw finally put him out with the cat, he would go wake up Billy or Peter or whichever of his old schoolmates was willing to stay up till five or six in the morning. Night owls can't be choosy; Sam was a little shocked to discover that Ike had been propping up the Stateside with his former tormentors John Pulaski and Jay Thibodeaux.

That Isaac was feeling lost at college was clear. Neither father nor son mentioned it: Isaac, who never thought grades mattered, had a bad conscience nonetheless. Sam was at a loss. He had feared Ike might come home some kind of snotty disaffected radical. They had wandered around ages at Cambridge that Sunday trying to find a lunch place that served meat; Sam knew it followed ineluctably that people who ate chick-peas and bean curd in a land of cheap beef would hate any country friendly to their own. He steeled himself for an Isaac bearing banners opposing Reagan's intervention in Central America and a battered copy of Antonio Gramsci in his back pocket. But it never happened.

Sophomore year brought instead the *Gimlet,* a college magazine founded by Ike and his roommate Casey and designed precisely to pillory all those theories Sam had never heard of but which his son assured him meant the death of honesty and clear thought: deconstruction, feminist criticism, the New Historicism, Marxist art history. The magazine seemed to get a lot of people's goat; Isaac was once even threatened with suspension for libel or some such charge, but to Sam the rag didn't seem so inflammatory: fiction by various hands, drawings and poems by Casey the Tattoo, a piece by Isaac on Propertius and pornography, a column "The Chicken Little Watch" charting the latest panics: nuclear winter, greenhouse effect, the ozone layer.

Oppressed by his son's restlessness, Sam wished he would go back to doing the kinds of things he did in high school, chess clubs, debates, and would quit tilting at such unsavory and inconsequential targets. Isaac tried to explain. "Listen, you old hayseed, you haven't a clue what these dopes are up to. I've got teachers who think 'elitist' is a dirty word, who interpret works of art only in light of their makers' sex, race, and class, and say that literature is an assertion of power by white guys like Homer or the authors of the Bible. Don't you understand? They're denying that we can transcend our circumstances, speak a universal language, create something eternal. You either have to scourge this narrowing of vision or declare higher education dead."

"Why do *you* have to be the world's policeman?" Sam was skeptical.

The *Gimlet* occupied the energies that should have gone into Isaac's studies. As usual, Sam made his objections known by kidding. How's the *Whiskey Sour* going, he would ask, how's the *Singapore Sling*? Isaac sent him through the mail an index card, on its blank side a drawing of a twisted blade labeled "GIMLET," on the striped reverse the legend, in block letters, "THIS IS NOT A DRINK; IT'S A WEAPON."

Instead of coming home on vacations, he now stayed in Cambridge to work on the magazine. When the school kicked people out of their rooms, he and Casey moved in with Casey's father, who turned out to be not a second-story man or pool hustler but a well-known poet. And Sam, however he regretted this new passion, was also a little proud. The masthead showed three people working under Isaac, a regular sweatshop. His son was boss, even of so makeshift and democratic an enterprise as a college magazine; he was intrigued by their printing arrangements—they typeset and printed the magazine on an old press in Casey's father's garage—and gratified to be told of their distribution problems. It was Harvard, but it was the real world. Sort of.

Their pokey ground-floor room was immured in glossy black; they'd painted the walls black one night in honor of the Rolling Stones and commissioned a friend to draw constellations on the ceiling—rubicund Mars, pink-ringed Saturn, plus some kind of silvery slosh intended to resemble Aurora Borealis. Both boys were delighted with the results. It was handy being on the ground floor, right on the Kirkland courtyard: they kept the window wide open so you could climb in and out freely, receive late-night visitors, use the bordering flowerbed as urinal. With plywood and a shower rod, Casey had constructed a canopy over his bed, swathed it in heavy folds of red velvet fit for a Spanish *infanta*. Women seemed to appreciate his red-velvet bower. "Looks like a voting booth," objected Ike. "Yeah, but you should see 'em line up to pull my lever."

That was before their falling-out. Now Casey was packing up, going home for the summer. "Are we still blood brothers?" Isaac asked beseechingly, as his roommate stuffed dirty T-shirts into a shopping bag, dismantled yards of velvet. Two weeks ago, seething with ideas for the fall issue, articles raring for print, Ike had been planning to stay as usual at Casey's father's house. Then Casey broke the news: he had chosen a new co-editor, his friend Henry.

Isaac gaped. "You've done *what*? You asked that little trust-fund coke head to help run our magazine? That insufferable poser? And without asking me? You've got to be kidding, Casey. Tell him no."

Casey, a consummate social being, was incapable not just of saying no, but even of not saying whatever he suspected a person might want to hear. "I already asked him."

"Unask him. Blame it on me. Tell him you were drunk. *I'll* tell him. If he were just an honest junkie . . . But all that pretentious trilling about Baudrrrrillard and Derri-DA? How could you?"

"Chill, Ike. He won't show up; he just wants his name on the masthead."

"I don't want any double-barreled Thirds on my masthead."

"Don't be a snob."

"Will you promise me he won't ever show up on the premises?" Casey's train of thought was transparently clear. Henry had treated him all year; now Casey wanted to treat, and to a far more stupendous offering than a sleepless weekend in New York. Besides, it was going to be a long hot summer in an empty town, and Henry's provisions would liven things up. Casey was likely getting bored with Ike, wanted new company. Understanding made betrayal no less crushing. "You're ruining the magazine, Casey. You're whoring to pay a social debt."

Breathless, Isaac left the room, paced the streets till morning. As soon as he awoke the next afternoon, he went straight to the office above the garage. There was Henry, red-rimmed, snuffling. Isaac exploded. "Get him out of here."

Casey didn't.

In the two weeks since that scene, Casey had acted distant, no mean trick in a room twelve-by-twelve. Since his roommate had so clearly staked out his ground as the aggrieved party, that left Ike with no choice but to try and make amends. Daily he concocted different wooings. They had a hot plate; Casey liked eating in. After his last class of the year, Ike carted his entire library to Starr's, seven boxes of books, all but the few he couldn't bear to part with. With the proceeds he bought a bottle of single-malt whiskey, solemn in its gold-embossed black coffin, and three pounds of dripping red sirloin, imbedded with rivulets and lakes of white fat. That night the two young men ate like cannibals with fingers and teeth, blood dripping down their chops. Almost like old times, yet inside Isaac was inconsolable. He was beginning to understand that Henry was Casey's way of dropping him.

"'Course we're still blood brothers, Ike. Don't be such a lame-o," said Casey on his way out. No way out. Nothing worse than saying you're sorry when you're secretly mad and the other guy won't accept your apology because he says nothing's wrong but obviously everything is. "Forget about it. Enjoy your summer."

Casey gone, Isaac settled down on the floor with the bottle of Laphroaig. In a day or two a summer student would be moving into this room: he had to be out by morning. Where would he go? Home with his tail between his legs, to three months' captivity with his depressing and depressive family, moping till September? And even in September, what did he have to return to? He had made but one single friend he loved and that friend was now an enemy. The rest was laziness, inertia, debauchery, childishness. Casey was right; he was a boor. He couldn't bear the black room another moment, couldn't face a night alone in his putrid lonely bed. Poison, he whispered into the bottle's mouth, inhaling whiskey like pure peat smoke, breathing fire. Have to pack now. Pack. Drunken brute. But what shall I take? Nothing, because I deserve nothing. Drinking too much. Trashiness, desecration. I'm far worse than Henry—he at least is honest in his vice; I'm the hypocrite. One more pull, then stop. Casey's right. Human ordure. I'll burn my books, and go. His mind exploded. What? Yes, the books I saved. A sacrifice. In a fury of purpose he swept the few paperbacks, canvas-hided hardbacks into a heap. Luther's *Table Talk*, Sidney, the *Tractatus*. Was he fooling? Lit the burner, cradling its cobalt flame, stuck in a hand, waiting for flesh to melt. Funny smell. Cold in here, unseasonably cold for June.

He fed the flame Luther. The laminated cover wouldn't catch, letters briefly magnified like solemn old eyes behind drugstore glasses, *Melancthon* leaped forth enlarged, then became tarnished to a transparent gray, pages shrinking black, crinkling at the edges. *Melancthon*, he whispered. Smells nice, like . . . like . . . camping out. Luther screamed a little, whistled, belched sparks. Ike fed the tiny stove the *Tractatus*, paperback. A mighty flame, pages burned and not the cover. Spy books, Curtius's fat *Latin Literature*, Helen Waddell on the desert fa-thers—his chief treasure, seasoned, wise, and gay, yes, that too, he didn't deserve hearing of monks who forsook the cities for a cave, a palm-frond mat, parched prayer, all must go, burn, burn, a fearful smell. He was holding on to the half-charred book, its royal-blue-and-gold binding flaring quickly like martyrs, like the alphabet crowns Akiva saw ascending to heaven as the scroll they wrapped him in was set on fire. All must go. The small pile lay charred, half-devoured, like a wild animal's dinner, when Isaac emptied the last of the whiskey over the remains and clambered through the window.

On a June night at the end of his sophomore year Sam's older son came home unexpectedly. "Are you here to stay or are you going to leave in ten minutes?" He stroked the hair out of the boy's face. "I'm here, aren't I?" Ike reeked of liquor, wouldn't look his father in the eye. It was as many words as Sam heard from him for the next three months.

He had new habits, or rather his old ones were worse. He set fur-niture aflame with his smoking, he slept all day and played all night, watched television drunk with his friends. Eight A.M. found Billy, Justin James, and Isaac crashed out on the den floor, set still blaring, amid a sea of crumpled beer cans, ashes, butts.

One morning when Sam came down to breakfast, he found Isaac sitting at the table, exhaling sodden gloom. The affront could no longer be ignored.

"How was school?" his father inquired. "Our hours don't seem to cross much any more, so I better grill you while I can. Your grades are an undistinguished slur of B minuses. Was the work hard or were you simply goofing off? Are you learning anything? What do you do with yourself all day?"

Isaac, grimacing, waved the questions away. "There's nothing to learn. The place is full of itself." He pushed his lower lip way out. "Everybody is too busy putting on airs to think or talk."

Sam was shocked. The boy sounded like Mattie. "There have to be *some* interesting people at one of the best universities in the world. Have you tried making friends with your teachers?"

Isaac sighed. "They're a bunch of complacent yellow-bellied trim-mers who can only think of tenure and publication and fellowships and sabbaticals. No time for students. Nobody's interested. The big shots strut out into a lecture hall the size of a gunboat, read from their notes, and take off for Cape Cod or a spot on the evening talk shows. That's it."

Such whining was too much to bear. Why wasn't his son making better use of his illuminatory adventure? Why was he being such a baby? Hadn't he the independence to study without a Miss Urquhart holding his hand, cooing over every word? Had Isaac no remembrance of how lucky he was, no foreboding of the harsh burdened colorlessness of the life outside? Sam had sworn never to mention cost—he'd taken out a second mortgage to pay off the loans, but, "You should drop out if you're not going to take advantage of the place; I'm not bankrupting this family to improve your Pac-Man and hone your hangovers. I sent you there to learn and explore and distinguish yourself," he said, very low, voice trembling. He had never spoken to the boy so sharply, yet Isaac, astonishingly, met him with a glassy, indifferent look. "Yeah, yeah."

Throwing back his chair, Sam stomped down to the basement to punish a leaking pipe.

After a month of disrupting the household's new Isaacless rhythms and getting everyone's backs up, he suddenly vanished. Gone for days on end, only turning up once in a blue moon, sleepy as a hedgehog and claiming he wasn't hungry. Someone was loving Isaac. Who? Somehow, Sam realized, these last two years he had been waiting for the other shoe to drop, for a call from Harvard announcing that Isaac had felt up a twelve-year-old or walked through plate glass. No more. Maybe it was Lindy McCormick, several years older than Ike, clever and kind. Maybe just such an older woman was what was needed. It wasn't enough for the boy to get laid, he needed goodness, he needed his equal. Lindy had always been sort of sweet on Ike, proof of an independent mind. Daunting to think of Dr. McCormick as an in-law, but that was Ike's lookout.

Then Lindy and Peter Karolis announced their engagement, and Isaac, best man, was all astir, arranged the bachelor party, picked out a house for them to live in, bossed around parents and priest. And in September, to everyone's relief, he went back to Harvard. Sam, still half hoping his son would bring back one of those pallid Manhattanites in black he'd seen prowling the Yard, forgot all about the mysterious secret summer romance.

In short, no matter how foxy Sam considered himself in matters of love and in divining his own son's heart, nothing prepared him for the wintry afternoon two months later when Isaac telephoned, not collect as usual but from a pay phone nonetheless. Isaac wasn't at school; he was at a gas station near Cyrus, and don't worry, he had plenty of nickels and dimes.

"Do you remember Miss Urquhart?"

Sam's heart sank, he didn't know why. "Of course I remember Miss Urquhart. Miss Urquhart and I are colleagues, or rather *were* colleagues."

"I've moved in with her." And then, in case Sam hadn't understood and had merely taken this to be some boardinghouse arrangement, Isaac explained, "I guess we'll be man and wife, or as close to it as I can talk her into."

For the longest time Sam could not absorb this information. It made no sense whatsoever. Isaac, whom he thought safely away at school, was instead a few miles away. Isaac, who lived in Cambridge, Massachusetts, was instead going to be living with his former math teacher. As man and wife? What was he talking about? It was as strange as if he'd declared he was a spy for the Russians or a hemophiliac. First Sam thought he was going to faint, and then he felt sick, and then he got ready to yell, and in the end with the typical namby-pamby inadequacy of a modern father, he only said in a thin offended voice, "I think you're making a mistake."

"I think *she's* making a mistake," Isaac retorted gaily, "and I tell her so daily, but she's not having any of it. As for me, I'm the luckiest man alive."

For a good ten minutes, then, Sam yelled; afterward he couldn't remember what he'd said. "And what about your education?" he wound up.

"I wasn't getting anything out of the place, and I don't want to waste any more of your money. Anyway, I'll go back to Harvard next year, if I can talk her into going, too."

"You know, some people manage to get laid *and* go to school at the same time."

"It's not like that, Daddy. You know it yourself: there are things more important than college. Anyway, when we get a little more settled down, I'll go back."

God, it was revolting. It was a crime against nature, what she'd done. He could have wrung her neck for laying hands on his boy. Was this all because of his wretched magazine's folding?

"You're going to ruin that woman when you throw her over,"

snapped Sam, inconsequentially. That was hardly his worry, but at
least it succeeded in jolting Isaac out of his blissed-out cheeriness.
"Never, never, never. Let God strike me down if I prove unworthy of
her goodness."

Isaac and Miss Urquhart had carried it off neatly as a bank heist,
and when Sam thought of the planning entailed in their getaway his
shock was drowned out by fury. She had notified the school in August
that she wasn't coming back, and had even found them a replacement
teacher. Sam had gone to the goodbye party, where they presented her
with a pewter box with everyone's name inscribed. She was transferring to Menasseh Regional, smaller and more rural, fifteen miles away,
where she had been made head of the math department. She was sick
of town, she explained; she liked Menasseh, where there were only a
hundred students, and she could walk across the fields to school or
winters ski cross-country.

And in the meantime she'd got rid of her apartment, set up a safe
house for Isaac in a one-room shack up a dirt road somewhere out in
Cyrus Township. No telephone, no electricity. Had he put himself in
permanent hock in order to revert to Doucette-dom? The hillbillyish-
ness infuriated Sam almost as much as her taking up with a colleague's
son—there must be a commandment somewhere against that, a Hip-
pocratic Oath she'd violated—or her letting Isaac drop out of school,
even though Sam knew if the boy had a mind to, bulls of Bashan
couldn't have stopped him. She was keeping Isaac sealed off, incom-
municado: she had kidnapped his son, and taken him where his father
couldn't reach him. At least from Cambridge Sam could hear his son's
voice whenever he pleased.

And amid all this came the itchings of pure curiosity. Who started
it, and how? It was like the extraction of maple sap, the eating of
lobsters or sea urchins: you wondered who ever dreamed it up and
who first dared to try it. Had Isaac, utterly inexperienced, half-blind,
so wretchedly conscious of his great girth that he wouldn't be seen in
a bathing suit, ventured to put the moves on Miss Urquhart? Had Miss
Urquhart, a thirty-five-year-old spinster cursed with a prickly conscience, a fine sense of the ridiculous, and a morbid fear of rebuff
finally told him she was his, and showed him the way? Had they
deliberated and shilly-shallied tortuously, almost talked themselves out
of this improbable idea, or been borne along heedless by love's rage?
How long had she felt what she felt for him? Since eleventh grade?
Tenth? Before he shaved? Had she been holding back, or did she sud-

denly see him without his glasses on and—Why, Mr. Hooker, you're beautiful.

But when he next saw Isaac, who dropped by the school and then came home with his father to pick up some clothes and allow his parents to get angry at him, Sam knew without their exchanging a word on the subject, knew from the nasty twist of jealousy in his gut, that to Isaac's mind at least this was it, this was love of a high and solemn, Dante-and-Beatrice, Héloïse-and-Abelard order and that it hadn't even occurred to him that this thing for which he was willing to sacrifice his education, lay down his life, might to his friends and neighbors seem comical or scandalous. Once again, Sam was exasperated by Isaac's refusal to understand that he lived in a very small town. He talked of Agnes not the way he talked of Mattie or Turner, with scolding and abrasive fondness, but as something already incorporated, already internalized, as men who mean it talk, or rather don't talk, of honor or God, and worse still, Sam knew that his public manner covered for some wholly other order of private knowledge. Two had become one, and all else was excluded.

Isaac would find a job; Agnes would go on teaching math, and their real lives would be elsewhere, at home, wrapped up together in their wooden hut.

Who would have thought that his boy, who hungered so hugely for fame and the real world, could be undone by a corset hook, by the first dog who would have him! And what did this say about Sam as a father, to have raised a son so absurdly grateful to be wanted? It couldn't last a year, he reminded himself; Isaac was twenty years old, and no matter how dutiful or how horny, would soon feel smothered, starved for information and news, would come up for air, return to his mission. It was a detour, and God help Miss Urquhart. Occasionally these days to his own disgust Sam caught himself not only feeling a little sorry for Miss Urquhart, but also defending her against the truly inspired venom of his wife, who was outraged that the skinny old bag should *ever* get a man, let alone their son. Jesus, whistled Sam, man's inhumanity to man is *nothing* . . .

Chapter 3

AGNES AND ISAAC'S new house was near Cyrus, ten miles over winding mountain roads from Auburn. It belonged to the Daigneaults, a prosperous farming family with a logging business, who owned most of Cyrus—a village, like many in the region, that had been more thickly populated in 1860 than today. Set back from a rutted dirt road leading nowhere, the old house had been built as a one-room school for Cyrus's farm children. Until the previous spring the Daigneaults had rented it to an eremitical miser with a grudge against the government, who never bothered to install a telephone or get hooked up to the power lines that ran no more than a hundred yards away.

They kept meaning to call in the electric company, but meanwhile for the first three months they lived by gas lanterns, whose cotton socks emitted a chaste white radiance. Gaslight made popping noises like corn kernels in a pan but softer, and a small explosion detonated when you put a match to the mantle, like lighting a pilot; it gave daily life a certain ceremoniousness, a studiously inflected pace that was almost like religious observance: you thought about it.

In the old days Isaac loved to ridicule the sentimental hypocrisy of back-to-nature types who shunned the delights of progress for the imagined purity of a time when life expectancy was about eighteen years and people's babies all died of the diseases of dirt. Now he was thrilled by the little gas refrigerator and the wood stove, which needed replenishing every three hours, and proudly led rare visitors up to the springhouse guarding the underground source of their water supply. He was sad when they got electricity: it made life more heedless and automatic. They still didn't have a telephone.

Isaac and Agnes had had a rough breaking-in, no denying it. Isaac, who longed for love, never imagined how hard it would be to accept another person's ways or to conquer his own selfishness. The first couple of months had been a ride without muffler or shocks; every little tremor nearly brought the house down. Precisely because each had staked so much on this shot at love, who got to sleep on the right side of the bed next to the lamp and who got up to put more wood in the stove became a struggle over first principles. This, combined with the cold, and the terror that the other would come to regret their alliance, made for a horrible winter.

Isaac yelled. For a month he had a permanent sore throat. Her touchiness, her tendency to sulk and clam up, to go all tight-lipped and prissy on him, drove him mad. He had to make her share everything, keep no secrets or die. She wasn't used to talking about her life, or thinking about herself in the intense, determined, stylized way Isaac imagined one examined one's soul. Under his grilling about her sexual, religious, intellectual awakenings, how she felt about her father, mother, brothers, how they felt about her and about each other, and why she became a teacher, she could only repeat, helplessly, "I don't know; I never thought about it."

"Well, think *now.*"

"I can't. I simply don't know." The longer he waited the more banal her response. "I started teaching because I needed a job and they had a vacancy: it was that simple. I never thought about destiny and vocation and all those big words *you've* got under your bonnet. I didn't love math; I was good at it, that's all. I never expected I'd do it for the rest of my life."

He interrogated her about other men, and when she wouldn't tell him because she considered it dishonorable to blab, and anyway it now seemed irrelevant, he decided she was holding back on him and exploded. "We will have no privacy, no shame, nothing kept back, no scruples. I want to know everything you're thinking and you'll have to tell me because I can guess it anyway. I have a hole this big inside of me, a chasm of loneliness and a terror of dying that gets bigger every day, and you've got to fill it up. I don't want a wife to sew my buttons and cook my dinner; I want you here inside me, here in my gut, here. You know the Cossacks used to rip open women's wombs and sew live cats inside. That's how I want you, like a cat inside me."

"You can't live at this pitch, Isaac," she tried to remonstrate. "You've got to let up a little. You're a boy yet, and you don't understand there's nothing wrong with being ordinary. The body and soul need to rest, and that rest is sweet. Some nights you just have to eat and sit by the fire and go to bed: it doesn't have to be thunder and lightning or else you're out of love. If we last, we last at a low steady flame, at 98.6. Ordinary is good." The same lesson she had been trying to instill in him since twelfth grade.

At first she was shocked when he barged in on her in the bathroom or read her letters, and longed to be back alone on Franklin Street. Then bit by bit she yielded. By will, by sheer volume, by the pressure of his attention, he conquered her modesty and reticence, and was conquered in turn. She was his, he was hers, she made him cry from happiness, they wouldn't bear grudges or think at cross-purposes or be separate in any way, they would say everything that came into their heads without reserve, her arm was his and every springy copper hair on it thrilled him, her heart thumped in his chest and he only wished he could get at her innards too, weigh in his hand her liver and kidneys, squeeze her intestines, stroke her heart, suck on her gallbladder, get all the way up her bottom and out her throat.

In the middle of the night he awoke and stared at her in the dark, a warm bump under the blanket, a breath. His. His goddess. Every day he came more deeply to love and wonder at her guileless truthfulness, her almost mannish decency and utterly feminine reaches of tact and protectiveness, the archaic measures of her modesty unveiling. She was blander in love than in the classroom, more careful. This mildness, at first disappointing, was happiness. Slowly, slowly he began to feel that love lay not only in the wild confessions he felt compelled to make in the beginning, night after night, daring her to recoil, but also in the sewing-on of buttons and the cooking of suppers, in the soft and silent accumulation of little deeds, in days that streamed down the gutter of routine and into the ground.

As for Agnes, sometimes she was scared that her terrible joy was devil's work. She had to keep reminding herself, like saying prayers, that it wouldn't last, that the laws of nature dictated that she would be left, left soon and left forever. Should she stoke up on happiness and heat, then, for the cold winter of her remaining life, or restrain herself now, not wholly give in? This clumsy and passionately intrusive boy left her without choice, without memory or corners of refuge, and she gave herself to him, oblivious of all but this—this love, this rude genius God had put in her hands.

.   .   .

Sundays not long ago had meant waking up sick as a dog on someone's floor, afternoon sun craning around a tacked-up sheet, taste of ashes and dirty socks in your mouth. You puked into some communal toilet, explored your bruises, raided the medicine cabinet for anything potable. Dragged yourself into the glaring daylight of the Out-of-Town kiosk in the Square, picked up the *Times,* the *Globe,* the Washington *Post,* and drifted into Tommy's Lunch hoping to meet someone who'd buy you a meal and treat you to your favorite songs on the jukebox. Chances were good: Casey and Mac and Stella and John pretty much lived in this dive. John and Casey playing pinball, Mac and Stella making out while you guzzled your lime rickey, devoured the papers, talked to anyone who would listen, and played "Sittin' on the Dock of the Bay" maybe eighteen or twenty-two times in a row. Once some local with a perm complained the song was making him dizzy. "If you don't sit back and let my friend enjoy Otis," Casey warned, "I'll push your guido eyes out the back of your guido head and send your guido nose to Watertown." Casey didn't mean it: he just liked to impress the girls. It was dark already by the time you ventured outdoors, the day spent. This, just last year, had been paradise: big-city newspapers, a hangover, and Otis Redding.

Isaac and Agnes were sitting at the kitchen table on a Sunday morning. You could feel the sated decorous stillness, churchbells pealing in the valley below. She was reading yesterday's *Recorder,* he was reading the Bible. Agnes had to drive to the post office, which doubled as a general store, to buy the *Recorder* a day late, or else they listened to Robert J. Lurtsema on the radio. It left more time for spooning, for reading, writing.

Their first winter and spring, until she got around to assembling the mail-order shelves, Agnes's books had stayed packed in brown boxes, and Isaac at first felt so undeserving of print and binding he could hardly bring himself even to borrow from the library. Stranded, he read her Holy Bible four times cover to cover, Genesis through Revelation, memorizing even those portions—the construction of the tabernacle, the design of the high priest's breastplate, the sacrificial offerings of the twelve tribes—that most people (people with television sets, hobbies, children, lawns, friends, other books) prefer to give a miss. If Isaac Newton, in between inventing calculus, physics, optics, color theory, and the laws of universal gravity, could prise from the Old Testament's blueprint for the temple proof that the Hebrew prophets recognized the heliocentric universe, who was Isaac Hooker to skip Leviticus? At first tolerant, he became entranced.

Mr. Horton had told him a story about the war. Enlisting in the Navy, he'd wound up with another boy from Gilboa. Jordan Watts— he's dead now, you wouldn't remember him. A vacant soul, devoid of interest, the children used to tease him. Once at sea, though, sleeping in a bunk beside strange guineas and polacks from New York and Chicago, Mr. Horton discovered in his fellow townsman unsuspected reserves of intelligence, humor. Jordan had been underestimated! A great guy. They swore if they survived they would never be separated, they swapped Gilboa recollections, planned their joint homecoming and menus of their first mother-cooked suppers. Blood brothers. We dropped the bomb, the war ended, Watts and Horton went home. There awaited a world of work, pay checks, ailing parents, courtship. Mr. Horton met his wife-to-be and went to work for the railroad. And discovered to his surprise that Jordan Watts had been magically trans- formed back into the dumbest person he had ever met, all that Marine brilliance vanished. That was how Isaac insisted to Agnes he felt about the Bible. Only book in the house, it looked pretty good. His Latin, too, from cramming her Vulgate, had gotten so copious he used a dictionary only once a page or so.

It would be a mistake to suppose these two sat around a lot. In fact they had less leisure than Isaac would have imagined possible. Weekday mornings Agnes left the house at seven, while he didn't get home from the typesetter's till eight or nine at night. After supper she marked papers and he sat up reading sometimes till two or three, long after Agnes had gone to sleep.

Periodically, over the years, Isaac had felt as if he were riding a tidal wave of revelation that always seemed to break too far from shore, leaving him with a mouth full of sand, lungs of salt water. Now, it was time to try to transmit to paper, make good on his saline delirium. At night after Agnes was asleep, or walking by himself in the woods, he would scribble in a notebook his fizzy, impatient, and tremulous be- ginnings. Sometimes, mistakenly, he would test an idea aloud.

"I want to write a history of solitude."

"What do you know about solitude?" Agnes teased. "A man who jumps out of his skin if he's left alone for twenty seconds?"

Sam, on the other hand, when Isaac burst in on him in the bathtub to announce his undertaking, had said, "Solitude is for chimpanzees. If human beings were meant to live alone, they would have been made with arms long enough to scrub their own backs."

Isaac, trying to decide whether the early Christians were the first to turn solitude from a curse into an ideal or whether monasticism was born in India, ignored them both. When he wasn't making notes, he was firing off letters to New York editors explaining what was wrong with their magazines and how he might set them straight. For, instead of going back to Harvard, Ike had decided that he and his girlfriend should move to New York, where he would become a hack writer. Not a writer, a hack. He wasn't aiming too high: all he wanted was to feed the two of them, while leaving himself time for serious work. To this air raid of criticism and advice dropped on so many prestigious Manhattan offices he had received but one reply. Up on the bedroom wall it was pasted, like information about fire exits or how to help a choking victim: a real, typewritten letter, two lines long, from an editor at *Aurora*. "Dear Mr. Hooker, You are a presumptuous puppy. If you are ever in New York, come see me." He liked the AG:dt at the bottom. A secretary of one's own!

On weekends, Agnes kept insufferably busy. The house and backyard were still a wreck: there were closets to be plastered and floors to be stripped and sealed and snow to be shoveled.

"Why bother?" he protested. "It's only going to snow again tomorrow."

"Yeah, and we'll all be dead soon anyway."

"Wise guy. Next time I'm going to find myself a languorous slattern—a sultry Latin dish who doesn't like to wash and scrub."

Some rare blissful Sundays he could sweet-talk her out of dragging him to church or fixing the roof. They lay in bed late, lazed around the kitchen over coffee and pancakes and sausages and eggs, hiked along Mount Menasseh, took a nap, ate an early supper, and back to bed again. Isaac had known enough youthful misery not to let rapture go uncelebrated. This, he knew, was the real McCoy, bliss such as he'd never known and might never know again. Since his father's heart attack, the clingy Sunday idleness had an extra poignance.

So there they sat by the kitchen table, Agnes reading yesterday's papers, Isaac studying Deuteronomy and drinking cup after cup of strong black tea, sucking on a shirt button he was waiting for her to sew back on.

"Don't swallow it, you lummox, or I'll have to turn you upside down and fish it out with—with a button hook. Lord only knows what else you got down there. A couple of Jonahs, probably."

Outside they could hear the liquid pulse of the morning's downpour trickling along the drain in iridescent streams. June. Isaac began peeking at Agnes over his book. The way she frowned and muttered at the newspaper, or licked a finger turning a page, flooded him with such a rush that he climbed onto her lap, capsizing the chair and wrestling her to the ground, rolling her about on the kitchen floor, both of them yelping with laughter.

"Get *off* me, you great baboon!" He pinned her down, one hand cradling her head from the linoleum, gazed into her eyes. They had spots in them, brown and green speckles. He put out a finger and touched the wet globe, just as her licked finger had flecked the top of each page. Then he stuck his tongue into the corner of her eyeball. She blinked, squirmed.

"Will you let me up, or do I have to . . ." her sentence ended in a shriek.

"I think he followed his lower parts and not his head when he married, and he's never done regretting it since," said Isaac, when they got up again. It was weeks now they had been talking of this "he," and when they weren't talking, Isaac was brooding.

"It must have been more than that," Agnes objected.

"No, no, it wasn't. He was twenty-two years old and didn't know girls did it. Once he found one who would have him, he was scared to let her go."

"Like you and me."

"It's always the randiest who marry young," pronounced Isaac with great energy. "*And* she was bewitching and perplexing and mysterious to him, simply because he couldn't accept that a woman could genuinely be as crude as all that. Why men go for mystery in women I'll never know, but they do. Men who would never consider a business deal they don't understand inside out or buy a house sight unseen, as soon as they meet a woman who makes no sense whatsoever, whose ways and wants and opinions are utterly unfathomable, decide they've got to drag her to the altar or bust."

"I'm sure they must have had more in common than that. Children never understand what their parents see in each other. I always thought my mom was a wet rag—couldn't climb trees or bale hay—and I figured Dad had to think so, too. But he didn't care, he didn't want some Calamity Jane for a wife: he wanted a good housekeeper."

"You know, people don't want to marry their *twins*. Just because your mother isn't interested in poetry doesn't mean they don't love each other and don't get along in their way."

"Don't be so fatuous, you old bag. They *don't* get along: I know, I lived there. They have no conversation: Dad gets wretched thinking about money and Mom can talk of nothing else. Anyway, you're wrong, as usual: men and women *must* be twins. They must have common interests, common tastes, common outlook. Their minds and sympathies *must* move, if not in total unison, then at least like a second hand to minute hand on the same clock. There's too much *different* between them, too much else in the world that conspires to tear people apart and set them against each other.

"So there you have it: a man who might have been a decent scholar, and a woman who could have made a million dollars, become New England's tire queen, opened a chain of bowling alleys, run for governor. Instead they get snookered by holy matrimony and fret away two lifetimes in debt and discontent, my father's intelligence short-circuited by self-pity, my mother's employed in nagging to death a virtuous man. It's wonderful how busy you can keep, making other people miserable!"

"Well, why did she marry him, then? If it's money she's interested in, she could have found someone richer, more ambitious."

"She's a sow, and sows like the mud," said Isaac, shortly. "Anyway," he added, "how can you tell how ambitious someone really is, in his heart of hearts? I think my father may be the most ambitious man going. He's just too lily white and scared of being laughed at to do anything about it.

"You know, it's hard leaving home, going into the world. People make fun of you for all kinds of things you never even noticed. When I got to Harvard they put me in an entry full of snot-nosed prep-school brats who had nothing better to do than mimic the way I speak. You know the way these guys talk—they crunch down hard on their *r*'s, they speak through clenched teeth—lip reader's hell. So they made fun of my vowels. You know, they'd point outside, say what's that out there, trying to get me to say Harvard Yard. I'd go, 'Grass and concrete.' Brilliant. Seemed like Casey at least had more wit to him than thinking someone was slow or mockable because he pronounced his *a*'s different. Then one day I come into the room and there's Casey lounging with his little gang of punk girlfriends on the couch. He takes one look at my trousers—I guess they were too short, but who's got the money or inclination to go buying new trousers—and he says to me, 'Hey, dude, next time your pants have a party, try asking your socks along, too.' Except he said paatty. And the girls broke up at that."

"What did you do?"

"I grabbed him under the arms and lifted him till his feet were dangling off the ground and I said, 'Next party you have, buster, is going to be with the worms ten feet under.' Threw him back hard into the couch like a medicine ball, right on top of his favorite female. I thought she'd go splat. He liked that: man's always looking to get his jaw broke. But that's what I mean: you go out into the world and you meet a lot of people who are out to humiliate you just because of the way you talk or dress, and I guess Daddy didn't want any part of it. Who does?

"But as for why Mom married him, well, I guess she thought he was going places. And then again her kid sister was married already and Mom would have married a *monkey* not to be left on the shelf. Daddy was just an innocent bystander."

American cars from before the oil scare were meant to be flown. Turner's '69 Coronet, gleaming tomato red in the June sunshine, souped up with a motor befitting a jumbo jet, was just such a prelapsarian mammoth, built in the blissful days before OPEC to soar at ninety-five without a tremor. Modern highways, too, with their broad looping curves, were molded to smooth such speeds, to cradle them in the asphalt palm of the hand. Snailing along at fifty-five was downright dangerous, like riding a bicycle too slow: you fall off.

But Gilboa, Turner had found, was a speeder's mixed blessing. The police chief whose wife had just walked out on him was permanently out to lunch and his colleagues only booked cars with out-of-state plates, so getting pulled over was unlikely. The back roads—his dad's domain—were what hampered you: unpaved, vertical, pockmarked, hell on the suspension, transformed by spring flooding to valleys of the moon. You could be breezing along and suddenly find yourself at the bottom of a crater the size of a lion's den. Now on a clear Sunday morning he crossed the Walcott-Cyrus line at 92-93-94, sailing through forest, Ronnie Milsap singing—just for Turner—"She Keeps the Home Fires Burning." His favorite song in the world. Wry and homey. Turner liked country-western best (after blues)—the only white people's music written for grownups, with sad grown-up troubles. Not I-want-to-ask-this-chick-to-the-prom-but-my-dad-won't-let-me-borrow-his-car, but about being elbow-deep in debt and missing your wife and the foreman having it in for you.

Plus Ronnie Milsap was blind, so it was extra poignant when he sang about a world gone dark. Turner closed his eyes for a second, just to get a glimpse of what Ronnie Milsap was missing.

The Coronet was Turner's consolation for Kim.

That morning his dad, looking up from the newspaper, his face a matching gluey gray, said, "Turny, do me a favor. Go see your brother, find out how he's doing." Ever since his dad got home from the hospital, Isaac's visits had dried up. No surprise. Ike couldn't stay good for more than a few days, before native selfishness and sloth resumed their dominion. Lucky that somebody got to miss his father's homecoming; the last couple of weeks had been a slow scarring. Pure pain. His dad just didn't seem to get better, but hatchet-faced, slumped in a folding chair in the backyard, wrapped in blankets. It was as if he were in mourning for someone else. A surly listless invalid, seemingly determined not to get better. Family meals—the grim three of them—made you want to cry. It got to his mom the worst. Last night, she padded downstairs to the office. Turner was going over her books. "Dad asleep?"

"He corks off at eight now." Then she said it. "If he dies on us, it'll just be you and me."

And Ike? was Turner's unspoken question.

"Ike's written himself out of this family—no help to anybody, not even himself. It'll be Mattie and Turner, same as always."

Turner shivered, dread-struck and honored all at once. Now his gaunt pining dad wanted news of the prodigal son. Just the idea of setting foot in that house made Turner go blank. He didn't want to subject his car to their driveway, let alone suffer Ike mauling it. He should have borrowed the Dart.

It was painful even to begin to size up the gravity of Ike's treachery in taking up with Miss Urquhart, the wrong done their family, their father, their mother, even him—she was his math teacher, too. It put everybody in a difficult position, this perverted dissolution of boundaries. If his brother wanted to get laid, why couldn't he have done it at college where he lived, like a normal person, stuck some suitable freshman from Indiana or Georgia and not fouled his own nest and everyone else's too, with his corrupt noisy gluttony? No, Ike had to take up with a woman his mother's age, his father's colleague. She was my teacher, too, Turner thought again with a pang; he had always been kind of sweet on Miss Urquhart, appreciated her sharp tongue, thought she liked him too. Now all that was spoiled.

Cornhill Road, his dad had said. Mom was sore at him for going; but what choice did he have? Damned Ike. Here was Cornhill. Damn him twice. Apple trees on your left, hill, old schoolhouse, hut-sized, unpainted, set back a ways, hidden by growth. Could he turn back now? Just to speak to him of their dad seemed unthinkable, once you had seen the dead shut look in his eye, the mortal loosening of curiosity, engagement, Ike oblivious of all but his own desire to be reassured, to be told Dad was doing fine without him, arms above the blanket's plaid swaddling dangling useless over the wooden rest of the deck chair, closed book on lap, coming along great.

"You're lucky your dad got sick on you," she said. "It should jolt you into making sure you do right by him. Mine dropped dead one day out of the blue—just happened to be a day I hadn't called him for two weeks: we'd had some silly fight about who knows what. That's when you don't get over it, when someone simply vanishes, leaving you with a conscience like an empty stomach."

"You don't get over it?" repeated Isaac.

"No. The funeral is the best day; it gets worse after that. People expect you to snap back, go about your business as if nothing happened. They think it's morbid not to. Their life's gone back to normal, why shouldn't yours? I was shocked: half the teachers at school didn't even mention it to me. It wasn't rudeness or indifference: they were embarrassed."

"Of course," Isaac said, energetically. "Of course everybody expects you to shove death under the carpet: it's unseemly. Without God, without faith, without an afterlife and immortality of the soul, death's a forbidden subject, old age is a kind of incriminating breach of etiquette, and mere animal existence, racking up year after youthful year, becomes an absolute value."

"You say 'youthful' so contemptuously," chided Agnes. "I think it's wonderful older people today live such youthful lives. *I* certainly want to be climbing mountains and skiing when I'm eighty."

"It's not a question of living fully; it's a question of accepting death. That's what's considered morbid nowadays. Anyway, youthful ought to be an insult, not a compliment."

"Oh, nonsense. Don't you 'nowadays' me. Every time I hear that word I know someone's about to complain about something people have been complaining about for the last million years. Have you really got the gall to tell me people weren't scared of death before 1900 or whenever you've decided God died? Come off it. You're the one who's reading the Old Testament. All you hear about is how many years Adam and Noah and Methuselah managed to rack up; they *obviously* believe a ripe old age is a mark of divine favor, and short life a sign of bad character. Look at Jacob complaining to Pharaoh that his life has been short and unpleasant and he isn't going to live to be as old as his dad."

"That's because the ancient Israelites didn't believe in an afterlife any more than we do. Then came the Christians, who like the Romans and the Greeks were supposed to love death, or at least not make fools of themselves trying to run away from it. You can't fear death and love life, too. But it's not the fear, it's the fraud. I honestly think most people believe they can live forever, and that death is some kind of infectious disease that can be avoided. No wonder they don't know how to mourn any more. If you have an appendix out, you stay in bed a week and everybody wants to know how you're doing. If your father dies, you're expected back at work next day and no one knows what to say to you."

"Well, they're shy," protested Agnes. "People think it's private, they don't want to intrude."

"That's exactly it," said Isaac. "Death didn't used to be private. Deathbeds were public events with all your distant cousins who hoped to inherit showing up and everyone cocking an ear for edifying last words: people thought not about a painless death, but a noble one. The invention of privacy has been a mixed blessing: people shouldn't die alone."

"Even animals creep away to die alone, and damned right, too. I hope *you're* not planning to be breathing down my neck when I croak, young man. Don't expect any fancy last words from me. I can assure you I'm going solo and in silence," warned Agnes, enjoying her own brazenness in assuming (or pretending to assume) that she and Isaac would be together for life.

A knock on the front door, soft and hesitant. Isaac was already planning what he would say to Agnes's damned nuisance sister-in-law but when he opened there on the doorstep stood Turner. For an instant Isaac turned to stone, knowing his father had died, and then in a great flood of relief, he understood from the sheer orneriness on Turner's averted face that it wasn't bad news, Sam was all right.

"Dad sent me. Wanted to know how you were doing."

Isaac forgot to invite him inside, but just stood there beaming. Look how skinny he was, like a bony nag, all sinew, knobby elbows, stick-out ears. Pale, too. Someone should look after him. "I've been longing to see you, boy," he said at last, clapping him on the shoulder and pulling him into the house. "Agnes will be very happy, too. Come in and have a cup of tea."

"I don't drink tea."

"Don't be a fussbudget, you stupid Mormon, just come on in."

Agnes was washing up their breakfast things. This was the first Hooker she had seen since their elopement, except for Mattie, who had cut her dead at the Stop & Shop. Isaac could almost hear her heart racing under her birdcage ribs and saw her blush, all the glorious ruddiness seeping into her beak-nosed face. Could Turner tell what a handsome woman she was or was he still too young to appreciate so austere a beauty? Hard to figure what Turner thought of women at all, too keen on his own pulse rate and pectorals. That must be why they were so crazy for him, perverse creatures.

"Aggie, do you remember my brother, Turner?"

"Of course I know Turner," replied Agnes, laughing but unconsciously assuming her shrill, sarcastic teacher's voice, "I taught him algebra and calculus. I nearly failed you, too," she said to Turner. "You were an even bigger daydreamer than your brother."

"I guess I was thinking about other things."

"*Nobody* thinks about other things in my class. Nobody thinks, period. But I always feel sorry for you faculty brats. You never get to goof off without people pointing. You can never get out from under your parents' beady eye, and they're so busy not treating you special they end up ignoring you. So I sympathize when a teacher's son decides he's not going to be extra-smart, or extra-good, but just plain normal. Not that you *weren't* smart."

"Mmmmm."

"You want some breakfast, Turner?"

"I've eaten already."

"How's your dad feeling?"

"Mending," said Turner. "They plan to do the by-pass on the sixteenth in case you're intending to be around"—this thrown at Ike—"but he's got to get stronger before they open him up. Well," he stood up. "I guess I'd best be going."

"You just got here," reproached Isaac. "Where you going?"

"Thought I'd climb Mount Menasseh."

Isaac and Agnes spoke at once. "In those shoes?" she said. "Can I come too?" he asked.

Turner ignored Ike, inspecting his tennis shoes.

"Your feet'll get drenched. It's muddy up there," Agnes said. "Borrow a pair of Ike's and the two of you can go hiking together."

Turner edged his way toward escape. "Shoes won't fit," he tried. Isaac's feet were battleships, Turner's like his mother's, small.

"We'll give you a couple extra pairs of socks." While Ike went to fetch them, Turner inched toward the door, wondering if he could bolt, but his brother was too quick. "Those socks are totally *bald*," Miss Urquhart scolded, lovingly. "I don't know what you *do* to them."

"I walk in 'em."

"Well, you must walk in your stocking feet to Lourdes and back to wear them down like that. I've never seen so many socks without toes: you'd think they'd been through the war."

"Would you like the grand tour?" Without waiting for an answer, Isaac turned house proud on their two rooms. First the kitchen with its red-speckled linoleum and baby-blue-painted chairs, like a child's nursery. Bookshelves assembled by Agnes lined the walls, jostling spread-eagled pots and pans, a shabby brocade sofa in the corner. The bedroom was bare, with a small cast-iron stove in the corner, by the window a schoolroom desk laden with a fat inky notebook, a ragged midnight-blue-and-scarlet quilt over the iron-frame bed. On the wall one typewritten page—from a New York editor, Ike explained—and a glossy poster of a Renaissance battle scene: ocher-pink horses with globular rumps bearing baby-faced men with spears and gaudy banners, and, supine in the mud, the bodies of fallen warriors geometrically foreshortened. To Turner, the poster reeked of school: he remembered her shoving this particular round sweet painter, Little Bird, his name meant, down her art-history class's craw. Isaac must feel continually graded. Of course, he was something of a schoolmarm himself.

"That's who she likes best," explained Ike. "Those Florentine painters of the fifteenth century who loved perspective more than life. She wrote her college thesis on mathematics and painting in the Italian Renaissance."

To hide his discomfort at being in their bedroom, Turner stared out the window at the cedar tree and the Daigneaults' apple orchard, rising up the hill. "It faces west," Isaac pointed out. "Too hilly for sunsets, but every spring evening from this window, I sit watching Venus climb that cedar and sail into a melting violet sky. Come on, brother, let's scram." The sight of his notebook on the desk spooked him with thoughts of all he had left undone, might never do. His ideas were proving sparks that flew up into the night air, scattering. He had found peace of a sort, and yet instead of fruitfulness was come face to face with his own indomitable fecklessness. Had he nothing to say or too much? Who sits in solitude and is quiet hath escaped from three wars, said St. Anthony: hearing, speaking, seeing: yet against one thing shall he continually battle: that is, his own heart.

Turner waited outside kicking a stone with the wadded toe of his borrowed boot while Isaac kissed Agnes goodbye as lingeringly as if he were setting off with Lewis and Clark and might be eaten by fellow travelers on the way. Turner sneaked surreptitious glances at his Coronet, trying to resist the urge to wipe off with a handkerchief the flecks of mud on its white wheels. He wondered what Ike was going to say, would he pay it respect the way Turner'd been pressed into admiring Ike's new house. Not that he expected or wanted his blinky brother to notice the car, even if it *was* practically bigger than the house. Ike, emerging, faked a double-take, obligingly whistled, ran a hand over its glossy rump. "What a queen!"

"It's a 'he,'" corrected Turner.

Isaac mock-goggled. "Your car's a 'he'? I never heard of a car that was a 'he.' It's not allowed. Cars, boats, countries, they're all women."

"This one's a guy. Like Germany."

"What's the matter, Mom doesn't allow you to take a woman for a drive?"

"Leave Mom out of this," said Turner so savagely that Isaac backed off.

"If I were getting a car," he said swiftly, "I'd go for a little Karmann Ghia, lemon-yellow."

"You wouldn't fit in one. Anyway, you don't drive."

Agnes watched out the kitchen window as the boys set off at an ambitious clip into the woods that rose almost vertically from the narrow backyard. Though she'd been a little cross lately at Turner's unfriendliness to Ike, she now felt overcome with tenderness for the kid, who seemed to have grown even peakier and ganglier in the last year. In the old days his long hair had flopped into his eyes, hiding his face like a shy girl's. She could picture him in eighth grade tossing his head to shake away the blinding hair. Now his crew cut made him look naked-pale, worried, unhatched. He needs a girlfriend, thought Agnes. Really, you get these shy, inarticulate kids, they meet a computer and never have to learn to talk. Everything is command and control. I guess I used to think so too; now it seems more as if life lies in the uncontrollable. What should I make them for supper—did Isaac say Turner doesn't eat spaghetti or that he won't eat anything but?—and if I do a wash now, will it stay sunny long enough to hang the clothes out to dry? Yes, she decided.

The sky was like a fresh-scrubbed beaming blue saucer enclosing the forested and scented earth; the grass gleamed with blue-crimson diamond points of beaded rain. All the trees' extremities had burst into palest green. The lilac bush, kept back by a cold spring, was only just losing its purple clustered crowns of tight scented pellets, miters of bloom shriveling into gray. Everywhere were premonitions of summer's seedy, insect-swarming luxuriance.

"Which way do you want to go?"

"Up."

"You don't want to go along one of the trails?"

"Doesn't make any difference. You still reach the top, sooner or later."

Turner, Isaac on his heels, hacked his way up through the woods behind the house, up past the springhouse, charging through bushes and brambles with prickly fingers and wet, slapping arms. He leaped up heedless, flinging himself forward, not bothering to part the branches ripping at his arms and legs and face. You had to exhaust your first rush of energy quickly and break through to a calmer and sustained second wind. The forest was black and dense, barbed with pines and spruces interspersed with a few slim white birches, surprised-looking, ladylike, their pale pink bark flaking off like wallpaper. Isaac pointed to a blasted reach of shoulder-high vines that he insisted bore tart blue-black grapes, tiny, glaucous, and spherical, enclosed in thick rinds.

"She made jelly last year."

Spoon-fed. Coddled. Pussy-addled. Ike, boasting about *grape jelly*? What a comedown. She'd babyized him. Would he be going home soon for a feeding and a nap, and leave Turner be?

It was a good forty minutes of upward plunge through wet, almost impenetrable brush before they reached, puffing and silent, a curious kind of ridge, a clearing. They had come out into an avenue that stretched, straight and elevated, as far as the eye could see, its glistening green bordered by darker forest, a secret highway of grass bright as a jockey's silks, which advanced along the mountainside without regard for nature, unearthly yet inviting, like a corridor to another world. When it met up with a brook the boulevard simply hiked up its skirts and passed over the water; many feet below one could see stone culverts through which the streams were made to flow.

It was the old bed of some disused sideshoot of the Boston & Maine. The tracks themselves had long ago been dismantled and their iron removed for other purposes, sold for scrap, but down in the gullies beneath the elevated ridge one could still see piles of discarded cross-ties, massive spars of tarry wood, square-ended.

"See the ties?" Isaac pointed. Turner, marching even faster, didn't answer, annoyed by the bossy proprietariness—was it Ike's railroad?—but his brother, panting, was determined not only to keep up this punishing pace, but to talk. "Just imagine the Titans who built these leagues and leagues and leagues of iron track through mountains and gorges and rivers and desert all across the country," he said. "Just imagine the will and endurance of the workers, the engineering of it. Do you know how many railroad bridges there are in Jessup County alone? It makes the heart quail, just thinking of the gargantuanness of the task. I'd have given up at the first quarter mile, figured let everybody get their own coal, I'm going fishing. Ever seen the steam trains at Bellows Falls? That's a sight to be proud of.

"What kind of people have the constitution to build railroads? No free man you'd think would so ruin his health and break his back. In Russia the railroads are built by slave labor even today, the Baikal-Amur, for instance: prisoners and North Korean conscripts. But in nineteenth-century America it was free laborers, Chinese coolies in the West, Irish in the Northeast laid this line, escaping the potato famine. Yes, you'd only build railroads of your own free will if you were come to a strange land to escape famine, just like the Israelites wound up building pyramid cities in Egypt. Luckily the ancient Egyptians didn't have a Trans-Sinai in the works, or Moses might never have got 'em out alive.

"Don't you find railroads *terribly* romantic?" he concluded suddenly.

Turner, concentrating hard on the path and his pumping heart and lungs and the sun in little flames licking through the pine ceiling, nodded. Everybody did. When he and Ike were little kids he remembered their sneaking into the American Legion bar in Gilboa, where all the retired brakemen and signalmen and foremen congregated, to pester Mr. Hurd and Elias Littlejohn and Mr. Buonpastore for remi-

niscences of the Boston & Maine. Even when trains had gone the way
of the horse-and-buggy, little boys still hooted "Chooo-chooo," dreaming of locomotives and cabooses. But things in the air were *more* romantic, he thought.

It was inconsiderate to talk while hiking: it slowed you down. Better
to climb alone, at your own speed, unhampered by some asthmatic
motor mouth who insisted on looking at the view, smoking, philoso-
phizing. Still, better be outside with Ike, on territory of your own
choosing, than with that woman there, in *their* house.

But Isaac meanwhile had taken matters into his own hands. He broke
into a skip. A dancing gallop that proceeded headlong in ludicrous
girlish leaps. Ike had always been good at skipping, not one of those
talents a boy gets to use much after first grade. A six-foot, two-
hundred-twenty-pound escapee from Bedlam, he cavorted gaily down
the path, and Turner despite himself came skipping after. Down the
grassy avenue of the Boston & Maine the two brothers careered, roaring, until finally Turner, clutching the stitch in his side, subsided,
almost physically pained by this new uprearing of brother love. Christ,
would he always fall for him, always hunger for approval from this geek
he looked down on, abhorred? You're a sap; he doesn't have *you* on the
brain.

"What if—what if Mrs. Cartwright saw us now?" he joked.

"What if?" replied Isaac, indifferently.

Back to business. "I don't think we're going to find a trail. Let's just
cut straight up through here."

Isaac, scanning the maze of forest and underbrush, agreed automatically. It wasn't as if you could get lost: you just went up. Again they
plunged up into this prickly dense medium like swimmers with eyes
shut, gasping, tripping, grunting, shoving, wriggling their way through
the forest's sly obdurate enmity, its pine trees whose knobs reached
out and poked you in the eye. Higher, steeper, primordial, dark, path-
less.

By late afternoon, Turner driving them uphill at a pace befitting the
Bataan march, Isaac asthmatic but uncomplaining, both scratched,
bleeding, they reached the summit. Below this bleak, wind-parched
hummock lay the village of Cyrus, consisting of one needly white belfry
atop a white clapboard Church of Christ, one white clapboard town
hall with green trim, one store, with gas pump, comically named
"Stan's Primal Meats," one auto-repair shop. Across the blue wooded
valley Mount Elmo smiled at Mount Menasseh.

"Ready to go down?" asked Turner, abruptly. They had only just got there.

The two boys descended in silence, scrambling, till they reached a brook on whose banks Ike, flopping to his stomach, called a halt. They sat, fallen into exhaustion's heady speechlessness. Turner could feel his lungs swelling to take in the crisp June air—*les grands airs*, the French called it, Isaac had told him on their ascent—and all the blood vessels in his legs pounding. The brook was brown but very bright and noisy, Isaac reached cupped hands down, offering his brother a fleshy ladle. Turner shook his head.

Something hung in the dry scented air, and neither knew what to say. A golden scales poised before them. On one side, Miss Urquhart, who to Isaac meant life, that is love, an urgent and joyous subject, for like all lovers he was dying to hear Turner's opinion and impressions of his beloved. On the other side, their father heavy with sickness and mortality. In both boys' hearts leaped the same question, What will become of me?

Did he love Ike or despise him? Did he have a choice? He despised him, and blamed Miss Urquhart, too. No question. Loathed them. But did he? All year, while coward Ike hid from his family, Turner had silently counted up transgressions even as he defended him to Mattie—Sam refused to discuss the subject. And yet no sooner had he stepped into that small warm kitchen, wormed his feet into Isaac's socks and boots, watched Miss Urquhart put away her sewing, smelled the scorched buttery griddle scent of the morning's pancakes than these stern recriminations dissolved. Undermining judgment, the twinge of erotic bittersweetness that the sight of lovers inflicts on an onlooker, that mixture of yearning, envy, consciousness of one's own solitary state. For all his disapproval, he wanted to stare, even to cheer them on. Those arms hooked around each other's necks made a breathless-tight circle, shutting you out, yet his own parts involuntarily perked up when Miss Urquhart's hand lighted on Isaac's bottom (he wasn't supposed to see). When am I going to get mine?

He hadn't seen many couples up close, only parents who never touched or kids at school who went out for a couple of months. But that was nothing, a boy horny and boastful and a girl determined to lose it before her girlfriends lost theirs. When he heard about Isaac and the math teacher, he had felt not just indignation but also curiosity. And fear. It was frightening that the borders of sex could extend all the way to swallow up decent middle-aged spinsters, like a murder in your own town or a flood that carries away a neighbor's house. No one was safe. Turner could feel the tongue of flame inside him, and wanted nothing of it. People who didn't control themselves weren't fit to live. Animals. And yet he'd wanted to see them together.

Love had given Turner a hard ride. At the movies as a kid he and his friends used to groan, catcall, make puking noises when the smooching started. But by fifteen or sixteen everyone all of a sudden got awfully quiet and interested, except for Turner, still repelled. Soon enough his buddies, one by one, found girlfriends, and now when the hot stuff started, Mike and Justin and Jimmy had hands down their girlfriends' pants, tongues down their throats, sighing and grinding. It was hard to remain out of the fray, especially when girls began chasing him, not just girls in his class but older ones too, the prettiest girls in the school, even though he still wasn't very tall. He was flattered, nervous, angry, guilty. The less interest he showed, the more they called him up at home, turned up on his doorstep uninvited. Ike nearly popped a blood vessel when Christina Molina started telephoning his kid brother for dates.

Last fall Turner had started going out with Kim Macleod, simply because she had worn down his resistance and he didn't want to be mean to her. Kim was an extremely pretty girl, strawberry blond and slender as a frail boy, but as soon as they started going out, they fought like cats and dogs and Turner found himself more unhappy and humiliated than he thought it possible to be. Going out with Kim, he discovered, meant in effect going out with her girlfriends, and he was shocked at how, hamming it up the more cruelly in front of this willing captive, they talked about sex. It seemed as if all that mattered was the race to lose it first, and once it was lost, how heartlessly and graphically they rated their boyfriends' bodies, positions, moves. Here was no question of love or loyalty: boy they considered half-enemy, half–guinea pig. "Justin's got a raisin between his legs, and when he comes he goes like this . . ." Dawn made a yippy sort of squeal and the girls collapsed in laughter. How could anyone knowingly subject himself to such exposure?

The long and the short of it was that Turner did not want to go all the way with Kim. Or he wanted to, but he wasn't going to let himself, and the more aggressive she got, the less he felt like it. In a month's time, when he was no longer sure what they'd done and what they hadn't done, though doubtless Jamie and Eileen and Marianne knew, Kim broke up with him, and to his own surprise, he was devastated.

In a crazy fever of desire and shame, Turner obsessively replayed the forty-two days before he blew it, forgetting the misery and quarrels and her sheer nastiness, picturing only her slim pale body, hipless, the way she shut her eyes and raised her trusting mouth to his (she was a full six inches shorter than he, a child). He wore her favorite shirt day in, day out till his dad stripped him forcibly, threw it in the wash. "What's good about me?" he asked his mother in a small strangled voice she hadn't heard since he was about four years old. Was it really him Kim had liked—loved, she said, *he* would never have used the word so lightly. Why?

All senior year he carved her initials in desks, walls, his own arm, mingling the letters of their names for proof their love was fated destiny, tailed her to and from school, haunted the pizza parlor where she worked, waited outside her window in the middle of the night, made Mike Karolis go ask her why she had broken up with him. College went by the wayside; all he wanted was Kimberly Macleod. One Saturday night when Domino's closed he waited for her in the Coronet, got up especially for the occasion. He had it all planned out, sleeping bag in the back seat, they would hike up to Bear Ridge, sleep out under the stars, fuck. She left Domino's with Sal, the manager. Turner, who had counted on her being alone, jumped out of the car and grabbed her by the arm. From then on, everything moved very fast: Kim let out a little scream; Sal, elbowing him away, warned, "Beat it, kid. If I see you hanging around here again, I'm calling the police." Before he knew it, his girlfriend and her boss had driven off.

Left standing in the parking lot with these stupid words, these stupid feelings just hanging there. Turner stroked his car's glossy rump consolingly. Poor Coronet. Monday morning he confronted her gang of girls.

"Why did you break me and Kim up?" Jamie, the ringleader, just laughed, and called him a queer. A gun queer. "You and your brother— you're both pathological jerks. Go butt-pirate each other—you're not fit for anybody else." That stunned him, getting hooked with Ike in that ugly way. Somehow he blamed it on Ike. The trouble was, you couldn't hit a girl. All you could do was walk away, knees buckling. Afterward, snappy comebacks rolled through his head as cheerlessly as a slot machine's whizzing triplings of lemons and cherries.

In May Kim started going out with Mike Karolis, and Turner was sure she told him what a dud he was. He didn't really care, except it spoiled their friendship. He was almost grateful when his dad got sick and he took over his mom's cab: now he could be out on the road, instead of facing Mike and Kim, Dawn, Marianne every morning. Finally he was becoming a grown man. Soon he wouldn't feel anything.

Next Friday was graduation day. He knew he had to show up, but it was going to be the saddest day of his life. He was enrolled at Gilboa State for next fall and hadn't yet told anyone he had no intention of going. How could you explain to your father that you couldn't go to a college because that was where your ex-girlfriend and your ex–best friend were both going? Better keep on driving the cab. The customers talked and you barely had to answer. If they rattled on too distractingly, he just turned up the dial on the country-western station. When he wasn't on the road, he was dispatching cars from his mom's office, lifting barbells, corresponding with computer pen pals. He would never go out with anyone else, he felt sure of it.

"Do you think Dad's all right, Turny?" asked Isaac suddenly. "This operation . . . Is he frightened? How does he seem?"

"Ummm . . . tired. Try coming over and see for yourself."

"I guess I should, shouldn't I?"

"Mmmm."

"Well, but it's awkward. Mom is so vile about Aggie it's all I can do not to kill her, and Dad is so pathetic. It depresses me, you know what I mean? They're stuck in this pit together, and they want to drag us into it, too."

"No, I don't know what you mean," said Turner. He and this fat blond lummox, they talked a different language. Every word Isaac uttered was alien. How could a human being, his own brother, be so affected, so unself-knowing?

"He's wasted his life and he knows it."

"Huh? Who?"

"Dad. You know—he should have finished his studies, become a college professor, left Gilboa far behind. Even his sisters managed to escape and get out into the world."

"What's so great about being a college professor?" Turner burst out, furious. "What's so great about the world? How can you say Aunt Ellen's done better than Dad? Dad's done his duty, he helps run the town, he's raised a family—that's no waste. All she knows how to do is spend her husband's dough. Why turn against him now, once he's sick? That professor business's kid's stuff—this is what's real: getting roads fixed, school budgets, teaching your sons what's right, and not—"

"No, he *hasn't* done his duty, and don't preach at me, Turner. It's your duty to exercise yourself to the fullest, do what you were put on earth to do and rejoice in it, not hide and cringe and whine and prevaricate," shouted Isaac, suddenly equally angry. "Do you know that Dante reserves a special ring in the Inferno for people who waste their lives and weep when they should be happy? The second ring of the seventh circle—that's worse than murderers and tyrants. I'd rather he'd left home when we were babies and lived a hard, wild, happy life in a big city than wasted away in this . . . anemic discontent."

"That's what you think professors are? Wild, hard, and happy?"

"Don't be so literal-minded, I only—"

"Hey, you're the college boy. I'm just—"

"*You* have to go to college, too, Turner. No shirking. Don't be like me and Dad. Go to Gilboa next fall, then you can transfer somewhere decent. You need to get away from Mom, and to tell you the—"

"Ike, I think I'm going to kill you. Just shut up. You hear me? Shut up *now*."

Isaac shut up, surprised. You can't talk to Turner about anything any more, he thought. The simplest things are off limits. He's got such an inflexible mind, black-and-white, no questioning. Maybe he ought to be a soldier after all. What's so great about *you*, that's what Turner was really asking him. What have you done to live up to your own bombast? Nothing, I guess. Will we ever get along again? Does he even remember when we were kids together?

"Do you ever think about when we were little, Turner? Remember the time we made a fort in the Ostriches' hayloft and I let you down in a pail tied to the beams and the rope didn't go far enough and you fell five feet?" Isaac tested, dipping a finger down into the brook.

"No," shot back Turner.

"Do you remember . . ."

"No, I said. I don't remember."

"What about the time I tried to smuggle you to school in my knapsack—you desperate to go wherever I went. Remember what happened? Mom caught me trying to haul this wriggling bundle down the stairs and threw a fit. 'You coulda *smothered* him,'" Isaac mimicked their mother's yelp. "You didn't mind. Only when you figured out you weren't going with me after all, then you busted out sobbing. Grownups were always pointing out that I cried more than you: *you* only cried when they tried to separate us. That was then, I guess."

Have you got any memories about me in which I'm more than just your sidekick? Turner was wondering, but he didn't speak. He was remembering other things—the time college-bound Isaac turned his back and wouldn't say goodbye, leaving him standing in the driveway like an idiot, the time Isaac closed the car door on his finger and wouldn't open it. Ike was the forgetter, not him.

"Where is this stream rushing off to, with such busy purpose?" Isaac pondered now, paddling with his hands in the brook, scooping up water and splashing it over his flushed face.

"It's got a date with the Ashuelot, and the Ashuelot runs into the Connecticut, and the Connecticut runs from Canada, almost, to Long Island Sound, four hundred and seven miles," Turner replied, unexpectedly.

He always got a thrill from saying that name—the Connecticut River. He'd even learned to spell it, although he couldn't spell the state of Connecticut. A handsome river, wide yet untouched, the only *big* American river that didn't have a large city at its mouth but expired in a sandbar, so that its wildlife was preserved intact. You could find all kinds of weird plants and animals along the Connecticut River that no longer existed elsewhere, or at least were awfully rare—dwarf wedge mussels and piping plovers and showy lady slippers. There was even a place farther down in Lord's Cove in Connecticut where forty bald eagles lived in the winter.

"Dad and I went up to Norton Pool by Plainfield last fall, camped out a couple of days when it was real cold," he said aloud, all the words spilling out in a muttered jumble. "It's a fine place: four hundred acres of virgin balsam and white spruce and granite cliffs. It's the only spot in the world where Jessup's milk vetch grows. The ecology has stayed the same for three hundred years, but now all these plants and animals are endangered."

"When did you go camping?" asked Isaac, jealously.

"Thanksgiving. When you were at school."

"Jessup's milk vetch, huh?" Isaac snorted. "I hope you're not becoming an environmentalist. I get a little nervous when people start talking ecology—I know next thing they'll be asking me not to smoke because it's bad for the trees," and he lit his pipe.

"Oh, I think sometimes it's sort of nice to be reminded of the connectedness of life—that we're cousins to grasshoppers and bears and not to lawn mowers and modems," Turner countered, a little bemused by his own loquacity. That's what happened when you were alone too much, either you couldn't string two words together or you couldn't shut up. "Not that I don't like modems, but sometimes after twelve hours in front of the screen you get to feeling like a machine yourself."

Isaac puffed on his corn-cob, brooding, savoring the ache in his legs and the cooling heat of the climb and wondering why things had to be so difficult. "Do you still believe in God?" he asked, instead of asking his brother if he liked Miss Urquhart.

"Why?"

"Just wondering. I remember you always used to. I hope I didn't jeer you out of it when I stopped believing. You do, don't you? But what kind of God?"

"What do you mean what kind of God? The usual kind—a God who created the hills," replied Turner, wary of what was coming next. As he saw it, faith was private, something between you and your conscience. Talking about God in company was a creepy kind of showing off.

"A God who made the hills?" repeated Isaac. "Mount Menasseh and Mount Elmo? Do you mean that poetically and metaphorically or literally?"

"Literally." Turner was beginning to feel like the fall guy in one of the Platonic dialogues he had read under Isaac's tutelage. He had noticed with disgust how Socrates would ask one foolish question after another: you would agree, of course, that it is impossible to be brave unless one is without fear. And the idiot respondent would agree and from that false premise an even more ridiculous proposition would be assented to by the luckless Glaucon or Phaedrus, step by step, until the guy was well and truly bamboozled into some conclusion so monstrous it dizzied the mind. It was like three-card monte: whatever you picked you were screwed, yet you were too proud and intimidated to quit. And here came Isaac swooping down on him, talons sharpened.

"You say you believe in a God who created the hills, which is a very beautiful thought, but as you know the hills have been around about twenty seconds," he pursued. "The earth is five billion years old, and its surface has been shifting and yawning and stretching and heaving ever since. The hills as we know them have only been here a blink of time, and they sure aren't here to stay. Would you say that God, when he was hanging around at that infinitesimally tiny fraction of pretime when matter was created, made a note to himself not to forget to arrange things so that in another billion years the motion of tectonic plates might momentarily toss up a Mount Elmo and a Mount Menasseh, not to mention a few milk vetches?"

Turner stared out over the valley. "I don't want your boots." He suddenly slashed open the laces, unpeeled sweaty paddings of wool, wriggled his naked feet free, and threw shoes, socks Isaac's way. "Listen," he ventured, "I've read as much as you about the creation of the universe. Big deal: you go into a store, there are books on quantum physics for people who only read *True Romance*. That's fine, and in a couple of years we'll have forgotten all about quarks and red dwarfs and implosion and we'll be spouting a different theory about the creation of the universe. But when it comes to God, I don't have a theory: I believe, and my belief doesn't need proof. In fact you might even say that unlike in science, the validity of my faith depends on my believing without any proof. It's moronic, guys using science and computers to prove the existence of God, like we're doing him some favor, like he's one of Saturn's suns or some supernova or something. *Jesus*. Computers are the coolest thing in the world, but they've got their limits. So this is it, here's my creed: I believe what believers have believed for the last four thousand years: that there is one God who made the world and who judges what we do in it."

"Amen," said Isaac. Turner gave him a dirty look.

"Do you believe in him—God—all the time?" Isaac inquired, in a different tone of voice.

"I think—this subject—is—now—closed." Turner spoke between gritted teeth.

"I asked because . . . because I believe, too. I think. Hills and all," said Isaac, almost shyly. "Anyway, look who's praising milk vetches over modems. I thought you wanted to be a fighter pilot when you grew up."

"Not fighters, helicopters. They're slower, more stately," explained Turner, relenting. "But I'm not gonna be a pilot. If you're going to be a pilot, you know you're going to be a pilot by the time you're ten. Like Jimmy Watts. Remember how they always sat him away from the window in school so he wouldn't spend all day looking at the sky?" He imitated Jimmy Watts, right in the middle of history class announcing periodically, "A Boeing 707. Two Northrop Tigerlilies. A Cessna Double Engine," and not even knowing he was talking aloud. "Jimmy Watts is stationed in Turkey now. That was years ago I wanted to fly. I'm too old already," he concluded.

"Jeez, if you're too old, I'm *history*."

"You are," said Turner, quite serious now. "I think about death all the time. Already, I have to push my body twice as hard to do what came easy two years ago."

Both at the same time remembered their father, who nearly had died, who wasn't yet out of the woods, and a chill ran over them, and they felt ashamed of their self-absorption, but couldn't shake free of it either.

Why won't he tell me what he thinks of Aggie, wondered Isaac, and if he doesn't say anything can I ask? Turner is the only one who would understand—has to understand. Doesn't he know how precious such a woman is, and that when you find joy you must grab it, or risk never living?

"Do you believe in love?" he asked aloud in a half-joking way. His brain was gone mushy, to be asking such questions.

"Is this twenty questions?"

"Well, I don't get to see you alone very often any more. I like to keep track of these things. Do you?"

"Between who?"

"Between a man and a woman."

"No," said Turner wryly. "But maybe between a man and a dog."

"Now you're talking." He was a little relieved to be back on teasing territory. "Tell me, how are things going between you and . . . what's Preston's mutt called . . . Brunhilde? Getting anywhere?"

Turner dipped his hand into the brook and watched his fingers turn green and bubble-logged like dead man's flesh. I'm going to kill him, he thought without even knowing he was thinking it. I'm going to kill that insolent ape. Someday he's going to get his: I'm going to drown him just like he tried to drown me in the Hanesworths' pond. He's too annoying to live.

"Why don't you believe in love, Turny?" Isaac persisted, undaunted.

"What's the point? Everything important you have to do you do alone." Don't bother me, don't bother me, stop asking stupid questions. Here they were high up near the top of a mountain in the early summer light, with all the world spread beneath them in squares; you could even see a yellow dog looking rather like the maligned Isolde trotting purposefully along the road to Agnes and Isaac's house; he saw a hawk circling, immobile wings outstretched like a glider, and sounds from the valley arose with lightning clarity, giving you a funny sense of how God might after all be able to hear and see everything at once. All this majesty, freshness, wind, and awe, and Isaac, deaf, blind bully, desecrating nature.

"Everything important you have to do you do alone," repeated Isaac. "You mean like having babies? You planning to get pregnant?"

"I don't think it's right to have children, and I don't think I'd make a good father," said Turner, in a final sort of way. End of discussion.

"So what are you going to do?" his brother demanded scornfully. "Are you going to live all your life as Mom's minion?" Uh-oh, he thought even as the words were spilling out of his mouth, now I've gone and done it. I've gone too far. No taking it back, either. He leaned down into the stream, cupping water.

Turner watched the shaggy dirty-blond head, the broad back, the immense up-ended bottom like a Muslim at prayer. His heart was pounding. Now. Grab that flushed bullneck in two hands and push his head under. Dunk, press, choke, bubbles signaling to the surface, until mountain stream soon to be joined with Connecticut River flooded windpipe, till breathing ceased, life fled. His mother's words sounded in his ears, "Ike came into this world like a drowned puppy." Now. Hands twitched just as gasping Isaac, water dripping from his jowls, raised his head. Frightened, Turner stood up, started to speak, and then, wordless, took off, leaping back down the mountain.

"Turny, where are you going? Wait up!" Isaac, fumbling over the abandoned pair of boots and socks, went bounding after, stalled by the thickness of the trees. "Turner, wait up!" But barefoot Turner was leaping like a gazelle. "Are you angry? I didn't mean it about you and Mom! I'm a brute, forgive me!"

By the time he had untangled himself from a prickly pine tree and blazed a new path he could no longer hear below him the crackling of his brother's swift descent. He was alone in the forest, lost. It was almost dark by the time Isaac, emerging into the open air, found that he had wound his way half around the mountain and come out above the quarry. Below him he could see the ghost-town metal tenements of machinery, a four-story shantytown of conveyor belts and separators, the conical tower of crushed stone, a couple of Mack trucks fifty feet below. He sat on his bottom and began to slide.

Chapter 4

"DID HE SAY ANYTHING?"

"No," said Agnes. "Just took his sneakers and went."

"Run me over to Mom and Dad's, Ag, see if he's there."

The Hooker house was lit up, and Turner's Coronet was parked outside. In the kitchen, Mattie was fixing supper. "Where's Turner?"

"That's a fine way to greet someone you haven't seen in a blue moon. Don't you even say hello any more?"

"*Hello.* How are you, Mom? What's new?"

"I think the muffler's got a hole in it. If I had a son who could drive, I'd ask him to take the cab down to Jim's and have it checked."

"You got two sons, luckily. How's Dad?"

"He won't tell me. If you want to know, go find out for yourself. He's cranky enough."

Sam came out of the study. His face seemed a little gray, but his eyes lit up when he saw the boy. "Let *go* of me!" he protested as Isaac enveloped him.

"How you feeling, Daddy?"

"Just fine, thanks to Florence Nightingale here. It's amazing the tender nurturing instinct your mother has. What a gentle touch, a heart of gold," he intoned, eyes rolling.

"Well, why should I bother?" Mattie retorted. "If I tell you to lie down, you get up. If I tell you to get up, you lie down. If I try to get anything for you, you nearly bite my head off. He goes, Stop treating me like an invalid. So now he complains that I neglect him. I think I ought to get a medal for sainthood."

"Anyway," said Sam to Isaac, "I'm ready to get out of the house and back to school. Only trouble is school's about to break up. I don't know what the hell I'll do with myself all summer: I'll have to go vandalize the graveyard so I can call a selectmen's meeting to fix it. The only good that's come of all this, aside from banishing hopes of ever being able to afford a new car, is I'm back to reading novels. I've read two hundred pages of *Moby Dick*. You ought to try it; it's not half bad, if you like fish."

Isaac headed upstairs. Turner was at his computer, eyes glued to green columns. Isaac cleared his throat, paced, flung himself face down on the lumpy cot, heaved up again.

His brother kept hacking. He was checking into a bulletin board for old car buffs. Will Riley from Bellows Falls was offering a '62 Nash Ambassador, mint.

"Turny?"

Only 200,000 miles on it. Asking $750. A beaut.

"Ever feel like you got a demon inside, making you do and say dreadful things?"

Ridiculous price. Come to earth, then we'll talk. $500.

"Turner, so help me God, I didn't mean it."

No way, José. $725.

"Will you ever forgive me?"

It was a game. He didn't want an Ambassador, though he might well drive over to Bellows Falls to take a peek. $550.

In a grisly flash Turner saw Ike tumbling to his knees, like an elephant in a circus. Can't do it, flashed Riley. "Stop playing the fool," Turner growled, jumping up and retreating to the other side of the room as if polluted by a drunk's sloppy kisses.

He'll never forgive me, Isaac thought. There are things I did when he was six months old I don't even know about that he's never forgiven me for.

"We destroyed that country," asserted Mattie. "It's a disgrace."

"What are you talking about? They killed two hundred and forty-one of our Marines. It was a wreck *decades* before we got there. Only disgrace was pulling out, instead of dropping a bomb on Damascus." Penitent Isaac was washing dishes after a family supper, slopping china into soapy water.

"We shouldn't have been there to begin with," she continued, undeterred. "First of all we kill their prime minister. . . ."

"What prime minister?"

"Oh, you know, the brother of that twit who's in there now. Don't use so much detergent, Ike, we'll be swimming in suds."

"You mean Bashir Gemayel? We never killed Gemayel."

"Of course we did, or the Mossad did. What's the difference?"

"He was an Israeli ally—he was about to sign a peace treaty with them." Isaac stacked still-soapy dishes in the rack.

"That's why they killed him, probably. They don't want peace. They just want our money."

"Mom, this is where you go berserk and I sign off. I want to have a talk with Daddy." Pausing in front of his father's study, he knocked gently and pushed the door ajar.

Sam was lying on the floor. He was soaked in sweat and his skin had blanched to the color of Cream of Wheat and there was an expression of inward concentration on his face such as Isaac had never seen. It was this expression more than anything else that terrified. Isaac knelt, peering into his father's face.

"Don't come near me," breathed Sam. "I'm fine. Go into the other room. I'm fine. I'm just a little sick to my stomach. It'll pass in a moment. Go on, son. I'll join you in a minute."

Isaac held his father's gluey wet hand while Mattie called the doctor and Turner got the car. They bundled him into a blanket—he was shaking and sweating at the same time, and concentration had shellacked his gaunt gray features into a mask as composed as a hunter stalking prey, as a priest at sacrifice, as a matador on tiptoe raising his dagger and willing the blade's entry into precisely that fatal cavity in the spinal cord that leads to heart and lungs, as a man preparing to die.

I'm going, Sam was thinking as he lay stretched out in the back seat, head on Isaac's lap. Resolve vanished, he was rent by a powerful convulsion of grief and rage.

Turner was driving, Mattie up front, here he was, staring up at the dark hurtling aisle of maples and a broad moon blazing bluish light. If only I were spared I'd be happy just gazing at the stars, or lying in a field under the sun, digging my fingers into soil, savoring with full lungs and a grateful heart each season's bounty, and then the moment's fierceness passed and he smoothed once more into supreme calm, an anticipatory loosening of his lifelong clutch at the this and this and this.

The pain wasn't enormous but irritable, a panicky cramp as if he'd been swimming too long on a heavy stomach. He knew the pain was what waited for him, that there was no avoiding it, no stalling. He thought of his father, whose diary he had been rereading these last months, finding himself more and more in consonance with that mild humility, wishing he could tell the old man how alike they had grown. He worried about Turner, who had the hardest row to hoe and whom he hadn't quite done right by, mother-cursed, who would have to soften his inhuman notions of manhood and duty or be crippled, and he wondered what would become of Mattie and would she marry again, and discovered to his surprise that he most violently didn't want her to. Oh Isaac, said Sam, but he didn't know whether he said it to himself or aloud, oh Isaac, my precious lamb, my blood's blood, my turtledove. Oh Isaac, joy of my heart, my bouncing boy, oh my Isaac, comfort yourself and be happy, my pride, my bullock. He saw Isaac gazing down at him, trying to be brave and smiling and probably wanting as usual to bury his head in his father's chest and howl. He tried to speak, he thought he was speaking, singing the song of love that came bubbling up in his lungs, but nothing came out. The pain swept in once more, on its stinking tide of nausea, and the world blackened into a blinding light.

Mattie decided that her husband's funeral should be as civil as possible. By civil she didn't mean polite, she meant no religion, or as she put it, no hypocrisy. Sam hadn't believed, she didn't believe. A funeral should be down-to-earth and genuine, nothing phony. They would have a brief service at the funeral home, a couple of friends would say a few words, and after the burial she would serve a big meal back at the house. A buffet. She would bake a ham, or maybe roast a turkey, make potato salad—if only Sam'd held on a month later they could have had corn on the cob—and ice cream. She scribbled down these items with a certain relish, pencil stub grinding down on the lined paper of an old school notebook of Turner's. Her head bobbed, her eyes glittered, her mouth moved as she wrote; Isaac could tell from her haughty glance that she was already welcoming the guests, assuming the somber imperious garb of widowhood.

"Who's going to talk at the service?"

"Not too many people. Better keep it snappy. No one likes memorial services that drag on forever. You boys should each say something about your dad, and maybe your Uncle Jim."

"*Uncle Jim?* Am I hearing right? I mean, Jim's pleasant enough, but he can't open his mouth without getting himself all tied up in knots. You'd just embarrass him, asking him to deliver a eulogy. Anyway, Daddy just tolerated him, barely," Isaac explained. "You have to think of people Daddy respected who know how to talk. Jeez, even Mrs. Cartwright would be better than *Jim*. At least ask Dr. McCormick: he's a great speechifier."

"Isaac, is this *your* funeral or what? When you die, you can ask whoever you like, but this one's my call. I don't need Emily Post to tell me what's right. Your Uncle Jim is a decent man."

"Cows are decent, too. How about Christopher Scannon? He sure was a big influence on—"

"That little vampire didn't influence your dad, he suckered him. Your dad hasn't spoken to him for twenty years."

"What about Jack Ellsworth? At least he can string two words together. What's Uncle Jim know about anything? He'll just get up there and say, 'I always told Sam he oughta have got his oil checked more regular,' or 'Knowing Sam Hooker was as good as a new carburetor.'" Isaac was desperate; his father, he was realizing for the first time, had no real friends. "What kind of flowers are you going to get? Will you have pallbearers? Are you going to—"

"Don't start with me, Ike," warned Mattie. "This isn't your affair. The one who pays the piper calls the tune." When Isaac lowered his head like a bull, she snapped, "You go do things the way you like over in your schoolmarm's house. Here we do things my way, and you're not going to have an easy ride any more now that your daddy's not here to spoil you."

"Don't you want a last chance to do Daddy proud?" Isaac countered. "Or are you going to bury him on the cheap?"

"You got some nerve, buddy boy. You're the one who worried your father sick. Don't talk to me about cheap. Do you know how much money we threw away on that college education you begged and bullied for? Who's going to pay your loans now? Not me. No more free lunch. You're grown up now. Turner didn't drive us crazy insisting he go to Harvard, prancing all over town playing big shot, but Turner seems to know how to make his way in the world *without* all the fuss."

Turner didn't look up. He was concentrating on the words he would have to say. He had timed himself: 130 words a minute, that meant 400 at the very least, yet every one that surfaced in the chilly timid pool of his mind he threw back as skimpy, inadequate, or too revealing. Dumb. Tell a story, Isaac had instructed him, a story about you and

Daddy. Turner didn't understand at first. He had seen his father every day of his life. How could breakfast, lunch, and supper, a camping trip, a basketball game, a drive to the store, be a story? If there were stories about him and Daddy, they were private stories, just about him and Daddy, stories that told him in retrospect how much Daddy cared about him.

Sitting clenched upright in bed at night, must have been nine or ten years old, his stomach roaring and tossing like a storm at sea, listening to the sound of his parents quarreling next door, sarcastic ugly voices. A catfight. "Have it your way," he heard low, and his mother, who would sooner burn at the stake than be deprived of the last word, screamed after his departing dad a torrent of curses. Then the sound of the door closing, not slammed, merely shut, with a frighteningly gentle finality. How fluent nervous children become in the language of doors—the slam, the loving closure, the final walkout!

Holding his breath, listening for the car's rumble, gnawed by certainty: Dad's leaving, Mom is going to be left all alone and defenseless, and I'm the only one can protect her. Will I have to quit school and get a job? Will we leave Gilboa? Go on welfare? Who's going to look after us? I don't know how to drive a car or fix the furnace. How will I know how to pay the bills? Suddenly, instead of the scream of tires on night gravel, his father's feet climbing up the stairs, going not to his own bedroom but, yes, to Turner's.

"You awake, Tiger?"

Turner played dead. Creak of father lowering onto bed, squashing him into a corner, sighing, lonely weight. And the strangest thing was, instead of being relieved, Turner was absolutely livid. "You're crushing my pillow," he snarled, pushing Sam off.

"Sorry."

"Well, it's all very well to say you're sorry, but now it's *ruined*." Turner, an early insomniac, was indeed fanatical about the unsullied crispness of that downy wafer—if it got hot or creased too soon, there was no point even *trying* to sleep. Also, as a younger brother, you had to guard those few things that were yours alone.

"Want to go fishing tomorrow, Tiger?"

"No."

"How come?"

"Because."

"Because what?"

"Because we don't even own a proper reel and it makes you sick to see things die and because, Dad," he was too proud at that age to say "Daddy" any more, "you and I have *nothing in common*."

There, the look of exaggerated hurt that crinkled his father's face by the half-light of the open door. "How can you say that, Turny? We've got *everything* in common."

"Like what?"

"Like guns and soldiers and blood and guts and war . . ."

"You don't like blood and guts and war one bit," admonished Turner. "You *faint* when you see blood."

"Yes, I do like blood and guts and war. I like 'em because you do."

No, his father wasn't going anywhere, but would stay by Turner's side till he fell asleep and be there still when he woke up, would follow him like goodness and mercy all the days of his life, loving what Turner loved with a wry face and squeamish stomach. And Turner, half-mollified, pushed his father off the bed a second time. "You messed up my pillow" was his parting shot.

Such remembrances should be locked in his heart, not spiced up for a roomful of staring strangers. His mind was cramped, salted and blanched of imagery or language, his mouth dried up at the obscenity of standing before a crowd and telling what his father meant to him. Well, either they already knew he was a great guy or they didn't. It wasn't anyone's business, anyway. Nobody now would ever know that somebody had once called him Tiger.

He shouldn't have died. Turner should have died instead. Daddy had two sons, he wouldn't miss Turner, but he, Turner, only had one father, whom he couldn't spare. It didn't seem right to lose the only father he would ever have.

The service was intolerable, to Isaac's mind. Perfunctory, nasty, ignorant, antiseptic. The reception room in the funeral home, a red-plush jewel box robbed of its jewels, looked empty and awry. Without a priest to lead, or a prayer book to go by, or an Almighty to whom one could commend the dead man's spirit or by whom his life might be sanctified, it was just one awkward man getting up and offering lame platitudes and two miserable boys stammering before the unsay-able.

Something incomplete. Funerals were supposed to make you realize the dead were really dead, but this one signally failed to convince. Life couldn't culminate in something so quick and shabby, so unresonant, like a visit to the dentist, or applying for a new gun permit. The only satisfying part was the crowd—swarms, reams of Sam's former and current students; there were Billy Ostrich and his father and mother and grandparents and brother and sister, and Isaac's Hooker aunts flown in from South Carolina and California, whom he hadn't seen in years and who looked like Sam but plumper, his California aunt frumpy but kind, his South Carolina aunt golden as tooled leather, the Mc-Cormicks and the Karolises and John Preston and the Hanesworths and Herringshaws, and all Sam's fellow teachers, the school janitor and the cleaning ladies and their children, and Gilboa's everybody, farmers, store owners, people Isaac didn't even know by name, come to do his father proud. And Agnes. Beside him, knee caps white, sitting straight, as on the first day they had gone to hear the Reverend Popper.

So much had passed since then; so much was irrecoverably lost. It seemed to Isaac he had slipped backward and backward into a slough of anonymous indolence. Drifting was life on the fast track compared to his murky and motionless regress. He knew less and had done less at twenty-two than at seventeen, was a greater ignoramus, slept later in the mornings, could barely hold down a menial job, had become ever more ingrained in the petty vices that came of sloth, was ever more neglectful of even the most automatic, trifling, and instinctual obligations. Love he had used as a chicken-hearted pretext for dropping out. He had gone nowhere in the world and yet did nothing for his family either, had so much time on his hands that he couldn't be bothered to pay bills or answer letters. His projected writings had run out of steam, pretend though he would that it was simply for lack of reference books. With his father gone—and Isaac was too childish not to feel this death as a sign his dad didn't like him any more—there was no one left but Agnes. She was his consolation, his spur, his dreamboat, his hope. His wife. He thought of her as his wife, and wondered if she thought of him the same connubial way. If only his father had let him talk about Aggie, and hadn't cringed so when Isaac tried. If only his father hadn't gotten so disgusted with him. If only he'd been as good a son as Turner.

After the funeral they drove out to the cemetery. This, too, entailed a tussle: Mattie had hired a car and driver from the undertaker but wouldn't let Agnes ride with them (Agnes would have been horrified to know that Isaac had fought for her inclusion). Sandwiched between mother and brother, he was oppressed suddenly by the meagerness of their diminished sliver of a family, this lopsided three, without husband and father. A mother and two sons—why hadn't his parents had the solidity to produce more children, thicker buttressing against annihilation without trace? It was time to be a man, but Christ, how he longed for the one who was gone.

The churchyard was crowded as a county fair. The gravediggers lowered Sam into the grave—a good gleaming black casket like a Cadillac sedan with lots of gold filigree, Isaac had picked it out in the mistaken belief that it would delight his father's secret flashiness, make him laugh. And after this nailed-down box was summarily dispatched to the worms—oh my poor dad, Isaac chanted over and over to himself—they drove back without him and the festivities began.

It must be said that Mattie Hooker knew how to throw a party. The kitchen table swayed under the weight of her provisions: there was a ham, ruddy and freckled with cloves, its ample rump corseted in strings, giving off a scent of roguish good cheer; there were clotted mounds of potato salad; bottles of Wild Turkey and Canadian Club bristled like soldiers arrayed for battle, while five latticework pies, baked by Aunt Sue, their surfaces yellow and granular as sandcastles, coquettishly revealed their velvety and aromatic innards. Her famous stinginess in abeyance, Mattie worked the room, plying her guests with drink, determined that everyone relax, eat, talk, have fun. Great bosom and hips enveloped in black lace, pale eyes aglitter, curly scarlet lips. An empress. Isaac had never seen so many people in his own house before; with a twinge of disloyalty he wondered whether she might not have led a more rowdy and gregarious life without his dad.

Agnes, whom Mattie in her dowager grandeur tolerated but wouldn't greet, let Isaac have too much to drink. He needed it if he was going to talk to every single person in the room, persuade them all how glad he was they were there, how much each had meant to his father, so that at last his father might be properly memorialized. Underneath this more respectable compunction was the secret mystical conviction that if everyone in the room were thinking of Sam hard enough, loving him hard enough, maybe then he might be resurrected in some form— three days at least you were allowed to stay among the living—might dwell in their midst, tangible and pleased, and maybe Isaac could be joined in some way to his father's diffused spirit, touch him as one touched fog or a jellyfish. That was the first, expansive stage in his drunkenness. Later on intoxication and bereavement mixed in him as savagely as whiskey and gin, reaping a furious, nauseated depression. As he moved around the room, lurching a little, he caught snatches of conversation about children and grandchildren, about school-board politics, about plans to convert the old mill into new boutiques, about politics.

"I never thought I'd live to see the day when there'd be a Mohammedan President of the United States," said Dan Herringshaw.

"Oh, Jackson's not a Muslim—that's his friend with the bow tie out in Chicago," corrected his son-in-law.

"What's the difference? In my day, colored people were very religious, and they sure weren't Muslims. They went to their church on Sundays, we went to ours; we never asked them which one, that was their business. Of course, there were a lot of colored people in Rockingham, and I guess there was some kind of Baptist church they all went to. No, they sure weren't Mohammedans back then."

Why weren't they talking about his father, whose day it was, his father who was dead and who was better than anyone alive, who was dead at forty-six years of age, before he'd even begun to live, his father who by his goodness shamed the living? Suddenly he didn't feel like seeing or talking to anyone except Turner, but Turner was busy being wept on by Aunt Ellen. Only let this great hot crowd in his father's living room and kitchen stop eating and drinking and making nuisances of themselves and go back home where they belonged, taking their levity, their gabby windbag damned rhinoceros-hided talkiness with them. When Billy Ostrich and Peter Karolis and Paul Chen attached themselves lovingly to him, he shook them off with a frown. That was stage two.

Had to find Agnes; only she would understand. Agnes was perched in a corner with Jack Ellsworth. He was telling her about a weekend he and his wife had spent in New York. "We went to see *Cats*, which was fun, though Eliot must be turning over in his grave to see what they've done to his poor little book of poems."

Agnes, red-faced and nervous, nodded, smiling, and Isaac, remembering that Christina Molina had once told him Agnes and Ellsworth were an item, hated her. He pulled her aside.

"Ag, we're leaving."

The smile vanished.

"You hear me?"

"I hear you, but you can't go."

"I can't bear it a moment longer. Please."

"Isaac, it's your dad's funeral. You can't leave early. You can't do that to your mom."

"If I don't get out this second, I'm going to take a hatchet to everyone in this room."

"It isn't right. It's not fair to your mom and your brother."

Isaac walked out. When she finally joined him he was sitting in her car raking its vinyl interior with his fingers. The party they left behind was diminished but still hopping. Isaac, over his shoulder, saw the yellow house aflame with lights and liquor, shaking with noise and (he imagined) laughter, and truly understood that it wasn't his father's house any more, and if it wasn't his father's house, then there was no room anywhere on earth for Sam. And so he must be gone. He felt he must scream to burst.

Mattie never forgave him. His own father's funeral! She was right, Isaac's selfishness was chronic. It was Sue and Margery and Sam's sisters who remained afterward, pressing pie carcasses and pineapple garnish into plastic wrap, decanting gravy into glass jars, easing crumbled latticework into the garbage. It is women who help you out every time, who stick around for the nitty-gritty. Turner was upstairs locked in his room, Isaac had made off with the Aged Slut, and downstairs the women sat, smoking and talking.

Mattie couldn't believe Sam was gone. Just up in smoke. She'd known him since he was a child, a shy skinny eager-to-please eleven-year-old, with a hank of slicked hair falling in his eyes and a shit-eating grin baring two big front teeth. They didn't make 'em like Sam any more: he was a real gentleman. They'd had a good time for all their differences. Where did the dead go? Her man was gone, and all she had left was a twice-mortgaged house and a mountain of bills and two sons without a grain of gumption. Not that Sue's or Marge's or Sam's sisters' kids were much better.

"If I was growing up today," Mattie confided, "I wouldn't have saddled myself with a husband and children. No way. Of course, back then we didn't know any better."

"What would you do instead?" asked Ellen, intrigued.

"Oh, I don't know. Travel, maybe. See the world. The *last* thing I would do is get married, and that's the truth."

BOOK
FOUR

Chapter 1

LORD . . . LORD. LORD . . . Holy Christ, let me not wake up to another hideous desperate morning, to the squalor of days. Let me never, never, never have been born. Let me not face this yawning howling moron vacancy, let me smash myself to smithereens, let me be destroyed and canceled out, let me *not* have at my feet this gaping endlessness of time, dank black years, let there be time no longer. Die, I want to die and be done with it and not have to witness this botched mockery of a life. Like a cow. Worse than a cow, cows aren't wicked or lazy, don't do dirt. Christ, to be dead and gone, a goner. A dead cow, and not drag on, mad and useless. Better a dead cow than a live . . . fool. No God, no truth, no life, no light. No end and no re- demption. Only meaninglessness, cycles of vacuous treachery. No light but only a mockery of light, a puling, sputtering whore light, no truth but smirking lies in frilly skirts baring sky-blue baboon bottoms. No God but a devil.

This, he realized, was the century's great discovery. There was no God left—maybe for others but not for us—but there *was* a devil, and that devil was a monodevil and an omnidevil. Everywhere. Ever since that day Isaac could see the devils, that was the difference. In Egypt holy fathers who lived in the desert could see them, St. Anthony and others, Martin Luther threw his inkpot at the devil, but to foul Isaac by virtue of his extreme worthlessness and sloth and cowardice, to Isaac the Luther burner the desert father destroyer had also been granted the gift, here in his own bedroom, out of the corners of his eye, late at night, little gibbon-sized wall crawlers with plumy gray tails that buzzed in his ears and fled when he looked straight on. Not real, my imagination. Not real, but that's worse. Nothing real. And this is what they said: all human endeavor comes to nothing. And Isaac answered, Let me be dead and *not* see before me eternal triviality and waste, treachery, mediocrity, bad faith, the disappointment of hope, not this abyss, not this infernal chickenshit lie of a seamy life. I was born a liar, said Isaac, everything I've ever said or done was fake, now I've lost heart even in my own deceit.

Darkness and cold, darkness and cold, darkness and a cloying weight, his idiot Hong Kong clock on chicken legs whose idiot tick strummed out the useless minutes. Hide the clock in a drawer, throw it out the window, but to think of the clock rusting and rotting in the earth . . . Well, it was too sad. Who wound it? Why did it keep going? What was the use? Everything rotted, turned to dust. Darkness and cold—he would never be warm again—heaviness. The heaviness was the insufferable burden of time and the welcome weight of the blankets he had pulled down from the wardrobe to bury himself alive, meta-morphosing into a great wool sausage, a monstrous papoose shuddering and chattering to the marrow of his rotten bones from the cold. No, this worm would never hatch into a butterfly.

If Isaac wasn't going to do anything ever—never leave Gilboa, never be great or even decent, never write volumes of history and philosophy, never sit in cafés in SoHo or up by Columbia drinking and talking and saluting the pretty girls, never perch his provincial rump on a red-velvet seat in the Metropolitan Opera House to hear a white lardy Don Giovanni chalk up his thousandth squeeze and mock damnation, never help people worse off than himself, never see his name in print over breakfast not if he lived to read his own obituary, never join that noble band of companions whose intimacy he dreamed of more than of wife and children—if he would never go back to Harvard, never leave his bedroom again but rot in Cyrus a disappointed and unfriendly lunatic, then better to die at once. The devils were coming fast and furious. A heavy one expanded inside his lungs and made his cramped heart gasp. Abandon hope, half-wit, failure, lazy as an ox, vicious; there is no God, no heaven, no inferno where you could meet your father and kiss his dear haggard cheeks, his attenuated hands. Now when Agnes tried to talk to him, Isaac the gusty gabber, fierce and voluble, unmannerly as a hurricane, couldn't answer. If he found words they ached too much, bored holes in the throat and choked him, he lost heart and clammed up, gulping and twitching, longing to be left alone. This battle to keep his wits, not to scream and foam, not to fly off into space, not to carve open his chest, was too bitter and unremitting.

Isaac was no longer Isaac, but merely the bloody bog, the plain, the knotty Megiddo on which this battle was being fought between life and lunacy, freedom and slavery, the devil's death.

"How's the patient?"

Agnes gave Peter a wry and sorrowful smile. How delicious, that mournful, lopsided feminine grin of irony: "Not so hot."

"May I go in, Agnes?"

He'd been the first and only of Isaac's friends—her former students—to fall comfortably into using her Christian name. Paul Chen and Justin and Jimmy Randall, even Billy, still couldn't look the teacher-turned-girlfriend in the eye, but Peter Karolis had been gracious, as if putting at ease a much younger person of inferior station. He'd been like that even in eighth grade; she remembered the slick part in his hair, the gentle edifying way he answered questions in class as if she'd asked because she honestly didn't know. He'd been too good, that was the truth; it made her uneasy. Boys needed to be naughty sometimes. When and how would he break out?

She wasn't sure Isaac would see him. Maybe if he came back another time?

"Agnes, this *is* another time already. I came last Sunday. Remember?" Peter bent toward her kindly. She's scared of Ike, he was thinking. He was olive-skinned like his mother, a matte green-brown tincture to his flesh, a long face so narrow it seemed perpetually in profile. Straight on, you could hardly see both his eyes at once. Everything about Peter was the same olive brown, like army issue; his hair, his skin, his eyes hedged and shaded by very straight eyelashes, his long nimble fingers, even his voice was a soft brown burr with more *r*'s in it than most New Hampshire throats had, a voice that elicited trust. He was in his first year at law school, and even Agnes saw that Peter couldn't keep on running over to Cyrus in the hopes that his crazy friend might finally deign to receive him.

"Oh, all right, go on, then, give it a shot. But don't be put off. He's not well," she said sternly.

There was no answer to Peter's knock, but he pushed the bedroom door ajar. It was pitch dark, and there were voices. Someone else is in there, was his first thought. Then his eyes adjusted to the darkness and he stopped short. An unmade bed, the sheets twisted into knots, and on the floor, on his knees, was Isaac Hooker, writhing, shaking, tears pouring down his cheeks, muttering words so wild that afterward Peter couldn't repeat them even to himself.

His instincts were mannerly, discreet: his reflex was to retreat with an apology as if he'd barged in on someone on the toilet or a couple *in flagrante*. But it didn't matter, the young man was possessed. Rocking back and forth on his knees, gabbling incantations, face contorted by a wretchedness so unearthly, so animal-like it made your hair stand on end, Isaac hadn't heard, didn't see; he was fully occupied. On his knees, brokenly invoking the ceiling through his tears. Peter the rock stared dumbstruck, for to witness this derangement was a sight as bloodcurdling as a shipwreck, as a volcanic eruption from whose molten rivulets it would be bootless to flee.

That's what is so horrific about mental disorder, he thought, the fear, no, the knowledge that it's contagious, like seeing someone yawn. No one is safe. You adjust your watch not by the sun but by other people's watches: if everyone's is a little fast or a little slow, how will you ever keep true time? If everyone sings off key who can retain perfect pitch? The sun itself is irregular in its motions. If whole families and towns went mad, who would be left to be sane? Who would know?

"Ike," soothed Peter, in his burry chestnut tones. "Ike." He was by Ike's side now; lips were moving but nothing came out, a tongueless Philomela. Up close, Isaac's flesh and joints appeared swollen and discolored; his ankles and feet beneath his pajama bottoms were bloated, the circles under his eyes purplish, puffy, his cheeks coated with tears and snot.

"Ike," coaxed Peter, and "Ike," he repeated, until at last Isaac calmed down, lifted his head, fastened his mad blue eyes unseeingly. Then, focusing suddenly, Isaac roused himself and bellowed, "This isn't a *zoo*! Get the fuck out of my house, you goddamned tourist!"

"Isaac," protested Peter, "I'm your buddy. I'm here because I want to be here."

Isaac hadn't shaved in a while, but someone—probably Agnes—had taken a recent swipe at his cheeks and chin and then given up; he was sprouting great swaths of golden stubble, like a bib of cropped corn. He was dirty and he smelled. When Peter refused to scat he lurched to his feet, ominously, and fell upon him.

"Out! Get out!"

"So he kicked you out?" Agnes, elbows on the red kitchen table, was preparing the week's classes, setting homework in advance. Why is Romanesque called Romanesque? Compare Autun (see photo) with the Erechtheum (see photo). How are they different? Here in this kitchen autumn sun poured through the window in streams so pure and airy you could see the motes of dust dancing in them. Here all was playful light and spaciousness, fresh paint, linoleum bright as head-lights, boots and spades and gardening gloves by the door, vines creep-ing across the window—and just a few yards away, dark stenchy hell. As if hell were a pit, an open hole in the backyard, anywhere, into which unsuspectingly anyone might fall.

Peter pulled a face, humiliated and unnerved. Everyone knew Ike had quit his job, was depressed about his dad, had dropped into some kind of slump or rut or whatever. As a kid he had always had his gloomy fits; his friends were accustomed to having to remind him periodically to pull himself together, things weren't so bad. With such a rallying exhortation in mind, Peter had buckled on his armor and pranced over to Cyrus. But before this wall of fire words went mute, fizzled out.

How could she have let things go so far? At least she could keep him clean, for Christ's sake. She was twice his age; she ought to know how to wipe his nose. How had he *got* like that? A few months ago at Sam's funeral, Ike had seemed manly, formidable, as if death and love had wrung the last traces of clownishness from his piebald soul. His eulogy made Lindy cry, and not only Lindy. He'd captured Sam just right. And now? A beast. Agnes ought to put him in a hospital for a while, before he hurt himself, or her.

"I'm going." Maybe in a couple of days he would call and tell her what was on his mind, what he thought best.

"Don't go," she said, unexpectedly. "You ought to stay a while, try again. I know Ike. He'll feel so awful when he comes to, and realizes he's sent you away." She pushed aside her textbook and papers and got Peter a can of beer, offered him some pie.

"When he comes to?" repeated Peter, with an incredulity that was accusatory. There was something about her flippancy—yes, she just wasn't being serious, she of all people—that made him lose patience. "Agnes, the guy's a gibbering loon. He ought to be locked up."

"I know Isaac," insisted Agnes. "He's not crazy, he's the sanest, most sensible man I ever met. He's in trouble, that's all, but he'll come through."

"He ought to be in a hospital, Agnes. Has my father-in-law seen him?" Maybe she's crazy, too. She sounds crazy as Isaac's mom. Trust Ike to pick another Mattie.

"He'll get through it on his own or he won't get through it. If you go into a hospital, you don't come out. That's my experience anyway."

Sure enough, a little later Isaac calmed down and was even persuaded by Agnes to come into the kitchen for a cup of tea. There he sat, rocking to and fro, but less vehemently, warming his huge raw hands around the teacup's steamy globe. He seemed unaware of Agnes or Peter, but sat in gloomy dignity, aloof.

They hadn't the heart to make conversation. Silence, but for Isaac's humming and rocking. He was cold, Peter realized, he was rocking to keep warm. The circulation gets sluggish from inactivity. He was lying around too much. Was that what lunacy was? No skin, no thermal layering, but flesh and sensibility raw as a burn?

Isaac spoke, in such a loud, deep voice they both jumped. "You're married now, aren't you?" He spoke with great effort, from the bowels of his unreason, as if straining to fix in his mind certain inalienable truths.

"Yes," said Peter, not reminding Ike he had been best man at their wedding.

"You and Lindy have been married some time now, haven't you?" Isaac, answering his own question under his breath, "Thirteen months and nine days. Four hundred and one days of marriage." And then aloud, to Peter, sternly, "Is Lindy pregnant yet?"

Peter felt like an idiot. "No, sir."

"Are you trying to get her pregnant?"

"Nah, we've decided to wait a while."

"I very much doubt Lindy wants to wait," muttered Isaac to himself, with a great and somber certainty, and then aloud to Peter as if speaking to a scoundrel he was willing to leave masked, "Well, don't wait too long."

The next time Peter came to visit—much later—Isaac again asked him if Lindy was expecting and again advised him to get a move on, not half so much like a deranged twenty-two-year-old as like a father none too enamored of his son-in-law. Go to it, or let her find a man worthy of her.

PPpp-pp-pp-pp-pp-pppppp-pppp-pp. He wasn't sleeping, no, it wasn't sleep, but it wasn't waking either. If it was waking, waking surely brought calm, relief, and freedom. Joy comes in the morning. Awake you could banish the pests and compose your thoughts.

But in this state—when he wasn't asleep, but was trying to sleep, it was nighttime, that's what people did at night, they slept because they had to sleep sometime or die—lying clenched, trying violently to relax, Isaac became a roll of printing paper on whose flimsy shiny swaths some immense and cruel ironmaster was clackety-clacking at lightning speed, printing out scrambled computer garble, left to right, right to left, unceasing. Clackety-clack pounded the unstoppable characters, laser quick, unpunctuated, unintelligent, like a hundred hefty amateur dancers foxtrotting on the shivering membranous floor of his brain.

Every night certain songs ran through Isaac's mind over and over in a continuous reel, extra fast, from beginning to end and back to the beginning. Every night for twelve hours while he tried to sleep till daylight broke and he gave up and just lay there, the same hideous tune would taunt him. Mostly it was Buddy Holly, perhaps because Buddy Holly sang in his hiccuping baby voice lyrics so inane that the combined arrangement was destined to get unshakably stuck in one's head, to drive one around the bend faster than would more varied or sophisticated music. Sometimes Ritchie Valens or on lucky nights Chuck Berry. Isaac detected in this possessed insomniac brain of his a thing for guys who sang falsetto.

So all night, over and over, Buddy Holly, who died twenty years ago over Iowa in a plane that also took down Ritchie Valens, not to mention the Big Bopper, sang in his tinny, teasy marmalade hiccup "That'll Be the Day" like a bird caught in an unreachable recess of Isaac's head singing itself to death. Like a starling fallen down the chimney trapped in a room, chirping incessantly as it batters itself against the walls in a frenzied elusion of your freeing.

There was a cheap garrulous songbird stuck in his head that didn't share his taste in music, and he couldn't get at it. Meanwhile hours passed, night fled. Maybe, went Isaac's insomniac logic, maybe if I could set loose a *cat* in my brain, then the cat would hunt down the bird and silence the song. But how to get the cat in and out again? Everything was ugly, everything was poisoned. If he didn't sleep tonight, he would surely go mad. If he didn't sleep tonight he would die.

He steeled himself not to think of words that might trigger unwanted songs, but the harder he tried, the more irresistibly they surfaced. "Maybe," he said to himself, and Buddy chimed in with "Maybe baby," "bird," he said, and came the chorus, "Bird. He's a bird dog."

Even a too vigorous "not" turned into "not fade away." Itchier still was when he forgot a line and spent the night scrabbling for words that would lead up to "blue" or "you" or "true" or maybe even "Suzie-Q."

This is what Isaac discovered: all the mind's glorious complex of faculties, designed to make us noble and free, can be turned against themselves to ensure binding enslavement. You, lofty builder, build your own prison. What is made to give God glory passes over into the devil's service. In Isaac's case the gift was total recall. He remembered everything he had ever seen, heard, or read. He lacked only the power to control his memory, to repress its indiscriminate retrievals. Sanity is control, inhibition. Isaac would never sleep again, and Buddy Holly would never shut up.

PPPPppp-ppp-pp-pp-p. The noise was rhythmic, intermittent, labial, but Isaac couldn't decide whether it was a *p* or a *b*. *B* was for "brother." Isaac had a brother named Turner. But why would Turner be at the window? The thought excited him, nonetheless. Ppp-pp-ppp-ppp. No, no, a *b* undeniably. *B* stood not just for "brother" but for "Bramley," his father's middle name. "Bramley" stood for his father. *B* was for his father's middle name. I wore out the other names wishing for him. Only the middle one is left, still good. So his father was at the window, for from there came the noise like a slip or a sigh.

Yes, definitely a *b*. *B* was also for book. But what book? Did Sam know about his arson? The only Sam-steeped book he could think of was the *Columbia Encyclopedia* he'd offered him as consolation for the ruined prize Bulfinch. If only he had taken it, he would have it with him now. How sweet to stroke its cover, sink a little under its weight, maybe someday he'd be up to reading it, although not now: so many ports, treaties, astronomers—oppressive. Maybe his mother would let him bring it back here someday. But did he deserve any relic of his dad? Or any books, after what he'd done? He was unsafe, he'd destroyed his books and neglected his dad. Unsafe. Bbbbbb-bbbbb-bbbbbbb.

Isaac understood now that this sound, which had gotten all entwined with his father, which had become his old man calling him at the window—rise up, my love, my fair one, and come away; for, lo, the winter is past, the rain is over and gone—was coming from the army blanket he had bunched around the spool of the shade to keep out the light. He was awake, and the puttering noise like a tiny boat's motor was no dead dad's serenading but a blanket creakily slipping loose from its moorings. For a moment it looked like the whole house was falling down, then he confused the blanket at the window with the blanket on his bed, which perhaps he was pulling so hard about his ears that its tails were slipping off the window.

No, no one was waiting for him at the window, and no one ever would. Nothing but him and Buddy, and even Buddy wasn't Buddy but only the loose broken parts rattling around in his brain. Back in bed, Isaac ran through all the entries he could remember from his father's encyclopedia. The words slowed his pulse and acted as a more tranquil antidote to the singing in his brain. Didn't silence Buddy Holly entirely, just reduced him to a miniature insect voice in the background, like a radio turned low. Three-forty-seven, and birds up soon. He was well into *A*, comforted by the thought that no matter how many more insomniac years remained to him, there were still twenty-five letters to go. Agadir. A city in southwestern Morocco, on the Atlantic Ocean. Processor of metal, exporter of fruit and vegetables, nearly caused an early outbreak of World War I when the Germans landed a gunboat in 1911 to prevent the French from establishing a protectorate. France ceded a substantial—sub-stant-tial—portion of the French Congo to make the Germans go away. Or something like that. Don't forget about the earthquake of 1960. Agag. Biblical King of the Amalekites. Saul supposed to kill him and didn't. Aga Khan. Agamemnon. Agog. Gag. Gog and Magog.

It was five-thirty and white-hot light was curling through the windows around the edges of the army blanket and Isaac rolled over in his dirty bed, pulled the covers over his head, and slept all morning without dreaming.

If you had asked Mattie Doucette if she was a dreamer, she would have smirked, "Get out of here!" But she was, although dream is too ephemeral and wishy-washy a word for Mattie's gut-felt desires. She wanted what she felt was hers, although quite by what title she was owed it she couldn't have explained. She had grown up contemptuous of her elders, of family, education, authority, convention, of everything ordered and accepted and revered—except for one thing. Money. Money and property. Property was house and land and all those chattels that lay in it and on it: refrigerator, radio, car, cattle, tractor—but these, concrete as they were, were perishables that rusted and broke and sickened and waned in worth, and so were less important than land and house or plain cold cash, things that appreciated in value.

Her parents had nothing. People who had nothing deserved nothing. Rare times her dad held a job he pissed away his pay, went on a roaring drunk, beat her mother, yelled, wept, trembled, snored, woke up crawling on hands and knees blubbing for more. She could see her mother's grim scared face when it was time to get to work and Dad was still comatose. Another job lost. Word gets around: soon it was five, seven, ten years since the last time anybody had tried hiring Roger Doucette. Her mother took in laundry, hid her earnings where he couldn't root them out. What bellowings this caused about the conniving wickedness of a wife secreting money from her deserving man. And her mother usually gave in. What was the lesson? Don't drink, and don't do laundry. Soon as she was old enough to be employable she went and got herself an afterschool job in the department store. That way, she could put away money and at the same time get smart clothes and knickknacks at a discount. Study the customers, too. She was a handsome girl and a snappy dresser who deployed her tight vivid skirts and sweaters as a general his army. Her sister Sue would spy some tacky overpriced bolero in a window and pine, then splurge; Mattie understood that in themselves smart clothes were no more than unused cleaning rags. Properly employed, they were a means of getting men to do for you what you couldn't do for yourself.

Money and property were what lasted, what people respected you for, what gave you power. It wasn't for their pretty faces that people kowtowed to the Driscolls, who owned a chain of drugstores, or the Herringshaws, who had married insurance money once the mill closed. These local grandees had summer homes the way Mattie had—or hadn't—summer dresses, and their children didn't know what to do with what they had, sometimes pretending to be just like you or me, sometimes looking down their noses at you.

"How much money does your dad have, Connie?" They were sitting by the river; funny how they never went either to Mattie's or Connie's after school, but met in between like married lovers. It was seventh grade.

Connie looked clumsy, coughed. "Really, I don't know."

"Imagine not knowing how much money you have," Mattie said scornfully. "Why don't you ask your dad?"

"I don't think that would be right."

"How come? It's yours too, isn't it? I mean, it's no state secret."

Connie obediently trotted off and asked her dad how much money they had, and evidently the answer was, Don't play with that Doucette girl any more. She denied it frostily, when pushed.

"Don't be a sissy, Con. There's still a lot of tricks I got to show you. Don't mind your dad." Connie had a certain hankering after excitement as long as it wasn't too exciting. On days when Mattie liked Connie, she decided this appetite was growing; other times the girl seemed intractably lifeless.

"What kind of tricks?"

"Well, the main one has to do with a tennis court."

This really was tricky. Everyone knew that the Driscolls had a tennis court on their land, and Mattie, who didn't know what a tennis court looked like, passionately wanted to see it. All year she had demanded an invitation, and all year Connie made lame excuses. Now she hesitated.

"Well, we have a tennis court, but . . ." She started stammering. "What kind of trick?"

"It's a fun game."

"Like tennis?"

"No, much better."

"What's it called?"

"It's called . . . Elbow."

"Elbow? That's a funny name. How does it go?"

"I can't explain it; I'd have to show you. When can I come to your tennis court?"

Connie was stumped. "Well, um, you see, I'm not really allowed to use it." Poor liar.

"You're not allowed to use your own tennis court?" Mattie was savage. "What are you, a prisoner in your own house? Doesn't your dad trust you? I got an idea. Why don't you sneak out of your house at midnight when everybody's asleep, and we'll go play on it."

"Can you play in the dark?"

"Why, stupid, you're supposed to play this game in the dark. With flashlights."

Connie, terrified, refused. It took a whole week for Mattie to coax the goose, and even then Connie looked miserable. The agreed-upon November night at ten, Mattie with borrowed flashlight sneaked out her bedroom window, walked six miles in the icy dark to the Driscolls' house in Auburn. Shadows leaped out from the woods. Ice underfoot. Strange animal howls. Flashlight waned. She was worried that she wouldn't be able to recognize the court, not knowing precisely what one looked like, especially in the piney gloom. But there in the middle of the Driscolls' woods—her eyes were getting used to the dark—was something fenced, walled, boxed-in. A tennis court. Flashlight wavering, she found a door in all that fencing, pushed. Just then, behind her, lights flooded the dark house, the sound of barking dogs racing toward her, a man's voice shouting, "Robbers!" and Mattie took for the hills pursued by hounds.

Only a mile later—didn't know she could run so fast—did she realize Connie had betrayed her. She was awake all night, fuming, hopped up from fright, plotting revenge. The Driscolls' dogs could have eaten her alive! Next day, Connie looked petrified. Mattie walked up to her, casual, and said, "So sorry, I fell asleep early and didn't wake up till morning. Hope you didn't wait for me long."

Connie's jaw dropped. "N-no. Is-isn't that funny. I didn't wake up either."

Mattie could be patient. She waited until the Driscolls went to visit their Boston relatives for the holidays. Christmas night, she made Frank Olszewski drive her all the way to Auburn on his snow plow. They plowed the tennis court under, ripping up its sticky tape, knuckling clay surface to choppy brindled mud. They built a bonfire, leaped and danced under the moon, high with silliness, giggling, whooping. Then they explored the property, peering in the big picture windows, played Mr. and Mrs. Driscoll. Best Christmas she ever had. Childish maybe, but it served Connie right for sicking her dad and his dogs on her own friend. Afterward, they put the Olszewski plow neatly in its shed, wiped the tires clean. The Driscolls couldn't lay a finger on her: how could a thirteen-year-old girl bulldoze a faraway tennis court? They checked tire prints, but lots of people roundabout had the same John Deere. Word was that the court was ruined for good. But truth to tell, Mattie had been a little disappointed. Was that it? A big square wad of string and clay?

This was what got on her nerves about rich people—they pretended money didn't matter, that nothing stood between you and them, that they only cared about higher things. But money was *all* they cared about. There was a kind of vague distant look that used to come over Connie Driscoll when you talked about things everybody else had to worry about that made Mattie want to kick her pasty face in. She could afford to look distant because she knew her future was provided for and she only had to tolerate this obstreperous guttersnipe another couple of months. Next fall she'd be going away to boarding school, and after that she would be attending some rich-girl college in Connecticut with a name that sounded like pinched shoes, never to see her former playmate again unless she and her country-club husband-to-be happened to stop by whatever department store or luncheonette Mattie was working at, assuming Mattie was lucky enough to escape the assembly line.

Well, it wouldn't happen like that. Mattie had it all planned out. She was going to marry a rich guy herself and come back and buy up all of Auburn, build a house with a big spiral staircase and an indoor swimming pool and servants.

When their paths crossed again, it was through their offspring. Connie married her own cousin—wasn't that adventurous?—and Mattie married Sam, no millionaire but still someone Driscolls couldn't altogether look down their noses at. The fruits of these local pairings were Macy who turned out smart and Isaac who tried to do to Macy what the snow plow had done to her mother's tennis court.

Time ran haltingly, stretched long as Silly Putty, twisted like a hanged man on a gibbet in high wind. In fact, it didn't go slowly—inactive eventless undifferentiated days hurry by, for it is memory's pressure slows time down, makes hours distinct and careful as stones strung on a strand. Rather, time rattled along like bulk on a circular conveyor belt, round and round and round, each loop indistinguishable from the last, and the next.

Most days Isaac didn't get out of bed but tried to recoup the night's losses in stupefaction. The more he slept—and now he'd been sleeping longer than bears, and when he reached the anniversary of that day, which was soon, he would go truly mad from the certainty that he had crossed a kind of chronological Styx bearing him irrevocably farther from his father, each moment that passed took him farther—farther—away—the more Isaac slept the less he could sleep. Now he seemed crouched at the horizon where sea blends into sky, no boundaries any more between wake and sleep but fluid diluted monotony. The more he slept—or waked, no difference really—the weaker he became, the faster he drifted from the dock at whose moorings he might someday regain mastery of himself. As even the most pitiable brainless creatures do daily, he reminded himself aloud in a burst of rage. Soon he would be on the high seas of hopelessness, bob belly up all his days without sight of land.

You, it's up to you, no one else, not fate, *you*, you can master yourself, you must. Never too late. Live free or die.

He slept in the hope of meeting his father, of blotting out this time of loss in a dream reunion. Dear God, bring me to him, let us not be parted. Where was he? What was the "it" that stood between them, what element parted father from son? Only in dreams was there possibility of bounding over the border, of reentering life, of finding the dear lost darling. Maybe he was still on earth—behind the cherry tree in the garden, behind the blanket curtain, in the bathtub—might come streaming out of the rusty faucets, wasn't dead, was alive, not just clenched tight in Isaac's lacerated heart but externally *there*. In the room.

Once he woke up in twilight and his mother was staring at him in a kind of sorceror's joke. You conjure up an apple, you get an orangutan. There she was, a jowly gray tigress, sitting on the edge of his bed, staring down at him gimlet-eyed as she had stared down at his dad in the hospital.

"I thought so," she said with grim satisfaction. "Just faking. Just pretending to be asleep. You're your father's son all over—spineless and crazy as a gib-cat." A gib-cat? thought Ike later. A *gib*-cat? "Your dad never did a lick of work in his life. He was a phony. A phony and a shirker. Only muscle he ever moved was his willy. Now you're the man of the family, Ike, and that's another pretty sad joke, if you ask me. Haven't heard a peep from you since your dad died. It's not as if we live on opposite sides of the earth. You could have sent a card. Turner's my only child now. You're worse than dead."

Those were her characteristic intonations, that was her very mode of delivery, like artillery fire in monotonous unstoppable little bursts, punctuated by discomfiting silences if you didn't answer. Pause, fire, pause, fire, pause, fire.

"You know I'm selling the house," she said finally.

Isaac tried to think of something to say back, but his arm wasn't long enough to reach down into that liquidy well where words hid, squiggling about like tadpoles. Too disheartening. So he closed his eyes and dozed off, hoping she would go away and that his father would come back. When he woke again, she was gone, no one was there, he was starving-thirsty, didn't know if it was day or night, some undistinguished *heure bleue*, too weak to drag himself to the bathroom for water and didn't want to face Agnes in case it was a regular human hour after all. Was it his mom or merely a night phantom, a specter of his bad conscience, a kind of succubus of guilt? It sounded like her, but would his mom *really* use the word "willy"? No, there the devil had slipped up, betrayed itself. But she'd mentioned selling the house.

When he woke for the third time it was so dark and hot and he felt even weaker but so wakeful he would never sleep again. He thought it had been she. That was the trouble with this beclouded condition; you couldn't really tell. Was it an angel impersonating his mother or a devil or nothing more supernal than the ghost of his conscience fulminating rebellions against his own undutifulness, beaming him corporeal "Call home!" commands, fleshly telegrams.

But this was no time to chew over his treachery, to count how many people, even *things* he had let down—the thought of the burned books, that blind cruel massacre of so many wise leathery little lives, was enough to make him go off his head. No, none of it bore contemplating, his wholesale betrayal of friends and family, neighbors and teachers, Casey, the magazine, the books he would never write, everyone who had helped him and counted on him and had thus been befouled by his defection, his backsliding, his willful destruction. By now his class at Harvard would have graduated, advanced past his ever being able to catch up.

"I have to write *Aurora* and tell them I want a job," he told himself hollowly.

When he turned his mind away from himself long enough to recognize another soul, he saw her and hated her too. She could do nothing for him, because nothing was enough. In the early days' cyclical surges of hope that he might be saved and cured, not by himself but by another, he periodically threw himself upon her, wanting only to bury his misshapenness in her freckled collarbone, dissolve into this more serene and resolute entity, this rock of peace and sense. (Everyone else at that time seemed so happy and so worthy!) He begged her to help him, to say he was all right, would mend and be useful. She told him; with her sarcastic disbelieving schoolmarm look she snapped, "Of course you'll be all right."

But telling never did the trick. Only say the word and I shall be healed. . . . The word grudgingly delivered only scarred you the uglier. When she proved unable—unwilling—to save him, disappointment soured to colicky recriminations.

It wasn't couldn't, it was wouldn't. It was *her* fault . . . only say the word . . . she just wasn't trying. He forgot this was the third time today he had hysterically demanded to be told everything would be all right, that each time she had told him just what he begged to hear, but either she'd said it too curtly or else the charm had worn off from making her say the words too often in one day. *She* doesn't believe it. She despises me. She doesn't think I'll get better. She doesn't care whether I do or not. All she cares about is her ninth-graders. She came in and out of the room. When she was in it, she drove him crazy, he longed to be alone, shouted her away, and as soon as she was out the door he wept for her return, made wretched by the look of irritation he knew would wrinkle her nose if he were to call her back, and yet couldn't control himself, would die if he didn't. Hating the sound of his own puling howl he shouted, "Agnes!" and cringed at her cross look when in she came.

At more lucid, disciplined moments Isaac told her she should leave him, go back to Gilboa, find a man worthy of her, have children—that was a low blow. He begged her to forgive him for leeching her strength. But the unspoken import was accusatory: he was finding her a little too independent, too brisk in her attentions. When he worried aloud that she wasn't getting enough exercise, he was actually bullying her to abandon those four-mile walks to and from school that consumed minutes during which she might be at his side. He said he didn't want to hamper her work or take her away from her students, but he meant, "Quit your job. I'm your work."

This was early on, in the long afternoon of his mind's sickness. For jealousy, though dismal and monotonous, is an imaginative exercise, requiring enterprise, curiosity, and gusto enough to read deceit into a raised eyebrow, a yawn, a sudden taste for Hemingway or strawberry ice cream or the Boston Patriots. During the months that followed he was too stagnant, too unsexed to wonder what Agnes was up to all day, even to notice her absence, incapable as he was of supposing that she or any human soul might be having fun.

> *Is it not passing brave to be a king,*
> *And ride in triumph through Persepolis?*

How much sharper the letdown if you conceived yourself to be on the high road to that great city, indeed halfway there, and then to turn back, to realize that cowardice, laziness, and lunacy have brought your journey to an end in a provincial ditch.

I've ruined my life. So many years left of failure unless I do it now. Kitchen knife, window—in a one-story house, that's a joke—belt, belt would snap, he was still so fat, despite his new indifference to food, still so grotesquely enormous an animal it would take a quart of rat poison to do the job. Several times a day—waking, that was the worst, and just as it got dark, the two nadirs of a lowly existence—Isaac was seized by the impulse *now* to cut his throat, gouge out his own eyes, suffocate himself, murder the usurping body, the parasite, the wicked ungrateful ox. And yet even at those moments when he felt decisively on the brink of an action he pretended to believe was right, inevitable, even honorable—for someone ought to put this subhuman ball of blubber out of its misery—just then, when he summoned up the resolve never to see Agnes or Turner again, maybe to see his father, curious scruples attached themselves like crumbs to the chin or stains on the tie from a dinner he had long since eaten and digested. The chief scruple was vanity. Just as very old ladies who quite sincerely have lost the fear of death along with their teeth and husbands and friends still complain that the hairdresser has given their curls too blue a rinse and this year's skirt length doesn't suit them, so too Isaac, who hated life and wanted to die, was halted at death's door by vanity.

If he killed himself, everyone in Gilboa would look down on him. No way around it. His death would give smug idiots like Raymond Doucette or the Gilots, who ran the Corner Store in Auburn, cause to feel superior and think him in retrospect pathetic. All his former Harvard classmates if they ever heard would gloat. A poor boy. Too much pressure for him. No favor letting them into such places, confuses 'em, makes 'em discontented. Casey too would think in disassociation, he was crazy all along, nothing *I* could have done.

Great as was his own self-contempt, the thought that genuine morons would assent to it was intolerable.

So Isaac lived that Ray Doucette might not crow. Or maybe, he admitted, the will to live was so hardy and multiform that like certain plants or germs it took on the appearance and attributes of other organisms, now parading as a proper concern with posterity (how could you die until you'd published at least one book?), now as compassion for his family.

But still other days he was past caring, could only concentrate single-mindedly on getting the kitchen knife past Agnes's eagle eyes. She watched over him, and said little. He had crushed the talk out of her over these months, cowed her. He could see her watchfulness, not love's providence, she couldn't love him any more and didn't, but duty. And a certain fear and dislike. She couldn't *but* dislike him.

Chapter 2

"Toy."

"*Toy* . . ."

"Toy! Well, Toy *is* your name, isn't it? I mean, *I* didn't name you Toy, did I? I would have named you Mike or Bill. Or is it your alias? Have you got another name you prefer?"

Giggles from the small class. She had already, she couldn't remember why, explained the concept of an alias, which intrigued them mightily. It had taken much longer for them to realize that Miss Urquhart (they called her Miss Evans, after their art teacher; they called all their teachers Miss Evans) might be cracking jokes. Now they laughed, a little late, at everything she said.

Of course Toy was his name. There, he had written it across the blackboard, not in chalk but in impermeable laundry marker: THE GOOD TOY, a slate banner unfurled for her as she walked into the classroom, a neat and triumphant self-approbation. She had scolded him—butter-soft, for her—now he was staring out the window, deaf to her coaxing, his face dark and ugly with sorrow.

In fourteen years' teaching Agnes had encountered three categories of students: farm kids, hoods, and a tiny band of the college-bound, children whose parents commuted to jobs at IBM or Wang or worked for insurance companies or else were local gentry—not that certain Driscolls and Herringshaws hadn't become worse trash than Doucettes—and who resisted the enticement of drugs and bikes and heavy metal. These last took care of themselves; but for the majority, well, you needed a power drill to penetrate their skulls. They sat there staring at the clock waiting till they could go smoke. When the Grateful Dead played in Boston, half her class was gone two days running: one to get there, one to recover.

What then were you to make of a small tawny orphan weighing ninety pounds and clad in pressed pants and white shirt buttoned to the throat, a twelve-year-old who might refuse to eat if you told him he wasn't being a good Toy at all but on the contrary a rather naughty one?

Six Cambodian refugees had been sent in a rare stroke of bureaucratic empathy to two Catholic families in Hebron: they weren't sons and daughters of cabinet ministers but rural children from a steep insect-green region not entirely unlike New Hampshire in June, or so Agnes imagined, children who had never seen stairs or flush toilets.

They each spoke two words of English when they arrived, "goodbye" and "okay," which they parroted in a high-pitched litany of reassurance. Agnes volunteered to teach them English, get them up to scratch till they could be absorbed into a regular class. Inasmuch as (to Agnes's mind) everything in the schools was done to discourage either learning or teaching, this had meant taking a special course at the state college and passing an exam in Teaching English as a Second Language. Now she had the six children every afternoon after school and before Truon, the eldest, went to work. Already she was overloaded, and the Cambodian children proved draining, but unlike her boyfriend Agnes had been brought up thinking that if you felt mopey (not that you thought about these matters) it was because you didn't have enough to do.

Besides, it was a challenge. Her great-grandfather had been a missionary in Japan, and she had in her an unsatisfied streak of wanderlust. As a child she'd read books about Tibet and Nepal and Burma and Korea and dreamed of temples shaped like incense cones and plum-colored water buffalos and saffron-mantled youths with round shaved heads. Almost timidly she pried these sealed golden youngsters for stories of home: a delicate and perhaps tactless undertaking, since home was forced-labor camps decorated in tall pyramids of human skulls, parents mowed down before their eyes, sisters raped, famished and diseased treks through jungle, beset by brigands, and, once across the Mekong, years of sitting behind the chicken wire of refugee camps at the Thai border, waiting.

Ieng Truon was seventeen, Khieu Thirith eight, the rest in between. Together they represented a meager remnant of a people consigned to oblivion. At an age when Agnes had spun out her waking moments agonizing over the invisible pimples on her invisible chest, Ieng Truon spent his nights—after, that is, he got home from his afterschool job as a clerk, finished his homework, and did his chores—writing senators and petitioning the U.S. government and the UNHCR to track down his one surviving sister, kidnapped by a Cambodian suitor at the Thai border. Determination to succeed and prosper and learn in the New World—a thirst to understand football and rock 'n' roll and presidential elections, to become indispensably lovable to their new families—coexisted in these children with a fixed and constant memorializing, an adamantine will to regain the old.

Before their gentle courtesy and perseverance, as much as their knowledge of human evil, you felt an inhibiting reverence. At first. Agnes soon wangled her way out of this perplexity by teasing: they loved to laugh, adored to be made fun of, and Agnes, too, was sent into fits by their disarming lilts from inconsolable solemnity to infantile hilarity. Of course, it could go the other way, too. Darkness and light dappled their faces. Toy, the madman of the gang, clowned and scowled, giggled and then was seized by a blackness she did not dare approach. Thank God, they were frequently naughty and obtuse.

Toy liked to be driven to Sears and ride the elevator. He laughed like a bell, one hand cupped over his mouth to hide dark, soft teeth. They wrote compositions in class and read them aloud.

"I have a sister," recited Toy in his birdlike twitter, sneaking her a questioning glance. "When I last see her, my sister is little."

"Last saw her, my sister was."

"When she come to live with me . . ."

"When she comes."

"She say."

"She will say."

"'Hey, you are now American boy.' I take her to Sears and we ride up and down and down and up in the elevator and then we go eat a sang-ich."

Truon had use of his foster parents' antiquated pickup, and he drove them all to school and back. Every afternoon the children asked to drive her home, and she explained that she liked to walk, which they, having undergone a headlong baptism into American culture, found incongruous, until Truon explained, "Miss Evans loves *Nature*." (They knew her name, it was their way of teasing back.)

But that afternoon, after the truckload of children had roared off, Agnes stayed at her desk, chin resting on her hand, staring out the window at a shorn muddy football field, visited by a sadness dense and tangible as fog. I'll just straighten up a bit, she muttered insincerely.

She didn't want to go home.

. . .

Agnes was thirty-five years old when she took up with Isaac. Sometimes it felt like a hundred, sometimes, seized by a teenager's strong-headed restless impatience with human stupidity, she'd have said fourteen.

When she'd lived by herself in the room on Franklin Street she'd been lonely as a stone or a horse, without knowing it. On the contrary, she had considered herself happy in a feckless, minor sort of way. Her days were unclouded, uneventful, and securely regimented: her walks and meals ran like army hours, in the evenings she read magazines and books over a salad and was asleep by midnight. This was freedom. Weekends she went to church, worked in the garden, rehauled her apartment, drove out to Boone Farm to visit nephews and nieces. She talked to herself, but cheerfully. An old lady's life, selfish and sinless; it kept her serene as an abbess, although she had read that even abbesses in old age are grueled by doubts, the canker of unsatisfied ambition.

When years later Isaac asked her what she'd wanted to be in life and Agnes replied she'd never thought about it, that wasn't quite the truth. Growing up, she had suspected in herself untested reserves of valor and fortitude, a capacity for deeds of bravery. A daredevil, she liked to scale walls, jump off bridges, and swing from ropes into the river. Like many girls, she regretted the lost days of hand-to-hand combat, and wished herself a man so that she might lead a crusade or live among the Bedouin. It turned out to be one of Isaac's more charming gifts that he recognized and flattered this would-be manfulness, that he understood how fluid are the borders between the sexes, that just as he loved in lazy fits not to stand like a man to pee but to sit on the pot and daydream like a girl, or lie in bed all day weeping over sentimental novels, so Agnes still wanted to practice her batting. On sunny days that first spring they played a kind of backassed baseball in the yard, Agnes a wild pitcher, he too blind to catch, and amorousness prevailing when Agnes vanished into the tall grasses after a pop fly and he trotted after and threw her to the ground for a premature and prolonged seventh-inning stretch. That was *then*.

Once grown, instead of joining the Foreign Legion or trekking in Nepal—was it timidity, succumbing to the pull of gravity, that kept her home?—she had chosen teaching as the most exerting of the professions and felt her mettle sufficiently tested, trying to keep weak teenagers off drugs and conquering the invincible indifference of eleventh graders who drag-raced their big-wheel pickups out by the quarry and thought calculus—not to mention art history or French—was for guys who couldn't get laid. Sometimes she wondered what it would be like teaching kindergarten. Kindergarten was the word for it: like tilling a garden where every month was May and the gardener had only to poke at the buds in awed joy. High school was more like a chaplaincy in the Salvation Army: you were there to save souls, but it turned out to be enough that your charges were sober and awake.

"Were you ever in love before?" Isaac pressed. "Did you meet anybody you wanted to marry? Who did you sleep with before you slept with me? How did you learn all this?" (This being motion, instinct, a pealing into joy.) "Was it so ecstatic with other guys?" Deceptively casual, as if any answer but "No. No. Nobody. No" wasn't going to pitch him into torment.

"Jerks, mostly," Agnes admitted. Summers before Ike she went hiking or rafting in the White Mountains or the Berkshires, even once in Utah, and it was then she dallied in love affairs that compared to her work were cautious and lukewarm. The summer before Isaac's senior year she'd almost married a painter from Amherst. They camped out, they went to summer theater, they drove to a concert at Monadnock and sat out under the stars with a bottle of champagne: well, that was thrilling. She had no idea how culture-starved she got in Gilboa. But in the end she found him a little wet: he was secretary of Artists Against Nuclear War, which struck her as either dim or disingenuous. Who was *for* nuclear war, for Pete's sake. She was sure her late father would have thought Jim a perfect drip. What was a normal man doing unmarried at such a great age, she caught herself wondering before she remembered she'd reached quite an age herself.

This was the funny thing: as a teacher, she'd always fastened upon misfits who gave her a hard time; in romance, it was the milksops who took a shine to her. Bored and irritated by her suitors, Agnes found the more she snapped, the more they pined. Jim was a little tricky to throw over, if only because this really might be her last chance—at motherhood, anyway—and the thought of concerts under the stars tickled her. Then she gave him the boot, and for a whole week after gloated over her reclaimed selfishness: the apartment now appeared positively cathedral without him underfoot, her bed ten degrees cooler, she could read over meals again and be asleep at eleven, could walk as fast as she pleased without being dragged down by his meandering, heavy-footed amble, and the crisp snappiness of conversations conducted in her own head beat their lame sententious quarrels.

She'd met Jim during one of her periodic assaults of massive dissatisfaction with school. Ellen Cartwright was a narrow-minded shrew, the new textbooks were criminally dumb, her independence was being eroded. Now she skipped into class with a new spirit of attack. Sam Hooker's weird older son, whom she'd always found arrogant, attention-grabbing (she preferred Turner, the underappreciated runt), was in three of her classes and proving infinitely more feeling, more independent-minded a man than the sap from Amherst she'd almost married. The kid was a math whiz, that she knew already. What startled her was his fierce greediness for art: most atheists she'd met were utter philistines. You put him in front of El Greco's "View of Toledo"—myopic, he pressed the print to his nose—and watched him turn scarlet, roar with happy laughter, lose his breath, swoon. She tried to describe to her class the unearthly quality of El Greco's light, neither night nor day; Isaac, smiling, stuttering a little, interjected, "It's the crackly bluish illumination of a lightning bolt, a kind of rending of the sky, electricity without heat." Of course, lightning, as if every day were Calvary. Why hadn't anyone else seen that?

His aesthetic communings weren't always so benign. When Macy Driscoll decided Rembrandt was egocentric for painting a hundred self-portraits, and ugly besides, Isaac nearly bopped her in the bean. She wished she could take him to New York: it would be worth manufacturing a school trip just to unloose Isaac Hooker upon live oil, pigment, brush strokes. All her career she'd been half-consciously, out of the corner of an eye, waiting for a Gödel or a Ruskin. Here he was, easily mistakable for a retard. She watched him in the school cafeteria dump a pound of sugar into his tea and then pour in milk till it flooded his tray, humming tonelessly all the while. His entire body rotated as he stirred the milky cup, slopping down his shirt front and lap. "Ike, you only need your wrist to stir," she pointed out. Her genius, too screwed up even to apply to college. Strangely enough, he had recognized her before she recognized him. Other students were scared: Isaac Hooker sought her out. It made her blood sing. Agnes remembered quarreling with Jack Ellsworth about him. Jack practiced a lordly detachment from his students: teaching was a job with mercifully short hours and long vacations. You came home at four-thirty and real life began. She could tell he believed it was spinsterhood that made her overemotional.

"You're wrong about Sam's son," he told her. "I know you think you've discovered a diamond in the rough, but that boy is going nowhere."

"What do you mean?"

"He's got bats in the belfry. Take a good look at his eyes sometime: they go every which way. Remember he's a Doucette. Doucettes don't go to Harvard. Sam's a nice man, but he's no match for his wife's genes. Remember when Isaac punched Caroline Ailes in the stomach and threatened to kill Ellen Cartwright? That kid is going to end up butchering his mother or jumping off a bridge."

"What a horrid thing to say." She never quite forgave Jack for that smug prediction. Her interest in Isaac was chiefly pedagogic, and there was no one around to tell her any different, except for her new half-guilty constraint in the presence of Sam and the suspicion that he in turn was looking at her oddly.

Well, it turned out she didn't want to snatch Jerusalem from the Saracens or parachute into minefields after all; she simply wanted a man to believe in and boss around. Revelation inched upon her the wretched month they weren't speaking, hit home the midnight he showed up at her apartment with his college applications. It was all she could do not to throw herself into his arms, declare the loud truth. Miss Urquhart was in love! Not in some high-minded way; no, she could hardly keep her hands off the child. Funnily enough, what seemed incongruous was not that the object of her passion was seventeen, but that she had fallen for such a butterball. Painter Jim she had despised for the soft white sling of his unmuscled belly; Isaac's girth was weirdly arousing, you wanted to be pressed breathless by it, bulldozed.

Then he went away to college, and she nearly died from missing him. If a student was talented, the smartest thing you could do was get him out of town. Her best she'd seen wind up local winos or playing banjo in bluegrass bands doing occasional gigs at Sadie's. Not that the region wasn't booming: the Massachusetts miracle of the early eighties had spread to southern New Hampshire, and Preston and Stash were two of the richest men in town, with more construction jobs than they could handle. All along Route 101 new stores and businesses were opening, red-brick Victorian factories being converted into fancy malls. You could buy tarragon mustard and white chocolate or a sequined miniskirt at what once was a paper mill in Rockingham or spend your lunch break at the tanning salon. The New Age had even dipped its toe into Jessup County's cold waters: there were more acupuncturists and astrologers now than GPs. But no intellectual life in Gilboa to speak of. For that you headed south.

At Harvard Isaac would be studying with famous poets and scholars, forging intense intellectual friendships, falling in love. Someday he would become a great man and make a name for himself, come back once a year to visit his parents, and she'd be happy to read about him in the paper, a historian, a man of letters, a thinker—she couldn't figure out exactly where his talent lay, except in a masculine largeness of mind and spirit that piqued her sympathy and made her own mental quarters seem cramped. For Agnes, life suddenly was parched of meaning, shriveled. She felt old and tame and fussy. Why hadn't *she* ever done anything while she was still young? She was crabby all the time, hated her apartment, dreaded coming home at night, her beloved nephews and nieces got on her nerves, and she didn't know why.

"It's the old noonday demon that stalks the desert, preying on the monks in their beehive cells," said the Reverend Popper mischievously. "Take a year's sabbatical. Even an old warhorse like you needs a rest. Go on a cruise. Quit your job; go teach children in the Andes or up the Nile. Better yet, quit teaching."

Agnes simply rolled her eyes. Nothing more irritating than good advice one has no intention of following. She couldn't go to Egypt or Peru, even if she had the money, because she was waiting for news of her boy. Once she even sank so low as to approach Mattie Hooker at the supermarket to ask how Isaac was getting along.

"At fourteen grand a year he better be getting along," snorted Mattie, not even unfriendly, just amused. Sow.

Would Isaac be repelled to know his old-maid schoolteacher had a lech for him? Terrible to think of. Jim called her again; she assented to a disastrous hiking trip. By Sunday, neither of them was speaking, and Agnes realized it was Isaac or nothing. Which meant nothing.

November brought in the mail a fat manila envelope stamped "Cambridge, MA." Inside were *three* letters in Isaac's surprisingly meticulous hand. Blood rushed to her head like a burst dam, and she found herself grinning like an idiot in the empty hallway. He's telling me he's got a girlfriend, she warned herself. She tore open the first letter standing up, read the second on the stairs, and saved the last for dinner, laughing aloud as she pored over them, commiserating, contradicting, admonishing, wondering. From then on Isaac wrote regularly, even though she barely answered—she just wasn't a writer, that's all, and his fluency embarrassed her—packets and packets of them, eight- and ten-page comic epistles complete with copies of the *Gimlet*, campus notices, descriptions of his friends. Still, a strange evasive aimlessness hung over these letters. No mention of studies. Why did he dwell so elegiacally on Gilboa days? Wasn't he working? Now she sent off a stern note, telling him to buckle down to his books. A waste of ink.

Without quite knowing why, she delayed her trip to the White Mountains; she wanted to know when Isaac was coming home, but wouldn't ask. Finally, Labor Day weekend, she took off in a huff.

It was late on an August afternoon a whole year later, the summer before his junior year, that Isaac turned up on her doorstep.

Was he different? Was he civilized, more normal? How old was twenty? His skin was russet as an apple, fleeced with golden stubble, streaked with sweat and dust, and his face with its beaky nose and double chin looked like the face of a Roman emperor. He was wearing a red tartan shirt with one remaining button and a pair of sawed-off army fatigues and he was carrying a paper bag and he was even taller and even fatter than she remembered and his glasses were held together with masking tape, and he still puffed loudly as he breathed, and she had to fight back her tears at the sight of him.

"Aren't you even going to ask me in?"

"What's *that* that's dripping?" She pointed a finger at the paper bag.

"It's our picnic. Ham and Swiss on rye, tunafish salad, soda, corn chips, and a fifth of Jack Daniel's."

"Don't you know you should *never* carry around mayonnaise in the summer? Who brought you up, anyway? Don't they teach you anything at Harvard?"

She was smiling and teary-eyed all at once. She loved him, a boy just out of diapers who didn't know how to shave or pack a sandwich.

"Get your bathing suit," said Isaac. "We're going swimming."

He'd been back for a month. He had borrowed Turner's car, though he had no license, his eyesight was worse, and he seemed almost drunk already. "Turner's the most generous man in the world if you just prod him." He must be drunk. Whatever you could say about Turner—and sensible was now clearly one thing fewer—generous he wasn't.

They drove out of Gilboa at high speed, barreling past the outlying plains of shoulder-tall straw-colored cornfields surmounted by silver silos shimmering and undulating in the muzzy declining heat of the day, to the sinuous cool of dark mountain roads. They rode with the windows down, rattling in their loose sockets, wind blood-warm gusting in their ears, Isaac talking nonstop, Agnes too happy to take in more than sweet snatches of his babble, or even to remind him to look at the road. Only later did he tell her that these were the first civil words he had spoken all summer. I put off seeing you all month I was in such a state. Not until she asked him about his roommate Casey and their magazine did Isaac falter, darken.

They pulled over at the foot of Menasseh, where the Ashuelot was straitened to a crooked and mossy finger of green over whose glistening murk, silent but for the fricative devotional hum of congregations of insects, weeping willow trees met, locking their bowed fretwork horns. Agnes and Isaac unpacked and slid down the bank to the water hollow. It was deserted. There they stretched out under the shade of a willow with their feet dangling in the cool muddy green water, watching insect-boatmen flit their skiffs across the surface. Agnes was grateful for Isaac's sudden quiet, that they might lie supine for a while, slapping at the mosquitoes and wondering what was to be with the two of them.

When it got too buggy, they stripped down, Isaac laying his glasses in a sneaker, exposing a body snow-white below his farmer's tan, baggy underpants. "Lucky I didn't wear my Space Invader ones today." Inching into the shocking cold river, they splashed, whirled, dived, yelling with laughter. His shorts turned see-through in the water, and she was seized by a shameless childlike desire to stare, to see what was underneath the transparent cotton plastered tight to his flesh. Poised on a rock before diving, had he caught her—he was still an innocent, it wasn't right, he would think it was because he was fat or freakish—peeking not quite surreptitiously enough at the solid globe of his belly, picked out in startlingly black hairs, his dimpled knees and large round behind, at the parted opening of his underpants? And yet now she couldn't keep her rude eyes away until, encouraged by her forwardness, he waded to her like a water buffalo, waist high in water, and her arms went right around his neck, tight and trusting, their mouths met, her legs clasped promptly around his waist.

They clambered up the bank shivering and suddenly serious from the mystery of cold water under pale green vegetative crust, baking sun, the entwining of slippery arms and legs, mud, longing, cicadas, solitude. The sun was low over Mount Menasseh, no one around. Isaac pulled her to a more horizontal embankment curtained by willow streamers, laid her out in the shimmery fragrant grass. He peeled off her suit like a mother undressing a child and then without even kissing her or asking permission, abruptly drew back and entered her with the suddenness and majesty of a river god disguised as a near-sighted math whiz. Up on the riverbank, where anyone might come along and see.

Years later it made her melt inside just thinking of the unheard-of things this clumsy virgin had done to her and called forth from her that day. Where had he even dreamed such stuff? How did he know what he wanted?

Love is brutal, love is deaf, love has no pity, love is strong as death, it has its marching orders and it knows no retreat. Well, from then on she was his, and there was no thought in her head but the hunger to feel again and again the deep, violent current of sensation he unloosed, the desire to serve and make happy this strange peremptory king, her boy, her pain, her pride. You think you're a monotheist and you turn out to be a pagan, worshiping human flesh and dreading fate's vindictive envy.

For days afterward she would find ribbons of grass or strands of sedge in a pocket, between her toes.

Late that evening, after he'd fed her soggy sandwiches cupped in hands that smelt of river and her, and they'd smeared each other in corn chips and bourbon to add to the seamy paste of sweat and reek and ardor they'd lathered up in a hot day's rut, they drove back to town in wet clothes that stuck to the car seat, the muggy darkness teeming with farm dogs' howls and insect throbbings, Isaac at the wheel with one arm around her like a very short rein, strangulation tight, singing loudly and kissing her ear.

> "By the rivers of Babylon
> There we sat down
> And there we wept
> When we remembered Ziii-iii-on. . . ."

Bliss to lean against his wet shoulder smelling of mossy river and bourbon and be enveloped by this immense solidity, which promised she would never be alone or unprotected again and revealed to her in a clutch of surprise how very lonely she had been.

What is between a man and a woman no one on the outside can understand or even guess. No one would ever know that it was Isaac who protected and reassured Agnes, who made her feel safe and adored. She had done nothing for him but interrupt his education, ruin his future prospects, keep him stuck in New Hampshire, alienate him from family and friends. Well, maybe she had improved his shaving.

That night he came home with her. Just before daylight she woke up in a panic; instinctively he pulled her tight, like a mother gorilla corralling a gamesome straying babe. "What's the matter?" he demanded in his sleep.

"I just remembered you don't believe in God." (It did sound a little silly.)

"Well, if I did, you'd be out of business already." What a wonderful boy, to shake off sleep and plunge into cheerful lucidity so instantly. "Anyway, don't despair. The *least* permanent and fixed thing about a person is his beliefs."

Everything moved so fast because Isaac insisted he was sure. Was it love? Yes, it was love. He was only twenty. But I've been waiting all my life; I knew you immediately; we can't live without each other. Why wait? He would finish up his last two years, but they'd be together on weekends and vacations. Was her rented room too tiny a birdcage for the two of them? Would it be too sticky facing his dad every day, and the town's talk? They'd find somewhere else. This was an interval; as soon as he was sprung from college, they could strike out for Alaska, the Northwest Pacific, or Europe. New York. Yes, they would go live in New York. He would get a job—anything, security guard, short-order cook—just so he could write at night, and on Sundays, they would stroll hand in hand through the Metropolitan Museum, visiting Rembrandt's mild gelid Bathsheba, El Greco's Cardinal.

Several times a week it was on the tip of her tongue to tell Sam; she was the grownup, she was his colleague, and she hated acting like a sneak. But she stopped herself: it was for Isaac to do, and maybe her impulse to come clean wasn't so much scruple as a kind of perverted boasting.

In the meantime she transferred to Menasseh and found them a house quite near the water hollow. She fixed it up in a fury, and on Thursday nights drove down to Cambridge to fetch him for the weekends. Did she already know he wouldn't graduate? Did she try to change his mind about dropping out—taking a year off, they called it then, though the year off began one Wednesday night in the middle of November when Isaac showed up and announced he wasn't going back. He got a job at the typesetter the next week. It was another month before he wrote his senior tutor to explain.

To admit she had known Isaac would drop out once they started up would be to recognize that she was ruled by selfishness, had no interest whatsoever in his good, that her crusade to get him into Harvard had been a mere pretext for getting him into bed. It was as if a Christian missionary had gone into business selling idols, rams for the sacrifice. She knew they would both be punished for her letting him drop out— let him: she'd probably willed him to. Her own sentence was certain: he would dump her in no time flat, it was only a question of when. She held long conversations in her head with Sam; he upbraided her with a cold fury and sometimes she defended herself, arguing that Isaac was doing better holding down a job than getting soused and cutting classes, and sometimes she agreed.

It didn't seem possible that Sam could die when Ike had so much left to say to him. Or at so ghastly young an age (ten years older than she). She felt sorry for all those Hookers, even Mattie. To such appetite, more life was due. Then, some months after, a year into their love, came Isaac's blackness. Retribution. She had ruined his life, left him with an inconsolably sore conscience. If he had stayed at school, if she'd demonstrated a little decent restraint, if they'd behaved them- selves, Sam would surely still be alive.

Now Ike had nothing. No family, even. His mother was hardly speaking to him, Turner, who did more or less what Mattie did, like- wise steered clear. They had closed ranks. Love conquers nothing. Agnes and Isaac had given up everything—he had, anyway; she had only switched jobs, dropped a few tiresome friends—now it seemed that the one lesson they were going to learn was that when trouble comes love is the first thing to fly out the window.

The day after the funeral Isaac woke up at noon too hung over to speak. She could feel on her own flesh sound's hurt, daylight like white- hot pins poked into your eyeballs. She drew a curtain; he covered his scorched eyes. He was propped up in bed, the sheets draped and twisted around his loins, and above this crumpled white plumage swelled his hairy golden chest, massive as a grand piano, and a head with its hawk nose and cleft chin imperial in its irritable internalization of pain. His torso looked suddenly useless, abandoned, a sandstone statue of a dead god. She sat on the edge of the bed and watched him, propped up, inert looking. "Come outside into the fresh air. You can sit out in the sun or we'll go for a walk."

"I don't want to see outside any more," he stated calmly, as if it were reasonable to forsake sky, soil, rivers, grass because they hadn't proved anchor enough to keep a parent earthbound.

"Shall I make you some tea?"

"No," he said unexpectedly, "I haven't time. I'm going to work."

"The *last* place you should be going today is work," she retorted.

He grunted, hauling himself out of bed. Agnes watched, disapproving. "You need mourning time." Life shouldn't resume so smoothly; mind and body needed a dark quiet place to count and absorb their shocks, their new privations. She remembered how after her father died she'd felt like someone lying in the middle of a busy intersection, with crowds hurrying over her. If only she could go sleep on his grave, like a little dog carved at the foot of a supine king in alabaster chain mail. "You haven't even cried yet, you blubbermouth. When are you going to cry?"

"Shall we set a date?" Sarcastic.

You couldn't tell a grown person what was best for him. Perhaps it was precisely the meticulous oblivion of typesetting he needed, sinking metal alphabets into liquid lead. But there was something a little frightening in the inexorable automaton way he rose, washed, dressed, and strode out of the house. She grabbed her coat and followed: there he sat in the passenger seat, waiting to be driven to Bellows Falls.

The shop, right across the Vermont border, was the enterprise of an old hippie, who stuck stubbornly to Linotype and had more business than he could handle—flyers, church bulletins, newsletters, the occasional monograph. It was a generous, slapdash operation manned by nonunionized freelancers paid by the hour: this free-and-easiness Isaac relished, though he was a little constrained by the need to arrange his ride home every day. As on an oil rig or at a jazz session, you could rake up inhumanly long shifts, then sleep it off. Also, he'd always liked fiddling with alphabets. Isaac stayed at work all that night, only showing up when Agnes was about to leave for school the next morning.

How grown-up Isaac's become, everybody said; his father's death has made a man of him. Agnes was silent. All that summer he set type fourteen, sixteen hours a day, came home, and went to sleep without eating. Agnes in a reversion to her salad days toyed in tart solitude over a boiled egg, a cup of tea, a magazine, unable to read, eat, concentrate. Listening for the sound of a car, sneaking glances at the clock, wondering when he would be back, reluctant to fall asleep and then be wakened by him, worrying that he wouldn't have eaten. She felt in her stomach the heavy restless indigestion of all the day's events, which wouldn't dissolve until she'd relayed them to Isaac and heard his reaction. She even got a telephone installed, so at least she could come pick him up when he was done instead of his having to wait for a lift, but he didn't call. Often he just slept on the sofa in the shop and went right back to work when he woke up. Evenings when he got home early, he went straight to the kitchen cabinet for the Wild Turkey. He drank, she drank, the drink made her talkative and him silent; he listened politely to her stories of students and her new assistant, Jenny Graves, who turned out to be positively two-faced, until he could go to bed.

Weekends he wrote editorials and columns for the Sturgis *Gazette*, and slept. He was making decent money, most of which he sent his mother: Agnes mailed these flimsy white envelopes, each stuffed with three one-hundred-dollar bills wrapped in a striped sheet from an exercise book, like a rock thrown through someone's window. What did Mattie make of these silent anonymous offerings?

He was always tired now, too tired to see his friends. Agnes, who thought maybe he was pining for fresh blood, urged him out and was disturbed when she heard him say over their new telephone, "Sorry, Billy-boy, I'm bushed. Maybe another time." All of a sudden their positions were reversed: she felt frolicsome, needy, irritating as a small child, and he, burdened, years older, wearily endured her caresses and her chatter. Isaac's become a man now, she agreed, not wanting to admit that she didn't like the man he was becoming.

It was a hot summer, and in the evenings he just wanted to lie in bed thinking, shot glass balanced on his stomach, didn't touch her any more. Too hot. Didn't talk much; didn't read; slept more, brooded. When she imagined him that summer, it was lying propped up in bed in the half-light, heavy, inert, morose. Shut off and distant, as he had been the day after his father's funeral, something beached, extinct, like the prow of a wrecked ship, the head and torso of a dead Hercules. "What are you thinking about?" she asked, desperate to clamber aboard, make him blink.

He didn't hear. Then he would shake himself, as if she were a fly on the end of his nose. "What are *you* thinking about?" Weekends he slept all day. My Snow White, she called him. He was tired. He was dog-tired. Then one Monday afternoon she came home and he was in bed and she knew he hadn't gone to Bellows Falls that day. The second or third day she asked, "Are you sick?"

"No, just tired."

It was four or five months after his father died and she knew he wouldn't get over it.

From then on Isaac was like a half-broken machine, heaving against its own damage, forcing wheels to move, engine to turn over, but ever more slowly. She watched him pull himself out of bed as out of a well, straining with an effort that left no room for talk or affection, watched him strap himself to the mast of his desk to write, and moan like a wounded beast when the words failed. And then the engine ground to a halt.

One afternoon Stan, a sparky young fellow from Springfield, Massachusetts, who edited the *Gazette*, came by to find out how come Isaac wasn't turning in copy. Isaac received him in bed.

"Are you sick?" Stan stuck a pen under Isaac's armpit, a palm against his forehead. Isaac smiled wanly, in spite of himself. He loved Stan.

"I don't have time to write any more."

"Buddy, you got to. You've got readers. If they got time to read you, you got time to write."

"I just can't. I don't have anything to say."

"You want me to print a newspaper with blank pages? One little editorial and one little column a week, that's all I ask. You're not old enough to retire."

"I can't," repeated Isaac, pitifully.

Stan played his trump. "Isaac, this is just fun and games for you, but Gary and Dave and me, we all got families to feed. This is how we make our living. I don't have another editorial writer. I can't go to press without editorials. If we don't go to press, we don't eat."

And so, face working with unhappiness, Isaac dictated off the top of his head an editorial on farm aid and one on Russia while Stan furiously scribbled. Three weeks later even Stan could see there was no point in asking: Isaac just wasn't making sense any more.

At his request she moved out of the bedroom and slept in the kitchen on her old pink brocade sofa. Like a fever patient Isaac could not bear the proximity of foreign flesh: he needed room to toss and moan, and her serene snoring drove him crazy. How heartbreaking and irrevocable that move seemed to her, how she lay at night waiting for him to call her back, praying he regretted the separation as much as she, although in fact it was plain he could no longer bear her. Almost overnight their bedroom, a bower of fleshly bliss, of sunlight, domesticity, and laughter, in which Isaac the proud lover had explored his beloved's body, plowed her to a delicious helpless satiety, had undergone a ghastly metamorphosis into sickroom, putrid with the smell of cooped-up, airless misery, of unwashed bedsheets, stale water, rancid snot rags, sleeplessness, lunacy.

Next door she heard him pacing and crying out. If she went to him, he drove her away. Pity for his suffering was curdled by resentment at her pitiless exclusion. What a tumult of opposing emotions rode her, all tainted by egotism. For if Isaac's desolation was punishment for her own sin, she also frantically resented it as a repudiation of their love. He was exaggerating, was being self-indulgent. Anything not to face the possibility that it might be the end of them, that their love affair was not a birth into healthy bliss but a sign of his sickness, that a cured Isaac might be cured of her as well. This was the terrible discovery: in Isaac's hour of need, all Agnes could think of was herself, a baseness she covered up in a rather antiseptic and unsympathetic efficiency.

"Aren't you the one who told me about Magellan?" she demanded. "How the kings of Spain and Portugal denied him ships and money, how all his men mutinied or shipwrecked and died, but he kept hammering away against the odds to find the southern passage?"

"They killed him. The Filipinos," muttered Isaac.

"And after his death they named the Magellanic Clouds and the Straits of Magellan for him. It's setbacks that make you strong, Isaac. You knew that when you were five years old. You just have to start all over again."

He sighed and rolled over.

They were utterly isolated. There was no one but Isaac to tell her her duty by him. When she suggested that he talk to Dr. McCormick he called her a conspiratrix, a witch; he could look after himself without some quack proposing idiot pills. So completely had she come to rely upon his judgment that she accepted him even on the matter of his own mental health. He explained to her one night, in a lucid spell: "People don't believe it any more, but there is a devil abroad in the world. A master thief who goes up and down the halls of human life, knocking at every door, and jimmying his way with a credit card or crowbar if he can't enter honestly. That devil is hatred, envy, and despair. Madness is the devil and he lusts after us with all his cunning, but we each have the power to choose between lunacy and health, darkness and light, life and death. It's not an arcane or once-in-a-lifetime choice but a mundane, commonplace, daily choice. Once you surrender to madness because it's easier than freedom and fills the empty plains of your soul, well, you're paying the devil for the rope he'll hang you with."

But the next day she couldn't get him out of bed.

Surreptitiously she watched his daily struggle, his muttering, "I *will* be well, I will, I won't be conquered, I will be well." Sometimes he went for a walk in the fields with her, absentminded, uncompanionable, but mobile at least, and she would think with a wave of relief mixed with ready anger—for she couldn't get mad at him while he was still sick—that he was getting better, perhaps next week she could persuade him to go rowing on Auburn Lake with her and the Cambodians, maybe in several weeks he might even return to his editorials. The next day he would be back in his dark lair, pretending to be asleep at her approach.

If he had been her student again, no matter how unhinged, she would have tyrannized him into health, industry, good cheer, with that harsh fearless compassion that scrubbed souls clean as sand. But now that he was her boyfriend, and she had given herself to him completely, how could she not see this breakdown as demonstration that he found her repulsive, that she had better not touch him or go near him lest she make it worse? And so, for the most part unprotesting, she allowed him to stay in bed, stew in his own juices.

If Isaac ever got better—and he would get better—the first thing he would do was leave her. They had been through too much ugliness together. Looking at her, he would always be reminded of his madness and fear that it might recur. Maybe that was why God turned Lot's wife to salt, so that Lot would be able to forget Sodom, and father a new race off his forward-looking daughters.

Chapter 3

IT WAS THAWING OUTSIDE. Though his bones had turned to permafrost, brittle and incurable, it made him want to cry when he woke up in the late mornings or early afternoons from a daytime slumber so treacherously total it was like a gassed stupor and became aware of a softer yet more persistent, more yellow and granular light than winter's raw whiteness straining against the blanketed window, seeking entry, deceptively aggressive as Zeus's diffused parts penetrating in a pressing torrent of gold. The snow was melting, spring was coming, summer on its heels. Soon buzzing flies and endless vacation, inflatable pools in backyards, waddling lobster women, baked basketball games, and depressing stupor. The warm days got him down, the thought of summer made him want to hang himself.

On Mars it was −70 degrees Celsius in the summer, and the Bostonian who decided a century ago that its scars were watery canals tooled by alien engineers had been proved irrevocably wrong. No water on Mars, no happy Volga boatmen, just polar caps of carbon dioxide. Just a planet of red craters and volcanoes, two-hundred-mile-an-hour dust storms raking the Plains of Gold. One afternoon Agnes working in the kitchen heard Isaac announce loudly and decisively, "No, I wouldn't like to live on Mars, no, not one bit." She felt cheered by his decision.

Someday people would go visit the sun, which after all was just another star that happened to be one million degrees hot. Daily now he considered going to the hospital; it would be a relief to know if he really was going nuts or what. It would be a relief to know. And if he were? Then he needn't bother worrying about the books he would never write or the books he'd already burned or Agnes's marriage prospects, but could give himself over to others' hands, reduce his expectations to good digestion, to an afternoon walk around the yard. Maybe his mother would let him take the encyclopedia. Weren't canvas, paper, and glue more lovable than flesh? Or maybe he wouldn't even want it any more. He mightn't hate himself so much for sleeping in the day. He would be an invalid; the sick need their sleep.

In his worst moments the prospect comforted. He used to read memoirs from Siberian, Chinese labor camps in a flush of secret envy; for prison sometimes seemed the only place one might be resolutely free, mindful of the essentials, incorruptible as the angels. (That was the danger: this cult of purity was a terrible delusion. Purity just wasn't a useful ideal.) Other days he knew that simply being told he was some . . . who knows? . . . some kind of *case*, some manic-depressive incurable, would be enough to ensure that he would go sailing over the edge and never come back. In uncertainty lay his only hope of cure.

What if he went to Dr. McCormick in private, or better yet wrote him a letter explaining his condition, asking for a confidential verdict, not necessarily to be acted upon? It was Dr. McCormick's old-fashioned numskull country-doctor prosiness that made the idea inviting: Isaac suspected you would have to be very crazy indeed for him to notice, and the fact that Isaac, even though he frequently saw or thought he saw out of the corner of his eye something that looked remarkably like a two-foot-long mouse or beetle scaling the bedroom wall, nevertheless *knew* it was a figment of his imagination, a trick of the eye; this was proof that he wasn't yet around the bend. Not crazy yet, he repeated, smacking his lips with a certain juicy satisfaction. I won't die either. But the very next hour, like an overconfident swimmer plowing out beyond his depth, Isaac, seized by cramp, would flail for the side of the raft, long for the strait jacket.

Day and night he worked on his letter to Dr. McCormick, hiding it in a desk drawer when he heard Agnes's footsteps. The curious thing about putting pen to paper after a six-month spell of illiteracy was that he appeared to have no control over his spelling and made howlers of the simplest words, writing "ignoramus" when he meant "imagine" or "dog" when he meant "can't." He held long imaginary conversations with Dr. McCormick. Sometimes they talked about the planets. Sometimes the doctor, his homeliness bolstering Isaac's confidence, advised him to enroll—no, that wasn't the word—consign himself for a while to the mental hospital in Brattleboro, where people could keep an eye on him. "You don't want to be a burden to Agnes, lad; she's got her hands full already cleaning up after those troublesome brats—she doesn't need another full-time nuisance."

Almost weeping from guilt and relief, Isaac consented to go for a month, to transfer his carcass to trained, white-robed care. A new school, a new state; maybe he would even succeed in graduating from the Hospital of Brattleboro, get his B.A. in paranoid delusions. Dr. McCormick smilingly assured him, "You've made the mature, unselfish decision, my boy." Which was enough to make Isaac recoil. What looked like Dr. McCormick, he realized, was actually the devil. All we have to do on this earth is manage ourselves. Once we abdicate to paid professionals this one basic task, everything is lost. Animals care for themselves and their families, too. Are we lower than animals? A man who can't shave himself ought to cut his throat.

When spring finally burst upon the land Agnes got strict with her boyfriend. It was as if winter had benumbed her instincts, induced a kind of hibernation of thought, a suspension of love. Now, just as guerrillas and governments wait for the spring floods to resume their civil wars, so too, with the chaste sunlight of a New Hampshire May, Agnes launched her offensive.

Don't allow her too much credit. Like so many great breakthroughs, it happened quite by accident. One night, finding that Ieng Truon had so far outstripped her that she could no longer answer his questions, Agnes brought home a textbook of advanced mathematics, listing page after page of theorems and their proofs by the masters of modern mathematics. These cryptically compressed formulas amazed her: how could solutions that had taken their discoverers months and months to arrive at, hundreds of refutations having first to be refuted, be encoded in a mere three points? How could a reader, in turn, dilute and expand this concentrate into a full-bodied, loquacious demonstration, as lively and intelligible as a sonnet or a fugue? How might one make it speak?

Over supper, Agnes showed the book to Isaac, who, perking up, latched onto a theorem that had troubled him in high school. If you draw a line through one of two points, only one line parallel to it can be drawn through the second point. Euclid's proof was unsatisfactory. Was there another? No, every proof that could be devised was flawed. Did this mean it was untrue? In the doorway to the non-Euclidean, Isaac began recovering his sense of self. It wasn't only he that was wild, erratic: the universe, too. Outer space flouts every earthly law. (So do subatomic particles.) Three thousand years of advanced astronomy passed before Kepler, after filling nine hundred pages of failed alternatives, got it through his head that the planets might be elliptical in their orbits; Einstein declared that if electrons had a will of their own he'd give up physics and become a shoemaker.

Numbers: music, harmony, and health. Also thrilling disharmony. The tritones, the ellipses, the wiry waywardness of higher mathematics filled Isaac's imagination and cheered him vastly. After supper, he even consented to sit in the kitchen, math book and paper towel on his knee, exclaiming as he labored and drew. The fact that he had always regarded math as a pleasant escape from more serious vocations made solving theorems the more bearable an activity. The next morning, he asked, "May I keep the book?"

It was the first request he'd made outright in a year of voracious needs. "You'll have to fight for it with Ieng Truon," she teased, but then, seeing his crestfallen face, added, "Oh, all right. You can keep it for the *day*. Then we'll see."

"Bring the boy over," suggested Isaac, more heartily than he felt. "Maybe we can do the solutions together." In the evenings now after supper Ieng Truon rode over in the pickup truck. They sat in the kitchen, shoulder to shoulder, heads bent over notebooks. They played chess, too, and talked up a storm. Agnes hadn't heard Ieng Truon say so many words all year. They talked politics, they talked America; Ieng Truon told Isaac about the French Jesuits who had schooled him, they argued about solitude and family life, about the Church, about the Khmer character, the virtues of nonviolence, and whether it was worse to be enslaved by a foreign power or to be slaughtered by one's own.

Argument was foreign to Ieng. At first politeness obliged him, stubborn as he was, to agree even with Isaac's most outrageous assertions, but gradually he began to resist. Gently and ineluctably he would lead Isaac into logical quicksand, dead alleyways, much as Isaac had used to mislead Turner, and laugh to see him thrash his way back to safe ground.

"I see, so you think the United States is good to recognize Pol Pot as government-in-exile."

"Yes, it's better to deal with a native murderer than to legitimize a foreign occupier."

"I see. And you think the United States is not right to recognize Soviet Union."

"No, I don't think we should have diplomatic relations with the Soviet Union until they change their system."

"And last night you say the Soviet Union is worse than the Nazi

Germans because it fights a war against its very own people. So why is it better for Khmer to kill Khmer than Vietnamese to kill Khmer, but for Soviets anything is better than that they kill their own people. If Ayatollah Khomeini invades Soviet Union, is it better to recognize Soviet Communists in exile?"

Evenings Isaac walked the great masters through their proofs. At night, brain exercised to exhaustion, he fell asleep. Once he dreamed of his father, and took it as a good sign.

When it got warm enough, Agnes kicked him outdoors in the mornings and left him to wander in the fields till she came home.

Mattie and Turner were lying in bed. Turner was asleep, Mattie awake. It was the middle of the night. For the last month, Turner had been sleeping in his parents' double bed. Mattie was convinced the place was going to be broken into: she didn't trust banks and kept at home large amounts in cash and bonds. Sam's life insurance had finally come through, the cab company brought in lots of money, she was negotiating with George Hanesworth over some property in Sturgis for which he was asking too much and wanted extra cash on hand just in case he relented in a hurry. People knew when you had money in the house. Not to mention the stereo, the television, Sam's toolbox. As a consequence, that summer when she was supposed to be taking it easy she adamantly refused to sleep, sitting up with an ear cocked for the burglars. One night Turner had come downstairs to find Mattie roaming the halls in her white nightgown and Beretta, looking like Lady Macbeth on guard duty.

"I heard someone downstairs."

"Go back to bed, Mom, it's only the mice."

Turner put down D-Con and lent her his shotgun, more practical than a pistol. He set up skeets in the backyard and taught her to shoot, just as Preston had taught him long ago. But still she didn't sleep and still she heard noises and still she lay waiting for the burglars. Turner, worried by the black circles under her eyes, offered to sleep on the floor in her bedroom. It worked; she slept greedily for the first time in months, but now he lay open-eyed and rigid all night. They worked out a compromise: Mattie offered him Sam's side of the double bed. At first he complained in the morning that his mother snored like a goose, wouldn't keep to her side but hogged the whole bed, nearly pushing him overboard. But he got over it. She liked having him in bed with her, lanky, hunched, skeletal as Sam was at his age. She missed Sam more than she ever would have guessed, missed his wryness, his restraint. Somehow he'd kept a check on her; without him she felt almost too unfettered. If she decided Jim Randall was trying to cheat her or that Cindy Olszewski really was communicating with aliens, there was no one to kid her out of it. Turner did his best, but Turner didn't make her laugh. He took her at her word, and that only got her more worked up. Still, she leaned on him something fearful and worried if he wasn't in his room sloped at the screen when she came back at the end of a day on the road. The kid had changed; he did not bear her possessiveness easily. On moving home from Walcott, where he'd been sharing a house with Mike Karolis and Gabriel Hanesworth, Turner had presented her with a contract: "If I'm going to be living here looking after you, I want meat three times a week."

"Oh?"

"Yes. Not hot dogs, not baloney, not turkey roll. Beef."

"You mean hamburger?"

"No, beef. Steak. Eye round. I'm going to be bringing home money, and that's what I want you to spend it on. Meat."

Mattie, amused by this little power play, gave in. As long as he didn't get too bossy. Suddenly Turner had begun eating like a normal person; you could see him filling out. Jimmy nearly blew a gasket when she rolled up to his cash register behind a cart laden with forty dollars' worth of bloody red steak bursting from its plastic confines like ripe murdered fruit. She liked surprising people, shouldn't let them get too confident.

Next thing Turner wanted was his shirts and pants pressed. That plan capsized: her ironing was so abrasive he ended up doing it himself rather than go to town in shirts looking as if they'd been branded by a sadistic cowpoke.

Preston had offered him a job as a kind of office manager, keeping accounts, and Turner, pleased by the idea of working for a man he respected, had accepted. He would study business administration nights at Gilboa State, run the contractor's office by day. And Mattie in turn was pleased to be keeping him at home; it beat the Marines any day, though she would have preferred he worked for her. But Preston paid well and the experience would be useful for later on when she started up her real-estate company.

Women have certain drawbacks in the fortune-making department. Sam had made her quit work at Bolts; she'd wanted to have kids young while she still had the energy. For twenty years she had had to listen to her husband bitch about his job, griping about the incompetent new English major Ellen had hired and the good teachers she refused to promote, fretting about who was going to take over the math department when Agnes Urquhart left, carping about the gym's being revamped when the money should go to better textbooks or teachers' salaries. It was the pettiness of the obstacles and the stakes that irritated her. All that anxiety, insomnia, effort, and indigestion over peanuts. Better to be your own boss, even if all you owned was a couple of battered cars, than perpetually anxious your supervisor was looking at you cross-eyed. Sit it out, girl, she reminded herself, you'll have your business in good time. You just need a little capital.

Her time came. Over Sam's sulks she had started Mattie's Cabs. It was long hours, hard work, no end of headaches; it seemed like one car of the three was permanently in repair, and she couldn't decide whether Sears or her brother-in-law ripped her off worse. For the longest time it seemed there was no call for a cab company, nobody was ever going to get into the habit of paying to be driven, especially now gas was back down to a dollar a gallon. But finally it took, and she found herself with a body of loyal customers. The campaign against drunk driving was the only good thing the U.S. government ever did for Mattie. Every time a high-school kid got killed driving high, business soared. Now lots of parents wouldn't lend their kids the car on weekends, and if it got a little tedious ferrying pie-eyed teen-agers who threw up in your back seat and decided once you'd dropped them on their doorsteps that they really wanted to go back to Sadie's and then didn't have the scratch to pay the fare, that was life.

By now she had rented an office over Central Square and had hired a full-time dispatcher and a fourth car and driver. She had plans to expand her itineraries, start a regular shuttle between Gilboa and Rockingham, maybe even Gilboa and Boston, mop up the demand left unmet once Peter Pan canceled its Gilboa run. She had been checking out the competition—there was a Rockingham-based limousine service boasting air-conditioned, smoked-windowed vans that charged twenty-six dollars round trip to Boston and seated up to sixteen people. She could do it better and cheaper, but she'd need two vans to start with.

Anyway, taxicabs were nice but Mattie still craved earth, houses, fields. There was slow, fruitful money in land. You drove through big towns like Rockingham or Brattleboro and on their outskirts what once had been cornfields and orchards were now fast-food chains and little tract homes. It was only just beginning to happen in Gilboa, too.

Developers had built a ridge of cardboard condos out past the hospital, Stanwyck Green or some such British-sounding name. If you bought land now, in a few years you'd be able to sell it in little plots, quintuple your money.

She had dreams of making Mount Elmo into a ski resort, building a field of little chalets below. Stranger things had happened. Fifteen years ago, when she suggested this to her husband, he laughed. Gilboa was out of the way, would always be rural and remote, pokey, depressed. She was being primitive, with this land hunger. And anyway, even if prices went up eventually, who had the money to spend now, and if you did why spend it on a hunk of backwoods out nowhere? His dad had owned prime real estate on the main street of Hebron, and had had to give it away. Besides, if she wanted to be a millionaire why had she married him? She should have gone to New York and found herself a tycoon.

Even now it wasn't too late. The Sturgis property was good land, if expensive. She had finally paid off the first mortgage, one more to go; she would sell this house and its five-acre plot, conservatively assessed in this year's taxes at $45,000; let's say she got the roof fixed, put in some more repairs, maybe sold it for $100,000, which even she knew was totally out of line. If she got Hanesworth's land for forty, she might get a smaller apartment for her and Turner in town, where you could still rent three rooms for two hundred a month. No, renting was a waste . . .

Crash. She must have dozed off. The noise came from downstairs. Turner, bolt upright, leaped out of bed in his T-shirt and pajama bottoms and headed for the door. "You stay here, Mom."

Down the stairs he tiptoed as he had done so many grouse-hunting dawns when he didn't want to disturb his parents. At the foot of the staircase he paused and listened again. There had been a spurt of break-ins this year—even the Ostriches' store had been vandalized. Silence. Then, incredibly, just as he thought it must have been the wind, he heard rustling and the sound of low voices from the study next door, saw electric light streaming through the crack between door and saddle. Two of them, at least. Would they be armed?

"Freeze!" cried Turner, flinging open the door. Afterward it seemed to him that his hair, prickling like a million little hedgehog spines, had risen from his head, and his tongue cleaved to his mouth and his heart turned to ice because there, standing by an open window, with the wind whistling through, was his dead father.

"Daddy . . ." he whispered in dread, transfixed, and then he looked again and it was Isaac. Live Isaac, who didn't look in the least like Sam, but was standing barefoot in the middle of the wooden floor, hair on end, white shirt bloodied—he must have cut himself climbing through the window—and in his hands, cradled, a big book. A telephone book, a dictionary or something. So intent on his mission that he didn't even register Turner's dramatic entrance, at least not in a normal sort of way, but was starting to climb back out through the window rather as woodchucks sometimes don't see you creeping up on them but keep on rooting, burrowing oblivious.

"Isaac . . ." Turner grabbed his brother by the shirttails—a sound of frayed cotton rending. "Isaac, come back, what's wrong with you? Where are you going?" But still Isaac didn't seem to take him in. Hugging the book tighter, he lifted a leg up onto the sill.

"Isaac," he pleaded, pulling again and trying to haul him back into the room.

"Stop right there," said a voice behind them, and both stopped and turned. Mattie was standing in the doorway in her flowered nightie, stubbly oak legs planted far apart, shotgun grasped in two hands. She was aiming right at Isaac; that is, she was aiming at them both, for the two boys were entwined, Turner still foolishly clutching Isaac's shirttail and Isaac straddling the sill. Turner remembered what he had told his mother when he gave her the gun: Never point it unless you mean to shoot. She was pointing. "I knew you were going to try something smart," she told Isaac, grimly. "It didn't fool me, you trying to buy me off with your pay checks. A common thief. What have you got there, anyway? A book? Put it down."

Isaac seemed half-roused from his trance by his mother's voice, but roused to what, Turner didn't know. He swung his legs into the room and stood up, clutching the book still tighter, and spoke now with that overemphatic articulation that had grown almost idiotically pronounced during his illness.

"It's my dad's encyclopedia. I'm taking it. There are things I need to look up."

"Oh, it's your dad's, is it? Well, I've got news for you, buster. What was your dad's is now your mom's."

"He got it for *me*," Isaac explained. "He bought it for me to read, before I was born. He gave it to me in ninth grade. He told me I could have it. I'm sure there are many things he gave you, but *this* he meant for me."

"Do you have that in writing? Because I just happen to have a copy of your father's will and he doesn't say a word about any encyclopedia for Isaac."

"You are a brutish woman," said Isaac, almost blandly. "But I'm taking this book, whatever you say."

"Oh, *I'm* brutish, am I? That's very interesting. *You're* a common thief, that's what you are. A thief and a vandal, and what's more you drove your father to his death with your shenanigans, and you know it, too."

Did I? wondered Isaac. Did I? Sometimes I think I did and sometimes not. And does she really think so, and does Turner? He looked at his brother's pale face, and suddenly, out of the blue, not just in a blind hunch but in all its consequences felt what it was like to be Turner, felt himself Turner from inside out, and groaned aloud at the strain and sadness of it, the pressure, understood with almost unbearable clarity about Turner and their mother, that he would never leave her. No, I didn't kill him; he let himself die. And I've got to escape, too. And Turner?

"No, I didn't kill Daddy, and you're wicked to say so. You never let him live, and now you're going to feed off Turner, too, you old black widow," he said aloud. He turned back to the window, encyclopedia under his arm. He had the power to break free and not come back, now he had it, but a moment later he might not. Could he take Turner too?

"You drop that book or I'm shooting," said his mother's voice.

He swung both legs over the sill, leaning into the chilly darkness, turning his broad back on the woman who was aiming levelly, dead-eyed, fixing his bulk in the gunsight. He heard a shrill unearthly scream from Turner like a rabbit caught in a steel trap and a great shattering rang out. He slipped through the window and fell forward in a deafened blare of pain, still clasping the book, rolling over and over in the grass.

He was running through the outskirts of the forest, leaping over rotting logs, roots of trees. It was dawn, and as he came out into the marsh the sun was just peeping over the hills, plopping its enormous crimson yolk over the blue ridge of Mount Elmo, an immense palpitating blood orange sailing up into a clear cold sky. Isaac's bare feet were cut and bruised, his shoulder throbbed where the shot had gone in, the other arm ached from the heft of the encyclopedia, he was wet and cold and starving hungry and filled with exultation, a conviction of freedom and possibility, combined with a rush of sacredness, as if the sun peeping over the hill were a kind of covenant, and the morning star, still twinkling silver-white in the higher pale violet sky, a presiding priest. Yes, he could run forever, through woods and marshland and open meadow under that fixed white glittering star, into the mountains, across sleeping continents, only he, alone on the earth and under the clear firmament. He was free because he had been created free by a strong loving hand. Everything was terribly, terribly all right.

Crossing the marsh, Isaac heard a noise that started low and swelled to a strumming roar, a croaking tumult. He stopped, rooted. It was God singing; but it was ugly. Who? And then leaning into the little marsh-sea from which this huge song rose, he laughed. Not God but a swarm of newborn frogs, darting and leaping in their deep green pool, pouring out their song of wet mossy crevices and brackish shallows, of spring births. Even frogs praised their maker, bore witness to his providence. So I must, too. But how? He started to move again, more slowly now, in long-legged clumsy leaps from hummock to hummock, splashing occasionally into muddy pools, feet pulped to frozen lumps, shoulder quite disembodied, a separate continent, a map of pain, spelling new alphabets of duty and of joy. Yes, I must go. Leave New Hampshire and all this. I'm glad she shot me. Bless her, now things are clearer. I must go away, and not be scared to fail, not be scared to be absurd and unnoticed. And must never forget that throng of tiny wide-mouthed throats croaking their funny seasonable song of creation and praise.

"You right-handed, Ike?"

"No, sir, left."

"Interesting," said Dr. McCormick, amiably. "Interesting how a left-handed man can shoot himself in his own left arm."

"What can I tell you? I'm a contortionist."

The doctor shook his head. "Sometimes I think it's more dangerous living in Jessup County than in New York City or Detroit. Two weeks ago I had another lad in here with a bullet in him—shattered his shin. And it isn't even hunting season. He told me the same cock-and-bull story as you: he was cleaning his gun and it went off or some such, but I knew his lady love did it. Not to kill him, just to give him a good scare, stop him roving. I knew it because my daughter Frankie happened to be one of the many females he was glad-eying. I almost took a rifle to the little rascal myself—glad Cindy did it for me."

"Cindy Olszewski shot her boyfriend?" repeated Isaac, in scandalized amusement.

"Yes sir. Looks like he won't be playing ice hockey in a hurry. Love does lead a fellow into tight corners. How are you and Agnes Urquhart getting along?"

"Fine," said Isaac, faint suddenly from the operation. "I hope you don't think *she* put a load of shot in my shoulder."

"Oh no, with a tongue like hers you don't need bullets. You two sure are a funny couple."

"Yeah? Too damn funny: I don't mind being laughed at, but no reason she should be."

"People stop laughing. Why don't you marry her? That'll shut 'em up."

Instead it shut Isaac up. He hemmed and hawed to himself and then said aloud, decisively, "I don't like marriage."

"I don't know why you young people are so allergic to matrimony. And no sooner do you finally tie the knot than it's off to the divorce court. You know my Lindy is getting separated already?"

"What a *shame*. Poor girl. Want me to kill Peter Karolis for you?"

"No, you'd be sure to foul it up, and leave me with more work on my hands. What do I care? I didn't want her to get married to begin with. I'm planning to retire, move to Florida, give the house to the offspring. I'm tired of weather. Get married, young man. You need a good woman to lick you into shape, stop you getting shot up."

"I'm going to New York." It was the first time—superstitiously— he had dared say these words aloud and now they were uttered he knew it was true, done, destiny. Once you'd announced your departure, there was no backing down, no loitering.

"They allow married people in New York last I heard."

"I'll think about it," said Isaac, but he was listening hard to something else, trying to remember the frogs singing in the marsh.

Chapter 4

THE WALCOTT FAIR was in full swing. In one shed were the prize bulls and sheep and pigs, in another the prize pies and preserves and honey and quilts. There was an ox draw. There were rides, and a Moon Walk, and a man who guessed your weight, and goldfish to be won if you swung a hoop over them. It was a glorious hot day. Isaac dragged Agnes from exhibit to exhibit. With them were Truon and Toy, Toy solemn with excitement and then laughing because Isaac was laughing. They watched the 4-H contest, in which rams and ewes, wild-eyed, emitting strangled, retching gasps of protest, were hauled into line by farm children clad in white, with blue ribbons hanging from their back pockets. Mr. Hanesworth was judge. In between blasts of Ferris wheel rock 'n' roll his patter—hoary, amplified—resounded. "Lover gal, be mine tonight," sang the Ferris wheel. "Now here we got a fine Shropshire ewe," countered Mr. Hanesworth, "long hind saddle and a trim front end. A tad weak on the pasterns as Shropshires do tend to be . . ." "Lover gal, I want to hold you so tight."

Toy was crazy for rides, and Isaac accompanied him in a motorcar that spun from side to side, trying not to wince when it caught him on the shoulder, and spiked at every collision with new daubs of the child's cotton candy, but reinfected by Toy's shrills of apprehensive joy. "It's so FUN!" the little boy shrieked.

Agnes stood below. She was wearing a bright blue dress he had bought for her, sleeveless, so tight in the hips she kept smoothing it, hiking it down, embarrassed by its clinginess but pleased, too. It gave him a kick to see her looking so vampish. As the cars slowed, he jumped out. Toy and Truon went to watch twin oxen drag a chariot of cement while Isaac and Agnes strolled hand in hand, she blushing whenever they passed one of her former students.

"Come look at more sheep," he urged. They ducked into a tent to stare at a black-faced ram with a yellow pelt cropped dense as felt and a cynical, jaundiced look. They were alone in the tent, just them and the sheep and the warm burry smell of straw and sour milk and sun-baked fleece lying in bundles where the animals had been newly shorn. He lifted the yoke of her scoop neck and kissed the white freckled flesh beneath.

"Are you really leaving tonight?" She held on to his finger tight.

Isaac started to answer, found himself stuttering, dread-struck. "I've got to go, Ag," he said very slowly, testing each syllable's sturdiness. "And *now*, before I lose my nerve again."

"Don't you want me to drive you? It's no trouble."

"No, I'll take the bus. If you drove me I'd never let you go, I'd just follow you home again like this damned sheep. Will you wait for me? I'll be back in no time."

"I'll wait for you, but you won't be back."

"Oh Agnes, why don't you come with me now?" he pleaded, burying his face in her hair. "Come to New York. We'll sleep on a park bench and dine from garbage cans. Maybe we'll strike it rich and move into one of those welfare hotels where we can cook our suppers on the radiator and ward off the drug dealers. Come with me tonight, my apple blossom, my true one."

"I can't," she said, smiling now. "You know I can't. School is starting up in a couple of weeks, and well, I wouldn't want to leave the Cambodians in the lurch."

"All right. Maybe it's better that you not quit your job till I've found work. But you will come later?"

Agnes looked as if she wanted to humor him. "Oh Ag, don't look so mistrustful," he begged, putting both arms around her and clasping her tight. "Marry me, then. We'll elope to New York and starve in bliss. How's that? We'll buy you a pretty lace dress with a veil. We can even get hitched in a church if you like."

"No, I won't."

"Why not?" Isaac was staring over her shoulder at a ewe with a ribbon around its neck.

"Well, you're not such a catch, you know," she said, trying to make a trembling voice sound light and steady. "You're getting a little too old for me. Over the hill."

"Agnes, let this ewe be my witness: I want you for my wife."

She shook her head. "I don't want to," she said, smiling. "But go. I'll wait for you, if you like."

He didn't know he was crying until she reached up and took off his glasses and wiped his face.

"Go."

A NOTE ON THE TYPE

This book was set in a digitized version of Janson. The hot-metal version of Janson was a recutting made direct from type cast from matrices long thought to have been made by the Dutchman Anton Janson, who was a practicing type founder in Leipzig during the years 1668–1687. However, it has been conclusively demonstrated that these types are actually the work of Nicholas Kis (1650–1702), a Hungarian, who most probably learned his trade from the master Dutch type founder Dirk Voskens. The type is an excellent example of the influential and sturdy Dutch types that prevailed in England up to the time William Caslon (1692–1766) developed his own incomparable designs from them:

Composed by Brevis Press, Bethany, Connecticut.
Printed and bound by The Haddon Craftsmen,
Scranton, Pennsylvania.